THE

Yorkshire Coast

AND THE CLEVELAND HILLS
AND DALES

By

JOHN LEYLAND

Author of 'The Peak of Derbyshire'

With Illustrations
by ALFRED DAWSON *and* LANCELOT SPEED

LONDON
SEELEY AND CO., LIMITED
ESSEX STREET, STRAND
1892

PREFACE

THE purpose of this book needs to be briefly described. It is descriptive of the Yorkshire coast, and of the north-eastern hills of that great and historic county, and a chief object has been to give to localities which are attractive enough in themselves the added interest of the history and the legendary lore that properly belongs to them. The perusal of this book will, indeed, show that almost every village breathes of history, and that there is a host of notable events whereof the Yorkshire coast and its neighbourhood hold record. Most Yorkshiremen know this very well, and they may be glad to possess a book that will remind them of the interest of localities; but those who each year resort in great numbers for health and enjoyment to the watering-places of the coast from every part of the kingdom miss, as it seems to the author—saving a few of them—some of the pleasure their wanderings should bring them. There was, indeed, an initial difficulty in the writing of this book. Where should a limit be fixed for the district to be treated? It must be confessed that the boundary chosen is in a manner arbitrary, though it is based upon natural configuration; but it was dictated by considerations of space, and to some extent by the convenience with which localities are visited; but ever as the author went westward something attractive beyond seemed to beckon him on, until at length the far-off hills of Richmond would have lured him further still. This may serve to explain why a certain fringing district is treated briefly, or merely by allusion — why, for example, Byland Abbey has little more than a mention. In regard to the manner of the book, it seemed to the author that—though it is in no sense a road-book—a 'descriptive wayfaring'—wherein the wayfarer should by no means hasten when there were historical circumstances, or legendary stories, or geological conditions to beguile his journey—would, for the most part, be the best for the purpose. He adopted it in a like book upon the 'Peak of Derbyshire,' and it received the sanction of general approval. The advantage it presents is this: That it gives a possibility of picturesqueness to description, and makes it possible to convey a fuller impression of the characteristics of localities, while in cases where—owing to considerations of space or other circumstances — it may be possible merely to name some hamlet or stream, that hamlet or stream will at least be better understood from the picture unfolded of its surroundings as the wayfarer goes forward. And in regard to the convenience of the arrangement, it may be added that a full index renders access to any part of the book easy. To present a complete picture of the history of the region chosen has, of course, been impossible; but the author's aim will be accomplished if he succeed, by the incidents he has related, in adding something to the appreciation of an important district — his native county. He must express his indebtedness, in the first place, to Canon Atkinson's 'Forty Years in a Moorland Parish,' a book of singular fascination, which throws much light upon the early and existing conditions of an important part of Cleveland, and also to some extent to the same author's 'History of Cleveland.' To Hinderwell's 'Scarborough' he is indebted in a less degree, as also to Poulson's 'Beverlac'—a standard work—and to sundry other works he has named in the book. For many of his facts he has depended upon the 'Letters and Papers, Foreign and Domestic, of the Reign of Henry VIII.,' recently published, which are a veritable historical quarry, and thus his book may include some dramatic episodes scarcely known to the general public. It remains to be added that fragmentary portions of the book have appeared in a series of articles published in the *Portfolio*.

ELM LEA, FOREST HILL,
May, 1892.

CONTENTS

LIST OF ILLUSTRATIONS

'And he had trudged through Yorkshire dales,
  Among the rocks and winding scars ;
Where deep and low the hamlets lie
Beneath their little patch of sky
  And little lot of stars :

'And all along the indented coast,
  Bespattered with the salt-sea foam ;
Where'er a knot of houses lay
On headland or in hollow bay—
  Sure never man like him did roam !'
                    WORDSWORTH : *Peter Bell.*

The Yorkshire Coast and the Cleveland Hills

CHAPTER I.

INTRODUCTORY.

THE county of York, which contains within its bounds so much of varied and characteristic English beauty that it might well be described as a 'Little England'—

'A kingdom that doth seem a province at the least
To them that think themselves no simple shires to be,'

as Drayton says—falls, nevertheless, into certain natural and well-defined divisions. Through the midst of it, from north to south, runs that great, fruitful, and historic plain, known as the Vale of York, of which

I

the northern portion is sometimes described as Mowbray Vale, because of the great lords who once dwelt thereby. Westward, from beneath the new red sandstone and gravel of the vale, rises the glorious region of the mountain limestone, in which are excavated the romantic dales of the Swale, the Ure, and the Nidd; and southward of this, again, are the sandstone hills, capped with great moorlands, that range with the elevated tracts of northern Derbyshire.

From the eastern outliers of the limestone hills we look far across the Vale of Mowbray to the northeastern hills, which lie between its fruitful strath and the sea. Here, again, we have a district well defined, lying between the gentle slope that flanks the estuary of the Tees on the north, and the shallow saucer-like Vale of Pickering on the south, in which the waters of the Rye and the Derwent are joined before flowing southward to the Ouse. The Vale of Pickering separates these north-eastern hills from another very distinct region—the rounded chalk-hills of the Wolds— which look westward across the great Plain of York, and reach the sea in the huge water-worn cliffs of Flamborough; and southward of these, again, lies the diluvial district of Holderness, a tract of fragments drifted from far-distant regions, as well as of later lacustrine and peaty deposits.

Except in the long, low shore of Holderness, the Yorkshire coast confronts the Northern Sea, and the pitiless blasts of the north-east wind, with grim escarpments of seamed and shattered rock, from which the

rude violence of the tempest has hurled down, here
and there, the rugged undercliff that lies below. It
throws out huge headlands that half encircle, with
their protecting arms, its lovely 'wykes' and bays,
and it thrusts far out to sea the hoary scarps of Flamborough, that seem, like some ancient weather-beaten
foeman, to bid stern defiance to the storm. What
may appear at first weird and forbidding in this rocky
coast-line, discloses, nevertheless, when we explore its
recesses, rare beauties of luxuriant vegetation in the
deep sylvan glens of the northern hills, through which
peat-stained streamlets, from the lofty heather-clad
moorlands beyond, run their brawling course to the
sea; and it opens for us, beneath the venerable ruins
of Whitby, the glorious Valley of the Esk, through
which we may reach, amid scenes of surpassing woodland loveliness, the breezy Cleveland moors. Be it
noted that variety is a distinctive feature of this coast,
chiefly owing to the southern dip of the strata, which
causes the successive formations, chiefly Jurassic, to
emerge northward towards Whitby. From beneath
the low 'boulder' cliffs of the long coast of Holderness,
the chalk, rising beyond Bridlington, forms the mighty
mass of Flamborough Head; and then, turning inland
towards the Wolds, is succeeded by the Speeton clay,
opposite the Vale of Pickering, and the coralline oolite
strata, to which are due the new characters of the
rocks of Filey and Scarborough. Beyond these, again,
the sandstones, with bands of coal and shale, emerging,
give distinctive features, by their sharply-everted ends,

to the southern cheek of Hayburn Wyke, and rise
to the northern elevations of the long cliffs of Stainton
Dale.   Still advancing, the lias formation comes to
the surface, forced upward by a dislocation, stretches
along the length of Robin Hood's Bay, and, in con-
junction with the superimposed strata, gives their
character to the great escarpments north of Whitby.
According to the nature of the formation, too, is the
varied wasting effect of the sea and the storm upon
them.   The diluvial coast of Holderness is being eaten
away with almost measurable rapidity, so that parishes
which are mentioned in Domesday lie now beneath
the sea, the names of vanished villages are yet
recorded upon the maps, and the lacustrine deposits
of the interior are exposed upon the shore.   The
materials which are thus washed away are carried
southward, and serve to build up the pebbly isthmus
of the Spurn, which is maintained by the nicely-
balanced action of the Humber and the sea, and,
though but a shifting bank, is perhaps the most
durable portion of the coast of Holderness.   The
chalky mass of Flamborough is deeply worn into
twilight caves and fantastic isolated pinnacles, while
the sandstones to the north seem to be wasted as much
by aërial denudation, and scatter their fragments upon
the lower shore; but further north still, upon the rise
of the lias shale, there are water-worn caves again,
which—less durable than those in the chalk—have
undermined the cliffs, and thrown them down in huge
masses into the surf.

This region of the north-eastern hills—which forms
a principal part of our subject—presenting, as we have
said, its lofty cliffs to the sea, looks also, with wooded
hills over the sloping meadows towards the estuary
of the Tees, with greater heights and wider prospects,
across the Vales of Mowbray and York, and, from
gentle slopes, across the Vale of Pickering to the
Wolds. It is, however, a region divided into two
very distinct hilly tracts. The first of these rises
pleasantly in umbrageous slopes from beneath the
recent deposits of the Vale of Pickering, and is known
as that of the 'tabular,' or calcareous oolitic, hills,
which, characterized by their flat-topped heights, and
completely intersected by the tributary dales of the
Rye, present, between them, to the northward—to the
declivities of the more lofty moorland area of the
Cleveland hills, in which the tributary streamlets have
their source—a series of remarkable bluffs and escarpments, at whose base it is not difficult to fancy once
dashed the waves of the sea. The principal heights
in this range increase as we go westward—from 270
feet at Gristhorpe Cliffs, 500 feet at Oliver's Mount and
Seamer Moor, 700 feet at Brompton Moor, overlooking Trouts Dale, and 783 feet at High Dalby, to 1,078
feet at Rievaulx Moor, and 1,289 feet at Black Hambleton.

The second range of the north-eastern hills—the
Cleveland Hills themselves — which, by their great
precipices and rocky cliffs, have given its name to the
district — the Kliflond of the Norsemen — is of the

carboniferous, lower oolite and lias formations, resting upon the red marl and sandstone, and reaches its greatest altitude in the moorlands south of the Esk. The principal heights of the great ridge, parting the watersheds of the Rye and the Esk, going from west to east, are: At Urra Moor, 1,489 feet, Westerdale Moor, 1,422 feet, Ralph Cross, 1,409 feet, near Danby Head, 1,419 feet, Glaisdale Moor, 1,318 feet, and Egton High Moor, 1,071 feet. Northward of the Esk, by which the moorland tract is cleft in twain, the chief altitudes are, at Guisborough Moor, 1,078 feet, Brown Hill, 929 feet, and Danby Beacon, 988 feet.

These lofty hills of Cleveland, through whose moorland dells many a peaty streamlet winds its course, and, by rocky gorges and sylvan shades, flows down both to the Esk and the shore, form a fitting background, with a character near akin, to the mighty scarps and rugged steeps that are their buttress against the sea. Their elevated and lonely moorlands, where the dwelling-places of men are few, have a subtle distinction of their own; there is something of the vast, the wild, and the weird upon them; and—though all but a tithe of their beauty will escape the speeding wayfarer —they will not fail to impress him with a sense of stern magnificence; while, in the wooded ravines and rocky passes by which they are cleft, he cannot choose but linger, and cannot wish but to return.

The Esk follows for some distance the line of the great dislocation of the strata, whereby the hills to the north are depressed—there is another great fault at the southern cheek of Robin Hood's Bay—and it flows over the great whinstone, trap, or basalt dyke, which, from beyond Cockfield Fell, in Durham, to near the coast at Whitby, a distance of some sixty miles, has been extruded through the strata—in Yorkshire through the new red sandstone, the lias, and the lower oolite—and has left conspicuous traces in · the soil. This marvellous dyke, in a line almost perfectly rectilinear, enters our district a little south of Roseberry Topping, crosses Kildale moors, and part of Sleddale and Commondale, and reaches Castleton, whence it continues, passing the Esk twice in its course, to Parker Houe, above the south bank of the river, near Crunkley Gill, further on to Egton Bridge, Lease Rigg, near Goathland Station, Silhoue, Whinstone Ridge (as the Ordnance map describes it), Blea Hill, and Biller Houe, and loses itself at last in Fylingdales Moor. What is the depth of this great cleft, through which the molten matter has been forced upward, it is useless to speculate; but it is found at every altitude between 25 feet and 975 feet above the sea, and its width varies from 35 to 45 feet, but in some cases to as much even as 70 feet.

Our knowledge of the early conditions of the Yorkshire coast is scanty indeed, but it seems possible to discern dimly, through the mists of that long-past history, the traces of a double invasion, or, at least, of an occupation and an invasion. The investigations of General Pitt Rivers have shown that the so-called Danes' Dyke across the base of Flamborough Head was a defensive work thrown up by an invader—the Celtic incomer (the so-called ' Brython '), as we suppose —who secured thus a base of operations against the Gael (or ' Goidel '), and that, advancing further, this invader formed successively the Argam Lines, and the Scamridge Dykes.   The entrenchments that can be traced along the edges of the Wolds, upon the hills overlooking the Vale of Pickering, and across the moorland ridges south of the Esk, are probably all evidences of early strife between the Celt and the Gael for the possession of this part of Yorkshire.   The houes and grave-mounds upon the hills are apparently the work of the Celtic settlers, and they would seem to indicate a higher degree of civilization than has sometimes been suspected.   Some of them are of very large size, approaching even 100 feet in diameter; and they were not merely thrown up, as might have been supposed, but were laid by gradual accretion, with a regular stratification of vari-coloured materials, sometimes brought from a considerable distance.   It would appear that the bodies were invariably cremated, and the remains deposited upon the natural surface, often covered or accompanied by an urn, and some-times protected by an erection of stones.   As to the ' British villages ' which are so freely marked upon the Ordnance map, we cannot doubt, after the investiga-tions of Canon Atkinson, that they were, in fact, excavations made much later for working the iron-stone, on the ' bell-pit system.'   Many weapons belong-ing to this early time have been discovered — flint

blades in profusion at Bridlington, others at Seamer
Moor, Pickering, and elsewhere, with axe-heads, arrow-
joints, and ' sling-bullets,' as well as dagger-blades (as
with the skeleton and oaken coffin exhumed at Gristhorpe), and other implements of bronze.*

It would not appear that the moorland fastnesses of
Cleveland were ever brought under real subjection by
the Romans, but a military road passing north-eastward from York, through Malton, and leaving Pickering on the east, ascended to the camps at Cawthorn,
and crossed the heights by Flamborough Rigg and
Manley Cross into Wheeldale, keeping by July Park,
where Roman remains have been discovered, above the
left banks of the Wheeldale Beck and the Mirk Esk,
to a camp on Lease Rigg overlooking Eskdale, then
crossed the river near Grosmont, probably sending
down a branch to Whitby, and passed on by Swart
Houe Cross probably to Dunsley, and to a series of
camps on the heights overlooking the lower country
and the sea. Malton was an important Roman station,
in direct communication by road with *Eboracum* (York),
Isurium (Aldborough), and *Cataractonium* (Thornbrough,

---

* A most interesting account of houe-digging in Cleveland will
be found in Canon Atkinson's ' Forty Years in a Moorland Parish.'
Many urns and relics discovered by that patient investigator are
now in the British Museum, and the early history of the Yorkshire
coast and the neighbouring hills is further illustrated in the
museums of York, Scarborough, Whitby, and Hull. An article on
' The Weapons of the Ancient Tribes of Yorkshire,' by Mr. H. Syer
Cumming, in the *Journal of the British Archæological Association*,
1864, may be referred to.

near Catterick); and a road has been traced south-eastward from it by Wharram-le-Street to the Wolds, pointing direct to Beverley, then a port, and, as some have surmised, the *Petuaria* of the Romans. Roman roads also approached the coast in the neighbourhood of Filey and Bridlington.

Dunsley Bay, north of Whitby, may perhaps have been the *Dunum Sinus* of the Romans, and some have chosen to see the *Portus Felix* in the bay of Filey or Bridlington, while it seems not unlikely that Flamborough Head was the *Ocellum Promontorium*, though here, again, some have applied that name to the Spurn. It is not to be imagined that the Romans, who had crushed Carthage by gaining dominion in the Mediterranean, and whose invasion of Britain was made possible by the destruction of the maritime power of the Veneti, would be content to entrust the defence of the coast merely to camps overlooking the shore. We cannot doubt, indeed, that their galleys often put into the harbours of the Yorkshire coast, for we know that even Stilicho, the last of the Roman generals to wield effectively the decaying Roman power in Britain, was able, with his galleys, to sweep the freebooters of the narrow seas even to the distant Orkney Isles.

But upon the departure of the Romans the power of resistance to the marauders from the sea soon passed away, and the Angles, sweeping along the coast, having captured the city of *Lindum* (Lincoln), pushed up the Humber, and the network of its tributary rivers, established the kingdom of the Middle English, seized and wasted the 'altera Roma' of York, burnt and slew through the great central plain, and set up, in the region this book will treat of, the dominion of the Deiri. If we may believe Matthew of Westminster, Ida, the 'flame-bearer,' landed at Flamborough, with his twelve sons in forty keels, to found the Bernician kingdom (547 A.D.); but it is safer to conclude that the Bernicians made their way by the Valley of the Tweed. Their forces were measured against the Deirans in that fierce struggle with which the consolidation of our existing England began, and the kingdom of Northumbria grew from the fusion of Deira with Bernicia.

It is pleasant to think that from these very hillsides of the Deiran kinsfolk—may we say from the Wolds, or the wooded heights that slope down to the Vale of Pickering?—those youths were ravished whose fair faces awoke the apostolic zeal of Gregory in the market-place of Rome. It is pleasant, at any rate, to fancy this, when we remember the expression of Gregory, 'Non angli, sed angeli!' when he heard the strangers were Angles. 'Whence come they?' he asked, and, being told by the slave-masters they were from Deira, 'Ay, verily,' he replied, 'are they *de ira*, delivered from the wrath to come, and called to the mercy of Christ!' The preaching of Christianity followed, and later in this book we shall relate the history of Hilda's celebrated monastery, the Lamp of the North, on the cliff of Streoneshealh. The site was doubtless chosen because of its accessibility by sea, and we have, indeed, a record of ancient seafaring therefrom, when, in 684, after the death of St. Hilda, the Abbess Ælfleda sailed from Streoneshealh to hold speech with St. Cuthbert at Coquet Isle. It was this ancient journey that suggested to Scott the famous voyage to Lindisfarne, and let it not count to the disadvantage of him—*nihil tetigit quod non ornavit*—that he pictured it far later, at a mediæval date :

> ' It curled not Tweed alone, that breeze,
>   For far upon Northumbrian seas
>   It freshly blew, and strong ;
>   Where, from high Whitby's cloistered pile,
>   Bound to St. Cuthbert's Holy Isle,
>   It bore a bark along.'

It was from Whitby that learning was spread abroad through the North, and we shall see in this book how John, the fifth Archbishop of York, a disciple of Hilda, founded another home of learning at Beverley in the *Sylva Deirorum*, the Deirwald, or Wood of the Deirans.

Dr. Atkinson has contended, with a considerable degree of probability, from the evidence of place-names, folk-lore, and dialect, that the Angles never effected a complete occupation of the Cleveland hills. In fact, in addition to the ' hams ' and ' tuns ' of Holderness, the Vale of Pickering, and the hills flanking it on either side, we find there a long series of names showing clearly a systematic occupation by the Danes. Freeburgh Hill may, indeed, speak of the ' frithborh,' the peace-bond or frank-pledge, of the Angles ; but

Thingwala, the designation of a place occurring in the Whitby Register, speaks just as plainly of the 'thing,' or free-court, of the Danes. Equally significant are Odinberg, the mediæval name of Roseberry Topping, and Thordisa, now East Row, near Whitby, embodying the Scandinavian female name Thordis, with the suffix á, meaning a stream, while the 'by' or settlement severally of Orm, Asolf, Norman, Ailward, Ugleberd, Bergulf and Dane is indicated in the existing or recorded place-names of Ormesby, Aislaby, Normanby, Elwordeby, Ugglebarnby, Bergleby and Danby. The Scandinavian invaders, who devasted Beverley and Whitby under Inguar and Hubba about the year 867, have left, too, in the numerous 'wicks' of the Yorkshire coast the reminiscence of the 'viks' of their own home-land.

Of the coming of Harald Hardrada, we read in his 'Saga' that he first made the coast of Cleveland—the cliff land—where all men fled from him, and then fared southward to Scarborough, dealing with that place in a manner to be spoken of later in this book. 'Kom Haralldr Konung thar fyrst ath Einglande er Kliflond heita og flydi allt vndan Konung for so sudr til Skardaborgar.'

With the Norman Conquest our Yorkshire district fared very ill. In Holderness, the great Earls Morkere and Tostig, with Ulf, the benefactor to York, and many more, were replaced by Drogo de Beurere, the Fleming, and afterwards by Odo, Earl of Albemarle. In Cleveland, the thegns, whose names bespeak their

varied origin—Eadmund, Uctred, Magbanec, Levenot
(perhaps the same who had the Derbyshire holdings of
Edensor, Hathersage and Ballidon), Gamel, Ligulf,
Orm, Siward, Waltheof, Torchil, and many more—
gave place to the king and his thegns, and to Hugh,
Earl of Chester, Robert Malet, William de Percy,
Hugh Fitz-Baldric, and the Earl of Mortain (who
also had Helmsley), and the great fee of Robert de
Brus was carved out later. The same story of displacement reigns throughout. But what was more
terrible than any mere displacement of landowners
was the terrible harrying and wasting that marked the
vengeance of the Conqueror for the revolt of 1068.
With the unerring judgment that prompted him in
the administration of naval affairs, William saw that
the strength of the revolt lay in the presence of
Swein's fleet in the Humber, and, swearing 'by the
splendour of God' to avenge himself, he first procured
its withdrawal, and then turned in destructive fury
upon the North, and especially upon the coast, which
might otherwise have held out temptations to the
Danes. The story of that terrific wasting, in which
villages and towns were turned desolate, the crops
burned, the cattle slaughtered, and the implements of
husbandry scattered in fragments, so that famine
followed upon destruction, is too well known to need
repetition here. The words 'Wasta est,' often repeated in the Domesday Survey, mark the extent of
the ravaging, and, with Professor Freeman, we may
dismiss the story that the Conqueror spared Beverley

because of fear of or reverence for St. John. ' Eleven sokemen and two hundred and twenty-five villans and bordars !' exclaims Canon Atkinson in his ' History of Cleveland,' ' working among them no more than fifty-eight ploughs, in all of what is now well-peopled, well-tilled Cleveland !'

We must deal all too briefly with the circumstances subsequent to the Conquest that concern our chosen region, not in the vain hope of doing justice to them, but that what follows may gain somewhat by our survey. The wave of religious enthusiasm that digni-fied and elevated the century after the coming of the Normans had its highest flood in the very region that William had wasted, and covered Yorkshire with the splendours of monastic architecture. At the touch of the Benedictine hand the vacant walls of Whitby, which had been silent since the scourging of Inguar and Hubba, were invested with new magnificence, and, despite the seafaring marauders, whose harrying drove the abbot and his monks to their cell of Hackness for a time in the reign of William II., the abbey grew and flourished. The Cistercians built the splendid houses of Rievaulx and Byland, and many more to which it is beyond our scope here to refer; to the Augustinians we owe Kirkham, Guisborough and Bridlington; and the Preaching Friars and the Friars Minor secured their homes at Scarborough, Beverley, and elsewhere, and in 1291 were preaching for the Crusade.

The war with the Scots brought pitiable trouble

upon the North of England, and the terrible harrying of Northumberland and Cumberland in 1296 and 1297 drove the Augustinians of Hexhamshire to seek a home with their brethren at Bridlington. For some time Yorkshire itself escaped, but in 1318 the Scots swept southward, slaying and plundering, and the Black Douglas burnt Scarborough, and a fine was levied upon Beverley; in the following year the ' Chapter of Myton ' took place; in 1322 the harrying of the north-eastern dales drove the nuns of Rosedale to seek shelter elsewhere, and in 1327 the great Cleveland lords, Peter de Maulay, William de Thweng, and John de Falconberg were summoned to the muster at York. The nobles had built themselves castles in places of strategical vantage, and we shall refer in this volume to those of Skelton and Kilton at the northern outliers of the hills, to that of Mulgrave and the royal castle of Scarborough upon the coast, to the remarkable series of castles that kept guard over the dales that open from the north upon the Vale of Pickering —Ayton, Pickering, Kirbymoorside, and Helmsley —as well as to many more. The great plague of 1349 visited Yorkshire most severely, and the clergy were insufficient for their duties. ' The numerous vacancies recorded in the livings during the year show that the Yorkshire priests had fallen like leaves before the gale,' says Canon Raine. ' They at least did not shrink from the performance of their duty. Archbishop Zouche himself escaped unscathed, but from the circumstance that he made his will in the year of

the great sickness, we can see that he was not un-
prepared to share the fate of so many of his clergy.'*
When we come to speak of Scarborough, we shall
recount a remarkable piratical episode that occurred
there in 1377, which will serve to show the unsafe
condition of the seas at the time.

We pass on in this brief survey to the Pilgrimage of
Grace (1536). The region to which this book is
devoted was deeply stirred by the events that followed
the dissolution of the monasteries, and we shall see
how much of historic interest relating to them belongs
to the Yorkshire coast and its neighbouring hills.
Aske, Darcy, and the other leaders drew, indeed, much
of their strength from this region, Sir Robert Constable, of Flamborough, raised the surrounding country,
and Sir John Bulmer awoke the flame further north.
Readers of this book, when incidents connected with
this rising are referred to, will remember the course
of it — how the commons of Holderness, and the
coast generally, were attached to the cause, and how
Hull was taken; how the victorious pilgrims laid down
their arms at the coming of the king's pardon, from
which, indeed, certain men of Beverley were excepted,
and declared 'they would wear no badge but that
of their sovereign lord;' how they were deceived
and outwitted by Norfolk and the king; how Sir
Francis Bigod, of Mulgrave, fanned the flame anew,
and with Hallam attempted to seize both Hull and

* 'Historical Papers and Letters from the Northern Registers,'
xxxi.

Scarborough, and, finally, how terrible was the vengeance that followed, in which gibbets bore their melancholy burdens by the roadside, and terror-stricken widows stole out at night-time to cut down the bodies of their husbands, that they might bury them secretly ere dawn, while the leaders laid their heads upon the block—Sir Robert Constable being hanged in chains at Hull—and one lady among them was given to the flames.

In the Civil Wars, our Yorkshire coast region played a considerable part, and the feeling of the people, which will be illustrated as we deal with places where it was manifested, was exceedingly strong. The double treachery of the Hothams, first to the king and then to the Parliament, with the desperate defence of Fairfax against Newcastle's powerful attack, has given special character to the operations at Hull. It was at Bridlington that Queen Henrietta Maria landed, convoyed by Van Tromp, when she returned to England after her expedition to dispose of the crown jewels abroad. The two sieges of Scarborough, moreover, in the first of which it held out so late as July, 1645, are notable incidents connected with the region we have chosen. The Cavaliers here certainly found much support, and during the Commonwealth the privateers of the Royalists were often operating upon the coast.

All these, and many more, historical circumstances will be recounted as we go on, in order to beguile and make more interesting our descriptive wayfaring along the Yorkshire coast and amid the north-eastern hills. It is a region whose heights are haunted by memories, and whose dales are full of history. The very people, by their rugged speech, their blue eyes, and their hardy sun-browned or sea-tanned skins, bespeak a near kinship with the Dane. They are a very pleasant folk, too, to journey amongst. The wayfarer along the country roads may meet, perhaps, a teamster with a load of corn, or a farmer trotting homeward, or it may be a labourer bearing upon his shoulders a huge bundle of the stems of burnt heather, or, as he will call it, ' ling,' which he has gathered upon the moor, and which will make excellent ' kindling' for his housewife's fire; but he may be assured of a pleasant greeting or a cheery word, and if he ask information, the Yorkshireman will certainly give it to him, and sometimes will go 'agate'ards' with him along the road, or otherwise help him on his way. The frank and ready courtesy of the Yorkshire peasantry is indeed a pleasant experience to the stranger, and it has happened to the writer of this to be made welcome and to receive unsolicited hospitality and good cheer at a farmhouse where the brown harvestmen, at their mid-day meal, were doing ample justice to a huge Yorkshire pie. In such company the wayfarer is likely to hear many a shrewd remark and quaint saying, for has not Mr. Baring-Gould recorded the observation of a friend to the effect that ' every other Yorkshireman is a character·' ? Yet character is apt to be brushed away by the levelling influence of the board-school, and the conventional necessities of a 'code,' and it is to be feared that there are not a few even in Yorkshire who are shame-faced at the homely wisdom and rustic speech of their honest, down-right, plain-spoken sires. Still, however, happily, in lonely valleys and sequestered hamlets upon the hills lingers a quaint flavour of the eld, and he who can win the confidence—no easy task, let us say—of the Yorkshire peasantry, may even now hear an echo of the witch-craft-time, of elves, and hobs, and fairies, of the 'gabble-ratchet' that is the forewarning of death, and of many another 'eldritch' thing, to certain of which, in this book, some reference may be made.

CHAPTER II.

THE NORTH CLEVELAND COAST REGION.

The Northern Plain—Coatham and Redcar—Marske—Saltburn—
Huntcliff—The Skelton Glen—Skelton Castle and the House
of Brus—Country Roads—Upleatham and Kirkleatham—
Wilton Castle—The Bulmers and the Pilgrimage of Grace—
Eston Nab—Ironstone Quarries—Guisborough—The Augus-
tinian Priory—Roseberry Topping, and the Prospect therefrom.

THE Tees—having left behind it the racing flats of
Mandale Bottoms, and having glided, with strange
reflections upon its darkened waters, by the fiery town
of Middlesborough, where its course is flanked by
blazing blast furnaces and wide-spreading steel works,
by long stretches of refuse from iron-smelting, and dark
lengths of land reclaimed from its waters, by docks
crowded with varied craft, and by yards where ship-
wrights are busy—escapes from its lurid, fretful surroundings into the broad, sandy expanse of Tees
Mouth. Beyond Tod Point and Bran Sand the Yorkshire coast trends south-eastward, and for many a
long mile is yet low and of the superficial 'drift,' and
one may gallop, without drawing rein, along its broad,
level sands. It presents as yet nothing picturesque

from the sea, but beyond it rise the bold form of
Eston Nab and the wooded heights of Upleatham, from
which the ironstone is largely won that has given a
varied measure of prosperity to the whole country-side.
Between the hills and the Northern Sea lies a pastoral
country, without special features, rising gradually to
the foot of the heights.

From these outliers of the Cleveland hills, from the
height of Upleatham, and still better from the crest of
Eston Nab (800 feet) to the westward of it, there is
a vast prospect of this lower country, and of the sea,
with the Durham coast beyond.   Below us, as we
stand on the heights, it is not difficult to understand
that much was marsh before systematic drainage began.
There, away to the north, at the very angle of Tees
Mouth, Coatham Marsh still preserves the character.
Nay, there still remains, upon the edge of it, that
'camp of refuge by the Tees,' as we cannot doubt,
with its earthen ramparts inclosing a space some 90
feet square, protected, as Professor Freeman describes
it, on every side by marsh or sea, and approached only
by a narrow causeway of dry land, whereon the last
uncrushed remnant of the Cleveland folk—the band
of marauders, as Ordericus calls them — thought to
make their last stand against the Conqueror after his
terrific harrying of their dales.

It is not surprising, in old times, in a marshy country
like this, that fishing should have been more profitable
than agriculture; and, indeed, we find that, upon the
partition of the great Brus fee, at the end of the reign

of Henry III.—a circumstance to be referred to here-
after—the boats at Cotum and Rideker are recorded
as being paid for at the rate of twelve shillings, while
the value of an acre of arable was but eightpence, and
of an acre of meadow but fourteen - pence. East
Coatham and Redcar, in these days, stretch their long,
unpicturesque conjoined length upon the outermost
angle of the shore ; and with their firm level sands,
and dry, bracing air, their twin piers, and other attractions, have secured a large measure of popularity,
chiefly among the holiday-makers of Stockton and
Middlesborough. The whole district below the hills
is of the ' drift,' or boulder clay ; but off the coast at
Redcar the lower lias shale crops out in reefs—the
West Scar and the Salt Scar, with the Goat Hole
between them, and the High Stone, and the East and
West Flashes, to the south of these.

From our point of vantage upon the hill we follow
the coast-line south-eastward of Redcar, closely accompanied by the railway from Middlesborough, to where,
two miles further on, the boulder cliffs rising to a
height of about 50 feet, the village of Marske is seen,
standing by a brooklet that there makes its way to the
sea. It is a pleasant, sequestered little place, visited
by few, with a Jacobean hall, with cupolas and many
mullioned windows, built by Sir William Pennyman,
in the time of Charles I., and now the residence of the
Ven. Archdeacon Yeoman, as well as a modern church of
Continental aspect, and an old one where Captain Cook's
father lies buried. Indeed, the whole of the country

hereabout is filled with the memories of James Cook. They talk of him much at Marton, where he was born; the house which his father built is pointed out at Great Ayton, beneath the western slopes of the Cleveland hills; and we shall presently speak of Staithes and Whitby, where he first became a seafarer. The 'old church' at Marske, however, is not older than the year 1821, when it replaced a Norman structure, with a nave and aisles, separated from it by semicircular arches, resting upon round pillars. The destruction of this church is the first instance we have had to note of the lamentable ignorance and blind folly of church-wardens and others who, from fifty to a hundred years ago, swept away with ruthless hand much of the historical architecture of Cleveland. A relic of this church remains, in a square Norman font, characteristically carved, which once graced the vicarage lawn, doing duty as a flower-pot!

In the summer-time, when the sands hereabout are flecked with the shadows of clouds, and when the sea-gulls ride upon the billows, and the air has a salty savour, the coast is delightful enough; but it does not begin to assume its true character of sweetness and grandeur until we reach Saltburn, some two miles further on, where the cliff rises to the height of about 100 feet. There, issues the first of those deep wood-land gorges through the hills for which the Yorkshire coast is famous. You cannot know their beauty unless you traverse them. Walking upon the breezy hills, indeed, you would scarcely suspect their presence;

but, with almost startling suddenness, their sylvan depths are disclosed, and you hear the mellow voice of the rushing stream. Many such delightful glens will occupy our pen in this book, but, perhaps, none leads to places so interesting as we shall reach by ascending the Skelton Beck—once known as the Holebeck—from Saltburn.

It is this fact, combined with its glorious sands, bracing air, splendid coast scenery, and woodland beauties, that makes Saltburn one of the most attractive of the Yorkshire watering-places. Saltburn-by-the-Sea is built upon the bluffs to the west of the ravine at the seaward termination of the flanking hills of the North Yorkshire moors, which trend away inland in a somewhat southerly curve to Roseberry Topping, having, between them and the plain described above, a series of detached and wooded hills, cut off from them by an upland hollow. Eastward of the mouth of the ravine rises the remarkable conical height of Cat Nab, with the primitive village of Old Saltburn at its foot, a place where the facilities for smuggling were once taken full advantage of, and consisting still of a few fishermen's cottages. Beyond the village, the long, dark scarps of Huntcliff, consisting of the lower lias shale, with the ironstone and marlstone series superimposed, rising to a height of 350 feet, lift their weather-beaten faces, seamed and worn by unnumbered storms; and at every tide the waves deposit in the hollows and crannies of the Flat Scar, which lies at their feet, and stretches from the Penny Hole, by Bird

Flight Goit, and Seal Goit, even to Cattersty Sands, at Skinningrove, a hundred varieties of the flora and fauna of the sea. At low water, with great circumspection, it is possible to walk over difficult ground—from Old Saltburn, by the Old Haven, Rockcliff, and Jackdaw Crag, right round the promontory to Skinningrove, but the venture should by no means be made without good advice. In the platform rock, as in the several strata of the shale in the cliff itself, many varieties of lias fossils may be collected. From the hill of Brotton Warsett (549 feet), above the crest of Huntcliff, one may survey a wonderful panorama. A vast expanse of blue sea lies extended before one, green where the cloud-shadows rest upon it, and dotted with the white sails of many vessels; away to the northwest, with the conical height of Cat Nab in the foreground, the long coast-line stretches to where, in the trembling haze, the shores of Durham are distinguished beyond the mouth of Tees; and inland there is a glorious prospect of the Cleveland hills, with the distant conical height of Roseberry Topping rising above the ridge.

The modern Saltburn on the west cliff has the character of a fashionable watering-place, with a splendid hotel, bearing the name of the great landowner hereabout, the Earl of Zetland, a sufficiency of other like accommodation, and many terraces of fine houses. There is a handsome pier, and an inclined tramway gives easy access from the cliff to the shore.*

* It may be useful here to note certain return driving distances to the resorts near Saltburn : Marske and Skelton, 7 m. ; Marske

It is now time that we should begin our inland journeying by way of the Skelton Beck; and here it should first be noted that another streamlet—the Saltburn Gill, a delightful, hillside, wooded, rock-bound brook—falls into its course near the mouth. This gill has its gathering ground in the hills above Skelton, by the Millholme Beck, and the Boosbeck, and many other streams and rills. The lower portion of the Saltburn Glen has been turned into charming gardens, where are a theatre and concert-room; and, passing beneath a light iron girder bridge, 140 feet high, and about 800 feet long, of good design, which connects the east and west cliffs, we find ourselves in pleasant walks between richly-wooded slopes, and amid trimly-kept grass-plats and flower-beds, and we come upon tennis-lawns, and a band-stand, and a grotto in the guise of a temple. But these evidences of the neighbouring watering-place are soon left behind. The gorge narrows between steep cliffs, and we advance further through the lovely sylvan scenery of Riftswood, catch sight of Rushpool Hall—a modern château, with peaked roofs and high tourelles—and descend to the picturesque hollow where Marske Mill stands, half

and Upleatham, 10 m. ; Kilton Castle and Glen, 8 m. ; Upleatham and Skelton, 8 m. ; Guisborough, 12 m. ; Kirkleatham and Redcar, 12 m. ; Lofthouse, 12 m. ; Easington, 14 m. ; Wilton Castle and Grounds, 14 m. ; Grinkle Park (Easington), 20 m. ; Roseberry Topping, 20 m. ; The Moors, by Skelton, returning by Guisborough, 20 m. ; Staithes, 20 m. ; Runswick Bay and Hinderwell, 22 m.

hidden by shelving crag and overhanging boughs.* Beyond this the railway crosses on a lofty viaduct, making a double horseshoe curve from Saltburn, by Brotton, to Skinningrove, and then Jackdaw Scar rears its stupendous form, and the stream runs below. Further on the way is pleasant enough, by woods and upland fields, to the village and castle of Skelton.

Of the village nothing need be said, save that it is very pleasantly situated on the slope, for the church there, too, was replaced by an uninteresting structure in 1785. The modern Skelton Castle, the residence of W. H. A. Wharton, Esq., Master of the Cleveland Hounds, who here has his kennels, is a large embattled building of tolerable architecture; but it stands upon the site of the great *caput baroniæ* of the house of Brus. Skelton and Guisborough were granted by the Conqueror mostly to the Earl of Mortain and Robert Malet, but upon the attainder of one, and banishment of the other, both were conferred upon Robert de Brus. This powerful noble was the ancestor by his son Robert of the great Robert Bruce, and from another son, Adam, were descended the lords of Skelton, and of a vast stretch of Cleveland. Adam was succeeded by another Adam, and he by three Peters in succession, the last of whom was a diligent

* Near the narrowest part of the glen the Saltburn mineral spring has its rise. Its chief constituents are chloride of sodium and carbonate of lime (respectively 27.78 and 11.20 grains per gallon), the other elements (in no case more than a grain per gallon) being carbonates of magnesia and iron, sulphate of lime, chloride of magnesium, alumina, silica, and a trace of chloride of potassium.

judge, learned in the law. Peter de Brus was one
of the confederate barons who wrung the charter
from John, and, in 1216, John, in retaliation, either
reduced Skelton by siege or captured it by stratagem.
What was the strength and character of the castle we
may infer from the wealth and importance of its lords,
and it is recorded that the Peter de Brus of John's
time was delighted 'soe much in the beauty of the
chapelle, that he gave certain landes to Henry Percye
upon condition that every Christmasse day he should
come to that castell, and leade his wife by the arme
from her chamber to the chapell '—a tenure perhaps
unique. Upon the death of the last Peter de Brus,
his estates were divided among his four sisters
and co-heiresses, and in this way Skelton came to
Walter de Fauconberg in right of his wife, Agnes de
Brus.

From the Fauconbergs it passed to the Nevilles
and the Lords Conyers, the last of whom had three
daughters and co-heiresses, of whose husbands the
story runs that, in mutual despite, each destroyed that
part of the castle of which he was possessed. Steven-
son, the author of 'Crazy Tales' and of 'Macarony
Fables,' better known as the 'Eugenius' of the 'Sentimental Journey,' lived at Skelton Castle in the last
century, where Sterne often visited him, and it is
related that, the host having a particular objection
to leave his bed when the wind was in the east, his
guest once bribed a boy to tie the vane with its point
to the west. Mount Shandy, near the castle, upon

the right bank of the Skelton Beck, will remind the
wayfarer of these visits, as Hob Hill above the other
bank, with Hob Hill Wood upon the slope, will of
those quaint wayward sprites who aforetime have, as
legend hath it, done so much that was mischievous or
useful for the Yorkshiremen.

The region to the west and south-west of Skelton is
one presenting many attractions to the wayfarer. He
may pursue the Green Lane which climbs the hillside above Skelton village, and gives a magnificent
prospect of the hills, the lower country with the Skelton
Valley winding through it, and the sea, and he may
drop down by that way into the Boosbeck hollow,
crossing the Guisborough and Saltburn branch of the
North-Eastern Railway, and so reach Stanghow Moor
beyond. Or, leaving the same road on his left hand,
about half a mile beyond the village, he may ascend
to the height of Airy Hill (700 feet), where on every
hand a glorious prospect is unfolded, not only of the
lovely lower country, with its varied contours of hill
and dale, but of the wooded slopes of Upleatham to
the north, and of Guisborough mapped out in its
amphitheatre of hills to the west, with the great moorland escarpments beyond, as well as of the heathery
heights of Guisborough Moor, and the conical height
of Roseberry Topping crowning the whole. The path
beyond Airy Hill will bring the wayfarer down by the
steep wooded declivity of Rawcliff Banks into the
sylvan glen of the Waterfall or Spa Gill (Guisborough
lying beyond), which, rising amid the heather and

ON THE CLEVELAND MOORS.   DRAWN BY ALFRED DAWSON.

bracken of Guisborough Moor, flows down, with many
a still pool reflecting the hills and overhanging trees,
and many a rushing shallow, by Wileycat Wood,
Slape Wath, Spa Wood and Waterfall Wood, and
falls into the Skelton Beck at the foot of Upleatham
Park. The direct road from Skelton to Guisborough,
however, approaches this point, dropping down into
the Skelton glen at Skelton Ellers, and a little further
on throws off a branch to the pleasant village of
Upleatham. That village may, however, be approached
from Skelton by the road to Marske, the wayfarer
turning to the left about half a mile after crossing the
beck. The country hereabout, it will be seen, is very
well provided with roads and by-paths, many of which
are most delightful to wander along ; but, inasmuch
as they are not very easily intelligible to the stranger,
he will find it an advantage to make inquiries before
starting upon his journey.

The old church of Upleatham, which was given by
Robert de Brus to the priory of Guisborough, was
once a fine Norman structure, and traces of two of
the arches of the south aisle may still be seen in
the portion of the old nave now used as a cemetery
chapel. There are some few remains of windows
and columns, too, in the chancel, which also had a
south aisle, with curious monumental remains, and
a row of grotesque Norman corbels may be seen externally on the north wall of the nave. A beautiful
Norman font, square in shape, without stem, and
with characteristic angle pillars, the flat sides covered

with varied carving, has been removed to the new
church, which is a structure of Norman design.*

Upleatham Hall, the seat of the Earl of Zetland,
is a fine modern structure, in a beautiful park covering
the top of the height, and with well-kept Italian
gardens and trim parterres. The northern side of
the hill is much quarried for ironstone, and a branch
of the railway ascends the acclivity to the height of
about 300 feet for the conveyance of it.

From this northern side of the hill, too, may be
seen, two miles away to the north-west, at the foot
of the slope, and upon the edge of the level, the hamlet
and hall of Kirkleatham, of which something may be
said here. The hall, which is the residence of G. H.
Turner Newcomen, Esq., is an old building, refronted
and enlarged by Carr, of York, standing in well-wooded
grounds. It was long the residence of the Turners,
the last of whom, Sir Charles, a well-known agri-
culturist, was here visited by Sir Joseph Banks, who
brought with him Omai, the 'gentle savage.' Sir
William Turner, Lord Mayor of London, founded in
1676 the hospital at Kirkleatham, which is a large
brick building surrounding three sides of a square,
the fourth being closed by an iron grille. The building includes a chapel, with fine stained glass, a
museum with a few interesting local objects, and a
library. Of the old church at Kirkleatham only a few

* By the old church a sequestered and beautiful by-path leads
down into the glen, crosses the beck by a plank bridge, follows the
bank for a little distance, and ascends to the road to Skelton.

fragments and memorial-stones remain. The present
structure, which has a statue of John Turner, sergeant-
at-law, by Scheemaker, and a characteristic full-length
late brass of Robert Colthurst (1631), was built in
1763, and is not so devoid of merit as most other
churches of like date in Cleveland.

Some two miles west of Upleatham, and a mile
south-west of Kirkleatham, at the foot of the great
escarpment of Eston Nab, lies the village of Wilton,
with Wilton Castle, the seat of Sir Charles Lowther, a
large modern house, of which Sir Robert Smirke was
the architect, in a commanding situation backed by
woodland. Here once was the castle of the Bulmers,
who, among the great families of Yorkshire, held their
post in time of need. Ralph de Bulmer was summoned by Archbishop Greenfield to a council of war
at Doncaster in 1315, to take measures for the protection of the North against the Scots, and again,
in 1327, the first year of Edward III., he was bidden
to betake himself to York, with such men as he could
assemble to aid in repelling the invasion. Sir William
Bulmer founded, in 1531, the chantry chapel of St.
Ellen in the village, of which some traces remain ; and
six years later Sir John Bulmer was hanged at Tyburn
for his share in the Pilgrimage of Grace, while Lady
Bulmer, suffering the fearful punishment awarded to
women for treachery, ' was drawn without Newgate to
Smithfield, and there burned.' She, with Sir John
and other persons, had plotted, if the confession of
her chaplain be rightly reported, to seize and carry

3

off the Duke of Norfolk, the king's lieutenant in the North, to Wilton Castle, and the lady is stated to have declared that she would as soon be torn in pieces as go to London unless the Duke of Norfolk's and Sir Ralph Ellerkar's heads were off, and then she might go where she would 'at the head of the commons.' As illustrating the feeling of the time, it is interesting to learn how that Parson Franke of Lofthouse, or Loftus, some six miles away, who had been prominent in the first rising, being asked for counsel on a point by Sir John Bulmer, replied to the messenger: 'Twisshe, straws! I can nother thee nother thy master thanke for sending to me for any such counsel. . . . And if thy master be sent for to London, let him go as he is commanded. I can give him none other counsel.'*

We read also, in the mutilated deposition of one whose name is lost, of a certain riotous storming of Wilton, at a somewhat earlier date, in those troublous times. It would appear that a party of the commons from Guisborough, reproaching the deponent with being 'a lollard and a puller-down of abbeys,' said that he should go with them, ' in spite of his teeth '; and so they went to Sir John Bulmer's, at Wilton Castle, apparently with the purpose of forcing Sir John to declare for them ; but we may infer that he was from home, for they were refused admittance. However, by threatening to burn the gates, they forced an entrance, searched

* 'Letters and Papers, Foreign and Domestic, Henry VIII.,' vol. xii., part 2, No. 12.

the house, 'and compelled the servants to take appointment with them.' Unfortunately, owing to mutilation and illegibility of the MS., the details of this assault cannot be made out.* There are some Norman features in Wilton Chapel, which was an appanage of Guisborough, with the effigy of a Bulmer and his lady, of the time of Edward I.

From Wilton the ascent may be made of Eston Nab, the bold contours of which are a chief feature of all this part of North Cleveland. A 'nab' in North Yorkshire is the steep, escarped end of a ridge, where it drops to the plain or the vale; and Eston Nab pre-eminently deserves the name. The greatest elevation is 800 feet, and some idea may be gained of the steepness of the escarpments from the fact that, within little more than the horizontal distance of a quarter of a mile on the north-western side, a drop of 500 feet is made. It is upon this flank of the hill that the famous Eston quarries are found, where vast quantities of ironstone are raised, and transported by rail from the foot to the blast-furnaces of Middlesborough. There is evidence, in the pits of the so-called ' British villages ' on the moors, of the early working of Cleveland iron; and record shows that the monks of Whitby and Rievaulx were among the workers. Of the modern industry, Grosmont, in Eskdale, may be said to be the birthplace; but its surprising development did not take place until the discovery of the vast seam of iron-

* 'Letters and Papers, Foreign and Domestic, Henry VIII.,' vol. xii., part I, No. 1011.

stone on the north-west side of Eston Nab by Mr. Vaughan in 1850; and the gigantic works of Messrs. Bolckow, Vaughan, and Co. have been the result. There is a rich growth of trees upon the slopes of the hill in many parts, but upon the top are the moors of Wilton, Eston, and Barnaby, covered with heather, bracken, and bilberry, and with pools and mosses here and there. Many tumuli are on these moors, testifying to early occupation; with a semicircular camp, perhaps British, but certainly occupied as an outlook station by the Romans, of which the foss and vallum may still be traced. Ord, in his 'History of Cleveland,' gives the dimensions as being 343 yards for the length of the arc, 706 feet for the length along the cliff, and 310 feet for the breadth across. From the north and north-western edges of the Nab there are vast prospects of the coasts of Yorkshire and Durham, and of the sea, as well as of the whole estuary of the Tees, busy with its shipping, while the wooded country towards distant Richmond is laid out like a map below.

Highcliff is that part of the Nab overlooking the town of Guisborough, which lies in a richly-wooded country, almost shut in by hills, and yet some 300 feet above the sea, at the foot of the broken and picturesque declivities of the south-eastern side. Camden compares the situation of Guisborough to that of Puteoli in Italy; but the new buildings which have sprung up in the town, for the accommodation of the iron-workers, have deprived the place of much of its charm.

Yet the splendid eastern wall of its priory—unsurpassed of its kind in England—may well continue to attract many thither. There is no such winding stream as flows by the sister Augustinian houses of Kirkham and Bolton; but the sylvan shades of Urchin Wood, Spring Wood, Cliff Wood, and Kemplah Wood, which clothe the precipitous steep of the flank of Guisborough moor to the south, are a fine setting for the splendid and melancholy fragment—a monument of blind fury and iconoclasm. It is beyond our scope to relate here the history of Guisborough (or, as often of old it was called, Gisburne), but some landmarks of that history are meet for our purpose. The priory was founded by Robert de Brus of Skelton in 1129 (or it may have been in 1119), and his family and all the great landowners of Cleveland were its benefactors. What was the character of the original buildings we are left to guess, for in May, 1289, as Walter de Hemingburgh, the historian, one of its canons, relates, a great conflagration consumed the church, with its library, its chalices, crucifixes, and vestments. The conflagration was due to the carelessness of a plumber, who had a fire on the roof for its repair, which he left to be extinguished by two lads who were with him, and the high wind carried the sparks among the dry and exposed timbers, and so the destruction began.

No time was lost, however, in the rebuilding; and we find that in 1302 Hemingburgh, then sub-prior, was despatched to Archbishop Corbridge to report upon the state of the house, with the assurance that its discipline and observances were strict and regular, and that the canons lived at peace with one another, and had contrived, since the last year, to pay off more than £225 of their debt, which in these days would be a very large sum. Guisborough was one of those houses asked, in 1319, to assist Archbishop Melton in his distress, owing to the losses caused by the Scottish incursion, and to the ' Chapter of Myton,' at which he had lost his plate; and in 1320 it was requested to shelter a canon of Bolton, the monks whereof were compelled to disperse, because of their losses in the same harrying. We may infer, too, that Guisborough itself had suffered, or, at least, was thought to be in danger somewhat later, for in 1375 the prior had license to fortify it. The last prior, Robert Pursglove, suffragan Bishop of Hull (*ob.* 1579), who lies buried, with a fine brass and later doggerel epitaph, in Tideswell Church, Derbyshire, founded a hospital and school in the town. At the dissolution, the site of Guisborough was granted to Sir Thomas Chaloner, whose family still hold it; and in 1867 Admiral Chaloner conducted some interesting excavations on the spot, when a stone coffin, with several others, was brought to light, which was assumed to be that of the founder, or of a later Robert Bruce, the competitor for the Scottish crown. This Sir Thomas Chaloner introduced the alum industry into England, having noticed, it is said, a resemblance of colour in the soil and foliage at Guisborough to that seen at the papal alum works near Rome; and further, so the story runs, having imported alum-workers from Rome, he was excommunicated with such forms as furnished Sterne for his celebrated cursing in 'Tristram Shandy.'

Of Guisborough Priory itself—in addition to portions of the transition Norman gatehouse, and, at the west end, an unearthed bit of the cellar under the 'frater' —nothing remains but the superb wall at the east end of the church—a splendid relic indeed—in looking at which, as Mr. Lefroy well says, 'the trained eye and educated imagination of the architect can restore, almost at a glance, the vast web of Early Decorated work which once made it a chief glory of its date.'* The tracery of the vast east window, which extended from just above the high-altar to the level of the top of the triforium, has been ruthlessly broken down; but the richly - carved mouldings remain to bespeak its splendour, and the shields of Brus, Bulmer, and Thweng on the jambs tell of the benefactors. There is a window above in the gable, and the three-light windows at the ends of the aisles are not less glorious in their rich details of tracery, their vine-leaf mouldings, and their oak-leaf capitals. The lateral buttresses are most beautifully composed in groups of three, with niches, now tenantless, and tabernacle work, and are surmounted by crocketed spirelets, while the thrust of the arches has been supported by the deep and lofty buttresses which still stand on the east. The responds of the lateral walls, and of the arcades, which remain,

* 'The Ruined Abbeys of Yorkshire,' by W. Chambers Lefroy, F.S.A., edit. 1891, p. 251.

make it not difficult to understand what has been the
grandeur of the aisle windows, the clustered columns,
the richly-moulded arches, the triforium, and the great
clerestory; but to reconstruct, except by analogy, the
domestic offices, is impossible, so thoroughgoing has
been the wanton destruction of Guisborough Priory.

In the western porch, under the tower of the
modernized parish church, are placed the separated
portions of an altar-tomb, which, according to Dugdale,
was once in the priory church.   It was probably that
of Robert de Brus, buried at Guisborough in 1294, or
of his grandson, the King of Scotland.   Other fragments—effigies of crowned and sceptred kings, one
holding the arms of Scotland—remain to tell of the
erewhile splendour of the Bruces.

Having now surveyed the ancient town of Guisborough—where, indeed, we might pause to write history
at length, and specially might we find something interesting to say concerning certain incidents of the
Pilgrimage of Grace — let us ascend to the well-
known peak of Roseberry Topping, which rises three
miles south-westward of it.   The way leads by a gentle
ascent towards Hutton Hall, and passes the railway to
Middlesborough, as well as the branch by which ironstone is brought from the quarries in the flanks of
Guisborough Moor, the conical peak being all the
way a prominent object; but the path becomes more
steep as it climbs the side of Hutton Moor and crosses
Roseberry Common, until, upon the crest, the breath-
less wayfarer stands 1,057 feet above the level of the

sea. The steepest escarpment is on the western side, where, within a quarter of a mile, there is a declivity of nearly 700 feet ; but the contour lines above 800 feet approximate all to a circle. Throughout the Middle Ages Roseberry Topping occurs in records and deeds as Othensbergh, wherein undoubtedly is expressed the name of the 'Hill of Odin,' which the Danes conferred upon it. How Odinsberg was transformed into Roseberry is not easy to discover, but Canon Atkinson suggests that, since Odin may be described as 'the lord of the air, who chases through the sky in the roaring storm,' Hreosebeorh, the hill of the 'rusher' or the 'raging one,' may be an Anglian translation of it. It must be allowed, however, that the first appearance of an Anglian translation, so late as the seventeenth century, requires some explanation, and to us it seems more probable that the name Roseberry is near akin to the old English word, now almost obsolete, 'rosland,' signifying heathery or moory land, which is near akin, again, to the Welsh *rhos*, a moor or dry meadow. 'Topping' is merely the local description of a peaked height. Roseberry is formed of the lias, with a sandstone cap, which gives it a broken, craggy crest, and its sides are clothed with fir and other woods. The cresset beacon upon the top is not yet quite forgotten. On the northern slope is a well, the waters of which once had a repute as a cure for sore eyes. There, says Ord, legend hath it that Oswy, a Northumbrian boy-prince, was drowned, while his mother slumbered upon the crest, she having brought him to the height that he might escape the doom of drowning which had been foretold for him. Upon the northern side of the hill are a number of pits, which the Ordnance surveyors and others have taken as evidences of a ' British settlement,' but which are much more likely to be evidences of early working of the mineral resources of the height. It now remains only to speak of the superb view from the crest. To the west and south-west, the whole of the Cleveland hills, with their heathery heights, green, or purple, or brown, according to the season, with broken and varied contours, and the traces of many a winding dale, and beyond them the blue North Sea ; to the north and north-west the tiled roofs of Guisborough, the wooded hills of Upleatham and Skelton, a vast prospect of Tees Mouth, and of the dim blue distance, where, beyond the smoke of Middlesborough, lies Durham, spread out like a map ; to the west the wooded and picturesque gathering ground of the Leven, with the valleys of Ayton and Marton, ever to be associated with Cook, further still the winding way of Tees, and the yellow cornfields and bosky woods that stretch out to where the far-off hills about Richmond stand out of the enshrouding haze ; to the south the neighbouring brother hill of Easby Moor (1,064 feet), as steeply and boldly scarped as that whereon we stand, with the monument of Cook upon its brow, and a little to the right, and further off, the massive contours of the Hambleton hills, that border the great Vale of York. Here indeed, on a clear day, for extent and variety, is the finest prospect that Cleveland can unfold.

CHAPTER III.

IT is, as we have said, a fascinating walk at low water
for the geologist, and the lover of rugged rock and
salt sea (the wayfarer being first satisfied as to the
safety of his journey), from Saltburn to Skinningrove,
along the talus of the lias cliff, with its water-worn
boulders, and still brown pools in the weedy rock,
where are anemones, starfish, urchins, and many other
things of the sea; but the journey may be made also
by a breezy walk along the cliffs.   On the right rises
the dome-like form of Warsett Hill, with the village of
Brotton, remarkable for nothing save its beautiful and
extensive views; and that here, as elsewhere in many
places in Cleveland, its ancient church has been replaced
by one of no interest whatever.   A descent to the
course of a wooded rill, and a climb over the end of

Skinningrove Ridge, brings the wayfarer to the village, which is chiefly dependent upon the neighbouring iron-stone quarrying. Skinningrove lies at the foot of one of the sylvan glens of the Yorkshire coast—that of the Kilton Beck—whereof the deep wooded character can be seen well by travellers on the coast railway, which crosses it diagonally on a lofty viaduct about a mile inland. The wanderer in the glen—and there are many paths through its woods—may hear the beck rolling over its stony bed, as he goes forward mid the trees and by gray scars, whereon ivy and lichens cling; and when the sun shines athwart the trembling leaves in the spring-time, they will gleam like living gold against the dark background of the further unsunned hill. On the left, as he fares onward, the railway having now crossed to the other hill, is the wooded hollow of Deepdale, through which a rill pours down from the upland fields; and further on, just before the viaduct is reached, is the confluence of the two main constituent streams. In our descriptive journey we pursue the Kilton Beck itself, to the right, which, receiving many a rill from the wooded slopes, giving varied contours to the hills by their several dells, brings us to the site of Kilton Castle, above the left bank of the stream.

These shattered gray walls are the remains of the baronial castle of the Thwengs, notable men of old time, of whom Marmaduke married Lucia, one of the co-heiresses of De Brus. The situation is typical of a Cleveland stronghold, being a tongue of land, some

300 feet long, protected on three sides by declivities to the beck, and defended once by an elaborate series of water-moats, which can still be traced, upon the north-west, towards the hill. Much of the massive masonry still standing is rough rubble, from which the dressed ashlar has been torn away, and is probably of the latter half of the twelfth century; but there are evidences of a still earlier building, perhaps of the time of the De Kiltons, who were here before the Thwengs. The principal portion of the castle now remaining is on the north-west front, and the northern angle has been flanked by a tower with loopholes, of which one is perfect, cross-shaped and deeply splayed, commanding the chief entrance. The entire width is about 88 feet, and the length of the inclosure, by the evidences, has been 256 feet; but the plan is irregular, and the structure bears traces of much alteration. There are still fragments of a large building at the western extremity, and in the place called the 'dungeon' indications remain of a staircase that gave access to the upper rooms. The tower and the eastern end are probably the most ancient parts of the existing castle. We hear of the place in the time of the Northern risings, associated with Sir John Bulmer of Wilton, mentioned in the last chapter, who is alleged to have resorted to Lord Lumley, who was at Kilton, saying he had already 'browyd and bakyt and sleyne hys beffes,' and to have prevailed upon Lumley to betake himself to the commons, when he 'was minded before to have tarried there unto Whitsuntide.'

Above Kilton Castle the wayward beck brings us, amid wilder scenery, and with scantier wood, by two main branches, the hamlet of Great Moorsholme lying between them, to the great moorlands north of the Esk, which will be described in a subsequent chapter. The constituent gills are Kate Ridding, Lockwood, and Swindale Becks, rising in the heather and bracken of Stanghow and Moorsholme Moors, and Skate and Girrick Becks, flowing down from the moors of Liverton and Girrick. At the headwaters of these tributary rills rises the remarkable tumulus-like peak of Freeborough Hill (821 feet), a prominent and impressive object from all the moorlands hereabout, which preserves the memory of the ' frithborh ' of the Angles, the mote for the peace-pledge, which once, we may assume, assembled here. Dim legend hath it, too, that somewhere within the conical height Arthur and the Knights of the Round Table lie hidden, like Barbarossa, awaiting the summons.

At Liverton, which stands upon the hill to the east of the becks we have described, in the midst of fruitful fields, with the great purple moorlands to the south, and the wooded ways of hidden becks making their course seaward on either hand, is a modern chapel, wherein still stands a Norman chancel arch, the finest in this part of Yorkshire, and worthy to be compared to enriched Norman arches at Adel, Iffley, and elsewhere. This arch is of three orders, each with a distinct capital and column, the front pair of columns being entirely detached from the mason work. The abaci are carved with interlaced scroll-work, and the capitals with grotesque subjects. The first order of the arch is made up of twenty-six projecting voussoirs and a keystone, severally carved with pairs of fine grotesque heads. Between each pair of voussoirs is a well-defined cavity, and each of the inner orders of the arch is adorned with a double series of the zigzag ornamentation, exquisitely carved.

About half a mile eastward of Liverton is the head of Handale or Grendale, through which another tributary of the Kilton Beck flows; and here, in 1133, William de Percy founded a priory for Benedictine nuns, whereof, sad to relate, so effective has been the work of the destroyer, not a single vestige remains. A stone slab or coffin-lid, sculptured with a sword, was dug up on the site some time ago, and popular imagination associated it with the sepulture of a traditional 'Scaw,' who, at Lofthouse or Loftus, a mile away down the glen, is fabled to have slain 'a loathly worm,' a story that reminds us of similar legends of the worms of Sockburn and Lambton. To the west of the village of Lofthouse is a circular mound with an entrenchment. There is a modern church of the year 1811. In the time of the Northern risings there was at Lofthouse a certain Parson Franke, often referred to in the depositions relating thereto, who is said to have done much in Aske's rebellion in 'raising' Sir Thomas Percy, and to have been himself a prominent captain; but, as we said in the last chapter, Sir John Bulmer found the parson himself

little disposed to be 'raised' when the rebellion of
Bigod began. Pursuing the Lofthouse glen for a little
distance further, we reach the Kilton Beck once more,
and the sea at Skinningrove.

Between Skinningrove and Staithes rises the mightiest
range of cliffs upon the English coasts, where Boulby
lifts his gigantic form to the height of 679 feet. The
grandeur of this range, exhibiting beneath its sandstone cap the strata both of the upper and the lower
lias, can nowhere be so well appreciated as from the
sea; but it is a magnificent walk along the edge, and
even the face of the cliffs, by the old alum-works, may
be explored by the venturous. Just beyond Skinningrove the broad reef of Hummersea Scar lies at the
foot of the cliffs, rich in its treasures of marine biology;
but the reef narrows further on by Rockcliff and the
White Stones, and beyond Hole Wyke is known as
Bias Scar.

Eastward, in a deep cleft, between the sheer pointed
precipice of Colburn Nab, and the rounder cliff of
Piercey Nab, lies hidden the quaint old fishing village
of Staithes.

Here is the first great dislocation of the strata we
have met with in our survey of the coast, and we cannot
do better than quote Phillips's account of it: 'On
arriving at Staithes'—from the Runswick direction—
'a much greater dislocation demands our attention.
The cliffs on the opposite sides of this harbour display
fine sections of strata; and it is with surprise we perceive that they are quite dissimilar. The signal cliff

STAITHES. DRAWN BY ALFRED DAWSON.

on the east has a diluvial covering, and beneath it
hard shale, irony and rugged, with great balls of ironstone; soft shale, with a remarkable sulphureous line
in it; and the ironstone series, consisting of layers
of ironstone nodules and beds, alternating with shale.
But in Colburn Nab, on the west side, we find a
diluvial covering, and beneath it a series of alternations
of shaly and sandy beds, in some of which are an
indescribable profusion of fossils, especially cardium
trunculatum, pectines, and dentalia; and at the
bottom the deeper lias shale, with a few layers of ironstone nodules. The extent of this dislocation is
obviously something greater than the whole height of
Colburn Nab.'*

You may see the village of Staithes now much as
James Cook saw it—a red-tiled place, nestled in the
hollow, grouped about a steep, narrow street which
leads down to the staith or landing-place, where the
brown, laborious fisher-folk stand, smoking, talking,
and looking out to sea, or gazing at their cobles, drawn
up in rows upon the beach, just as for generations
their ancestors have done, and as if fishing were the
idlest craft that any man can follow. Blue-eyed,
ruddy-skinned, picturesque fisher-girls wander along
the beach in search of 'flithers' for bait, or trip through
the narrow ways and steep courts of the village with
baskets of fish poised on their heads, while at the
doors sit their elders, in the summer-time, knitting, or
occupied in the mending of nets. Mr. Besant has

* 'Illustrations of the Geology of Yorkshire,' 1829, p. 99.

4

reconstructed a picture of Staithes and its fishermen
in the time of Cook—the men given to drink, perhaps,
but never careless or reckless : ' that kind of fisherman
is not common on the Yorkshire coast.' ' When it
rained or snowed, or when the east wind was too
bitter even for their hardy frames, they sat together
in the bar of the Cod and Lobster, the Shoulder of
Mutton, and the Black Lion, drinking over a pipe of
tobacco. On the south side of the main street the
narrow courts rose steep and confined, each with its
flight of steps; beyond the bay, under Coburn Nab,
they were building ships—always one ship at least on
the stocks; perhaps a whaler, perhaps a collier, perhaps no more than a fishing smack or a coble; but
all day long the cheerful hammer rang, and the ship-
wrights went in and out among the fisher-folk.' The
grocery and drapery shop of Mr. Sanderson, where
James Cook served a part of his time, coming from his
father's house at Great Ayton in 1740, and from which
he ran away, escaping the rest, was long ago washed
away. There is a wooden pier, and a new lifeboat
station in the little bay, that Cook never saw, and the
railway brings strangers to a place where in his time
strangers were few indeed, except such as came by
sea. It was these same strange seafarers that poured
into the eager ears of the 'prentice-boy wild tales of
whaling in Arctic regions, of strange adventures in
southern climes, episodes of battle, piracy, and ship-
wreck, wherewith they entranced him, even as Othello
entranced Desdemona. But Cook was a boy, and soon

thereafter, with the fabled shilling, he forsook Staithes for evermore and betook himself to Whitby.

Like Old Saltburn, like Skinningrove, like Whitby itself, like the village at Robin Hood's Bay, Staithes lies at the foot of a glen, through which streams that rise in the heather of the moorlands make their way to the sea. It is an experience specially delightful, having left behind the great escarpments of the coast, to pass by the course of such streamlets through the fruitful lower country, to ascend by some umbrageous way, and, having traversed a space of breezy moorland, to descend into the peaceful valley of the Esk.

Such an experience may be begun at Staithes, even on horseback, by pursuing the Ridge Road, so called because it lies along a high ridge that separates the courses of the Easington and Roxby (pronounced Rousby) becks, which for two miles or more, within a couple of hundred yards of one another, pursue an almost parallel course. Its charm, however, is of the things that are but half revealed, for, though the waters are heard purling far below, they are rarely seen through the trees, and the wayfarer will not regret, if he have the opportunity, though the paths are few, the labour of descending to the stream. Then having passed, beyond the beck on the right, Grinkle Park (the residence of Sir Charles Palmer, M.P.), embosomed in woods, the foliage becomes more scanty as the hamlet of Scaling is approached, and at last the purple edge of the rounded moorland rises in the view, with roads that lead across into Eskdale. The village of Easington, which is upon the hill above the left bank of the Easington Beck, is a place of great antiquity ; but its church of All Saints was replaced about the middle of the last century by a miserable structure. In 1888, however, a good and dignified edifice, designed by Mr. C. Hodgson Fowler, F.S.A., was erected, and, in taking down the barn-like edifice, a perfect treasury of carved stones was dug up, including hog-back tombstones and fragments of early crosses, Norman examples, and fifteenth-century memorials, thus testifying to the Christian faith of Cleveland for many hundreds of years. All these are ingeniously built up in the tower of the new church, except a splendid gravestone, with floreated cross, which has a place in the chancel. It bears the inscription—and portions of the lead-filling still remain in the Lombardic letters—' Robert Buscel gyt ici Priet pvr la alme de li,' and is supposed to be the memorial of Robert Buscel, of the neighbouring hamlet of Boulby (*vix.* 1284), a member of the great house of Busli or Buscel.* The beck of Borrowby Dale, a sylvan glen

---

* As we are dealing in this chapter with a district that played a considerable part in the Northern risings, and again with Sir John Bulmer, it may be well to supplement what was said of him and Lady Bulmer (who appears, by the way, to have been in fact the wife of a certain Cheyney) by extracts from an interesting confession of Sir John Wattis, parson of Easington, in which he relates a conversation he had with Sir William Staynhus, Sir John Bulmer's chaplain. 'Then I said, " Fie, Sir William, that ever your master should be tempted against his prince " . . . for I daresay, on my conscience, he would never have been tempted with such matters

eastward beyond the hamlet of Roxby, is another streamlet that discharges its waters through the ravine at Staithes.

It is a glorious walk from Staithes to Whitby, whether we follow the road through the old village of Hinderwell, *i.e.*, the well of Hilda—where the mariners of Staithes lie buried by a church, which replaces a structure with a Norman chancel arch that gunpowder in the evil time helped to destroy—or whether we scramble with difficulty by the cliffs ; but perhaps the character of the coast, with its lofty scarps and deep inlets and bays, may best be seen from a boat. It is the region of ' wicks,' which remind us by their names of those northern Vikings who, from similar ' wicks ' or ' viks,' came pillaging hither. Passing Staithes, we come to Jet Wyke, separated by the old Nab from Brackenberry Wyke, and this, again, by the Twixt Hills from Rosedale Wyke, beyond which rises Skittering Cliff, and the cliffs that form the western cheek of Runswick Bay. Hereabout, too, ingeniously enough, but without sufficient evidence to justify the

but that she [Lady Bulmer] is 'feard that she should be departed with [from] him for ever. I said she peradventure will say, " Mr. Bulmer, for my sake break a spear," and then he, "lyke a dow," will say, " Pretty Peg, I will never forsake thee." Thus I said she showeth things and trifles, and makes him believe that he may do things that are " unpossybyll." . . . He [Hew Cramer] had heard some of Sir John Bulmer's folk say that they heard their master say " he had lever be racket thene to part frome his wyffe." '— ' Letters and Papers, Foreign and Domestic, Henry VIII.,' vol. xii., part 1, No. 1084.

surmise, Mr. Haigh has endeavoured to locate the
Beowulf Saga, recognising the name of Hron in Runswick, and identifying Bowlby with 'Beowulf's beorh,'
and Hartlepool, in Durham, with Heorot, the hall
of Hrothgar. The cliffs sink at Runswick Bay, where
a number of wooded streamlets make their way from
the upland breezy pastures in the neighbourhood of
Ellerby and Mickleby.

Runswick is one of the most beautiful bays on the
Yorkshire coast, disclosing a delightful broken country
of field, stream, and wood, backed by the fine contours
of lofty hills between its western cliff, known as Lingra
(or Lingrow) Knowle, and the bold and curiously
peaked headland of Kettleness, which projects far out
into the sea on the east. Upon the western hill the
village of Runswick, the home of fishermen and jet-
workers, climbs the steep in picturesque confusion.
The place has fought for its existence with the sea,
and in the year 1682 the whole of it, saving one
house, was sucked down, though no man was lost.
The fisher-folk of Runswick are a brave and hardy set,
fighting also with the sea for their livelihood, with the
cobles that you may see drawn up upon the beach,
and the nets that lie stretched out to dry upon the
sand. They are shrewd and quick-witted, too, but
Young, the Whitby historian, credits them with many
superstitions. Before the return of the little fishing
fleet, we are told, the good wives, for luck, would
make an end of certain cats, while in bad weather
the children would light a fire upon the cliff-top, and

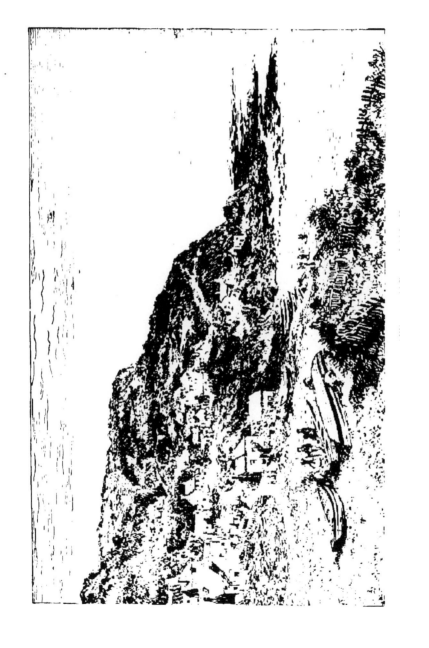

dance round it, invoking the spirit of the winds with the words :

> ' Souther wind, souther,
> And blow father home to my mother.

It is on record, too, that the 'bittle,' or beating with battledores, of clothes, which the fairies were wont of old time to wash in Claymoor Well, a mile away upon the hill, was plainly audible at Runswick by night. The cliffs south-westward of the village are low and broken, consisting of boulder clay and pebbles, but in the midst of the bay the High Cliff, of the hard shale, rises ; and it is here that the arched caves known as Hob Holes have been excavated by the action of the sea. The jet-diggers, however, have now destroyed the cavernous features of the haunt of Hob, whereto he was wont to beguile the unwary that there they might be destroyed by the incoming sea. Yet, with the characteristic waywardness of the Yorkshire Hobs, it was his pleasure to cure whooping-cough, and at low water, we read, the mother would carry her child to the mouth of his cave, and invoke its tenant with the words :

> ' Hob-hole Hob !
> Ma bairn's getten t' kink-cough :
> Tak't off—tak't off !'

The bold and curiously peaked form of Kettleness, with the ruins of its old alum works, closes in the picturesque bay on the east. The flanking reef, going from west to east, is known as Kettleness Scar, Barton Scar, Scab Ness, and Fillett Tail.

South-eastward of Kettleness the coast continues with striking and varied contours of steep and cliff, and in places the hard shale is curiously water-worn. Loop Wyke is overlooked by the height of Tellgreen Hill, and then comes Overdale Wyke, with its beck. Above is the ancient village of Lythe, which has a few Early English features in its otherwise uninteresting church, and gives a splendid view of the coast and the hills towards Whitby and beyond. Passing the mouth of Overdale, we reach Deepgrove Wyke, where the cliff is deeply scooped, shut in to the north by a curiously-shaped projection known as the Long Head, and to the south-east by the bold form of Sandsend Ness, steeply scarped, and with disused alum-works—the termination of the long rocky wall which began at Saltburn. Just beyond the Ness are the charming village of Sandsend, at the mouth of a glen, and East Row, the site of the ancient Thordisa, a name which, as we said in the introductory chapter, implies the beck of some Scandinavian Thordis. At this place two streams descend from the magnificent woodlands of Mulgrave, where the wayfarer may linger amid sylvan beauties and mossy dells, by the Wizard's Glen, the Waterfall, the Devil's Bridge, and the Eagle's Nest, and may dwell upon the ancient glories of Mulgrave Castle and its long history—viewing the splendours of the existing house, and the entrancing prospect from its 'quarter-deck' terrace, where Charles Dickens is said to have 'danced upon the green' in ecstasy. The two becks are the Sands-

end Beck and the East Row Beck, which have a course
approximately parallel through the woods, the former
deriving its waters from the becks in the neighbourhood of Mickleby and Barnby, and the latter, known
in its upper waters as the Birk Head Beck, from
several gills in the vicinity of Ugthorpe. This last
is a sequestered upland village near the margin of the
moors, interesting from the fact that there lived the
venerable Nicholas Postgate, the seminary priest
who, after labouring many years among the Catholic
recusants hereabout, was taken and hanged, drawn,
and quartered at York in 1679. This is a circumstance
we shall recur to in speaking of Sleights in Eskdale.
From that day to this Ugthorpe has been a centre
of Catholic life in North-East Yorkshire. The village
is doubtless of great antiquity, and there was a 'find'
of Roman silver coins there in 1792.

Upon the ridge between the two streams that flow
down through the midst of the woods, and in a position
of great vantage, stand the ruins of the ancient castle
of Mulgrave. They say it was founded originally by
the giant Wade, a hero of Scandinavian or Teutonic
origin, sometimes called Vada, who lies buried at
Goldsborough, upon the hill above Kettleness, between
stones that are about 100 feet apart. This giant's wife
was wont to milk cows a long way off upon the hill, and
for her convenience, so the historian hath it, he laid
down his 'causeway,' being part of the Roman road
that approaches Dunsley, she, however, helping in
the work; but, as ill luck would have it, her apron-

string broke upon one occasion, and she dropped about twenty cartloads of stones, which may still be seen upon the moor. What is more certain concerning Mulgrave is that it came to the Mauleys (De Malo Lacu) in King John's reign, from the Fossards. There were eight Peters de Mauley in succession, one of whom was a captain against the Scots in Edward II.'s wars, and the last of whom died about 1415. Mulgrave then came to the Bigods of Setterington, and here lived Sir Francis Bigod, the leader in the rising of 1537, who lost his head for his convictions, but who, though he had earnestness and conscience in what he did, has been sneered at by Mr. Froude as a 'spendthrift,' and as a 'pedant,' apparently because he had written an honest book against the royal supremacy in religious matters, a book that certainly had a very powerful influence upon his followers. Mulgrave passed from the Bigods to the Radclyffes. Charles I. created the third Baron Sheffield Earl of Mulgrave in 1646, whose family, after gaining the dukedom of Normanby and Buckingham, became extinct in 1735. Mulgrave is now the seat of the Marquis of Normanby, who is also Baron Mulgrave, of the creation of 1767.

As was said, the old castle of Mulgrave stands between the two becks, upon a steep ridge, whereof almost the whole width is occupied by the works. On the north side the walls are upon the very verge of the bank overlooking the precipitous slope to the Sandsend Beck, while to the south there has been a system of outworks extending even down the slope towards the East Row stream. Approach was cut off on the east by a wide and deep moat, on the edge of which rise massive walls, and a tower of considerable strength, with crenellated loopholes; while the western side, where was the chief entrance, had also a moat with a drawbridge, situated at a point indicated by two round towers of solid masonry. Southward of the southernmost of these towers is the oldest part of the existing walls, supported by late Norman unstaged buttresses. The total length of the irregular area, inclosed by the curtain walls, was about 180 feet from east to west, and 80 feet from north to south, exclusive of the walls themselves, which were about six feet thick, with towers at their many angles. The different levels have caused the walls to bulge, and these are now supported by huge buttresses. Within the area, now entered by steps on the west side, is the picturesque main building, which has the general plan of a parallelogram, about 66 feet square, with the remains of round towers at the angles, in the north-eastern one of which is a semicircular arch, built up with brick and stone, the bricks, many of them placed herring-bone fashion, being probably of Roman origin. The principal window on the east side is divided by mullions and a transom, and is deeply splayed; and there are two other three-light windows, also divided by transoms, on the west side, now built up, and against which the later fireplace of the 'great hall' is built. The castle bears evidences of considerable alteration, and it seems natural to suppose that a Norman structure of the Fossards has been further improved by the Mauleys, and perhaps by the Bigods. Having been garrisoned for the king in the Civil Wars, it was dismantled by order of the Parliament in 1647 (22 Charles I.), evidently with the aid of gunpowder.

The modern castellated mansion of Mulgrave was built by Catherine, Duchess of Buckingham, a natural daughter of James II., and has since been beautified and extended, and it occupies a magnificent situation, in well-kept grounds, above the Sandsend Beck. A summer-house in the grounds is said to mark the site of a hermitage founded about the year 1150 by William de Percy, in fulfilment of a vow. Also, in the Mulgrave woods, not far from Foss Mill, there is a circular camp, probably Roman, with a mound, about 130 feet in diameter at the top, and surrounded by an earthen parapet. The arboretum, near the Sandsend entrance, is a place where a great variety of trees were planted by the Maharajah Duleep Singh, when he was resident at Mulgrave some years ago.*

We may now betake ourselves from Sandsend and East Row, along the sands of Dunsley Bay, perhaps the Dunum Sinus of Ptolemy, or by the low cliffs, towards Whitby, the great scaur, and the abbey of St. Hilda, ever the chief features in view, while the sea rolls in on the left. Above, on the hill, is Dunsley,

---

* Mulgrave Castle is not shown, but on certain days the beautiful woods, with the old castle and the glens, are thrown open, but tickets must be obtained at Whitby.

the point to which the Roman road from York was directed, and doubtless an outlook station, marked now by the mound upon which the chapel of Dunsley stands. About half - way between Sandsend and Whitby the Upgang Beck pours down the steep, and soon thereafter the wayfarer finds himself at the mouth of the Esk, where the ancient town of Whitby lies hid.

CHAPTER IV.

WHITBY.

IT has been said with truth by a recent writer that
the 'ancestral hush' of the Yorkshire coast rests upon
Whitby. What memories are awakened, what pictures
of bygone events evoked, by its very name! We think
at once of Hild and the Synod of Streoneshealh, of
Caedmon, the Saxon singer, of the fount of learning
to the Angles. The salt smell of the fish-market by
the pier, too, is enough to call up for us many a vision
of hardships at sea, and of smacks running close-
hauled, helpless before the gale, of broad-beamed
whalers, and of the old Baltic trade.

There, between the two tall cliffs, where Esk pours
his waters into the sea, the picturesque houses of the
old town are grouped upon the eastern hill. You will

say, in looking at them, that here is a place to which
old-world associations cling even as moss clings to
the stone. It is morning, and you stand upon the
quay, where the brown-skinned fishermen are bringing
up from the smacks by the wall the silvery freight, and
the ancient fish-like smell that belongs to men who
go down to the sea. They are laying out the fish
upon the flags, dragging along huge cod and haddock
by the gills; there are men with baskets of herrings
upon their shoulders; there is a crowd of buyers and
idlers; there is the washing of the fish and the packing
of it to send away. Turning then to the harbour, you
look out between the twin lighthouse piers, to where
the waves are bearing their snowy crests out at sea.
It is the summer-time, and earlier on you might have
seen the smacks as they returned from their night's
trawling on the herring-ground, some unsuccessful and
lightly burdened, others labouring heavily with a catch
that weighed them down almost to the gunwale, lower-
ing their brown sails as they brought up at the quays.
But it has been a heavy night, and you see hauled up
in the harbour that concourse of smacks, not from the
neighbouring shores only, but from almost every important fishing station on the English and Scottish
coasts, that makes up the herring fleet. The large
and graceful boats from far-off Fowey, Penzance, and
St. Ives; the heavily-framed craft from the further
North—you know them by their build; the roomy
Manxmen; smacks from Berwick, Hartlepool, Harwich,
Lowestoft, and the Channel—all these may be recog-

nised by their different trim and rig, or, failing that, you may know them by the distinctive letters, 'F. Y.,' 'P. Z.,' 'S. S.,' 'B. K.,' 'H. L.,' 'H. H.,' 'L. T.,' or other like sign, painted in white, with numbers, upon their bows, to indicate the port of their origin.

Opposite to you, the gray cliff, with the brown growths clinging to it, is lighted up with sunny hues, and the red roofs of the houses on the steep grow brighter, and the blue smoke curls up the hillside from their chimneys. Towards evening, you know, all will fade away in purplish grays. Above, the old church, now sadly fallen from its state, and the venerable ruins of the abbey, in piteous and speaking ruin, crown the steep. You pass along St. Ann's Staith, and, leaving for the nonce modern Whitby on the West Cliff, betake yourself, by the swing bridge— looking up the beautiful Esk to where, beyond the crowd of shipping in the inner harbour, the green hills rise, topped by the moorland—to old Whitby, on the right bank of the river. Here two streets run parallel to it, the upper one Church Street, where are the quaint houses of many curiosity dealers, leading you up the hill to the foot of the abbey steps, and you glance over the red roofs to the shipping below in the harbour. Near by, too, is the market-place, with the picturesque town-hall, built in 1788, resting upon pillars. The streets hereabout have changed very little since the day when James Cook walked in from Staithes, and many of the houses bear dates taking us back a century and a half or more. ' In the lower

WHITBY HARBOUR.   DRAWN BY ALFRED DAWSON.

of the two streets,' says Mr. Besant in his life of the great circumnavigator, ' courts nearly as narrow as the Yarmouth passages run down to the water's edge, or to houses built overhanging the water. Some of these are old taverns ; they have, built outside, broad wooden galleries, or verandas, with green railings, and steps to the water, where the captains or mates of the colliers could sit with a pipe and a cool tankard, and gossip away between dinner and supper, looking out to sea the while between the cliffs. . . . At the Raffled Anchor, for instance, even a sluggish imagination can easily discern James Cook himself, in his rough sea-dress and tarred hands, sitting among his friends and shipmates—himself already having gained the quarter-deck.'

The sojourner's conception of Whitby will grow clearer if he go westward, beyond the confluence of the Ellerdale Beck, and the shipbuilding yards, to Larpool, looking whence he will see the whole of the inner harbour, and the town upon both sides of the river, with the abbey ruins upon the height—a prospect of singularly picturesque beauty. He may go eastward, too, along Church Street, past the old town-hall, past the Fish Pier and Tatenhill Pier (two inner landing places), along the stretch of sand where the fishwives and laundresses of Whitby spread out their nets and clothes to dry, to where the spa-ladder, hanging in mid-air, leads out to the east pier. Or he may pass under it at low water, and make his way, at the foot of the sheer scarps, along the scar or scaur,

5

that long gaunt talus of the rock, with shattered fragments cast down from the inaccessible cliffs frowning
above, and still brown pools in its rugged surface,
while in a long white line the threatening sea breaks
loudly on the left. Let him hasten along to Saltwick,
or return, by no means being tempted to linger here
too long, for the sea steals in, and the channels are
filled, and the twilight grows deeper, and at high tide
the sea dashes against the cliffs which few can hope to
scale.*

Having now surveyed as much of Whitby as may
remind us of the old time, or, at least, as will not
distract us from the eld, let us turn to its history and
its memories, which, indeed, give much of its interest
to-day. To us it seems certain that Whitby was
known as a harbour to the Romans, for a clear infer-
ence from their history is that their galleys patrolled
the coasts, and such were the conditions of navigation
in Roman times that harbours were of exceeding
necessity. We choose, therefore, to believe that
Roman galleys were seen from time to time in the
lower Esk, and that the road from York, which

---

* The Eskdale fault depresses the strata north of Whitby about
200 feet, and the east pier is built on the alum shale, while the west
pier stands on an oolitic sandstone. The sandstone gives us the
sandy beach towards Sandsend, while the hard lias thrusts out the
waterworn scar. Vast numbers of shells and many varieties of
marine algæ are to be found in its cavities, while many remarkable
and characteristic fossils may be collected, more especially Belem-
nites tubularis, Ammonites Mulgravius, A. Bucklandi, and Nucula
ovum.

points to Dunsley, sent down a branch to Whitby,
where, indeed, some Roman remains have been found.
At any rate, when Whitby first rises upon our horizon
as Streoneshealh, it doubtless is because it was a place
easily approached by sea. We have, indeed, instanced,
in the introductory chapter, a very early notice of seafaring from Whitby, when the successor of Hild sailed
thence to visit St. Cuthbert, and it is not to be doubted
that earlier, at the great synod, Colman and his monks
came hither from Lindisfarne by sea. Indeed, we
shall not be far wrong if we infer that it was this very
accessibility that led to the selection of the bleak cliff
of Streoneshealh for the site of the monastery of Hild,
and of Ælfleda, the daughter of King Oswiu of
Northumbria. Ere Penda was defeated in the Winwædfield, and paganism received its death-blow, Oswiu
had made a vow that he would build a monastery and
devote his daughter to God if victory fell to his arm.
The double monastery for monks and nuns, founded
at Streoneshealh about the year 656, seems not to have
been of the strict Benedictine rule, but to have been
somewhat on the Celtic model. From the circumstance that the body of Eadwine, slain in 633, was
buried there, we may infer that there had been a
religious establishment on the spot long before.

Legend has grown up about the memory of Hild,
but one fact shines clear through it all, that she was
a remarkable woman of great moral and intellectual
sway. From her, kings and nobles sought counsel,
and the house over which she ruled became the lamp

of learning in the North, from which, like rays of light in the gloom, went forth Bosa and Wilfred (the second) of York, John of Beverley, and many more less celebrated than these. When, after the long period of disorder that followed the departure of the Romans, the observances of the East and the West were to be reconciled, no place but Streoneshealh was deemed meet for the synod. Hither, then, in 664, came Oswiu with his court, Colman with the monks of Lindisfarne, Wilfred from York, and others. The points discussed appear comparatively trivial at this day—the fashion of the tonsure, and the time for the keeping of Easter—but much was implied by observances, and many were the difficulties that arose from a difference of practice; and Mr. J. R. Green has well said, after taking a view of the somewhat undisciplined character of the Irish Church, that 'it was from such a chaos as this that England was saved by the victory of Rome in the Synod of Whitby.' 'You own,' said Oswiu to Colman, 'that Christ gave to Peter the keys of the kingdom of heaven—has he given such power to Columba?' There was but one answer. 'Then,' said Oswiu, 'will I rather obey the gatekeeper of heaven, lest, when I reach its gates, he turn his back upon me, and there be none left to open.'

If Whitby occupies so important a place in regard to the religious history of our country, not less significant is its relation to our literature. For it is with the name of the lay-brother Caedmon, and with Streoneshealh, that we connect the first passionate

outpouring of Christian faith that followed the long
struggle with paganism—the dim outshadowing of that
earnest and soul-filling melancholy, of that inexpressible
sense of the new and terrible significance of life, which
the Angle drew from his knowledge of the mystery of
man's redemption. It matters not to us whether all
that we have of Caedmon's is Caedmon's own ; it was
with the lay-brother of Streoneshealh that all later
Angle singers associated the first expression of Angle
song. Though Caedmon was well advanced in years,
he had never learned, so we read, that rude alliterative
jingle with which his fellows beguiled the long nights
by the hearth-fire ; and so, often, when at the board
all in turn became gleemen, he would rise and go
homeward, sorrowing, we may believe, when the harp
came round. But once it happened, when thus he
had fled in solitude to tend the cattle by night, that
he fell asleep, and lo! One appeared to him, and said :
' Sing, Caedmon, some song to Me ;' but he, answering,
said : 'I cannot sing ; for this cause left I the feast
and hither came.' Then He who spoke said again :
' Howbeit, you shall sing to Me ;' and Caedmon
asked : 'What, then, shall I sing?' and the speaker
answered him : ' The beginning of created things shalt
thou sing.' On the morrow the cowherd recounted
his story to the Abbess Hild, and she and the brethren,
' comprehending the divine grace in the man,' when
he had given expression to a passage of Holy Writ,
bade him assume the habit, and thereafter he sang of
the creation, the fall, the history of the Jews, the

redemption, and of the judgment, the pains of hell, and the joys of heaven.

When Hild had ruled her house for many years, she died about the year 680, and her passing was witnessed in vision, as Bede recounts, by a nun at the daughter house of Hackness, near Scarborough, the manner whereof we shall relate when we deal with the historical circumstances of that place. Great was the sanctity of the departed abbess, and many legends grew up about her memory; and it was told how that she had turned to stone the venomous snakes that infested Streoneshealh, as may yet be seen in the ammonites of Whitby scaur. As Scott has it in 'Marmion,'

> 'They told how in their convent cell
> A Saxon princess once did dwell,
>   The lovely Edelfled ;
> And how of thousand snakes each one
> Was changed into a coil of stone
>   When holy Hilda pray'd.
> Themselves within their holy bound
> Their stony folds had often found.
> They told how sea-fowls' pinions fail
> As over Whitby's towers they sail ;
> And sinking down with flutterings faint,
> They do their homage to the saint.'

The Princess Æthelfled succeeded Hild in her rule but, from her time forward, we hear nothing of Streoneshealh until the wasting of the monastery by the Northmen under Inguar and Hubba, about 867-70, when Abbot Titus fled to Glastonbury with the relics

of the saint. Yet, from all we know, though the gap
in our knowledge is great, it is clear that Streoneshealh continued to flourish until that time. In relation to this event, let us not imagine that Whitby itself
lay waste and barren, for, as Canon Atkinson has conclusively shown, it continued to be a chief centre of
Danish colonization.*

Now we reach a different scene—the coming to
Whitby of Regenfrith or Reinfrid—the 'miles strenu-
issimus in obsequio domini sui Willielmi Nothi, Regis
Anglorum'—who, having been 'pricked to the heart
·by the tokens of ruin and desolation' at Whitby, and
having been ten years a monk at Evesham, resolved
to rebuild the abbey, and establish the Benedictine
rule. It was William de Percy, who died a Crusader,
that enabled him to do so. The house became rich
and powerful, and was favoured by the Conqueror,
William Rufus, Henry I., and Henry II.; but about
the middle of the twelfth century it was plundered by
the King of Norway, as often by pirates. We find that,
according to a legendary story, in the fifth year of the
last-named king, when William de Brus, Ralph de
Percy, and another, having so belaboured with their
boar-staves the hermit of Eskdaleside that he died,
had taken sanctuary at Scarborough, the abbot was

. * We need not here enter into the etymology of the name
'Streoneshealh,' nor endeavour to discern in it the 'sinus phari'
which Bede tells us is its significance. Canon Atkinson sees in the
word the personal name of some Streone, with which explanation,
for want of a more plausible one, we may well be content. Eadric,
of Mercia, slain in 1017, was known as 'Streona.'

so powerful that he was able to withdraw them from
sanctuary, whereupon they accepted the hermit's
death-bed forgiveness, and bound themselves to hold
their lands as tenants of the abbey, and by the curious
tenure of every year, on the eve of Holy Thursday
(some say Ascension Day), cutting with a knife of
the value of a penny sufficient 'stakes, strutt-towers,
and yethers,' and carrying these on their backs, and
setting them up in the bed of the Esk, as a barrier
against the tide, while the officer of Eskdale blew:
'Out on you! out on you!' in denunciation of their
crime. This curious custom, which has been in a
manner maintained, had doubtless another origin,
though perhaps a similar one, than that ascribed to
it. Scott thus alludes to it in 'Marmion':

> ' Then Whitby's nuns exulting told,
>   How to their house three barons bold
>   Must menial service do ;
>   While horns blow out a note of shame,
>   And monks cry " Fye upon your name !
>   In wrath, for loss of sylvan game,
>   St. Hilda's priest ye slew."
>   " This on Ascension Day each year,
>   While labouring on our harbour pier,
>   Must Herbert, Bruce, and Percy hear."'

It is now time that we turn to the pitiably ruinous
and deeply weather-seamed fabric of the abbey; and
at the outset it is sad to have to relate that in a great
storm in 1763 a part of the nave fell; while in 1830
the central tower gave way—that tower from which
we are told Robin Hood and Little John discharged

their arrows, in proof of skill, at the request of their monastic hosts. And here we cannot but express an earnest wish that those who are responsible for the existing remains may be induced to devote more watchful care to their splendid possession, lest it fall into still further decay. The choir is a glorious example of the Early English, with dog-tooth mouldings of the earliest character—its features, three lancets in each of the three stages at the east end, the uppermost ones rising into the gable; clustered columns supporting noble arches; a rich triforium, to be compared with those at Rievaulx and York, enriched with semicircular arches, each inclosing two pointed ones; and a clerestory with a lancet, and lateral pointed arches, in each bay. The north transept, of a later period of the Early English, is most beautifully composed, again with three tiers of lancets, but having a wheel window in the gable, and is adorned with beautiful mouldings of lilies, as well as externally with canopied niches. Of the other transept but a single clustered column remains. The three easternmost windows of the nave are Early English, but the others are Geometrical Decorated, with tracery of an unusual character. Of the same date and style is a curious lozenge window in the western end of the north aisle. The domestic offices are entirely wasted, but traces of them remain, as well as of the chapter-house, in mounds and foundations, on the south side. The large house known as Whitby Hall, built by the Cholmleys, the grantees of the abbey, about the year 1580, is on the site of the abbot's dwelling. An interesting relic of mediæval times stands in the 'abbey plain,' in the shape of the shaft of a tall cross, mounted upon a series of circular steps.

The town of Whitby appears to have flourished under its Benedictine patrons. It is mentioned as a port soon after the Conquest, and continued throughout the Middle Ages the centre of a considerable fishery, and there were fishing stations also all along the coast. The pirates of the Northern Sea seem to have done their best to profit by the growing trade, and there remains a legendary story of one such who was bold enough even to land at Whitby, as many actually did, to steal the bells from the church tower, and to carry them aboard his ship, which thereafter struck on the Black Nab, and went down at a place where still the sunken peal rings merrily at Hallowe'en. This church of St. Mary is just below the abbey on the cliff—a structure built early in the twelfth century, and still having some Norman features, but so woefully maltreated, so shorn of its true features, and so made up with ugly galleries within, as to be a pitiable, though in many ways an interesting, structure.

Whitby continued to grow in importance, and in the sixteenth century we find it contributing a quota of ships to the king's service. By the development of the resources of the alum shales upon the coast the trade of Whitby was wonderfully increased by the time of Elizabeth, and still more by that of the Stuarts, and the harbour became thronged with shipping. In-

deed, the concealed lands and alum workings which
Sir Paul Pindar and another had formed, and which
the Earl of Mulgrave had seized, were valued at
£11,600, and the king's loss in rental during sixteen
years was estimated at £184,000, while the earl confessed that his profits during three years had been
£11,000.

We can still hear, from the same century, too, the
sounds of forgotten party strife in the old town—can
picture to ourselves, for example, how, when the
Commonwealth men were in, one Christopher Wright,
rushing into the house of Thomas Norfolk at Whitby,
did call for drink, and declare loudly 'that he was a
Cavalier, and that he was for King Charles, and that
he would fight heartily for him so long as he did live,
though he were hanged at the door-cheek for it.' It
gives a touch of life to think of such things.

The coast hereabout has given its share of fine
seamen both to the fleet and the merchant marine,
and not seamen only, but ships too, for the vessels
with which Captain Cook made his first voyage round
the world were built in Whitby yards, and still a
considerable shipbuilding industry is carried on there.
The ship in which Cook embarked as an apprentice
from Whitby was engaged in the coaling trade; but
the coast from which he set sail is chiefly famous for
its very important fisheries. The whale fishery of
Whitby began in 1753, when the *Henry and Mary* and
the *Sea Nymph* sailed for the Greenland coast, and
thereafter a considerable impetus was given by whaling

to the shipping of the ancient port. In all, it is recorded that fifty-three Whitby vessels were engaged in the Greenland and Davis Straits whale fishery. During the fifty years from 1767 to 1816, 2,761 whales were brought back, together with 25,000 seals, 55 bears, and many other creatures of the Arctic clime. In the year 1814 alone, eight vessels brought back 172 whales, which produced 1,392 tons of oil, as well as 42 tons of fins.

Such are the historical events and legendary stories, here dealt with all too briefly, that give an unfailing interest to Whitby. These are the quaint features, the picturesque characters, the old-world aspects, whereby it has become the joy of the artist, and that have caused it to be made the background—as in ' Sylvia's Lovers '—of many a work of fiction. A new town has grown up upon the West Cliff, where there are terraces, hotels and boarding-houses, and here, as well as in the houses of the suburbs, many visitors make their home in the summer-time. The Saloon upon the West Cliff, with its concert-room, theatre, gardens, tennis-courts and promenade, was built by Sir George Elliot, who was then owner of the West Cliff estate, in 1880. And so, in its contrasts of the old and the new, the picturesque and the fashionable, and in the sharp line drawn between the two, Whitby is unique. There are interests enough for those who resort thereto, presented by the old town and the unfailing attraction of the sea and the sands, of bathing and fishing; there are cliffs to investigate, rich in geological treasures, and many a sylvan glen to journey through ; the museum illustrates the antiquities and features of the neighbourhood ; there is the whole glorious coast between Saltburn and Scarborough, or further still, to explore ; one may pull up the river to Ruswarp, and, taking the boat over the weir, row on by sunny waters and green woods to Sleights, and may reach a whole district of moorland and dale, of which we have yet to speak. All these places, too, are made very accessible by the coast and Eskdale railway lines.

An account of Whitby would not be complete without some particulars concerning ' Whitby jet.' Jet appears to be of ligneous origin, and the hard variety, which is the true ' Whitby jet,' occurs in thin bands, worked with great and increasing difficulty. It has a fine texture, is unaffected by temperature, is durable, takes a high polish, and lends itself to delicate manipulation. The scarcity of the hard jet has led to the importation of a hard Spanish variety of somewhat inferior quality, which is wrought at Whitby, and seems to stand midway between the best native kind and the soft Whitby jet, which is cheap and effective when new, but soon loses its polish or breaks. The use of the material for the making of ornaments is of high antiquity, for it occurs in the houes or burial-mounds of Cleveland, and, from discoveries of jet objects in the neighbourhood of the abbey, it was clearly prized in the Middle Ages. Drayton speaks of it thus :

' The rocks by Moulgrave, too, my glorie forth to set,
Out of their crannied cleves can give you perfect jet.'

The modern growth of the industry dates from the beginning of this century, when much encouragement was given to the workers, and is greatly due to the introduction of jet at court ; but, through change of fashion, and perhaps through the indiscriminate use of the soft kind of jet in past times, the industry is now somewhat depressed, though a period of court morning will usually give activity to it again.*

* It will be useful to give here a table of distances from Whitby by road : Aislaby, 3 m. ; Beggar's Bridge, 9 m. ; Brotton, 18 m. ; Castleton, 14 m. ; Cawthorn Camps, 21 m. ; Cockmill, 2 m. ; Danby Castle, 13 m. : Dunsley, 4 m. ; East Row, 3 m. ; Egton, 7 m. ; Egton Bridge, 8 m. ; Falling Foss, 6 m. ; Fryup, 12 m. ; Glaisdale, 10 m ; Goathland, 11 m. ; Goldsborough, 6 m. ; Grosmont, 7 m. ; Guisborough, 21 m. ; Hackness, 23 m. ; Hawsker, 4 m. ; Hinderwell, 10 m. ; Kettleness, 7 m. ; Lealholm Bridge, 10 m. : Lighthouses, High Whitby, 3 m. ; Little Beck, 6 m. ; Loftus, 16 m. ; Lythe, 4 m. ; Malyan's Spout, 10 m. ; Marske, 23 m. ; Mickleby, 7 m. ; Mulgrave Castle, 5 m. ; Peak, 9 m. ; Pickering, 21 m. ; Randymere, 9 m. ; Raven Hill Hall, 10 m. ; Redcar, 26 m. ; Rigg Mill, 4 m. ; Robin Hood's Bay, 6 m. ; Roseberry Topping, 27 m. ; Roxby, 12 m. ; Runswick, 10 m. ; Ruswarp, 2 m. ; Saltburn, 21 m. ; Saltwick, 2 m. ; Sandsend, 3 m. ; Scarborough, 21 m. ; Skelton, 20 m. ; Sleights, 4 m. ; Sneaton, 3 m. ; Staithes, 11 m. ; Stainsacre, 3 m. ; Thomasine Foss, 10 m. ; Ugglebarnby, 5 m. ; Ugthorpe, 8 m. ; Upgang, 1 m. ; Woodlands, 3 m. ; Westerdale, 17 m.

CHAPTER V.

LOWER ESKDALE.

Characteristics of the River—Larpool—Rigg Mill—Ruswarp—Aislaby—Little Beck, Iburndale, and Sleights—Falling Foss—Dr. Nicholas Postgate, the Seminary Priest—Eskdaleside and the Hermit thereof—Grosmont—The Alien Priory—Goathland—The Killing Pits—The Monastic Cell—Thomasine Foss and the Goathland Waterfalls—Julian Park—Egton Bridge—Egton—The 'Bargest'—East Arncliff Woods—The Beggar's Bridge, Glaisdale End.

WE shall now, in our descriptive journeying, leave for a time the immediate region of the coast, in order that we may make a further exploration of the north-eastern hills. First betaking ourselves through the lovely valley of the Esk, and bringing to an end our description of Cleveland proper, we shall cross over the high moors into the watershed of the Rye, where we shall find much also that is beautiful and interesting to attract us, and we shall then reach, as we turn eastward, the region of the Upper Derwent, which will bring us once more to the country fringing the sea. Five chapters having been occupied in this pleasant way-faring, we shall, then, resume our survey of the coast

south of Whitby, even, if it be somewhat briefly at
the close, as far south as the pebbly isthmus of the
Spurn.

The Esk, which is the chief waterway of Cleveland,
follows for some distance the general line of that
great dislocation whereby the strata to the north of
the river are depressed, and, in the neighbourhood of
Grosmont, it passes the well-known basaltic dyke, to
which we have already referred. The district thus
traversed is essentially a moorland area, the moors to
the south rising with the strata to a greater elevation
than those to the north. There are few river courses
more charming than that of Eskdale, for the constant
diversity of its scenery, the bold configuration of the
hills by which the dale is shaped, or the winding way
of the river amid pastures, cornfields and woods, or
where sometimes it is shut in by precipitous barriers
of rock. Of old time, before the drainage of the dale
began, the river spread out in marshy swamps, whereof
the traces remain to this day in the soil, and its way
was margined by dense tracts of forest, to such an
extent, indeed, that an old resident of Danby told
Canon Atkinson—as is recorded in that charming
book, which gives so intimate a view of many historical
and other circumstances touching an important part
of the Cleveland district, his ' Forty Years in a Moorland Parish '—how that an old uncle had told the
informant that ' he kenned t' tahm when a cat-swirrel
could gan a' t' way [all the way] down fra Commondale End to Beggar's Bridge [Glaisdale End] wivoot

yance tooching t' grund.' Nor are we without visible
evidences of the ancient forests of Eskdale in these
days, for the rich woods of Arncliff still remain, and
eastward, towards picturesque, salt-smelling Whitby,
as up-stream towards the moorland sources of the
river, though more scantily as we ascend, beech and
oak and rowan overhang its devious way, and clothe
the steep slopes of the hills.

In ascending the river from Whitby, the oarsman
may pull some distance up its stream, and the North
Yorkshire and Cleveland Railway makes the whole
dale accessible; but the wayfarer, leaving the town
by the quaint way of Church Street, will pass the
graving - docks and the Spital Bridge, which spans
the tributary Ellerdale Beck, and, passing the ship-
yards on the right, with the umbrageous slope beyond,
will proceed along the shady lane, past Larpool Hall,
whence retrospectively there is a splendid view of the
river and the town, until the pretty village of Ruswarp
appears in the landscape, with its Jacobean hall and
its church. Before reaching Ruswarp, however, a
tributary falls into the Esk on the left—the Rigg Mill
Beck—by the foot of which is a pleasant resort for
holiday-makers. Here we may take a path through
the Larpool woods, and, descending to the beck, and
crossing a footbridge on the left, may reach Cock Mill
Waterfall, which plashes down, in a fairy-like scene,
a distance of some 36 feet, by an old water-mill. A
further journey along a grassy ridge between two
brooks, having the hamlet of Stainsacre, with its wind-

6

mill, on the hill to the left, and that of Sneaton on the right, brings us to a point at which we can drop down through a lovely woodland to Rigg Mill in the same glen, where is a sylvan solitude given up to the music of the stream and the birds; picturesque, too, with the time-worn water-mill shut in between the dark wood and the stream, which has here eaten away its bank, and left the claw-like roots of the trees outstanding weirdly above. The constituent brooks are the Long Rigg Beck, the Intake Beck, and the Mitten Hill Beck, which rise in the neighbourhood of Normanby, and on the flanks of Filingdales Moor.

The way from Ruswarp to Briggswath and Sleights Bridge along the riverside, overhung by oak, birch, and ash, and presenting fresh and charming views at every turn, is known as the Carrs. Above, on the right, is the pretty moorside village of Aislaby, which may be approached from Whitby by the road passing by Sneaton Castle (a modern house), and Cross Butts, or from Sleights Bridge by a way leading amid the stately trees of the place known as Woodlands. Beyond the farm-houses and haystacks of that village (the dwelling-place once of a Danish Asolf), there is a splendid view of Eskdale, towards Grosmont and Egton Bridge, with the swelling moorlands above its deep woods and spreading corn-fields.

Just by the station at Sleights is the foot of Iburndale—the valley of the Little Beck, a streamlet that descends from the hills on the left, and gives us some of the sweetest woodland scenery in Eskdale. We

shall notice in our tracing of the Esk that every tributary of importance descends to the river from the
south, and the course of the Little Beck is, indeed,
characteristic of many other streamlets hereabout.
Some six miles to the southward, near Lilhoue Cross,
which stands, with the tumulus, more than 900 feet
above the sea, in the wet green swamps between the
dark purple heights of Filingdales and Widow Houe
Moors, rises the Blea Hill Beck, which flows downward in its lonely course amid the heather of Sneaton
High Moor, where the grouse and the wind are its
companions. Steeper and steeper becomes the descent
between John Cross and York Cross, and the purling
stream takes the name of its tributary, the May Beck;
then, flowing through plantations and rich woodlands
overhanging its rocky bed, it receives the Parsley Beck,
becomes itself known as Little Beck, and runs by the
hamlet of that name, as well as by Iburndale, lower
down, and so amid woods and fields reaches the Esk,
there about 75 feet above the sea.

In our descriptive wayfaring, however, we shall first
ascend the steep brow of the hill above it through the
village of Sleights, of which the red cottages soon line
the yellow, grass-grown road. They have little gardens
in front of them, gay with flowers in the summer-time,
or piggeries and poultry-yards; and, past the church,
the road sweeps round to the right, and the dark
heathery form of Black Brow, on the edge of Sleights
Moor, rises in front. Climbing Blue Bank, we reach
the moor, leaving behind us the sleepy village, and

a glorious prospect is spread before us of heathery heights, with the green dale below, and the ruins of Whitby Abbey far-off upon the cliff, and the blue sea beyond. The exhilaration that proceeds from the breeze of heathery moorlands, and the contemplation at the same time of the sea, is such as those only can know who have experienced it in some such place as this. Young, the Whitby historian, has preserved a curious legend concerning Sleights Moor. A little Wade, he tells us, the infant child of Giant Wade, and Bell, his wife—who, it may be remembered, having but one hammer between them, were wont, during their simultaneous building operations at Mulgrave and Pickering castles, to fling it to and fro across the hills—this child, being left upon Sleights Moor and growing impatient for his milk, picked up a stone weighing a few tons, and hurled it across Eskdale to where Bell was milking her cow at Swart Houe, on Egton Low Moor, and hit her with such violence that the stone had a piece knocked out of it, as 'could still be seen till the stone itself was broken up a few years ago to mend the highways.'

Passing a little distance down from the moor, there is a winding way that brings us by a steep declivity to the quaint hamlet of Little Beck in the glen. It is from this pleasant beckside starting-place that way-farers are wont to explore its upper course, where, amid ferns, wild-flowers, and pensile foliage, it rolls over its rocky bed. A curious fanciful construction, known as the Hermitage, may beguile the traveller, and there he may rest awhile. It was shaped by one George Chubb, in the year 1780, out of a solid rock, and there are two easy-chairs, also carved in stone, upon the top. Beyond this odd conceit is Falling Foss (42 feet), the third in height of the Cleveland waterfalls, situated in a beautiful hollow, where the sparkling water dashes down from the rocks into a pool overhung by trees and embowered amid ferns. The wayfarer may return to the Esk at Sleights Bridge, all the way by the beck. Above, on the hill to the right, between the hamlets of Iburndale and Sneaton, is the ancient village of Ugglebarnby—the 'by' of a Danish Uggleberd—where was formerly a chapel of great antiquity.

Before we ascend further the winding way of the Esk, an historical circumstance arrests us that fills the dale with memories. It will have been seen, from the share which the Cleveland men took in the Pilgrimage of Grace, that many of them continued to be attached to the old religion. The seventeenth-century lists of recusants testify to this also, and, indeed, the same is true even to this very day. Towards the end of the seventeenth century, one of them, a certain Matthew Lith of Sleights, was not only strong in his beliefs, but firm, and even rash, in his expression of them. At a wedding party on December 7, 1678, he made use of the words: 'You talk of Papists and Protestants, but when the roast is ready, I know who shall have the first cut;' and another heard him say: 'We shall have a sorrowful Christmas, a bloody "Fastnes," and a

joyful Easter,' all which was thought by some to imply
hidden plot or disloyalty. One John Reeves, 'gauger' of
Whitby, and a certain Henry Cockerill, went therefore
to search Lith's house, but, instead of discovering arms
or ammunition, they found there only one Nicholas
Postgate, a venerable seminary priest. Lith attempted
to hide him, but he was taken away, and, it having been
proved that he had exercised the offices of his religion
at Ugthorpe and Egton Bridge, he was condemned to
death, under the cruel statute, and was hanged, drawn,
and quartered, neither the reverence due to age, nor the
mercy due to all men, availing to save him from his
blood-thirsty pursuers. A copper plate was thrown
into his coffin, which gave his epitaph: 'Here lies that
reverend and pious divine Dr. Nicholas Postgate, who
was educated in the English college at Doway. And
after he had laboured fifty years (to the admirable
benefit and conversion of hundreds of souls), was at
last advanced to a glorious crown of martyrdom at the
city of York, on August 7, 1679, having been priest
51 years, aged 82.'* We are told that Reeves, who
apprehended him, never received the £20 usually paid
to informers in such cases, but, 'having suffered for
some time an extreme torture of body and mind, was
found drowned in a small brook.'

Three miles south-westward of Sleights is Grosmont

* Challoner's 'Memoirs of the Missionary Priests.' 'Depositions
from the Castle of York' (Surtees Society). From the occurrence of
the name Postgate (Poskit, Poskitt) in the lists of recusants at
Harwood Dale and Filingdales, it is evident that Dr. Nicholas
Postgate was a native of this part of Yorkshire.

(pronounced Gro-mont), approached in a few minutes by rail; but the winding way of the Esk is perhaps half as much again, and the wayfarer along the road on the steep slope below Sleights Moor, which is known emphatically as Eskdaleside, will find the miles very long ones. They are such as the writer once traversed hereabout, and concerning which the farmer who directed him remarked, with a sly twinkle in his eye, that the road was a hard one, and 'we give good measure.' About a mile from Sleights Bridge are the ruins of the ancient chapel of St. John at Eskdaleside, where, legend has it, dwelt the hermit whom Percy and his associates grievously maimed, because he had closed the doors of the chapel upon a hunted boar which had taken refuge there—a circumstance to which we referred in our chapter on Whitby. It was represented, in 1762, that the chapel was 'a poor, mean structure, covered with thatch, and situate in a low damp place near the river Esk, which very frequently overflowed its banks, and was anciently placed in that solitary part out of superstitious veneration for the memory of an ancient hermit who was said to have resided thereabouts; that the way to the said chapel was steep, commonly bad, and very often dangerous; and that, the chapel standing alone in a field at a long distance from any dwelling-house, there was no kind of shelter for the people who resorted thither before the chapel door happened to be opened.' The chapel at Sleights was therefore built in place of it, and opened in 1767.* The old chapel

* Lawton's 'Collectio Rerum Ecclesiasticarum de Diœcesi Eboracensi.'

stands by the Esk in the pleasant wooded dale; and, as the wayfarer approaches Grosmont, there is a sublime prospect of the dale, and of the river, here in the loveliest part of its course. Opposite, on the north, are Egton Low Moors, with Swart Houe Cross, behind which lie Hutton Mulgrave and the rich woods of Mulgrave Castle.

Grosmont itself is, it is true, something of a disfigurement in the dale, for it has become a busy place where ironstone is quarried, as well as sandstone, and has blast-furnaces of its own, whereof the evidences are very visible, and it is besides the junction of the Eskdale railway line with the line running thence through Goathland and Newton Dale to Pickering. The well-known basaltic dyke is exposed at Grosmont. 'Here,' says White, 'it has the form of a great wedge, the apex uppermost; and the sandstone, which is so rudely shouldered aside, is scorched and partially vitrified along the line of contact.' Grosmont may claim to be the birthplace of the modern iron industry in Cleveland, for, in 1836, the first cargo of Cleveland ironstone was sent thence by the Whitby Stone Company to the Birtley Iron Company. The traveller may be dispensed from the trouble of seeking any remains of the ancient priory of Grosmont, which gave its name to the place. This was founded in the reign of John by Johanna, daughter of William Fossard, and wife of Robert de Turnham, who invited hither, and provided with a site in Eskdale, a colony of monks from Grandimont, in Normandy. The priory thus was alien, and although, in a charter of De Mauley dated from St. Julian's in Goathland, the monks are said to be English, so continued until the Prior of Grandimont obtained leave, in the time of Richard II., to dispose of the rights in the cell, upon which the priory at Grosmont became indigenous, and thus escaped the suppression of alien houses by Henry V.

It is from Grosmont that the exploration of Goathland is often begun. Those even who have travelled by that most beautiful of railway lines, the one from Whitby to Pickering, have here learned something of the features of the smaller glens of Cleveland, though the finest beauties have of necessity escaped them, as well as of the wild moorland. After leaving Grosmont the line follows the course of the Mirk Esk, a winding tributary of the Esk itself, as far as Beck Hole, and far below in its devious glen the streamlet is seen in its rocky course, overhung by rugged scars clothed with ivy, bracken, and wild flowers, and flanked by the sylvan shades of Crag Cliff Wood, Spring Wood, Blue Ber Wood, Mirk Side and Combs Wood. The hill on the right immediately after leaving Grosmont is Lease Rigg, whence there is a splendid view both up and down Eskdale. Upon its upper slopes, in a commanding situation, about 500 feet above the sea, are evidences of the Roman camp, a station on the road from York and Malton, through the Cawthorn camps, to Dunsley, which comes over the eastern flank of Egton High Moor. The north-eastern end of that moor, too, at the place called Mirk Mire Moor on the

Ordnance map, near Struntary Carr, is rich, like all
the moors hereabout, in tumuli ; and, on the other side
of the Mirk Esk also, to the east, there are tumuli
and evidences of ancient defences on the moor. As
to the ' Killing Pits,' a mile and a half south of Beck
Holes on the Goathland Moor, between the Wheeldale
and Eller Becks, since the investigations of Canon
Atkinson, they can be no longer regarded as evidences
of a ' British village,' nor even perhaps of an ancient
battle, but rather as interesting evidences of the surface working of the ironstone. The two constituent
brooklets of the Mirk Esk, the Eller Beck and the
Wheeldale Beck, have their juncture at Beck Holes ;
and, if we trace the former to the left, by its stony
way, often called Goathland Dale, shadowed by the
trees, we reach Thomasine Foss, where, in a delightful
scene, the waters dash in a silvery torrent through a
rocky cleft and over a precipice into a deep pool,
about which the *Osmunda regalis* grows profusely, and
where the scars are shadowed by foliage and clothed
with trailing greenery. Water Ark and Walk Mill
Foss are other falls in the same glen ; and Friar's
House and Abbot House remain to remind the wayfarer of the ancient cell of Whitby where once Osmund
and his brethren prayed for the health of the soul of
Queen Matilda, and entertained the poor through the
benefaction of Henry I. This brook has its source
in a number of rills among the swelling heather of
Goathland Moor; and to a similar beginning in the
heights of Glaisdale and Wheeldale Moors we might

trace the Wheeldale Beck, through a somewhat richer woodland, and by Nelly Ayre Foss and Malyan's Spout, by which last a tributary rill descends nearly a hundred feet into the sylvan ravine. The waterfalls of Cleveland, to be seen at their best, should be visited after heavy rains, when, indeed, with their flashing waters and mossy rocks set in the tenderest of greens, they present most tempting subjects for the artist. Above the left bank of the Wheeldale Beck is the tiny hamlet of July (or Julian) Park, so called from a deer-park of the De Mauleys of Mulgrave which was here, and whereof the dyke is still traceable, as is also the Roman road upon the neighbouring moor above. Randay Mere is a lonely pool in a hollow near by. The site of the castle of St. Julian, a hunting seat of the De Mauleys, to which perhaps a hospice was attached, St. Julian being the patron of wayfarers, is still pointed out near the beck.

Returning to the Esk at Grosmont, we may walk along a very pleasant road, mostly by the river, on the left bank, to Egton Bridge, for the Esk from hence to Crunkley Gill is in the best part of its course ; but the railway, convenient as it is, cannot be escaped, and is, we may not hide from ourselves, a disfigurement to the dale. The moorland aspects of this region will be described in the next chapter, and therefore it is enough here to note that everywhere above the pleasant cultivated hill-slopes, with their farms embowered in trees, and their rich woodlands, spreads the heather and bracken. Egton Bridge is the prettiest village in

Eskdale, nestling by the stream, here with little islands in its course, with quaint houses snugly placed on the slope above the river, overshadowed by trees, and overgrown themselves by greenery, and with haystacks and ricks, and poultry-yards, and all the pleasant surroundings of rural life. Yet the village appears to be growing, and has at least one fine modern building in the Catholic church. Mrs. Macquoid has so well described the Esk at this point in flood that we quote her words: 'At the inn a pretty-looking girl said they could not lodge strangers, but that at a " house across t' water " we could get rooms. We went down the inn garden, and there was the river rushing along and eddying in yellow foam over a row of sunken stepping-stones, after which it curved round on either side under the shade of drooping trees; sunshine stole down here and there through the trees, and from the little plank bridge the subdued green light made the scene still more lovely. We crossed the stream, and found ourselves on a green island, and facing us the pleasant-looking house we had come to seek. Here was another row of stepping-stones, but, alas! we could not cross; the wide brown river was dashing furiously over them, and they were all deep under water. There was nothing for it but to go back; still, we could not regret having seen the Esk with its war-paint on.'*

The village of Egton is about a mile away from Egton Bridge, upon the slope of the hill to the north.

* 'About Yorkshire.'

The church there has Norman and Early English features, an aisle on the south side being separated from the nave by round pillars, with square capitals and bases, supporting semicircular arches, all quite plain, and evidently early. Here the old folk tell of a 'bargest' (bier ghost) or 'kirkgrim,' which aforetime haunted the neighbourhood of Egton Church—one of the strange, fearsome ghost-like creatures, 'neither beast nor human,' that Yorkshire once had many of, and whereof the footfall foreshadowed death. As we have in this descriptive wayfaring noted historical and other matters concerning places we have alluded to, so may it be of interest too, as illustrating party violence in troublous times, if we record that, in 1666, one William Kirk of Eskdaleside was had up for sedition in saying of certain soldiers in a public-house at Egton, where he was having a cup of ale : ' Their major is growne so high that he saith never a Papist shall weare a sword, not soe much as a stick in his hand; I say never a cavalier shall weare a sword ; within a few daies thou shalt not see a king in England.'

The walk from Egton Bridge to Glaisdale End, a distance of about a mile through East Arncliff Wood, may be made in two ways, either by taking the road leading to the right after passing the Catholic church, the most difficult way, or by going forward, crossing the bridge, curving to the right, and passing over a plank bridge, which brings one shortly to the entrance to the woods. In either case the walk is most delightful, especially in the spring-time, when the banks

are carpeted with primroses, and the beech and oak
trees put on their freshest green. The pathway is
often high above the stream, which roars through its
rocky channel ; now it leads amid dense foliage, now
where huge blocks of lichen-covered rock border the
way, beneath high scarps overhung by greenery, or
through brakes of waving fern, and at last we reach
the nab that the hill thrusts out between the Esk and
its tributary the Glaisdale Beck, from the top whereof
is a splendid prospect both of Glaisdale, save for the
blast furnaces, and the Esk.

The famous Beggar's Bridge here spans the Esk in
a singularly light, graceful and fairy-like segmental
arch, embowered in foliage, far above the stream.
High up on the eastern side are graven on a stone the
initials ' T. F.,' and the date 1619 ; and, inasmuch as
the bridge is spoken of as Firris Bridge in a document
two centuries old, there is little doubt that it was
built—shall we say rebuilt ? for there are stones in it
that have belonged to a fourteenth-century structure
—by Alderman Thomas Ferris, or Firris, of Hull. It
generally resembles in its appearance the Bow Bridge
at Castleton, a twelfth-century structure, now destroyed,
and Danby Castle Bridge, which was built about the
year 1386. There is, however, a graceful legendary
story concerning the Beggar's Bridge, to the effect
that an Eskdale lover—Ferris appears to have been
an Eskdale or a Glaisdale man—once unable to visit
his mistress on the eve of his departure to seek his
fortune afar, because the angry Esk could not be

swum, vowed, if ever he should return rich, that he would erect a bridge so that no Eskdale lover should ever be so tortured again. Further, they say that it is called the Beggar's Bridge because he went away poor, despised of the lady's father, and returned when he had acquired glory in the defeat of the Spanish Armada, and wealth among the treasure ships of the Spanish Main. As a singer hath it :

'The rover came back from a far distant land,
And claimed from the maiden her long-promised hand ;
But he built, ere he won her, the bridge of his vow,
And the lovers of Egton pass over it now.'

CHAPTER VI.

UPPER ESKDALE.

EVERYWHERE about us now, on the hill-tops, spreads
the rolling moorland, covered knee-deep in heather,
or 'ling'; and, in the harvest-time, the purple moor-
banks above the dale crest the upland cultivated steeps,
in rare contrast of colour to the yellow hue of the
ripened corn. The northern hills—the 'Low Moors'
of Egton and Danby, to which we shall presently return
—present to the Esk a far more regular breastwork
than those to the south, though several becks and gills
tumble down them to the dale. The great moorland
height on the south, however, that separates the watershed of the Esk from that of the Rye, thrusts out upon
the river several moorland ridges at right angles to its

course, and between these lie the 'dales' which are
a chief glory of Cleveland. It is the varied contour
and bold features of these long projections of the moor,
with the opening of the lovely dales between—Glaisdale, Great and Little Fryup, Danby Dale, and Westerdale—that lend such charm to the delightful valley of
the Esk, for almost at every step some new and charming prospect is revealed. In the words of a much-
travelled friend of Canon Atkinson, speaking of these
dales: 'They differ from all others I have ever seen,
and in this particular especially, that elsewhere you
have to go in search of beautiful views; here they come
and offer themselves to be looked at.'*

Before, however, we traverse the dale further, or
describe the tributary dales on the south, it will be well
to complete our account of the northern moorlands,
which lie between Eskdale and the sea, and to which
the becks we traced upward from the coast in earlier
chapters bring the wayfarer. Above the Esk, between
Grosmont and Egton Bridge, is Egton Low Moor,
named Westonby Moor at its western end, and Briscoe
Moor to the north, where certain of the streamlets rise
that pour their waters seaward through Mulgrave
Woods. Beyond these Low Moors of Egton, the
Stonegate Beck, the most important of the northern
tributaries of the Esk in this part of its course, though
by no means important enough to have a 'dale,' comes
down through a delightful sylvan and rocky ravine,
and has its source in the flanks of Ugthorpe Moor.

* 'Forty Years in a Moorland Parish,' p. 185.

7

Beyond the beck the bold form of Lealholm (or Lelum) Rigg is thrust out towards the river from the height of Lealholm Moor, which, at Brown Rigg Houe, reaches more than 900 feet. We are now at the eastern end of Danby Low Moor, which rises, going westward, to 988 feet at the Beacon, and falls further on in the swampy region where the Clither Beck has its source, near which is Doubting Castle, where a meeting of moor-tracks may confuse the traveller, when the mists are upon the hills, as it has the writer of this. The western end of Danby Low Moor rises to 850 feet at Job Cross, and the hills reach a greater altitude still, westward, on Commondale and Guisborough Moors.

In a previous chapter we described how the moorlands north of the Esk may be reached from the coast at Staithes by taking the ridge road between the Easington and Roxby Becks, and we may now pursue the journey hitherward toward the river. In taking this route the moor is entered at Waupley New Inn, beyond which all is heather, with patches of bracken and bilberry. In front rises the huge rounded form of Danby Beacon, a commanding height, and one of the lonely places of nature. It is a moor replete with the evidences of prehistoric life in the houes or grave-hills, which may be seen here and there upon the crests, and of which Canon Atkinson has opened many. There is, besides, a reputed 'British village' on the hill, wherein men will now choose rather to see the evidences of ancient superficial iron-working. 'What a panorama it is that greets your eyes!' Canon Atkinson says, with worthy enthusiasm, of the prospect from the Beacon. 'Bold mountain ridge and coy shrinking dale from left to right as you face the south, and spreading round so as to overlap on the right side ; and then, turning seaward, the sea from Redcar sands to almost Whitby, and right away out to the north the coast of Durham, beyond Sunderland and north-ward still, with an outline that seems to lose itself in the dim distance beyond. And a moment since you saw but a barren ling-covered moor-bank !' What is here said of the surprise of scenery is equally true of the surprise of aërial effect upon the moors. The writer of this has seen the hills all glowing in their purple vesture, every ridge and undulation bright and clear in the vivid sunlight, their heights alive with the sharp cries of the grouse and the rapid beating of wings, busy with flocks of moor-pipits and blackbirds, and with the horned moor-sheep browsing upon the banks. Again, when the hazy air has been flooded still with sunlight, it has suffused the whole landscape with yellow, and he has found the heights filled with a silence broken only by the murmuring of the breeze in the long growth of ling. At other times he has seen the moorland when its vesture all was brown, and when the patches of bracken were turned to red and gold. Many moods of the moors are, indeed, coy, and must be wooed, not by the speeding wayfarer, but by him who can linger and return. There are seasons when the ling is long, and difficult to make one's way through ; and there are places on the moors that are

boggy and dangerous; and, indeed, let the wayfarer
be warned against certain spots which assume a hue of
most delicious green, and seem to lengthen out in
tempting pathways downward from the hills, for these
are but the mossy vesture of wet swamps, in which
one may easily sink, but whence it is far more difficult
to escape.*

This journey across the moor towards Eskdale has
led us into a general description of moorland wayfaring,
such as it is found in Cleveland. Let us imagine now
that we have reached the southern border of these
Danby Low Moors, and are about to descend into the
dale. If we should chance to be at the edge of the
declivity in the early morning, it might well be that
the valley would be filled with a light mist, and that
the opposite ridge would stand out brilliantly in the sunlight,
with a strange and charming aspect not unfamiliar in
this region. Then, as we descended to the cultivated
slopes, and the mist cleared off in wreaths, the objects
of the lower landscape, farmstead, stack, and tree,
would steal into sight, and so, one by one, the beauties
of Eskdale would be disclosed, and we should soon
reach that river which we recently left at Glaisdale
End.

The reader who would gain a true conception of the
dales opening into Eskdale on the south must picture

---

* In traversing the moors, the roads, which cross them in white
lines from village to village, may always be kept to, but in journeying upon the moorland itself, it may be necessary upon occasion to
take account with the gamekeepers.

to himself first of all the steep moor-banks that shut
them in. Glaisdale is typical of the rest. Broad and
fruitful, the cornfields and meadows cover the bottom,
rising gently from its beck, and above them stand
the farm-houses dotted about the hillside, each—as
you find them often in Yorkshire—with its clump of
trees, places seeming so peaceful and sequestered on
the sunny slopes that you might fancy trouble could
never enter at the door. Close behind them rises the
steep moor-bank, where perhaps some 'intake' has
been won from the heather and fern, and gives a scanty
herbage to the husbandman ; and so, beyond, you climb
the craggy acclivity to the topmost moor. The descents
of Glaisdale fall in some places more than 500 feet
within half a mile, and while, in its midst, the beck
is 400 feet above the sea, Egton High Moor, which
shuts in the dale on the south-east, speedily scales more
than 1,000 feet, and the greatest elevations of Glaisdale Ridge, which separates the dale from Great Fryup
—the next dale of Esk—on the other side, is 1,069 feet.
The woods of Arncliff (erne, an eagle), which we passed
through in approaching Beggar's Bridge, clothe the
lower part of Glaisdale also, and, with beetling, ivy-
grown cliffs, and leafy shades of oak and beech and
rowan, and glades carpeted with primroses, or rich in
bluebells in the spring, make a delightful approach to
the dale. But the road through it is up above the left
bank of the stream, and, soon after leaving the hamlet
of Glaisdale End, passes near Hart Hall, a farmhouse
where the old folk tell of a 'Hob,' in whom, though un-

canny, the milk of human kindness ran; for, when hands were scarce at the haymaking, or the wain stuck fast in the 'gait,' or there was much corn to be threshed, or there was work that it passed the power of man to do, then the little brown 'Hob' would haste to his labour when men lay asleep, or, half fearful, waking, listened by night to the heavy thud of his flail. And once, forasmuch as 'Hob' was 'amaist as nakt as when he wur boorn,' the good folk, since the winter nights were cold, made him a 'hamp,' a garment of ancient fashion, wherewith he might be clothed, and put it in his way. But Hob, so it is written, with that freakish inconstancy so characteristic of his kind, took their thoughtfulness amiss, and went off, exclaiming:

> 'Gin Hob mun hae nowght but a hardin' hamp,
> He'll coom nae mair, nowther to berry nor stamp.'

Near the 'head' of the dale, too, is a farm bearing the name 'Hob Garth,' and above it, on the high moor, indeed, upon the ridge between Glaisdale and Great Fryup, not far from certain pits resembling the 'Killing Pits' at Goathland, is a 'Hart Leap,' where a fabled hart, sore pressed by the hounds, leaped a distance of forty-two feet, as is marked by stones even at this very day.* The upper end of Glaisdale derives great character from the descent, on the right bank of its

---

* The accomplished vicar of Danby has collected from an ancient informant much deeply interesting folk-lore concerning Hart Hall Hob, which will be found, with a great deal else of like sort, in his 'Forty Years in a Moorland Parish;' and he has spun a delightful story for boys, in his 'Last of the Giant Killers,' based upon the 'Headless Hart of the Hart Leap.'

THE ESK IN GLAISDALE.   DRAWN BY ALFRED DAWSON.

beck, of the Wintergill, through a deep cleft in the steep side of Egton High Moor, and from the bold moorland nab that is thrust out between the gill and the dale 'head.' There is tangled woodland, too, before we reach the heath of Glaisdale Moor, which is part of the lofty transverse ridge that separates the watersheds of the Esk and the Rye, and across which the moorland tracks lead into Rosedale. It is in this great ridge that all the southern tributaries of the Esk have their source.

Return we now to Glaisdale End, in order that we may continue our wayfaring up Eskdale. The splendid woods of Arncliff are left behind, but still there is plenty of foliage in the dale, and there are pleasant farmsteads and cultivated fields; and, as we go forward along the road on the slope of the southern hill, the river is seen in a tortuous course below, winding about with many a dimpling curve, accompanied always by the railway, and beyond is the sunny slope of Lealholm Side, with the varied contours of the hills, divided by the tributary Stonegate Beck. Above, on the left, rises the broader extension of the end of Glaisdale Ridge, dominating the vale, for the Esk curves round the base of it, and presently we reach the pleasant hamlet of Lealholm Bridge by the stream. Just beyond the hamlet the Esk takes a wide sweep, perforce abandoned by the railway, through the deep rocky cleft of Crunkley (or Crumbeclive) Gill, where the steep scarps of naked rock, with trees and ferns rooted in their clefts, overlook, in scenes of surpassing beauty, the river, which rolls in yellow foam over its rocky bed, and lingers in still pools in the hollows. In this delightful spot there is not a little to remind the traveller of Chee Dale on the Derbyshire Wye. Crumbeclive appears as a manor in Domesday, with Danby and Lealholm as its berewics. It had belonged to Orm, and was granted to Hugh Fitz Baldric, but ultimately formed part of the great Brus fee, and Danby then became the *caput manerium*.

Beyond Crunkley Gill, Great Fryup Beck falls into the Esk, and we are at the 'end' of Great Fryup, another of its 'dales,' shut in between Glaisdale Ridge, before alluded to, and an isolated hill to be presently described. The lower course of this tributary resembles that of the Glaisdale Beck in general character, for the steep slopes of the boldly contoured hills, diversified with wood, are cultivated, and there are pleasant tree-sheltered farmsteads upon them. As we go towards the dale 'head,' the elevated moorland is before us, and presently we climb the hill with growing difficulty, and in a strangely wild and picturesque scene, for there the rocks are scattered in chaotic confusion, hurled down from the tall scars above, and covered with a rough clothing of bracken, heather, and rough grass; but a plenteous growth of fir, oak, birch, and mountain ash softens the savageness of the scene.

The isolated hill on the west of Great Fryup separates it on that side from Little Fryup. It is a ridge in some respects singular, for unlike other ridges hereabout, it is not continuous with the great transverse

moorland ridge, but is separated from it by Fairy
Cross Plain, which it dominates in a sharp 'nab,'
1,014 feet high. Concerning the folk-lore of the Plain,
Canon Atkinson has recorded much that is curious in
his 'Moorland Parish,' as elsewhere certain 'fond'
stories of the trolls who dwelt long ago beneath Round
Hill, which in appearance is a kind of gigantic anthill,
of remarkable aspect, in the hollow near by. The
isolated hill sinks towards the Esk, but confronts the
river with the sheer scarps of Danby Crag far above
its course, and the romantic thickets of Crag Wood
upon its sharp declivity. A road from Great Fryup
by Fairy Cross Plain, brings us to Little Fryup 'head'
—the dale lying between Danby Ridge and the isolated
hill—and we pursue the pleasant course of its beck,
a distance of two miles at most, until we reach the
Esk once more.

At the foot of Little Fryup, on the slope of the
moorland hill that shuts it in on the west, facing the
Esk, and with a wide and beautiful prospect of its
dale towards Lealholm, stands Danby Castle, an
ancient house of the Latimers, now the property of
Lord Downe, a great landowner hereabout, who has
a house at Danby Lodge across the Esk. It will be
remembered that, in speaking of Skelton and Kilton
Castles, we referred to the partition of the great Brus
fee among the sisters and coheiresses of the last Peter
de Brus. In this way Danby came to Marmaduke de
Thweng, of Kilton, and became afterwards the heritage
of Lucia, the only child of his eldest son. In 1296

she was married to William le Latimer, and, within the next ten years, Danby Castle was built. It remained a seat of the Nevilles, Lords Latimer, until the time of Elizabeth, and afterwards came by purchase to the Dawnays. The situation of the castle is exceedingly fine. Its plan was originally an oblong square, 117 feet by 81 feet, inclosing a court, which was about 54 feet by 20 feet. The peculiarity of the plan is that rectangular towers stood at the corners projecting diagonally beyond the outline. On the north side may be observed the shields of Bruce, Thweng and Latimer. The kitchen was on that side, and two enormous fireplaces, with indications of the sites of two ovens, may yet be seen. On the east side stands the west wall of the great hall, which seems to have been a noble apartment, and parts of four two-light windows, 16½ feet high, under square hood-mouldings, looking upon the court, still remain. The area of the hall is now occupied as a barn. On the south side the angle towers gave place at an early date to extended angular projections, the south-eastern one of which is occupied as a farmhouse. The 'Jury Room' is richly panelled in oak, and has a fine late mediæval fireplace in it, and within the court is a characteristic corbelled chimney. The gateway was on the western side. Evidences of considerable alteration are visible in the castle, and, though fallen from its high estate, and partly ruinous, it is a most interesting remain; and the gray walls, in which green growths have found root, with the angles, doorways and windows, are very picturesque.

Tradition has it that an English queen once dwelt at
Danby Castle—perhaps Katherine Parr, who was first
married to John, Lord Latimer.

Below the castle, spanning the Esk, and carrying
the road from thence to Danby Lodge, and beyond
it to Dale End and Castleton, is the castle bridge,
now known as Duck Bridge, a hipped structure with a
single arch, built at the end of the fourteenth century,
and bearing upon its keystone the arms of John, Lord
Neville of Raby, doubtless its builder, who, in right of
his wife, was summoned to Parliament as Lord Latimer.
From the bridge to Castleton the distance is about a
mile and a half, there being roads or paths on both
sides of the river. On the left, as we go forward, is
the hamlet of Ainthorp at the foot of the hill, and
opposite to it, across the bridge, that of Dale End,
through which a steep road leads up to Danby Low
Moors, with the opening of the Baysdale Beck.

Castleton, a pleasant village, as you find them in
Cleveland, at the very edge of the moors, stretches
along the country road, at the 'end' of Danby Dale,
where the Danby Beck comes down from the hills.
We may call it the 'capital' of the large parish of
Danby, for Danby village there is none, and the church
even is some distance away up Danby Dale. It is a
village where those who do not exact luxuries may
find pleasant quarters; and there is fishing in trout
streams, and shooting over moors, and many an interesting place to explore, and an invigorating air,
moreover, such as is ever found in the neighbourhood

of the heather. One hostel in the place will tempt
the traveller with the lines, painted upon a sign :

> ' Kind gentlemen and yeomen good,
> Step in and sup with Robin Hood ;
> If Robin Hood be not at home,
> Come in and drink with Little John.'

Long ago the little village clustered about the hill,
whereon stood the great castle of Brus, the site of
which is now marked by a farm. Before the Conquest
Danby, and much more with it, was in the hands
of Orm—probably the Orm, son of that Gamel who
was foully done to death by Earl Tostig in 1064—and
it came to Hugh Fitz Baldric, and, after his death or
forfeiture, to Robert de Brus. Brus, indeed, had his
castle here before the grant of Skelton, which led him
to transfer his headship thither. The position of
Castleton was very important, and existing evidences
show that the castle was of great strength, and its
garth of large extent, protected by walls of prodigious
thickness, and by moats at different levels. Peter de
Brus was one of the northern barons who opposed
John, and, in 1216, either by force or stratagem, the
king took Skelton, in his vengeful harrying of the
North. Canon Atkinson conjectures with great probability, from a number of circumstances, that it was
at this time that the fortress at Castleton was dismantled and wasted, for certainly very early it lay
ruinous, and probably scarce habitable.

At Castleton the exploration of Danby Dale begins.
In character it resembles the dales we have already

traversed—at the bottom meadows and cornfields by
the beck, tree-embowered farmsteads on the slopes,
and, above, the steep moorland ridges that shut in
the dale. On the east, above the dale side, are Danby
Moor and Danby Ridge, rich in barrows, and with
traces of ancient earthworks thereon (as, indeed, we
may see on many of the ridges hereabout) ; and on
the west rises the long narrow moorland tongue of
Castleton Ridge, along which runs a road from the
village that strikes southward across the moors, and
whence, indeed, it is delightful to look down into
Danby Dale on one hand, and Westerdale on the
other. In the midst of the dale is Danby Church,
dedicated to St. Hilda, rebuilt, if tradition be trust-
worthy, from stones quarried out of the dismantled
castle of Brus. The existing edifice, however, is
modern, and of no great interest. It is to the vicar
of Danby, Canon Atkinson, that we are indebted for
a whole world of quaint and curious information concerning the folk-lore, history and characteristics of
Danby and its people, embodied in the ' Forty Years
in a Moorland Parish,' a book which has made Danby
famous. Canon Atkinson is also known as an inde-
fatigable barrow-digger, and hence it is that the
British Museum is enriched with a large collection of
prehistoric remains from the houes hereabout. His
' Cleveland Ancient and Modern ' threw great light
upon the Danish colonization of the neighbourhood,
and his ' Glossary of the Cleveland Dialect ' is rich in
its illustrations of our folk-speech. With a lighter

touch, moreover, in his ' Last of the Giant Killers ; or, the Exploits of Sir Jack of Danby Dale,' he has peopled the dales with imaginative creations, based nevertheless upon the legendary lore of this part of Cleveland. Two miles above the church we approach Danby Head, and a steep footpath brings us out upon the heather of the great transverse ridge. Hereabout, in mediæval times, wolves had their haunt, as is testified still by the Wolf Pit on Danby Moor, and by other place names of the region.

Half a mile beyond Castleton the railway leaves the course of the Esk, here shrunken to the dimensions of a considerable brook, and passes north-westward up Commondale, a pleasant valley in the high moors, with scattered farms, and the shade of many a rowan. If we should ascend the Seddale Beck, which here comes down between Commondale and Kildale Moors, we should reach Percy Cross, upon the border of Guisborough Moor. Roseberry Topping to the west lifts his conical head, and Easby Moor holds aloft the Cook memorial column far over the lower country of the gathering ground of the Leven and the tributary waters of the Tees, which was the scene of the great circumnavigator's early years. It is a country of vast and varied prospects, from the far-off hills towards Richmond, and the dim coast of Durham, to a splendid moorland landscape of the heights that flank the Esk, but to these things we referred in speaking of Roseberry Topping in an earlier chapter of this book, and it is therefore unnecessary to dwell upon them here.

Another tributary of the infant Esk is the Basedale
Beck, which comes down in a long curve from the
great heights of Basedale Moor, which borders upon
the great escarpments from which the Cleveland hills
look westward across the Vale of Mowbray. Basedale
is the loneliest valley we have met with in our wanderings. Shut in between steep moor banks, with a rough
growth of trees here and there, and but a dwelling
or two in its whole course, which is of some four miles,
few sounds accompany the music of its waters, save
the sharp cries of the grouse, and the voice of the
wind as it sings on its way through the long growth of
heather. Yet here, in the solitude, in the midst of the
dale, is the site of a Cistercian nunnery, which was
removed hither from Nunthorpe, near Stokesley, in the
reign of Henry II., Basedale having been given to the
nuns by Guido de Bovingcourt.

Let us, however, turning south-westward, trace the
Esk itself through Westerdale to its source in the great
moorland ridge from the slopes of which it has received most of its tributaries. Westerdale is divided
from Danby Dale by the Castleton Ridge, and is
bounded on the west by Hograh, Stockdale and Basedale Moors. It is a wide pastoral dale, with tree-
encircled farmsteads, and through the lower part of it
the tributary Tower Beck, as well as the little Esk
itself, runs down from the moors. In the midst of
the dale, the hamlet of Westerdale stretches along the
road that crosses it, and near by they will show you
the pits known as Ref Holes, as evidence of a ' British

village,' but much more likely as an evidence of the old working of the surface iron. It would appear that the Templars had a Preceptory at Westerdale, for a certain William de la Fenne is named as having been preceptor there at the time of the suppression of the Order in 1308. As we reach the ' head ' of the dale a nab confronts us, thrust out between the Esk itself and a tributary gill, and we trace the former further through a deep cleft in the moor, to where it has its sources in a number of little streamlets among the heather of Westerdale Moor.

To such a moorland ending has our tracing of the tributary becks of the Esk in every case brought us. And now, having reached the great ridge dividing the watersheds of the Esk and the Rye, from which the other ridges we have named run out as promontories towards the dale, let us consider for a moment its physical characteristics. It is to be noted that the descent towards the Esk is much sharper than that towards the Rye, and hence the tributary dales of the former river are much shorter than those of the latter ; and that the transverse ridge grows higher and higher as we proceed westward. At the Three Houes on Egton High Moor the altitude is 867 feet ; it reaches 1,071 at Pike Hill Moss, a mile further west ; 1,075 feet at Yarlsey Moss ; 1,212 feet at Shunnor Houe ; 1,318 feet on Glaisdale Moor ; 1,350 feet opposite the Castleton Ridge ; 1,422 feet west of the sources of the Esk, and 1,419 feet at Burton Head, above the steep escarpment which gives such a superb view to the west ; but

the greatest elevation is on Urra Moor, a mile south-
west of this point, where the height is 1,489 feet.
Burton Head and Urra Moor flank, in fact, that angle
in the great western escarpment from which the Ingleby
Beck flows downward to the Leven.

The views from these high moors are splendid in
their extent, and most impressive in their character.
Northward, we scan the coy, retreating dales of the
Esk, shut in by the ridges, which are green, or purple,
or brown, according to the season; and, beyond the
river, with rare atmospheric effects of distance, rise
the northern moors of Danby, with the Beacon and
the conical crest of Freeburgh Hill, while, more westward, the greater cone of Roseberry stands out boldly
in the view; and, indeed, whichever way we turn,
there is such a prospect of rolling moor and boldly
contoured hills as will not soon fade from the memory.
Southward down the heathery slope we look towards
the watershed of the Rye, where, in their moorland
gathering-ground, the streams of Bilsdale, Bransdale,
Farndale, Rosedale, and Newtondale have their sources.
But the beginning of these streams, though it gives
character and variety to the moorland landscape, does
not distinguish it so much as the vast prospect across
the intervening hills to where, far off in the great plain
of York, the venerable minster may be seen standing,
in the clear atmosphere, conspicuous in the view. It
should be noted that the southern slope of these
Cleveland hills is met by the long series of sharp
'nab'-like bluffs which the 'tabular' oolitic hills, that

rise gradually from beneath the recent deposits of the Vale of Pickering, present to the north. Terminating thus southward, in broken slopes and spurs, the Cleveland hills present bolder escarpments to the west, where, shutting in the heads of Eskdale and of the lonely dales through which its early tributaries flow, in bold wooded escarpments, they look over a fair prospect of the gathering-ground of the Leven to distant Durham and the Tees, while scarcely rivalled in their kind are the wide views from these western steeps, over a broken and picturesque foreground, and across the great and richly cultivated plain to where, in the blue distance, rise the far-off western hills.

CHAPTER VII.

THE RYE.—BILSDALE, RIEVAULX, AND HELMSLEY.

Characteristics of Ryedale—Bilsdale—The 'Tabular' Hills—The Winter March of William the Conqueror—Walter l'Espec and the Coming of the Monks to Rievaulx—The Fabric of Rievaulx —Descent of the Site—The Rievaulx Terrace and Temples— Duncombe Park—Its Art Treasures—The Park—Helmsley— Its Castle and History—George Villiers, Duke of Buckingham —Seventeenth-Century Quakers at Helmsley.

IN crossing over the great moorland ridge south of the Esk, we leave behind us the more characteristic part of the region known throughout the Middle Ages, and as late as the time of the Stuarts, as Blackmoor, Black-amore, or Blacomoyre—a name generally applied to the Cleveland hills—to enter the gentler-featured dale of the Rye. Not all Ryedale, however, belongs to the province of this book. Our wayfaring will carry us scarcely further west than Bilsdale, through which the river Seph flows to its confluence with the infant Rye, nor further south than the well-defined edge of the hill-country that looks from gentle wooded slopes across that great saucer-like plain known as the Vale of Pickering, in which the Rye and the Derwent unite

their waters before flowing thence southward, by a
narrow valley of denudation, through the oolitic hills
that extend eastward from Castle Howard to Malton
and Langton Wold. Roughly speaking, this region
of our inland wanderings is defined on the south by
the line of railway from Helmsley, by Pickering, to
Seamer Junction, and by the country road that accom-
panies it.

Nevertheless, it will be well to begin by describing
generally the configuration of the interesting and fruitful vale of the Rye. The river has its source in the
moorland hills that lie between Osmotherley and the
Clevelands; and in a south-westerly direction it flows
through a narrow and picturesque dale, soon shut in
on the west by the long line of the Hambleton Hills.
Many becks and rills descend from the heights, but the
first important tributary is the river Seph, soon after
receiving which the swift-flowing Rye sweeps by the
venerable ruins of Rievaulx, and, with a great and
sinuous curve, reaches, by the foot of Duncombe Park,
the ancient town of Helmsley. Many places hereabout, westward of the Rye, may tempt the wayfarer.
He may choose to linger in the beautiful scenery of the
Hambleton Hills, to explore the great rocky escarpments, differing, as Phillips says, only from sea-cliffs
in that no water beats against them, with which at
Boltby, Whitecliff (or White Mear), and Rolston they
overlook the picturesque country to the west. The
majestic remains of Byland will lure him wistfully down
to the quiet sequestered dale, where he will gaze in

admiration and pity upon the great ruined façade
standing in solemn dignity against the dark slope of
the hill. He will wander thence to the delightful
village of Coxwold, where he will bethink him of the
writing of 'Tristram Shandy' and the 'Sentimental
Journey,' and will picture Sterne in how 'princely a
manner' he lived, 'sitting down alone to venison, fish,
and wild-fowl, and all the simple fare which a rich valley
(under Hambleton Hills) can produce.' 'I have a
hundred hens and chickens about my yard,' wrote
Yorick of his place at Coxwold, 'and not a parishioner
catches a hare, or a rabbit, or a trout, but he brings
it as an offering to me.' As the hill-country that flanks
the Rye on its right bank ranges more directly to the
east, the tourist will find much to attract him at
Newburgh Priory (the seat of Sir George Wombwell),
with its Cromwellian relics; at Gilling, with its beautiful scenery, and fine old castle of the Fairfaxes; at
Slingsby, also with the remains of a very interesting
castle, and at many another place thereabout. The
Rye in this part of its course flows slowly south-westward from Helmsley, through the midst of a wide
and fruitful strath, with the flanking hills at a considerable distance on either hand. It receives the
waters of the Costa Beck, a famous fishing stream, from
the neighbourhood of Pickering, and falls, three miles
above Malton, into the Derwent, which, having issued
from Forge Valley, where we shall find it later on in
this book, has flowed through a similar wide and
pastoral plain bordered on the south by the Wolds.

Now, however, the Derwent, with its increased volume of waters, having passed by Malton, flows through another picturesque part of its course in that green and narrow valley, the only opening from the Vale of Pickering—which but for it would be a lake, and discharge its waters into the sea near Filey—where it has the rich woods of the Earl of Carlisle's splendid seat of Castle Howard on one hand, and the exquisite remains of Kirkham Priory on the other.

Such a brief account of the general features of Ryedale and the Vale of Pickering, as they are bordered on the south, must suffice for our purpose, for it is time that we now betake ourselves to our wayfaring among the tributary dales of the north. And, first, let us begin with Bilsdale, the way of the Seph, because it is the most westerly of the dales we propose to describe, and because it presents this advantage to the wayfarer: that a tolerable road from Stokesley or Ingleby Greenhow passes down it from end to end, leaving the river only in the neighbourhood of Rievaulx to cross over the hill to Helmsley. From the dale-head to Helmsley the distance is about thirteen miles. The scenery of the narrow dale is very beautiful, and in parts even grand. The Bilsdale Beck, for so the river Seph is called in its upper course, rises west of Burton Head, at the south-western termination of the Cleveland hills, its earliest waters being derived from the flanks of Urra Moor; and below the hamlet of Urra it flows southward in a valley flanked by steep hills that rise almost from its margin to a height of

about 500 feet above its bed. Many little gills descend
from the slopes below the moor, upon the rounded
edge of which is an ancient earthen rampart, as well
as from the Bilsdale East and West Moors, which
flank it on either hand, the Raisdale Beck being the
most important of its early tributaries. The lowei
slopes are cultivated ; there is much wood in the dale ;
the rock crops out in picturesque and precipitous
scarps here and there ; there are lofty, peak-like nabs
between some of the becks, and the dark moorland'
edges crest the steeps. At Chop Gate, where there
is an inn, the valley widens, but again grows narrow
where Nab End Moor, an outlying portion of Bilsdale
East Moor, rises boldly, facing the hamlet of Orterley,
with tumuli and the broken circle of the Bride Stones
upon its top. The 'nab' is thrust out on the left
between the river and the Ledge Beck, which, from a;
tangled woodland on the edge of the moors, brings down
the waters of the Tripsdale and Tarn Hole Becks. Now
again the moorland edges recede, and the wood grows
thicker in the dale, as the river hurries southward with
increased volume, receiving the waters of the Fangdale
and other becks.

The hill upon the right, dominating the river with
a very steep escarpment, is Helmsley Moor; and the
wayfarer, having reached the southern angle of it, past
Birch Wood, will have an opportunity of examining one
of the remarkable features of the configuration of this
region. We have already said that the 'tabular'
oolitic range presents, to the slopes of the transverse

moorland ridge, a series of sharp bluffs or nabs, the range being completely intersected by the tributary dales of the Rye. Here is an example of it, for the northern end of Rievaulx Moor meets the southern slope of Helmsley Moor with a well-defined semicircular escarpment, clothed with the thick larch plantations of Roppa. Beyond this point the oolitic moor descends to the dale with an exceedingly precipitous wooded escarpment, below which, near Shaken Bridge, the Seph joins the Rye, overlooked on the west by the bold form of Easterside Moor. That river, well stocked with trout and grayling, has come down through a very picturesque dale of its own, already alluded to, and it flows hence to Rievaulx in a rapid winding course—which justifies the surmise that its name may be derived from *rhe* (Brit.), swift—over a rocky bed, margined by green sward, in a narrow valley clothed with a glorious woodland upon its boldly-featured hills, that is delightful in the fresh green of spring or the full leafage of summer, but magnificent when autumn turns the foliage of oak and elm and beech to red and russet and gold. Above, on the hill, is Old Byland, with traces yet of its occupation by the monks, who afterwards removed their house to where we now see the splendid ruins of it near Coxwold; and there is also at Old Byland a most interesting Saxon dial, which may be compared with that at Kirkdale, of which we have yet to speak.

The road through Bilsdale is of great antiquity, and was perhaps a Roman way from York to the mouth of the Tees. When William the Conqueror had crushed the last remnant of the Cleveland men at the camp by Tees Mouth, it seems to have been across the moors and by this dale that he descended in winter time (January, 1070) to Hamelac (Helmsley), on his terrible march to York. Mr. Freeman thus paraphrases the account of this celebrated march as given by Ordericus: 'We now read how his course led him through hills and valleys, where the snow often lay, while the neighbouring districts were rejoicing in the bloom of spring.' [The march, however, was made in January.] 'Through that wild region William now made his way amid the cold and ice of winter. It needed the bidding and example of a leader who was ever foremost, and who shrank from no toil which he laid upon others, to keep up the spirits of his followers. The march was toilsome and dangerous; the horses died in crowds; each man pressed on as he could, thinking only of his own safety, and recking little of his lord or his comrade. At one point William himself, with six horsemen only, lost his way, and had to spend the night in utter ignorance of the whereabouts of his main army. A chance attack from some band of wandering outlaws might perhaps have freed England. It might at least have undone the work of the Conquest, and thrown the conquerors into utter anarchy and confusion.'*

It was a region of untamed solitude still—*locus vastæ solitudinis et horroris*—when the white-robed monks from Clairvaux first seated themselves by the Rye,

* 'Norman Conquest,' iv. 305.

where William and Waltheof and the brethren raised up, in the narrow valley, that magnificent example of our Early English architecture whereof the maimed fragment evokes at this day the diverse sentiments of admiration and horror—of admiration for them that earnestly and laboriously built, and of horror for them that ruthlessly destroyed. Let us first picture to our-selves the great founder, Walter l'Espec, and then think of his work. The neighbouring castle of Helmsley, of which we have yet to speak, was his, and some fragments of it still remaining belong, it may be, to his time. We hear of him as a valiant soldier and skilful leader of men, whose trumpet - voice harangued the English forces at the Battle of the Standard, from that car whereon the four sacred banners were displayed, ere he led them to victory. Long before this, however —if legend and recorded tradition be true—the only son of L'Espec and of his wife Adeline had been killed by being thrown from his horse, which was startled by the rushing of a boar across the road, against a stone, that is still shown as the base of a cross, at Kirkham Priory, in the green dale of the Derwent. Upon this sad event L'Espec resolved to devote the greater part of his worldly goods to the service of God, and thus he founded first the priory of Kirkham for Augustinians, in 1121, placing the high altar, it is said, on the spot to which his son's body had been dragged by the steed, and next the great Cistercian abbey of Rievaulx, some ten years later, as well as subsequently the house of Wardon, also Cistercian, in Bedfordshire.

A monastic verse in record of this triple foundation remains :

> ' Pro reorum veniâ Kirkham domus bona,
> Rievallis deinceps, et hæc tria, Wardona
> Est fundata primitus a dicta persona,
> Pro quorum meritis datur illi trina corona.'

St. Bernard had at this time been minded to send over from Clairvaux a colony of monks to his friend Archbishop Thurstan, and it was at Thurstan's counsel that L'Espec established them by the Rye—in the Rieval, or Rievaulx, from the tributary dales. William and Waltheof, the first abbots, were friends of St. Bernard, and soon the Cistercians became a *gentem magnam*, widely known for their piety and their labours. At length, weary of the world, the aged founder himself entered the house of Rievaulx, and died there in 1153. The third abbot, Ælred, has left us his portrait : ' An old man full of days, quick-witted, prudent in counsel, moderate in peace, circumspect in war, a true friend, a loyal subject. His stature was passing tall, his limbs all of such size as not to exceed their just proportions, and yet to be well matched with his great height. His hair was still black, his beard long and flowing, his forehead wide and noble, his eyes large and bright, his face broad, but well featured, his voice like the sound of a trumpet, setting off his natural eloquence of speech with a certain majesty of sound.'* Fittingly, indeed, would the venerable soldier, entering the house he had founded, exclaim with the Psalmist : ' I have loved,

* ' De Bello Standardi.'

O Lord, the beauty of Thy house, and the place where Thy glory dwelleth.'

The abbey became rich with endowments, and in 1160 Pope Alexander III. granted it exemption from tithes, and it otherwise was greatly favoured. It was from Rievaulx that Abbot Ælred, the historian, sent out the colony of monks who founded the celebrated house of Melrose in Scotland. The abbey seems to have suffered somewhat from the incursions of the Scots, and in 1314 the abbot was summoned, by the Archbishop of York, and the Bishop of Durham, whose ambassadors had made a fruitless journey to Scotland, to deliberate, with the abbots of St. Mary's at York, of Selby, of Fountains, and of Byland, as to measures of defence. It was from Rievaulx, according to the Lanercost chronicle — though other authorities say Byland—that Edward II. fled hastily in 1322, as the Scots, under Douglas, swept down from the moors, and was conducted by two monks towards York, his treasure, however, falling into the hands of the enemy, who also plundered the abbey. Many other historical circumstances concerning Rievaulx tempt the writer's pen, but it is now time that attention should be turned to the fabric itself.

And first it must be noted that, owing presumably to the narrowness of the dale, the church was not built east and west, the ritual 'east end' being actually to the south. It was, indeed, the rule of the Cistercians to build in such lonely dales as this, and, as Mr. Sharpe points out, in the narrowest parts of them. We remarked of Whitby that its stonework has been deeply seamed and worn by the blasts of the Northern Sea, every interlamination being searched out and deeply eaten away. The contrast at Rievaulx, sheltered in its dale, is very marked, for the carving of the pleasantly-coloured sandstone is still almost as sharp as if the monastic sculptor had but just laid down his chisel. The remains which we see are those of the choir and transepts, rough grass-grown mounds, covering the bases of the columns and walls, alone testifying to the existence of a nave; but on the 'south' side (actually the west), across the space of the cloister, are the exquisite remains of the refectory. Such fragments as are left of the nave, and the lower parts of the western walls of the transepts, where there are a few round - headed windows, formed, in all probability, portions of the original church built by Walter l'Espec, and they appear to be the earliest Cistercian work in England.

Mr. W. C. Lefroy is inclined, and we think rightly, to attribute the splendid extension of the choir of Rievaulx to emulation of the neighbouring Cistercians of Byland, for the homeless monks who had found a home upon the moor, some two miles away from Rievaulx, at the place now called Old Byland, after remaining a time there, and a time at Stocking, had built their magnificent church, 328 feet in length, some five or six miles away, near Coxwold, where we now see the remains of it.* The splendid six bays, that

* 'The Ruined Abbeys of Yorkshire,' ed. 1891, p. 51.

were added to the choir of Rievaulx late in the Early
English period, and are now the chief remains of the
abbey, are indeed a departure from the primitive
simplicity of the Cistercians, such as may be seen also
at Fountains, Byland, and elsewhere. It would be
very difficult, indeed, to find a more gloriously con-
ceived, a richer, or a more characteristic, example of
the late lancet style. True to the Cistercian model,
the ritual ' east end ' is square, with two tiers of lancets,
three in each, the lower ones separated by lancet
panels ; the upper ones, whereof the middle one is more
lofty than the others, by clustered shafts ; and, doubtless, other lancets were in the gable. Each of the
seven bays of the new work measures more than 20
feet, and consists of a richly moulded arch resting upon
clustered columns, the vaulting shafts rising from
corbels in the spandrels, and showing the spring of
the vault to have been at the string-course of the clerestory ; two pointed arches in each bay, forming the
triforium, rise to this string-course, exquisitely moulded,
and resting upon clustered shafts ; and there are
coupled lancets in the clerestory. In the transepts
the arrangement of lancets is somewhat different. The
transepts are separated from the choir by a lofty arch,
resting characteristically upon clustered shafts, corbelled
out above the level of the choir pillars, which now
frames a lovely view of the wooded hills of Ryedale,
looking north. The total length of the church has
been 343 feet, and it seems likely that explorations of
the site of the nave would disclose Norman features,

such as still remain at Kirkstall and Fountains. Of the conventual buildings, the refectory is the only one that remains in anything like completeness. It stands at right angles to the church beyond what was the cloister, which, according to the usual plan of the Cistercians, was upon the 'south' (here, in fact, the west) side of the nave. It is of somewhat earlier date than the choir—Mr. Sharpe suggests about 1175—and rested upon the vault, now fallen in, of an undercroft, made necessary by the slope of the ground. It is entered by a round-headed doorway, with four orders of characteristic mouldings, and resembles the refectory at Fountains; but the wooden roof, of which the corbels can be seen, was in a single span. The pulpit, or reading - desk, from which a monk read to his brethren during meals, remains recessed in the 'west' (here the north) wall, beneath an arcade, approached by a staircase from the refectory itself, and by another from the undercroft. Of the other buildings, there are traces of the chapter-house, an exploration of which would yield much of interest, the fratry, the kitchen (whereof the fireplace remains), and the abbot's chapel; but visible evidences of the *domus conversorum* and other buildings are few.*

---

* An architectural description of Rievaulx will be found in Sharpe's 'Architecture of the Cistercians,' and complete illustrations of the choir are given in the same author's 'Architectural Parallels,' as well as of the moulded detail in his 'Mouldings of the Six Periods.' See also 'The Ruined Abbeys of Yorkshire,' by W. Chambers Lefroy, and a paper on 'The Cistercian Plan,' by Mr. J. T. Micklethwaite, in the *Journal of the Yorkshire Archæo-*

The quondam Abbot of Rievaulx lay in the Tower in 1537 for his share in the Pilgrimage of Grace, 6s. 8d. a week, it appears, being charged for his maintenance. A new abbot was intruded, who seems to have been more complaisant, for he surrendered the abbey at the dissolution, upon which the site was granted to the Earl of Rutland, and came by marriage to the family of Villiers, Dukes of Buckingham, and afterwards by pur- chase to the Duncombes. The Earl of Feversham, of that family, is the present owner. A very interesting document shows that at the time of the dissolution all the conventual buildings were standing, but were about to be unroofed and wasted. Doubtless jacks, levers, or gunpowder were used for the destruction of the nave. The elements have since had a destructive influence in causing the crumbling away of the upper walls, and the rooting of ivy in the clefts of the stone- work has had a disastrous effect also.

Rievaulx Abbey is usually visited from Helmsley, either by the country road, a distance of about two miles and a half, which crosses the hill, and descends by a steep way through the woods, or by the rcad through Duncombe Park, which is somewhat longer. In either case, the first view is usually from the cele- brated terrace above the Rye.* This terrace, which

---

logical and Topographical Association, December, 1881. Canon Atkinson has edited the Rievaulx Chartulary for the Surtees Society.

* In order to control the influx of visitors, Lord Feversham has devised a system of tickets, which are procurable at the estate office

has been spoken of with justice as one of the finest in England, was formed in 1758 by Thomas Duncombe, Esq., and is about half a mile in length, high up upon the hillside, covered with a trimly - kept greensward, overhung by magnificent trees of varied growth, and margined by flowering shrubs and evergreens. The whole hillside is indeed, covered with a splendid woodland of beech, oak, and ash, many of the trees being of great size, with enormous boles overgrown with closely clinging ivy. At the northern end of the terrace stands an Ionic temple, with pillared portico, and ceilings within painted with classical frescoes by an Italian artist; while a circular Tuscan temple, with a colonnade, is at the southern end, its dome-like ceiling also painted, and its floor laid with a tessellated pavement found at the abbey. It would be difficult to do justice in words to the entrancing beauty of the prospect unfolded as the visitor walks along this terrace. The lovely choir of the abbey stands far below, hard by the swift-flowing Rye; meadows and cornfields line the dale, and dense woods clothe the steeps of Ashberry Hill on the opposite bank, and of every height hereabout; while, above, the moorland edges crest the gracious scene. A steep pathway through the wood, not easy to descend after heavy rain, gives approach to the ruins, which may also be

at Helmsley, a charge of one shilling being made for each. On Mondays and Saturdays these admit the visitor to pass through Duncombe Park; and, in addition to the Rievaulx terrace, the home terrace overlooking the Rye at a lower point is at times accessible.

reached by the lane that leads down from the high
road to the river among the pretty cottages that still
stand thereby.

A mile south-west of Rievaulx the Rye enters
Duncombe Park, having above, on the right, the village
of Scawton, where is a chapel dating from the twelfth
century, which the monks of Old Byland built upon
their migration to Stocking, and it still possesses the
bell they gave it, bearing the shield of Abbot Roger,
and the inscriptions ' Campana Beate Maria' and
' Joh'nes de Copgraf me fecit.' The scenery of the
dale, with its well-cultivated fields and splendid woodlands, betokens at once the neighbourhood of a great
demesne. The park at Duncombe is tree-encircled,
and the Rye traverses it in a wide course, with far-
winding sinuosities in its way. The house stands
towards the eastern end of the park, at a point of great
vantage, commanding the finest reaches of the river.
It was built originally in 1718 by Thomas Duncombe,
Esq., nephew of Sir Charles Duncombe, secretary to
the Treasury under James II., who had purchased the
estate from the executors of the Duke of Buckingham.
Vanbrugh was the architect, and the house had much
of his ' gloomy grandeur'; but it perished, save the
north wing, almost wholly in a disastrous fire in 1879.
The great collection of works of art, however, suffered
little, and will erelong grace a new structure that is
being reared. The most celebrated work in the collection is the so-called ' Dog of Alcibiades,' which is
attributed to Myron, a most expressive and life-like

marble, resembling in character the 'Dog of Alcibiades' at the Uffizi. It was bought by Mr. Duncombe at the sale of Henry Constantine Jennings for a thousand guineas. 'At this rate a dead dog would indeed be worth more than a living lion,' said an interlocutor of Johnson, referring to the purchase. 'Sir,' answered the sage, 'it is not the worth of the thing, but the skill in forming it, which is so highly estimated; everything that enlarges the sphere of human powers, that shows man can do what he thought he could not do, is valuable.' There is also a good Roman 'Discobolus.' Among the pictures are several splendid Guidos, including 'Charity,' a very impressive picture, 'St. Catherine,' and 'The Daughter of Herodias'; a 'Circumcision' of Giovanni Bellini, a 'Head of St. Paul,' by Leonardo da Vinci, a very fine Titian, and examples of Domenichino, Correggio, Rubens, Rembrandt, Wouvermans, Hogarth, Reynolds, and many more.

The park is finely diversified with hill and dale, the encircling woodland clothing the slopes with varied foliage, and alive with hares and rabbits, and with squirrels leaping among the boughs, and the banks are bedecked with wild-flowers and ferns. The great upland stretch of greensward in the midst of the park, to the west of the house, may perhaps be thought a little dreary, but it is a favourite haunt of the fallow deer. Some 300 head of red deer also have their home in that neighbouring part of the demesne known as the Black Park, and the coverts are well stocked with pheasants and partridges.

The late Earl of Feversham was widely known as a most successful breeder of shorthorns, and many celebrated animals have come from the farm at Griff, which is about half-way between the house and Rievaulx; and the present earl has made the Duncombe herd most decidedly representative of the best Yorkshire breeds.

As we turn now our faces towards Helmsley, it will be well to glance at the fair scene spread out below the home terrace, with its well-kept greensward, its terminal temples, and its gay flower-beds. Below is the far-winding Rye, curving like a golden serpent in the sunlight, and reflecting in its glassy surface the dark woodlands, beyond which lies a vast prospect of the pastoral vale; while on either hand rise richly-wooded hills, and away to the left stand the grey walls of Helmsley Castle and the tower of Helmsley Church.

In a chronological account, Helmsley Castle would have come before Duncombe Park, at the foot of which it stands, overlooking an angle of the Rye, and just westward of the town. Helmsley is a most delightful place to stay at—the headquarters of upper Ryedale, in the midst of a country of surpassing interest, with trout and grayling fishing, for those privileged, in the neighbouring waters (the Ryedale Anglers' Club preserves them), and with access to romantic wooded dales and rolling heathery moors. It is, besides, a charming little town, enjoying the purest of air, with a grey castle and a wide market-place, surrounded by picturesque houses, in the midst of which is a statue of the late Earl of Feversham, robed as a peer, by Noble, beneath a rich Gothic canopy designed by the late Sir Gilbert Scott. There still remains, moreover, a picturesque black and white timbered house testifying to the greater picturesqueness that once characterized the place. Nothing remains of the ancient church save the base of the tower and a few fragments, the present edifice, in the Norman style, and somewhat heavy in character, having been built by the Earl of Feversham, in 1869, at a cost of £15,000.

Helmsley, named Elmeslae in Domesday, and subsequently Hamelake, or Hamelac, was granted to the Earl of Mortain, and came to the L'Especs in the time of Henry I. It passed with the sister of the founder of Rievaulx to Peter de Ros, or Roos, whose great-grandson Robert, one of the barons arrayed against John, built, or rather rebuilt, at Helmsley, a stronghold, which he called Castle Fursan, about the year 1200, parts of which still remain. The builder of this castle married Isabel, daughter of William, King of Scotland, and, after her death, he joined the Templars. His effigy may still be seen in the Temple Church. One of the co-heiresses of the last De Ros married Sir Robert Manners of Etall, and conveyed to him not only Helmsley, but Belvoir, which last had come to the family by marriage with the heiresses of William de Albini. It will be remembered that another member of this same family of Manners

married the celebrated Dorothy Vernon, and thus not
Helmsley and Belvoir only, but Haddon, too, fell to
the Earls of Rutland — truly a glorious heritage!
Francis Manners, sixth Earl of Rutland, had an only
daughter, who married George Villiers, first Duke of
Buckingham, who commanded the unhappy expedition
to the Isle of Rhé. When the duke was assassinated
by Felton in 1628, his son, who succeeded to Helmsley,
was but sixteen months old, and he remained abroad
during the Civil War. Helmsley, however, was
garrisoned for the king, and was besieged and reduced
by Fairfax, to whom the Parliament had granted it,
Fairfax being wounded in the shoulder during the
siege. It was afterwards dismantled as a fortress by
order of the Parliament. The younger Buckingham,
'the sated man of pleasure, who turned to ambition
as to a pastime,' was enabled, by marrying Fairfax's
daughter, to secure many of his forfeited estates, and
amongst them Helmsley, whither he retired from the
court. He died miserably at Kirkby Moorside, as we
shall see in the next chapter, his body being brought
to the castle; and then, to use Pope's ungracious
sneer,

> ' Helmsley, once proud Buckingham's delight,
> Slid to a scrivener, and a city knight,'

when, as we have already seen, it was purchased
from his executors by Sir Charles Duncombe, in
1695.

The remains of the castle, which add no little
picturesqueness to the town, stand just westward of

it, within the bounds of Duncombe Park, upon an isolated mound, in no very commanding position, between the Rye and its tributary, the Elton Beck. The plan is rectangular, and the works cover some ten acres. They were protected by a double moat, now dry, and wherein trees have found root, and by very extensive earthworks, upon which stood barbicans. The principal entrance was on the south side, where, between the two ranges of moats, an extensive barbican, 333 feet in length, still remains, with flanking towers at each end, and returning angles, and drum towers projecting on each side of the gateway, which is in the middle of it. The front of the gateway is Edwardian, but the gatehouse itself is Norman or Early English. It has a 'joggle' arch, and portcullis groove, and both the ditches were crossed by drawbridges. It probably belongs to the Castle Fursan. Of the keep, in the inner ward, a considerable portion remains, though it is rent from top to bottom by the explosion with which the Commonwealth destroyed it as a defensive work. The west side of the keep still towers to a height of 96 feet, in three stories above the dungeon. The lower walls are ancient, of late Norman date; but the upper works are Edwardian, the curtain wall being embattled, and having at each end, projecting a little beyond its face, square embattled turrets, which rise considerably above it. The later mansion-house, of three stories, is on the west side, though here again portions of the walls are of a very early date, and have evidences of Decorated work.

The main features, however, are Tudor, and are probably of the time of the third Earl of Rutland, whose shield, with those of Villiers and others, remains on the walls, some of which are still panelled in oak, with plaster work above.

The moats of Helmsley Castle were filled, and might be again, from the Elton Beck, which flows down, through Beck Dale, in a course approximately parallel to the Rye, from the edge of Rievaulx Moor. It is very pleasant to trace it upward, by the ripening corn-fields, with here and there a peep at the heather, and through the woodland of oak and ash, where, over the brown, mossy rocks in its bed, reflecting the over-hanging foliage and the blue sky, it hurries downward, sometimes silent in still pools, and anon brawling over a stony shallow. The pedestrian who does not visit Rievaulx Abbey in a hurry—and no pedestrian should —may take this way with great pleasure to himself, for the country is exceedingly varied in its character. He will ascend from Beck Dale, westward, cross the upland ridge, and drop down into Ryedale above the abbey; or the walk may be extended through Ouldray Woods, and to the edge of Rievaulx Moor, the descent being made at Shaken Bridge, a little below the con-fluence of the Seph and the Rye. The return may then be made through Duncombe Park.*

Before we close this chapter it will not be without interest to refer to an incident that took place at

* Tickets for the abbey having been first procured at the estate office at Helmsley.

Helmsley in the year 1665, because it throws light upon a phase of sectarian feeling that lends a picturesque and curious interest to the seventeenth-century history of the North of England, and perhaps especially of the district this book treats of. The Quakers, a body whose youth was far less sedate than its age, had a considerable following in Yorkshire, more particularly in Holderness; and the dissatisfaction of these sectaries took the form of plotting against authority, and of publicly abusing clergymen and judges. A curious eccentricity characterized the Quakers of those times, and their long faces and wild expressions betokened that they were somehow possessed. A few of them were even disposed to use the physical arm, or, as we may say, the sword of the Lord and of Gideon. It was so at Helmsley. On April 29, 1665, the vicar, Thomas Slinger, was about to read the service at the funeral of a parishioner, when a party of excited Quakers, five in number, without any visible explanation of their action, rushed at him, and tore his surplice and book. They were brought up for their assault, but how they were punished we are unable to say. The eccentricity of the Quakers, however, generally took the form of reproaching the minister as a ' liar,' a 'priest of Baal,' a 'Babylonish merchant selling beastly ware,' or with some other telling epithet. Our account of the Quakers—though we may meet with their eccentricities later on—must conclude with an amusing illustrative anecdote of what took place—not, indeed, hereabout, but on a certain occasion at Orton, in Westmoreland.   The vicar there, one Fothergill, had exchanged pulpits on a particular Sunday with Mr. Dalton of Shap, who happened to be possessed of but one eye.   However, a Quaker, presumably hatted, stalked into Orton Church during the sermon, and, in a loud voice, called out to the preacher:

'Come down, thou false Fothergill!'

'Who told thee,' asked the minister, 'that my name was Fothergill?'

'The Spirit,' quoth the other.

'Then that Spirit of thine is a lying Spirit,' exclaimed the minister conclusively, 'for it is well known that I am not Fothergill, but *peed* Dalton of Shap!'

CHAPTER VIII.

THE RYE.—KIRKDALE, AND FARNDALE.

Riccaldale—Kirkdale—Limestone Features—Kirkdale Church—
The Saxon Inscriptions—Orm, Son of Gamel—Kirkdale
Cave—Sleightholmdale and Bransdale—Kirkby Moorside—
Castles of the Stutevilles and the Nevilles—The Death of Buck-
ingham—Keldholme Priory—Douthwaite Dale—Farndale—
The View from Gillamoor—The Farndale Hob—The White
Friars of Farndale.

A MILE eastward of Helmsley the road and the railway cross the river Riccal, which flows down through
Riccaldale to the Rye. This is one of the minor
waterways of Ryedale, lying between Bilsdale on the
west and Bransdale on the east; but the wayfarer,
who may have an opportunity of traversing it, will
find very much of varied and beautiful scenery along
its course, in its three regions of the moorland, the
wood, and the pastoral. The Bonfield Beck, which
rises in the heathery ridge of Helmsley Moor, at a
height of 1,300 feet, flows southward in a lonely hollow
in the moor, which has not for some miles the
character of a dale; but, as the Bogmire and other
gills come down to join it, cutting the moorland into

the ridges of Collis and Lund, dark woods of larch and fir appear upon the slopes, and soon the Riccal, made up of many becks, flows beneath a steep wooded escarpment on the right, and thenceforth, until the railway crosses it, its dale is clothed with a rich and varied woodland, through which delightful sylvan paths may be threaded, where primroses and bluebells make the banks gay in the springtime, and where rock and rushing stream add to the beauties of a charming dale.   But south of the railway the woodland character ceases, and the Riccal winds slowly across the almost level pastoral vale, by the hamlet of Harome to the Rye, after a course of several miles, in which it flows almost parallel to it.

Our eastward wayfaring along the Pickering road brings us, about a mile beyond the Riccal Bridge, to the twin hamlets of Beadlam and Nawton, which lie between the wooded and pastoral uplands on the left, and the rich strath of the Vale of Pickering on the right.   They have no special character of their own, but, with the neighbouring rural hamlets of Pockley, Harome, Wombleton, and Welburn, testify to the agricultural richness of the vale.   As we go forward there is a wide prospect southward to the distant wooded hills of Gilling, Hovingham, and Slingsby; while far off down the vale are seen the level edges of the Wolds; and something more than a mile further on we reach another tributary dale of the Rye.   The dale is Kirkdale (pronounced locally Kerdel), and the stream the Hodge Beck.   Now, Kirkdale is known somewhat higher up the brook as Sleightholmdale, and still further northward as Bransdale, which last name, according to the thinking of some, it derives from a certain Brand the priest, whose name occurs upon the inscribed Saxon dial at Kirkdale Church. The road which we are pursuing in our descriptive journeying drops down into the richly-wooded glen, through which the Hodge Beck flows south-eastward, and crosses its rocky bed by a ford, overhung by ash and other trees, but a wooden footbridge is provided for the pedestrian. The scene is highly picturesque, for on the left a huge scarp of the rugged rock is exposed, decked with the green growths which have found root in its crannies, and from the boughs of the ivy-grown trees is heard not seldom the cawing of rooks and of crows. And one thing, as the wayfarer will notice, gives a special character to the scene, for, except after very heavy rains, he will miss the murmuring voice of the beck, and, looking down, will see that the bed is dry, or, at most, that still pools fill the deep hollows in the rock. We are, in fact, here upon the oolitic limestone, and the Hodge Beck, with the curious characteristic of limestone streams, has 'sunk' at Hold Caldron Mill, a mile or more higher up its course, and is here pursuing an undergound way to issue again, a full-bodied stream, at Welburn, about half a mile lower down. In the mountain limestone region of North Derbyshire, the place where a brook suddenly disappears in this way is called a 'swallow,' and here, as there, by the shrinkage and erosion of the stratification, caves and underground fissures have been formed, which have a very interesting character.

The course of the Hodge Beck brings us to several places to which we may well turn aside in our journeying; and as we followed the Seph in its downward way, let us trace the beck upward in a manner to its source. It loses its identity a mile south of Welburn, in the plain, where it has its confluence with the Dove, which descends from Farndale (to be alluded to presently) on its way to the Rye. Welburn was a possession of Rievaulx, but the manor place there was the property of Sir John Bulmer, who lost his life, as we saw in our earlier chapter, for his share in the Pilgrimage of Grace. In the survey of his estates in 1537, it was described as standing on a plain high ground in the midst of the town, with a fruitless orchard, and in a state of great decay, with a gatehouse ready to fall down. The picturesque edifice which remains is also ruinous, but mostly of a later date. It belonged in the seventeenth century to Luke Robinson, a diligent magistrate hereabout, who represented Scarborough in Parliament, and was driven out of the Commons at the Restoration. He is scoffed at in an old political ballad, thus:

> ' Luke Robinson, that clownado,
> Though his heart be a granado,
> Yet a high shoe with his hand in his poke
> Is his most perfect shadow.'

An avenue of fine beeches leads to the house on the west, and on the other side are some enormous oaks, while close by stand Scotch firs of great size, and a fine cedar. The most ancient part of the edifice is of timber, and the rest, of later date, has much that is picturesque, with an embattled oriel window looking over the fishpond; while, within, the wide-chimneyed kitchen, the staircase, the oak-panelled corridor, and other features, are good and characteristic.

Much more interesting, however, than the house of Luke Robinson is the ancient church of Kirkdale, which stands in a meadow by the beck a quarter of a mile above the crossing of the railway line. The situation is one of exceeding loneliness, for no house stands within a considerable distance of the edifice, and few are they who wend along the path that leads up the romantic sylvan dale. The writer of this has remained long thereby with only the cawing of a rook and the rustling of the leaves to break the silence of the spot.* The very name of Kirkdale is enough to assure us that here is an ecclesiastical site of great antiquity, nor are we without other evidence of the fact. Within the primitive south porch, built in above the door, and well preserved, a Saxon dial and inscription, carved upon a stone some seven feet in length by two in width, still remain. The stone is incised in three compartments, the dial occupying the middle one, and the principal inscription, beginning in the space to the left, is concluded in that to the right. It reads thus:

'✛ ORM GAMAL SVNA BOHTE SC̃S GREGORIVS MINSTER DONNE HIT WES ÆL TO BROCAN &· TO FALAN &· HE HIT LET

---

* The key of the church is kept at Welburn.

MACAN NEWAN FROM GRVNDE XPE & SĈS GREGORIVS IN EADWARD DAGVM CÑG IN TOSTI DAGVM EORL ✠

whereof the translation may be made as follows:

'Orm Gamalson bought S. Gregorius' minster when it was all to-broken and to-fallen, and he it let make new from the ground, to Christ and S. Gregorius, in Eadward's days the king, and Tosti's days the earl.'

Now, Tostig was earl only from 1055 to 1065, so that we know within a narrow period the date of the rebuilding of Kirkdale Church by Orm, son of Gamel. In the middle compartment of the slab is the incised dial, divided into eight hour-spaces, and having across the top the inscription:

'✠ ÐIS IS DÆGES SOL MERCA ✠'
('This is the day's sun mark,')

and below, on the semicircle:

'ÆT ILCVM TIDE'
('At every time');

while across the bottom we read:

'✠ & HAWARD ME WROHTE & BRAND PR̃S'
('And Hawarth wrought me, and Brand the priest').

This dial may be compared with the one at Edstone, two miles away, in the Vale of Pickering, which is inscribed, 'Orologium viatorum' ('The wayfarer's clock'), and 'Lothan me whrotea' ('Lothan wrought me'), as well as with one at Aldborough, in Holderness.

It is not to be doubted that the Orm who rebuilt Kirkdale Church was the same who is mentioned in

Domesday as having been lord, in Edward's days, of Chircheby (Kirkby Moorside), something more than a mile away, and it is a safe surmise that he was the son of that Gamel (son of an earlier Orm) who, with Ulf, son of Dolfin, was treacherously slain at Tostig's bidding. Here, then, at Kirkdale, was a church so ancient in 1055-65 as to be in utter ruin (unless we surmise that it had suffered in the later incursions of the Danes), and the dedication to St. Gregory—to him who, moved by pity for youths enslaved from this very Deira, sent Augustine and his fellows to England —is enough to mark its high antiquity. A gravestone of very early date is built in on the north side of the tower, which has an incised cross, surrounded by most graceful scrollwork of unmistakable Saxon character. The Rev. D. H. Haigh, of Erdington, a well-known authority, has discovered a runic inscription upon this stone, in which he reads ' Cyning Æthelwald,' and hence infers that it was the gravestone of Æthelwald, son of Oswald, who was sub-king of Deira in the reign of Oswiu, and who treacherously joined the pagan Mercians under Penda in their attack upon North-umbria, but abandoned them, and returned to his faith, upon the eve of the battle of the Winwædfield, A.D. 655. Other early stones are built up on the south side of the tower, in the south wall of the church (a rude crucifix), and beneath the east window of the chancel (knot work).

The church consists of nave and chancel, north aisle, and a low tower. It is mostly Early English,

10

but the plain round-headed south door may belong to the time of Orm, and there is a remarkable early arch within the tower. The roof of the north aisle has been raised curiously at a late date, and the eaves of its old roof still project through the wall. The church is a humble edifice, with much that is modern about it, and it has undergone a ' restoration,' during which the monuments of the successive owners of Welburn Hall were removed from the chancel to the neighbouring stable, provided for the use of those farmers who come from long distances on horseback. There is some evidence seeming to show that a monastery anciently existed at Kirkdale, founded perhaps by St. Cedd, who established the neighbouring one at Lastingham.

Passing this interesting church, the Kirkdale woods are entered, where, in the thick leafage of the great oak and ash trees, many a squirrel may be seen leaping from bough to bough. If we cross the dry bed of the stream, and ascend a steep pathway on the right, through a narrow gully known as Kirkdale Slack, so thickly grown with grasses and ferns, and so overhung by the branches of trees, that progress is difficult, we may reach the hamlet of Fadmoor upon the hill, and beyond it Gillamoor, whence is a splendid prospect yet to be described. The wayfarer may at first be surprised to find in the woodland of Kirkdale Slack a series of huge constructions of masonry, over-grown with mosses and ferns, and with bushes rooted in their crevices, but presently it will dawn upon him

that these are abandoned limekilns. In fact, we are
upon the calcareous limestone area, and in the immediate neighbourhood of the celebrated Kirkdale
Cave, the opening of which is about thirty feet above
the Hodge Beck.

The cave was one of the first ossiferous caverns
ever scientifically explored in the country. It was
investigated by Dr. Buckland in 1821, and the record
of his observations aroused the greatest interest at the
time. It is now known that here was a den, in the pre-
glacial age, of successive species of carnivora, especially
of hyænas, bones of a great number of which have
been found. Vast quantities of gnawed bones have
also been unearthed, from which we learn that these
savage occupants of the place dragged in their prey
piecemeal. In the sandy mud which covered the
floor of the cave, and was overlaid with a stalagmite
deposit, were discovered, in addition to the bones of
hyæna, tiger, bear, wolf, probably lion, and other
carnivora, the gnawed bones of the elephant, rhinoceros,
hippopotamus, horse, ox, and of three species of deer,
as well as of many of the rodentia and birds, which
these savage creatures made their prey. The cavern
is something more than 250 feet long, and varies from
two feet to fourteen feet in height. The entrance
is difficult, and some other parts of the cave have to
be crawled through, so that the explorers are now few;
and, though the cavern cannot but interest the geologist,
it will be vain to expect to discover bones there now.

Instead, however, of ascending the hill, let us trace

the Hodge Beck itself still further. Above Kirkdale
Church the aboriginal woodland grows richer, and
clothes every steep with dense banks of foliage.
The stony bed of the stream is overshadowed by the
outstretching boughs, beneath which, on its margin,
the sward is bejewelled in the spring with primroses
and bluebells; while the woodland is redolent with
the sweet scent of the lily of the valley, whose gentle
bells lie half hidden by the ferns. A mile above the
church we reach Hold Caldron Mill, where the stream
has disappeared below ground. The scene is pictur·
esque, with the quaint footbridge, the rushing water,
and the dark background of Skiplam Wood, through
which we fare onward by the sinuous course of the
beck a mile further still to Lily Wood, which is
celebrated for its luxuriant and far-spreading growth
of the lily of the valley, which fills the dale hereabout
with its scent. Beyond this point we are in the part
of the valley known as Sleightholmdale, where the
scenery becomes wilder, and the moorland rises in
front; while the great belt of larch plantations stretches
away to the left round the northern scarps of the
'tabular' calcareous hills. A view of the dale sur-
passingly beautiful may be gained at Tatie Nab, at the
edge of these tabular hills. There is a chalybeate
spring, known as the Spa, in Sleightholmdale, and
soon beyond it we are in Bransdale (pronounced
locally Brancedel) proper. Few tourists ascend the
stream further than the Spa, yet the deep moorland
course of the beck is well worth pursuing for the

wayfarer who is not sparing of his miles. The dale
expands further on, and there are farmsteads and
cultivated slopes deep down amid the moors. The
source of the beck is some eleven miles north-west
of Kirkdale Church as the crow flies, and within half
a mile of the steep westward escarpments of the
Cleveland hills at Burton Head. No regular roadway
runs through it like that through Bilsdale, the main
road from Kirkby Moorside to Ingleby Greenhow
being along Rudland Ridge, which is the crest of
Rudland Moor, the great heathery height on the east,
but many tracks and bridle-paths lead down to the
dale, and traverse the hillsides by the farms.

Return we now from our journeying through the
long dale of the Hodge Beck to the country road that
crosses it below Kirkdale Church, by which we came
from Helmsley. Another mile eastward along this
pleasant way, between high hedgerows whereon we
may often see the long wheat-straw caught in the
harvest time, betokening the recent passage of some
freighted wain, will bring us to the straggling little
market-town of Kirkby Moorside, with its houses of
brick and stone, some whitewashed, mostly with red-
tiled roofs, but some thatched, a place of no very
attractive appearance, but well named, from its
proximity to the moors. Kirkby is a place of very
great antiquity, but of the church that gave name to
it probably scarcely a fragment remains. There are,
however, Norman pillars in the nave, much of the
rest of the structure being Decorated; but it has been

so many times 'restored' that it remained for Sir
Gilbert Scott only to convert it into a fine and, in
large part, modern church. In fact, it is one of the
most beautiful churches in the district. The brass of
Lady Brooke (1600), with her six sons and five
daughters, is curious.

The Stutevilles had a castle at Kirkby Moorside,
of whom was Robert de Stuteville, a comrade in arms
of Walter l'Espec at the Battle of the Standard. The
site, for there are no remains, is upon Vivers Hill,
where the encircling moat may still be seen amid
lofty trees. There is a splendid prospect from the
hill of the whole Vale of Pickering, from Helmsley to
Pickering itself, with the Howardian Hills in the
neighbourhood of Castle Howard beyond it, and away
to the left the level edges of the Wolds. The castle
passed from the Stutevilles to the Nevilles, Earls of
Westmoreland, who also had a castle at Kirkby
Moorside, whereof a massive tower remains to the
north of the town in a strong position at the edge of
a declivity. Upon the attainder of Charles Neville,
Earl of Westmoreland, for his share in the Northern
Rebellion of 1569—tradition says that he escaped
hence across the moors to the border, deluding his
pursuers by reversing the shoes of his horse—Kirkby
Moorside, with his other estates, was confiscated. It
was granted by James I. to the first Duke of Buckingham, and the second duke — of whom the vivid
portraiture in 'Peveril of the Peak,' as well as in
Dryden's 'Hind and Panther,' has fixed him for ever

in the public mind — retired from the court to this part of Yorkshire. It was while hunting hereabout that he was seized with the sudden illness that brought him to his end, and he died, abandoned and in poverty, in a house in the market-place at Kirkby Moorside, adjoining the King's Head Inn. Although Pope's picture of his death in the ' Moral Essays ' is not strictly true to fact, it will never be dissociated from the profligate spendthrift's end :

> ' In the worst inn's worst room, with mat half hung,
> The floors of plaster and the walls of dung,
> On once a flock bed, but repaired with straw,
> With tape-tied curtains never meant to draw,
> The George and Garter dangling from that bed,
> Where tawdry yellow strove with dirty red,
> Great Villiers lies—alas ! how changed from him,
> That life of pleasure and that soul of whim !
> Gallant and gay in Cliveden's proud alcove,
> The bower of wanton Shrewsbury and love ;
> Or just as gay at council, in a ring
> Of mimic statesmen and their merry king ;
> No wit to flatter left of all his store,
> No fool to laugh at, which he valued more.
> There, victor of his health, his fortune, friends,
> And fame, this lord of useless thousands ends.'

Lord Arran, who was present at the duke's death, thus wrote of it to his chaplain :

' I have ordered the corpse to be embalmed, and carried to Helmsley Castle, and there to remain till my Lady Duchess her pleasure shall be known. There must be speedy care taken, for there is nothing here but confusion, not be expressed. Though his stewards have received vast sums, there is not so much as one farthing, as they tell me, for defraying the least expense.'

Buckingham's entrails were buried at Helmsley, but his body afterwards found a resting place with his father's in Henry VII.'s Chapel at Westminster.

Eastward, below the slope of Vivers Hill, in the direction whither our wayfaring takes us, is the site— and nothing more, for not a vestige remains, save that some stone coffins are built up in neighbouring walls— of the Cistercian nunnery of Keldholme, founded in the reign of Henry I. by the Robert de Stuteville of the Battle of the Standard, who also founded Rosedale, and was a large benefactor to St. Mary's at York. The site of the priory is by the river Dove (a stream well stocked with small trout), which winds southward through the meadows to its confluence with the Rye. In its upper course this stream flows approximately parallel to Bransdale, through Farndale, one of the most beautiful of the tributary dales, having its source far up in the great transverse moorland ridge, within a mile, indeed, of the sources of the Esk.

Wider than Bransdale on one hand, and yet not so expansive as the upper part of Rosedale, on the other, Farndale presents some most magnificent prospects to the wayfarer ; and especially delightful is it to journey along Blakey Ridge, the moorland height which separates Farndale from Rosedale, and gives in places most delightful views of both. A good pedestrian, indeed, for whom an invigorating walk of fifteen or

twenty miles would not be too much, may leave
Castleton in Eskdale, and follow the Castleton Ridge,
with its delightful views of Westerdale and Danby Dale
on either hand, already alluded to, cross the great
transverse ridge of moorland by Ralph Cross, and
descend by Blakey Ridge ; and he may pass over the
Dove at Lowna, and ascend to Gillamoor, whence
there is a most glorious retrospective view of the dale,
and may so reach Kirkby Moorside.*   The lower part
of the course of the Dove, where it traverses the
'tabular' oolitic hills south of Gillamoor, is sometimes
known as Douthwaite Dale (pronounced locally
'Doothit'), and is a gorge of singular loveliness.   It
is usually approached from Kirkby Moorside, either
by the road, or, more advantageously, by a footpath
across the fields, which climbs the hill eastward of the
town, giving, in clear weather, most extensive prospects
of Ryedale to the south, and then drops down the
precipitous slope to the little hamlet of Yoadwath,
where a picturesque bridge spans the Dove.   In the
rugged descent, and still more in climbing the opposite
steep of Hutton Common, the character of the narrow
dale unfolds, with the river winding its sinuous course
below, and the lofty hill on the left clothed from base
to summit with dense woods of fir, while up the dale
the romantic heights towards Gillamoor appear, with
the purple moorland beyond.

* It is sometimes possible, by special permission, to reach the
head of Farndale, and the middle portion of Rosedale, from the
direction of Ingleby Greenhow, by the mineral railway, which crosses
the high moors and Blakey Ridge to the Rosedale ironworks.

Nowhere can the scenery of Farndale itself be better appreciated than looking northward from the little churchyard of the village of Gillamoor, about two miles north of Kirkby Moorside, where, at an elevation of some 500 feet, we gain one of the most splendid prospects in all Yorkshire.   Looking up Farndale, with its cornfields and pastures, and the woods hiding the course of its stream, the heather-clad hills rise on either hand, and shut in the prospect to the north; while on the right hand one of these heathery nabs of the calcareous hills (locally known as Squire Nab) boldly confronts the dale.   Never, perhaps, is this prospect so entrancing as when—and the writer has seen it thus—the westering sun suffuses the' landscape with yellow light, while the moorland grows deeper in its hue, and all the shadows take transparent purplish tones in the clear air of the evening.   New charms will be added to the prospect, too, if the traveller, having first gained a retrospective view down Douth-waite Dale, walk westward round the edge of the calcareous scarp at Storth Head, with Ramsgill Grave below.   It may be observed of Farndale, as of Brans-dale and Rosedale, that, just where the high moorland slopes to the foot of the escarped edge of the calcareous hills, the heather advances upon the stream, and the signs of cultivation become fewer.   In this part of its course the scenery of the Dove is very impressive, for the heathery flanks of Harland Moor descend very precipitously to its margin.   Further north the dale widens, and between the steep and lofty moor-banks there is a well-cultivated space of pasture and corn-field, while the pleasant farmsteads, embowered amid their trees, seem to nestle beneath the escarpments of rock that lend their picturesqueness to the dale. Bold contours are given to the hills by the nab which is thrust out on the left from Rudland Moor, between the Dove and its tributary, the little West Gill Beck, and by the rounded heathery bluff that separates it on the other hand from the Blakey Gill, which rises in Blakey Moor. The height about the upper waters of the Dove is known as Farndale Moor.

Where Rudland Moor on the west overlooks the dale with very precipitous scarps, there is upon the height a tumulus known as Obtrush, or Obtrush Roque, which is thought to be Hob Thrush's Ruck (or heap), and is associated with the Farndale sprite, spoken of sometimes as Hob o' th' Hurst. This wayward wight will remind the reader of the Hob of Hart Hill, in Glaisdale, and of that other sprite who woned at Runswick Bay. Professor Phillips has given a version of a story concerning him in an embellished and picturesque form, and with sundry defects of language, which Canon Atkinson—our best authority upon North Yorkshire dialect and folk-lore—has rendered somewhat more into the matter and manner of the folk-speech. This Hob, then, was a 'familiar and troublesome visitor of one of the farmers of the dale, and caused him so much vexation and petty loss that he resolved to quit his house in Farndale, and seek some other home. Early in the morning, as he was on his way, with his household goods in a cart, a neighbour meeting him, said: "Ah sees thou's flitting!" "Ay," cries Hob out of the churn — "ay, we'se flittin'." On which the farmer, concluding that change of abode would not rid him of his troublesome inmate, turned his horse's head homeward again.'*

It will interest the wayfarer through Farndale to remember that the Carmelites, or White Friars, had a house there in the Middle Ages, founded, in the 21st of Edward III., by Thomas, Lord Wake, who also established the Augustinians at Haltemprice in Holderness. Hugh Wake had married the heiress of Nicholas de Stuteville early in the reign of Henry III., or in the previous reign, and thus the Wakes had become landowners in Ryedale.

* 'Forty Years in a Moorland Parish,' p. 66. Professor Phillips, in his version of the story, has made a play upon the vowel in the word 'flitting,' causing Hob to use the form 'flutting,' but, as Canon Atkinson points out, and as the author, too, from his knowledge of the Yorkshire dialects, chiefly of the West Riding, can asseverate, no such play upon the vowel would ever be heard in the speech of one of the 'folk.'

CHAPTER IX.

FROM FARNDALE TO THORNTON DALE.

Moorland Wayfaring—Lastingham—Cedd and Ceadda—The Angle Monastery—The Church and Crypt—A Resourceful Curate—Cropton and Tallgarth Hill—Rosedale and the Seven —The Roman Road and Cawthorn Camps—Sinnington— Pickering—The Castle—The Church and its Wall-paintings— The Pickering Beck and Newton Dale—The Levisham Beck and the Moors—The Dalby Beck—Thornton Dale—Ellerburn and Thornton-le-Dale.

IN the last chapter mention was made of the splendid view of Farndale from the edge of the calcareous hills at Gillamoor, and now, in our descriptive journeying, we propose, instead of traversing the direct road from Kirkby Moorside to Sinnington, to conduct the reader by the foot of these hills from Gillamoor to Lastingham, a distance of more than two miles, and then to descend by the river Seven to Sinnington, having first spoken of some interesting places on the hills thereabout. The whole distance from Kirkby Moorside to the place last named, by way of Gillamoor and Lastingham, is not much more than ten miles, and it gives the tourist not only a prospect of Douthwaite Dale, and, from Gillamoor, of Farndale, but a taste also of moorland wayfaring, and a thorough understanding of the configuration of the 'tabular' calcareous hills, and brings him to Lastingham, which is one of the most interesting places, for its ancient historical memories, in the whole watershed of the Rye, and, moreover, both at the starting-point and the end of his walk does he touch the railway-line.

Standing, then, in the churchyard at Gillamoor, and looking eastward, there are meadows and cornfields, with hedgerows and trees on the steep sides of the dale, and the upper course of the Dove is marked to the left by the trees that overhang it in its course between Harland and Spaunton Moors. Below us in the hollow is Douthwaite mill, at the foot of the bold, heather-clad nab that rears its huge form as a northern scarp of the calcareous hills. Above the mill rise the cultivated fields, and the farmhouse known as Grouse Hall—let the wayfarer who asks his way pronounce it 'Groose'—stands at the very edge of Spaunton Moor, through which the way of the Hutton Beck may be traced by a depression in the hill. The path winds down to the rustic bridge at the mill. It was on the slope that the writer was once directed on his way by a countryman whose quaint figure might well have stepped out of a picture by Millet—a Rosedale quarry-man it was, who had walked a long stride across the opposite moor, wearing a wide soft hat on his head, and clad in a long blue coat, and with his trousers girt about the knee, and his brown, sharp-featured, shrewd and comely face looked out from beneath the shade of a huge faggot of burnt and tangled 'ling' from the moor that he was bringing back as 'kindling' for the good wife at home. Ay, well could he remember long years ago how an ox was roasted whole on the top of the nab when 'Squire Shepherd' of Douthwaite came of age! The way to Lastingham? Ay, the 'gainest' way lay yonder. He pointed across the valley to Grouse Hall, and by that way let us continue our journeying, passing over the Dove by the rustic bridge at the corn-mill, and ascending the opposite steep. Beyond the farm we are upon the open moor amid the heather and bracken, where the paths are few, and there is a rill in the moor margined by that fair, sweet, and tempting green that betokens where the swamp lies; but Barmoors Lodge in front, which we leave on the right, serves as a guide. Then another nab rises in front—another northward escarpment of the same 'tabular' hills—but, unlike the last, this is clothed with woodland. The Hutton Beck, which we cross by stepping-stones, and its tributary the Loskey Beck, come southward down the moor, having Hutton Ridge between them, and with conjoined waters flow through the long picturesque village of Hutton-le-Hole, well named from its situation between the two nabs, beyond which, in a picturesque little dale of its own, parallel with that of the Dove, the stream flows further southward to its confluence with the Seven. After crossing the Hutton Beck, our way is still eastward by the edge of the moors, and in a mile or more we reach the pleasant village of Lastingham, with the heather all in front of it, nestling in a quiet hollow, through which the Hole Beck flows south-eastward also to the Seven.

Lastingham is one of the few places that carry back the mind to the earliest dawn of Christianity in Northumbria, for it was here—at the Lastingaeu of Bede—but twenty-two years after the baptism of Eadwine, that Cedd, Bishop of the East Angles, at the prayer of King Æthelwald, established, about the year 648, a monastery—'among steep and solitary hills,' as Bede tells us, ' where you would rather look for the hiding-places of robbers, or the lairs of wild animals, than the abodes of men, so that, according to the words of Isaiah, " In the habitation of dragons might be grass with the reeds and rushes "—that is, the fruit of good works.' Bede himself visited the place in later years to hear tidings from the brethren of the lives of Cedd and of Ceadda, and we may be sure that it has changed little since, for still the lofty hills surround it, and the solitary moorland is all before. Fasting and prayer hallowed Lastingaeu ere Cedd established his monastery, for with his brother Cynibill he knelt through the Lent in the lonely dale. Cedd's East Anglian bishopric would draw him away from the scene of his beloved foundation, but he appears to have often returned thither, and it was in 664 that he revisited Lastingaeu when a plague was devastating Northumbria, and died there, and was

buried first in the open ground, and afterwards, when
a stone church had been built in honour of the Virgin,
on the right of the altar. He had founded a monastery,
too, as we are told by Bede, among the East Angles,
and thirty of the brethren thereof, hearing of his
death and wishing to be near where his body lay,
came northward to his Yorkshire house, but all save
one fell victims to the pestilence. Cedd's brother
Ceadda, the monk of Lindisfarne, afterwards venerated
by Englishmen as St. Chad, ruled the house after his
death, and it betokens the renown of the monastery
for sanctity that hither to him came Ouini, Ætheldred's
wealthy thegn of Ely, wishing, like his lady, to take
the religious life, but nothing bare he in his hands save
axe and hatchet, which—for that he had no 'booklere '
—he used for the service of the monastery when the
brethren were at their study. It was from Lastingaeu
that Ceadda set forth, after the fall of Mercian
pagandom in the Winwædfield—when, as Bede tells
us, the Mercians 'rejoiced to serve the true King,
Christ '— to assume his bishopric of the earlier
Mercians, the Middle English, and the Lindiswaras,
which was subsequently located at Lichfield. A man
so simple, humble, and laborious in his long mission
journeys was Ceadda, that only in his later days did
he mount a horse, and then it was at Archbishop
Theodore's behest. As he lay on his death-bed in the
narrow cell, legend tells us the soul of his brother
Cedd, who had died at Lastingaeu, came, with a choir
of ..... ls, to comfort his fleeting hours. The monastery

11

was standing at the date of Bede's death in 735; but probably suffered in the ravaging of the Danes, when Whitby was laid waste. However, it was restored for a time after the Conquest, when Stephen, Abbot of Whitby, with a colony of monks, removed thither, but only to be transferred thence to York a few years later.

The church at Lastingham, which presents points of interest worthy of its history, has gone through strange vicissitudes. It so happened that William Jackson, R.A. (1778-1830), was a native of the parish, and, with praiseworthy though ill-directed feeling, proposed to beautify the church. With that view he painted and presented to it not an original work, but a copy of Correggio's 'Agony in the Garden.' He also 'restored' the south porch, and, in order to find a place for his work, the Norman apse was woefully altered, and a circular dome-like lantern above it, filled with yellow glass, thereafter cast its curious glare upon the picture.* The church, however, was 'restored' afresh in 1879, and this time with better taste. The semicircular apse of Norman character was brought into being again, the tall and plain pointed tower arch was opened, much work was done at the nave, and some absurdities were cleared away; but these re-constructions and rebuildings, as will readily be imagined, have served to deprive the edifice of part of its interest. The embattled western tower, with angle buttresses, has Decorated features, and there is a two-

* The picture is now at the east end of the north aisle.

light Decorated window in the west end of the south
aisle, which is broader than the one on the north.
The buttresses supporting the thrust of the nave
arches have Norman features. Within, the reconstructed apse, with its round-headed windows, is
noticeable. The stone vaulting of the nave is new,
and resembles that of the celebrated crypt, and the
pillars and pointed arches have an early appearance.
But the chief interest is in the crypt, which is approached by a new stone staircase in the middle of
the nave, and in the direction of its axis, and is a
perfect church, extending wholly under the upper one,
with the exception of the westernmost bay, and has a
nave and aisles of three bays, as well as an apsidal
chancel of two. From this crypt the hand of the
'restorer' has been withheld, and the massive masonry
and dim twilight of the Norman vault have a very
impressive effect. It is not unreasonable to suppose
that some parts of the walls of the crypt belong even
to the stone church in which Cedd was buried, but
its main features are of a period shortly after the
Conquest. The ground falls towards the east, so that
light reaches the vault through three narrow round-
headed windows, with deep splays, severally at the east
ends of the aisles, and in the apse. The round stunted
pillars are very massive, with characteristic capitals
rudely carved and broad bases, and the vaulting is
round, plain, and quadripartite. Towards the west
end of the north aisle is a doorway opening into a
curious underground passage now only a few feet in

length, but tradition has it that it led once under the moor to Rosedale Abbey, some three miles away. We may dismiss this idea, however, because the passage does not point in the right direction for the abbey, and was, moreover, obviously intended to give access to the crypt from the lower ground to the east, without the worshippers having to pass through the upper church. The stories of subterranean passages, moreover, in connection with ancient structures in North Yorkshire are many. Fragments of two Saxon crosses are preserved in the crypt, with some curious early wood-carvings. Cedd's Well, an ancient spring in the village, still speaks of the founder of the monastery.

A curious book, published at York in 1809, gives a strange picture of clerical life at Lastingham in the last century.* It tells us that the Rev. Mr. Carter, curate of Lastingham, was reported to the archdeacon as a disorderly character who kept a public - house. The curate replied that, inasmuch as he had thirteen children, he was naturally straitened on £20 a year; but that fortunately the streams of the neighbourhood provided his family with fish, for he was an enthusiastic angler, and enabled him, moreover, to make presents to the gentry, which were requited seldom less than two or three fold. 'This is not all. My

---

* 'Anecdotes and Manners of a Few Ancient and Modern Oddities, interspersed with Deductive Inferences and Occasional Observations, tending to reclaim some Interlocutory Foibles which often occur in the Common Intercourse of Society.'

wife keeps a public-house, and as my parish is so wide
that some of my parishioners have to come from ten
to fifteen miles to church, you will readily allow that
some refreshment before they return must occasionally
be necessary, and when can they have it more properly
than when their journey is half performed?   Now,
sir, from your general knowledge of the world, I make
no doubt that you are well assured that the most
general topics in conversation at public-houses are
politics and religion. . . . To divert their attention
from these foibles over their cups, I take down my
violin, and play them a few tunes, which gives me an
opportunity of seeing that they get no more liquor
than necessary for refreshment; and if the young
people propose a dance, I seldom answer in the
negative; nevertheless, when I announce time for
return, they are ever ready to obey my commands,
and generally with the donation of a sixpence they
shake hands with my children, and bid God bless
them.   Thus my parishioners enjoy a triple advantage, being instructed, fed, and amused at the same
time.'

Leaving the pleasant village of Lastingham, and
the gentle, if genuine, philosophy of its erewhile curate,
which will remind him no little of the simplicity of the
'Vicar of Wakefield,' the wayfarer may scale the hill
by a plain cross which commemorates the coronation
of Queen Victoria, and, leaving the hamlet of Spaunton
on the right, descend the long straight road to Apple-
ton-le-Moors, which has a fine modern church—a

memorial of the late Joseph Shepherd, who left the place a poor boy and grew rich, erected by his widow. The way from hence to Sinnington is by a footpath down through the fields, giving most beautiful views of the winding way of the Seven on the left, pastoral and deeply wooded, and at length reaches the stream, where, in a thick woodland, it winds in a still deep pool at the foot of a huge mossy scarp of the rock. The way by the water on this side is impossible, but the wayfarer will keep high above the right bank, through the wood, following every curve of the stream, which reflects in its glassy surface the overhanging trees, and the great rocky scarps that here and there rear themselves from its edge.

Instead, however, in this descriptive journeying, descending by this—the most direct—way to Sinnington, let us go southwestward from Lastingham, and, crossing the river, ascend to the village of Cropton, by Tallgarth Hill. This name doubtless implies the garth of some stronghold or fortified house, for the site is defended by an inclosing fosse, with outworks, in the shape of a double ditch, round the base of the hill. From the top there is spread before us a magnificent view of Rosedale—the Valley of the Seven—shut in by the swelling purple heather of the moors. We need not here describe it at length, because its character is very much that of Farndale, though it is wider and scarcely so picturesque. Yet, especially to approach it from the north, and suddenly to find its richly-cultivated fields and tree-encircled farmsteads upon the slopes, nestled amid the moors, is delightful. There is much wood in parts of the dale, the moor-banks are steep and high, and rocky scarps look down upon the stream. The Seven rises as a tiny streamlet amid the heather of the great transverse ridge, scarcely a mile from Danby Head, but a tributary, the Northdale Beck, comes down in a little valley of its own from Glaisdale Moor, and this stream again is separated by the heathery Northdale Edge from the Hartoft Beck, which falls into the Seven lower down, while the Thorgill is a tributary on the other side. The beauty of Rosedale is somewhat detracted from by the iron-works, the lofty chimney whereof is a conspicuous object from Cropton ; and these works, and the mineral railway by which they are in communication with Middlesborough, have lent activity to the dale, for several hundreds of men are employed. The working of iron is of great antiquity here, for the Stutevilles had forges very early in the thirteenth century. But Rosedale was still a remote and lonely hollow in the encircling moors when Robert de Stuteville, in the reign of Richard I., founded there the priory for Benedictine or Cistercian nuns (there seems to be a doubt as to the order), of which the fragment of a turret-staircase, and an arched door that led into the cloister, are the visible evidences at this day. The house suffered so severely in the incursion of the Scots in November, 1322, that Archbishop Melton dispersed the nuns. The names given are those of Alice de Rippighale, Avelina de Brus, Margaret de Langtoft,

Johanna Crouel, and Elena Dayvill, who were received
severally at the priories of Nunburnholme, Synning-
thwaite, Thickhed, Wykeham, and Hampole.*   At the
dissolution the site was granted to Ralph, Earl of
Westmoreland.

The moorlands east of Rosedale have many traces
of ancient occupation upon them.   The Roman road
from Dunsley, which we have already referred to,
having crossed the Esk, and ascended by way of the
Mirk Esk, passes over them, by Flamborough Rigg,
descends to the course of the Sutherland Beck, a
tributary of the Seven, and then climbs the steep scarp
of the 'tabular hills' to the camps at Cawthorn, little
more than a mile from Cropton, which are thus strongly
defended by the natural configuration on the north-
west, and in that direction they have a beautiful view,
as in every direction an extensive one.†   The rectangular camp was a permanent station, presumably
a post of the ninth legion, for the entrances resemble
those raised by that legion at Old Malton, the others
probably being for the accommodation of large bodies
of troops moving along the road.   The earthworks
deserve attention, and the position is very remarkable.
The many evidences of sepulchral mounds hereabout
show that there was a comparatively large British
population on the heights, and it seems not unlikely
that the fastnesses were but imperfectly subjected by

* Reg. Abp. Melton, 240 *b*.
  † The Cawthorn camps are usually visited from Pickering, which
is about five miles away by road.

the Romans, for there are other camps upon the hills that were, it is fair to assume, outposts to overawe the dwellers therein.

We may now, having described Lastingham, and having said something of Rosedale and the neighbouring hill-country about Cropton, descend by the left bank of the Seven, a delightful way keeping by the stream, and bringing us, through woods and fields, to the picturesque village of Sinnington, which stands by the river that has given to it its name. There is a green, with a maypole, by the fine stone bridge that spans the river, and the village gives one the impression that no considerations of space ruled the builders, for there are broad expanses of grass and pleasant gardens as one enters it. The place is ancient, and there are some ancient features in its church, and the Latimers had a place here. From Sinnington eastward to Pickering by the hamlets of Wrelton, Aislaby, and Middleton, at which last place is a characteristic church, with Norman features, of type not unlike that at Pickering, which we are about to describe, the distance is four miles, along a quiet country road upon the gentle slope, with the pastoral hills to the north, diversified by hedgerows and trees, and a wide prospect across the Vale of Pickering on the other hand. As we approach Pickering we pass Keld Head—the word ' Keld ' always indicating a spring—where the Costa Beck rises, a pellucid trout and grayling stream (preserved by the neighbouring club, which breeds and turns into the stream 12,000 or 15,000 trout every year), that finds its way, with weedy waters, for there is a degree of warmth in them, across the Vale of Pickering to the Rye.

Pickering, an ancient market town, the capital of the Wapentake of Pickering Lyth, is a quaint, sedate, old-world place, picturesque enough in its way, without the vice of dull uniformity, and with not a few attractions as a headquarters for a district of many interests. You walk up a quiet street, between shops, and houses of the well-to-do, where trees hang over the garden walls, to where, north of the town, upon a height overlooking the Pickering Beck, whence is a lovely prospect of its wooded dale, stand the remains of its Edwardian castle, now happily well preserved by the local authorities, who, in a vacant place within the castle garth, have laid down a delicious greensward, where —most delightful and picturesque of places, surely— there is tennis-playing in the summer-time. The site was probably long ago seized upon as a point of vantage, commanding not only the opening of Newton Dale, but much of the broad strath of the Vale cf Pickering too, but it seems likely the royal castle here was built not long after the Conquest. Pickering had been retained by the Conqueror, and, in the reign of Henry III., Lord Dacre was the castellan. It was granted to Edmund Crouchback, and from him passed to his son Thomas, Earl of Lancaster, who was beheaded at Pontefract in 1322 for his leadership of the baronage against Edward II. Pickering was restored, with other possessions, to the heirs of the dead earl, and it has ever since remained an appanage of the Duchy of Lancaster. On the banishment of Henry of Lancaster, however, the castle was seized by Richard II., but, when Lancaster landed at Ravenspur in 1399, he marched straight to Pickering, and secured it, and the deposed king was for a time confined there. Leland visited the castle, and describes towers as existing that exist no longer. The ruin of the place was effected mostly during the Civil War, when it was besieged and laid waste, and the elements have continued the destructive work then begun.

The works of the castle cover an area of several acres, the outline being a somewhat distorted circle, and the massive outer wall remains, with fragments of towers at intervals, in a broken and ruinous condition. The ground descends very precipitously on the north and west, and there has been a deep fosse before the wall. Upon a lofty and grassy mound in the midst of the castle garth stands the shattered multangular keep, which approaches to a circular plan, and differs in that respect from other keeps hereabout. There are merely a few narrow openings in its walls. It is surrounded by a wide and deep fosse, and is connected with the outer circle by walls which divided the area into three distinct courts. The several towers are known as the Mill Tower, which has a turret approached by a staircase; the Devil's Tower, in the outer circuit, with doorways opening upon the walls, and a sally-port at its foot; and Rosamund's Tower, which is three stories in height, and has transomed windows in its uppermost chamber; and there is a square tower defending the inner portal. The broken walls present few architectural features, but there are a few Norman evidences here and there, and a small and ruinous Early English chapel remains. The fortifications belong mostly to the time of Edward I., though older portions are embodied in them. These gray and broken walls, clothed with ivy and mosses, and with ferns and wild-flowers rooted in their crannies, present a very picturesque appearance; and the ash and sycamore trees that have grown in the area add to the charms of a very attractive place that may well detain the wayfarer, both for its historical and architectural interests, and the superb views that are presented from its castle walls.

Leaving the enclosure, the wayfarer may retrace his steps down the road, and turning to the left, through a narrow way, may reach the church, which is hidden behind the houses. It comprises a western tower and spire, nave, aisles, and south porch, transepts, chancel, and organ chamber, with a vestry on the north side. The church has been 'restored.' Some portions of both aisles have been rebuilt; a difference of level between the north aisle and the nave has been done away with; the transepts, we believe, have been lengthened; the organ chamber is new; and a good deal has been done at the chancel. The oldest parts of the structure are the pillars and arches of the nave, which are Norman, massive, and of two distinct periods. There are four bays, and the semicircular

arches on the north side are of square section and
perfectly plain, resting on cylindrical shafts, with
' cushion ' or fluted capitals and square bases; on the
south side the pillars are a little later—square, with a
shaft on each face, and foliated capitals—and the round
arches are of two orders, chamfered.   Near the present
chancel arch one of the responds of its Norman predecessor may be observed upon the ground.   The
tower arch is Early English.   The transepts are
entered through pointed arches, that on the north
side resting upon grotesque corbels, and there are
Early English lancets in the south transept.   The
reconstructed chancel is Decorated, as are the aisle
windows, the embattled tower (saving its lower portion), and the spire.   The clerestory is ineffective, and
.there is a low-pitched post-Reformation roof.   The
font is Norman, and the sedilia capitals have remarkable carvings.   On the north side of the nave is the
cross-legged effigy of a knight, which may be assigned
to the time of Edward I.   He wears the *chapeau de fer*
and mail armour, with plates at the knees and elbows,
and his shield and surcoat bear the arms of Brus.
The head is supported by angels, and the feet rest
upon a dog.   In the vestry are also the alabaster
effigies of a knight and his lady, of the time of
Henry IV., upon a modern high tomb.   The knight
wears plate armour and a collar of SS.   His hands
are raised in prayer, and there seems to be a heart
sculptured beneath them.   The feet rest upon a lion.
The lady wears the *cote hardi*, a richly broidered

mantle, and a collar of SS., and her feet also rest upon a lion, while angels are at the head of each figure. These effigies have also been assigned to the Bruces, but the matter is less certain.

We have left to the last the most remarkable feature of Pickering Church—the wall-paintings in the nave. These were accidentally discovered in the year 1851, and were a good deal remarked upon; but the vicar of the date—fearing, shall we say idolatry, or that the venerable paintings would attract more attention than his sermons?—did his best to destroy them, causing corrosive chemicals to be applied. Happily for the cause of ecclesiastical art, his destructive power fell short of his iconoclastic zeal, and the sadly-injured paintings were again exposed in the year 1878. Such was their condition that restoration became necessary if they were to be preserved, and the work has been most conscientiously and carefully carried out. Happily, where doubts arose, access could be had to a series of drawings made for the Yorkshire Architectural Society when first the paintings were disclosed.* On the south side of the nave, above the transept arch, and extending somewhat westward of it, is a series of twelve subjects illustrating scenes in the life of St. Catherine of Alexandria. We see her rebuking Maxentius for his

* Much is due in this restoration to the present Vicar of Pickering, the Rev. G. H. Lightfoot, M.A., whose interest and care were chiefly instrumental in saving the paintings. He has described them in the *Antiquary* (April, 1890). The work of restoration was executed by Mr. Jewitt for Messrs. Shrigley and Hunt, of Lancaster.

OLD FRESCOES IN PICKERING CHURCH.

Engraved by permission from a photograph by Messrs. Boak and Sons, Driffield.

worship of Serapis (the idol being a horned image on a pedestal), and we follow her in her imprisonments, her scourging, and her torture upon the wheel, which breaks up miraculously, the whole being exceeding quaint and archaic. Then follow, after the manner of a frieze above the nave arches, a series of seven designs representing the corporal works of mercy; and we next find, without break, representations of the Passion of our Lord. We see Him in the garden and before Pilate (who is painted black) and being scourged and bearing the cross, and the crucifixion is depicted, with the taking down of our Lord's body, and the entomb-ment. Then follows the descent into hell—to the spirits in prison who stand within the jaws of death. Here, within the fierce jaws of a finely-conceived grotesque monster, stand the figures of Adam and Eve, and Christ is approaching to lead them forth. This subject was also one of those destroyed at Stanton Harcourt Church, Oxfordshire, but the monster there was inferior to the one at Pickering.* The south side of the church has also paintings between the clerestory windows, which seem to have been of events in the life of the Virgin; but these have suffered grievously, and not all are restored. Turning to the north side, and beginning at the west end, we find first a gigantic representation of St. George, clad in plate armour and surcoat, with lance and shield, slaying the dragon. Next beyond this is a huge and

---

* The Stanton Harcourt example is illustrated in the *Archæo-logical Journal*, ii. 367.

quaint St. Christopher bearing the infant Christ, and
lighted on his way by the lantern of a hermit, who
stands at the door of a cell. We then come to
Herod's feast, the royal guests, in fifteenth-century
costume, being seated at a long table resting upon
trestles, upon which we see three large salts and other
objects. On the left kneels St. John with his head
just smitten off, and the executioner with drawn sword
stands by with the daughter of Herodias. We see
her again further to the right, with the saint's head
upon a charger, and a little further on still she lies
upon the ground; while the Baptist, with the nimbus,
clad in a coat of hair, appears to be giving her his
benediction. In the upper right-hand corner of the
picture we read, in black letter, the single word
𝔥erodi. The coronation of the Virgin is over this,
she being seated among holy men, while a choir of
angels is depicted above. Next follows the martyrdom
of St. Thomas à Becket, the scene being actually
antecedent to the deed, for the saint kneels, while the
four knights draw their swords and Edward Grim
holds out a pleading hand. The last of the representations is of the martyrdom of St. Edmund, who is
bound to a tree, his body pierced with arrows, while
archers on either hand are stringing their bows or
winging their shafts. On the left are the words, in
black letter, 𝔈dmund 𝔓ryne and 𝔐artyr, while above, on
a scroll, we read :

> 𝔥even blys to his mede,
> 𝔥em sall haue for his gud dede.

The tone of colouring in the pictures is low, and the running patterns in black and red are characteristic. These are some only of the subjects that once adorned Pickering Church, for others in the transepts and various parts of the edifice have been entirely swept away.

The dale you survey from the walls of Pickering Castle is Newton Dale, the way of the Pickering Beck, which presents, as you ascend it, superb woodland and moorland scenery, changing at every step. The passenger by the railway to Whitby, which winds through it, will often remark that, in its kind, this is amongst the most beautiful railways in England. There is no road right through the dale, the one to Whitby keeping the eastern height ; but the adventurous wayfarer, to whom rough paths are no hindrance, may explore its character thoroughly, and the writer has journeyed with inexpressible pleasure through the woods on the left bank as far as Levisham station, a distance of some six miles. As you go forward by the water the hills rise on either hand crested by their rocky scarps, and the hillsides are diversified by wood and meadow ; the opening of the sylvan way of the Gandale Beck on the opposite side, shut in by hills of massive contour, adds diversity to the scene. You ascend a steep path through Kingthorpe Woods, and for two miles more make your way along the wood-top with nothing but cornfields on your right, and with glorious views of the winding dale, and of the steep wooded hills, whence a partridge will occasionally wing

his way, until you emerge upon the Whitby road.
Great oaks, ashes, and firs overhang the way, and
the thickets are redolent of the lily of the valley;
but again you descend through the woods, and, by a
doubtful pathway, take your course through the lonely
hollow, and by rough stretches of long grass, with
patches of meadowsweet and bog myrtle, to Levisham
Station, the scenery being especially beautiful where
the Levisham Beck descends from its narrow glen,
separated from the dale by the hanging woods upon
Ness Head. The village of Newton is on the hill to
the west. Beyond Levisham Station the scenery of
the dale grows more stern, the steep moor banks being
covered with a wild and rough growth of heather and
bracken. Killingnoble Scar stands out boldly on the
left, celebrated long ago for its breed of hawks, which,
as appeared at a commission held in 1612, the Goathland men were 'charged to watch for the king's use.'
All around now is the purple moorland, with rocky
scars overlooking the dale, and curious nodulated
conformations upon its edges — a stern, impressive
country with a character all its own. Soon the railway
reaches the crest, and then descends by Goathland to
the Esk, a region we have already described.

The interesting and boldly-featured moors to the
east of Newton Dale may be reached by the Levisham
Beck, or much more easily by the road from Pickering
to Whitby.* The beck has a course between steep

* It may be well to drive from Pickering to Saltergate Inn or
Lockton.

flanking hills, with the moorland villages of Levisham
and Lockton above it on either hand. Its source is
at High Horcum amid the heather, where, under
Saltergate Brow, at the edge of Lockton High Moor,
is a curious cleft in the hill known as the Hole of
Horcum or the Devil's Punchbowl. The moors
hereabout are most characteristically configured, and
present very bold and impressive features. An ancient
entrenchment, known as the Double Dike, across the
moorland, now serves a new purpose, being employed
in the driving of grouse. There are mushroom-shaped
Bridestones, too, upon a height, and the curious conical
hill known as Blakey Topping (more than 800 feet)
and the nab of Hazelhead Moor, dominate the
scene.

It is a region rich in waters, and we shall conclude
our long descriptive wayfaring in this chapter by
pursuing the Dalby Beck, which has its rise in a
curious lonely hollow named Doedalegrif, and flows
thence southward, approximately parallel to Newton
Dale, through Staindale and Thornton Dale. The
upper course needs no special description, for beautiful
and characteristic as it is, it resembles in features the
other neighbouring dales we have described. The hill
of Low Dalby on the left, however, is curiously cleft
by the hollows of Sieve Dale, Snever Dale, Flax Dale,
and Heck Dale, none of which appears to have a
streamlet, though a rill comes down through Sand
Dale. As the stream turns westward, and approaches
the little hamlet of Ellerburn, its course becomes

most beautifully wooded. Ellerburn itself is notable for its church, which has many Norman features, including short clustered and round piers, with capitals characteristically carved, and there is a cross with interlaced scroll-work in the churchyard. The way hence to Thornton - le - Dale, commonly known as Thornton Dale, is most gloriously wooded upon the slopes; and the village of Thornton itself, with its picturesque dwelling-places, its almshouses, its mighty trees overhanging the roadway, its rippling stream and rustic bridge, is perhaps the most picturesque in this part of Yorkshire. At any rate, it is a most attractive place in the springtime, when the hawthorn hedges are in flower, and laburnum and lilac overhang the garden walls. The church has been ' restored,' but is still interesting, and its features have not suffered as in some ' restorations ' we wot of. On the north side of the chancel is the recumbent effigy, within an arched recess, of Sir Richard Cholmley, known, from his stature and complexion, as the ' Great Black Knight of the North,' who died at Roxby Castle in 1578. The castle, which was built by Sir Roger Cholmley about the year 1520, stood westward of the village near the Pickering road, but its foundations alone now remain.

CHAPTER X.

THE COAST FROM WHITBY TO SCARBOROUGH.

The Saltwick Cliffs—Robin Hood and Little John—Hawsker Bottoms - Robin Hood's Bay—Description and Geology—Bay Town—Its Characteristics—Fyling Thorpe—The 'Evil Eye' —Stoupe Brow—The Peak—Its Roman Camp—The Great Geological Fault—Stainton Dale Cliffs—The Cliff Edge— Hayburn Wyke and Stainton Dale—Cloughton Wyke and Scalby Ness.

So far, in our descriptive moorland and riverside way-faring, we have traversed the Cleveland hills and the watershed of the Esk, as well as the more important portion of Ryedale, with all its tributary dales on the north, and we have descended Thornton Dale also, through which flows a tributary of the Derwent; but, instead of pursuing our progress further eastward towards Scarborough, we shall now return to Whitby, as a starting-point, and approach the great watering-place by the sea - coast from the northward. The description of the many-featured and romantic dales between Thornton Dale and Scarborough—and chiefly of that 'nest of sister vales, o'erhung with hills of varied form and foliage,' that have their meeting-place near Hackness—will most fitly follow our account of Scarborough itself, since it is thence they are most frequently and most easily visited.

There are two ways by which we may fare southward from Whitby towards Robin Hood's Bay, either by the road or the cliffs—the latter, for the pedestrian, very much more varied and beautiful —but we cannot go, except as far as Saltwick, at low tide, by the scar at the foot of the cliffs. It is a glorious walk along the cliff-top, passing between the abbey and the edge, whether for the pleasure-seeker who loves the invigorating scramble, with the blue sea on the one hand, and the splendid inland country on the other, or for the geologist who would investigate the fossiliferous strata of the Liassic shales and Dogger beds, or the wasting effect of the elements upon the face of the lofty scarps. A descent may be made at Saltwick, a delightful spot in the summer-time, where the sections of the Upper Lias may be examined, by going down the rude steps from the height to the level rock below. The cliffs here are very precipitous, and, with their own warm tones, and the rich hues of the wild vegetation that clings to them, including patches of heather here and there, present glowing colours in the sunshine. It may be observed all along this coast that, just as the sun is westering, deep shadows will rest upon the face of the cliffs, taking cool reflected tones from the blue expanse of sea, and making magnificent contrasts of colour with the huge out-thrusting masses and rugged nabs that the sun yet lights up with red and yellow and brown.

The configuration of the escarpments is very bold; and Saltwick lies hidden in a sequestered, restful cove, where the wayfarer will be like to linger in his journey. Saltwick Nab and the Black Nab are the seaward prominences of the rock, and the coast is a dangerous one indeed, where many a good vessel has been lost upon the pitiless reefs. A mile further on, with the white surf dashing below us as we go, and the sea studded with the gleaming sails of merchant ships, or the brown canvas of the fishing craft, stands the high lighthouse, showing, at a height of 240 feet above the tide, a white occulting light that is visible at a distance of twenty miles or more. It is managed by the brethren of the Trinity House, and, with the second lighthouse, was built in 1858.

From Ling Hill, near the lighthouse, there is a wide-spread view of the Northern Sea, and of many a head-land and nab boldly confronting it, with the abbey at Whitby away to the north, and the cliffs of Robin Hood's Bay, picturesquely broken, to the south. Our journeying soon brings us to Whitby Lathes, where, as legend hath it, fell those wondrous shafts that Robin Hood and Little John discharged from Whitby tower for the delight of the abbot and brethren, and in requital of the monastic hospitality. The story runs that the abbot manifested his pleasure at the feat of skill by putting up pillars at the places where the arrows fell, and Charlton tells us that in his days these still stood, and that the pillar of the outlaw himself gave the name of 'Robin-his-Field' to one meadow,

while 'John's Field' became the designation of another.
We are here, indeed, in one of those regions consecrated by tradition to the 'bold outlaw,' for he was
much in Yorkshire, as they say—do they not show
at Kirklees by the Calder the very window from which
he shot the last bolt that ever he sped, and the grave
where he still lies buried?—and we are told that, in
seasons of particular danger, he was wont to resort
to this part of the coast, in order that, in case of
pursuit, he might be able to betake himself to the sea.
If we imagine that the neighbouring breezy hill village
of Hawsker, to the right upon the Scarborough road,
takes its name from some 'hawk scar,' it will be easier
to fancy that Robin Hood and his merry men lingered
sometimes in the romantic hollow of Hawsker Bottoms,
down by the cliffs, where the little Raw Pasture Beck
makes its way to the sea.

Long before we reach this point, however, the lovely
bay, named, no one truly knows why, after the great
outlaw, has been spread out before us. The glorious
sweep of Robin Hood's Bay, full three miles from
cheek to cheek, presents a fair prospect as we look down
upon the sunlit waters surging on the long reefs and
yellow sands upon the shore, and across to the great
height of the peak, and to the huge form of Stoupe
Brow ranging thence inland, and upon all the lovely
country below, where woodlands climb the slopes, and
clothe the hidden courses of the streams; and where
farmsteads and cottages, embowered in roses, clematis,
and honeysuckle, are dotted about the steep brow of

ROBIN HOOD'S BAY.   DRAWN BY ALFRED DAWSON.

the hill, above which rises the purple moorland. Here, we say, is a prospect that will not soon fade from memory. The hills that shut in the bay, rising from 500 to 700 feet or thereabout, range away inland from the north cheek in a rough approximation to a semi-circle, cleft in the midst by Ramsdale, and reach the coast again at the Peak, and from their slopes many streamlets come down to the sea. Southward of Castle Chamber and the north cheek, or Bay Ness, the deeper Lias shales may be seen fringing the whole shore of the bay, even to the south cheek, some three miles away, in a series of reefs known as the West Scar, the East Scar, and Cowling Scar, opposite to Robin Hood's Bay Town, and as the Flat Scar and the Long Scar in the midst of the bay, while the point thrust out grandly from the south cheek is named Peak Steel. In the middle part of the bay the Lias is thickly overlaid with glacial deposits, and the boulder clay, which here chiefly constitutes the low cliffs, contains many rocks drifted from afar, some blocks of Shap Fell granite being washed out upon the shore.

It is to the softness of the boulder clay that Bay Town owes most of its characteristic features. One of the quaintest places imaginable, it hangs in picturesque confusion upon the steep sides of a narrow gully, and upon the very margin of the sea, and fights for dear life, as it were, with the waves, which have often sucked down its seaward dwelling-places into their depths. The quaintness of the place, the brightness of its sea, the purity of the air, and the many beauties of the country, have contributed to make Bay Town a place to which many resort for health and pleasure in the summer-time. Here, and at the neighbouring village of Fyling Thorpe, there is a quiet and retirement which many may prefer to the brilliant attractions of the neighbouring fashionable watering-place of Scarborough. The little beck by which the town is built has scooped out for itself a deep ravine in the glacial deposits, and it is upon and above the steep sides of this ravine that the red-roofed houses are piled. Many of them are built upon the very edge, propped up by walls that rise from the precipitous steep, their gaily-painted balconies overhanging, and almost every cottage seems to have been built independently of its neighbours, for they stand at curious angles to one another, and the plan of the place is not easy to discover. You may cross over the ravine by a bridge, and reach the houses upon the rock, which climb the steep in closely-packed confusion, and are separated from one another by narrow winding alleys, from two to six feet wide, paved with rounded pebbles from the beach, and with grassy staircases of stone leading from stage to stage. There are balconies to some of the cottages, and wooden stairways lead down into the narrow passages. A broader road, but a tortuous one, too, and a roughly-paved, brings you down to the shore, and, between two rounded buttresses of masonry, out upon the beach—an opening up which the sea dashes wildly in the storms. The soft glacial cliffs are honeycombed along the shore, and many of the seaward houses of the town have from time to time been washed away. So near are they to the waves that the bowsprit of a stranded ship has been known to drive through the parlour windows of the inn by the beach, the predecessor of which was sucked down by the sea.

The salt, seafaring character rests upon the whole of Bay Town. You may peep in at the open cottage doors, and the narrow interiors will remind you, with their nooks and corners and lockers, of what the cabins of old whalers must have been; and the Robin Hood's Bay men had their shares in the operations of the Whitby whaling-fleet. Fishing-nets and blue jerseys hang from the balconies, and the windows are gay with flowers—as the fisherman loves them—and every speck of paint is bright and clean; and there are white curtains at the windows—as the Yorkshire house-wife loves them, too. Rosy-faced lasses stand at the door, and you will hear as you pass the rattling of vessels within as the mother is making ready the meal—a brown-faced, plump, hardy 'throddy body' most likely, as in some parts of Yorkshire they call such a one. The men, too, are like those at Staithes—hard-working, laborious seafarers; but the 'fischar towne,' as Leland called it, has lost something of its fishery, and many of the lads are away at sea. Excellent seamen they make indeed, and not a few men in the fleet and the merchant marine have their homes at Robin Hood's Bay. These are the true sons of their fathers, who were not less bold as smugglers

in the old time than skilful as seamen, and their stow-
holes may yet be seen in the water-worn cliffs of
the bay.

The little hamlet of Fyling Thorpe is about half a
mile westward of Bay Town on the sunny slope
between Fylingdales Moor and the sea, and in one
of the 'dales' a little streamlet descends by it to the
shore. Behind it, above the meadows, is the spreading heather, with its patches of reddened bracken and
deep-toned grass; and before it lies the wide bay,
with the sounding surf breaking in successive lines
upon the reefs, and many a white sail out upon the
open sea beyond. The old cottages in this little
hamlet are exceedingly pretty, with porches embowered
in climbing roses and honeysuckle, and tall holly-
hocks and bright patches of marigolds and wall-
flowers in their gardens; but the Scarborough and
Whitby railway, which descends by steep curves from
the Peak by Stoupe Brow, and crosses the lower
country by the hamlet before ascending again to
Hawsker—happily opening up the whole delightful
country to the stranger—brings many people hither,
and not a few new houses have sprung up hereabout
for their accommodation. Before the railway was
made Thorpe was, indeed, a sequestered place, and
it is worth while noting—we have it on the authority
of Mrs. Macquoid—for the belief is somewhat rare in
Yorkshire, that the 'Evil Eye' was a superstition of
the district—we gravely doubt if it be so now—and
that 'till quite lately one of the inhabitants thus fatally

gifted always walked about with his eyes fixed upon
the ground, and never looked at anyone to whom he
spoke; his glance was cursed, and he dared not speak
to one of the rosy children, lest some blight should
fall on it.'

As we continue our wayfaring towards the south
cheek of the bay, either by the sands at low water
or by the road from Fyling Thorpe, we cross over, or
pass the mouth of, the Mill Beck, which, rolling over
its stony bed with several little waterfalls in its way,
presents in its course the most beautiful woodland
scenery to be found near Robin Hood's Bay. Near
by is Fyling Hall, an old mansion with mullioned
windows and high gables, and a huge fireplace and
much dark oak within. Still further on, beyond
Stoupe Beck, another pleasant wooded streamlet,
rises the huge form of Stoupe Brow, ending at its
seaward height in the Peak or Raven Hill, which
dominates the whole bay, and forms its southern
cheek. The tumuli known as Robin Hood's Butts,
which are fabled to have formed marks for the outlaw's shafts, are upon the brow of the hill, and urns
from them may be seen in the museum at Scarborough.

The commanding situation of Peak Hill was seized
upon by the Romans for a military outlook camp,
formed, there is good reason to believe, early in the
fifth century, under Constantine, whom the legionaries
in Britain raised to the purple. The memorial stone
thereof was discovered in 1774, when the foundations

of Raven Hall were being dug, and it is now in the
Whitby Museum. It testifies that Justinian, the
provincial governor, and Vindician, who was in
command of the forces in the North, were its builders.
This great elevation reaches 700 feet within half a mile
of high-water mark, and commands an unrivalled view
of the bay, and of the splendid inland country; and
Raven Hall stands boldly at the top, with its terraces
looking like fortified works upon the shelving scarp.*
The railway, by much skilful engineering, breasts the
height, and, by the station at the Peak, makes it easily
accessible both from the north and the south. The
Peak, moreover, will always attract the geologist by
the magnificent fault, with a throw of more than 400
feet, which can there be investigated. So tremendous
is this dislocation that the fossiliferous marlstone of the
Middle Lias, usually 400 feet deep in the formation,
is raised considerably above the top of it, and is juxta-
posed with the lower estuarine rocks of the Superior
Oolite.

In calm weather the stupendous cliffs southward of
the Peak may be surveyed in a boat, but the hardy
and adventurous climber may explore something of the
face of them, and may reach the wild undercliff which
for a considerable distance extends below. The highroad to Scarborough is about a mile inland upon the
edge of the moor. The cliffs from the Peak to

* On certain days of the week the grounds are opened to the
public, and an announcement of these days is usually made week
by week in the Whitby papers.

Hayburn Wyke are known as those of Stainton Dale, which is the delightful course of a wooded streamlet behind them. There is no well-defined pathway along the crest, but the climber who does not fear a giddy height, and is not averse to climbing walls here and there, and is willing to walk round a cultivated field at times, and to ask permission of the cheery and ever-courteous farmers, may journey delightfully along. All about him is the magnificence of nature; far below, surging against the rugged scarps and broken under-cliff, is the limitless sea, dotted with craft; his path is amid long grasses, heather, and wild-flowers; and the air is filled with the song of the lark, the cawing of crows, and the humming of many bees. As he passes the deep cove of Blue (or Blea) Wyke, where, far beneath, the sea dashes upon a rocky spur, he must be cautious and surefooted. At every step some new configuration is disclosed, some sheer declivity or broken steep, some deep cove, whose sober tones are lighted up with patches of heather, or some bare and buttress-like spur, and presently the huge Bees or Beast Cliff (sometimes called Darn Cliff) thrusts out its rugged form. Beyond it, reflecting with ruddy hues the sunshine, is the southern cheek of Hayburn Wyke, a scarp of grand characteristics, prominent in all the country hereabout; further still stands out the headland at Scarborough, with the castle upon the steep, and, when the day is clear, the far-stretching form of Flamborough is discerned upon the dim horizon.

Hayburn Wyke may be approached either from the

station of that name, on the Scarborough and Whitby railway, by the splendid woodlands by the farm there, or from Stainton Dale station, the latter a most delightful way, leading at the foot of heathery uplands, crossing to the left bank of the stream between hawthorn and blackberry hedges, and bringing down the wayfarer through the deep glen of the Thorney Beck and the sweetest of woodlands, shadowed by oak, ash, fir, and holly, and amid wild roses, honeysuckle, and ferns to a rustic bridge, and to where, in a brawling cataract, the brook pours down upon the pebbly shore of a deep sequestered cove.* Or Stainton Dale may be traced upward through a singularly picturesque country towards the Peak, and to where stood an ancient wayside hospital neighbouring the Whitby and Scarborough road. Sequestered and lonely as is the dale, a strange popular belief penetrated there two centuries ago, which illustrates a curious phase of disloyalty under the last of the Stuarts. The people would not for a long time believe that Monmouth, their popular hero, was really dead; and so we find that, in 1686, one Alexander Cranston, in the house of a certain Robert Walker of Stainton Dale, did declare stoutly, as was sworn in evidence, that Monmouth was still alive, and that he could go to him before night, for that Colonel White had been beheaded in his stead; and, further, that he hoped Monmouth would wear the crown of England within two years' time.

* The steep paths through these most beautiful woods are very slippery and difficult to traverse after heavy rains.

Between Hayburn Wyke and Scarborough the cliffs
descend, and soon are of the glacial drift, resting upon
shale and sandstone. They are broken into inlets and
points, and, especially at Cloughton Wyke and Scalby
Ness, present much that is picturesque; but they cede
in beauty to the neighbouring rich and lovely inland
country of Hackness and the Upper Derwent. Scarborough Castle Hill is now the most prominent object
in the landscape as we go forward, with the shattered
keep upon its height, and there are thick woods upon
the hill to the right. The road from hence to Scarborough passes through the pleasant villages, lying
between the hills and the sea, of Cloughton, Burniston,
and Scalby, at which last place is an Early English
church 'restored,' and in part rebuilt, but with good
features. Cloughton Wyke is a picturesque cove, with
Hundale Point to the south of it, between which and
the Long Nab there is a shallow sandy bay. A little
beyond the Long Nab a footpath from Burniston
descends to the sands, and to the sandstone scars that
here fringe the shore; and the pedestrian not averse
to some scrambling, nor to wet feet, may keep the
beach in season, considering the tide, the whole way to
Scarborough. It is more pleasant, however, to walk
along the cliff-tops. Two miles more of this wayfaring will bring us by Cromer Point to Scalby Ness,
which projects boldly out to sea, and shuts in the north
bay at Scarborough. Just beyond it, within the bay,
is the mouth of the Scalby Beck, with Scalby Mill and
much that is picturesque upon its course, making it a

13

favourite resort for visitors to the fashionable watering
place. We may now, having reached this point, paus
in our descriptive wayfaring, in order that we ma
devote our attention to Scarborough itself, to whic
we shall devote the next chapter.

CHAPTER XI.

SCARBOROUGH.

Its Varied Interests—Geology—The Castle Hill—The Harrying of
Harald Hardrada—William le Gros—The Religious Houses
of Old Scarborough—Piers Gaveston and the Baronage—
Mercer's Cutting-out Expedition, 1377—The Fabric of the
Castle—Attempts upon it in the Pilgrimage of Grace—Seditious
Prophecies at Scarborough—The Scottish King and Disloyalty
—Stafford's Stratagem—The Two Sieges during the Civil War
—Stuart Privateers—George Fox—The Old Tower and the
Parish Church—The Discovery of the Spa Water—'Spagyrical
Anatomy'—An Eccentric Governor—Growth of Popularity—
The Spa and its Buildings—The South Cliff—Oliver's Mount
—The Valley and Museum—The New Town—The North Bay.

IT is much to say for the Yorkshire coast that, with
rocky scarps of such grandeur as we have described,
and a neighbouring country so rich in landscape
beauties, it should possess watering-places so rare in
their attractions, and yet so distinct in their characters,
as Whitby and Scarborough—quaint and picturesque
Whitby, nestled in the deep cleft of the Esk; gay and
fashionable Scarborough, upon a hill, and spread out
along the bays on either side of its headland, which
is thrust out like a clenched hand into the sea with
its castle uplifted on the top. It is needless here to

raise again a useless discussion as to the respective
claims of rival watering-place 'queens.' It will be
enough to say of Scarborough that, if you seek a
splendid situation, and a picturesque coast, where bay
succeeds bay and where lofty escarpments of rock
rear their seamed and weather-beaten faces against
a blue and bracing sea, here you have them as few
other places can give them to you; if you would enjoy
the pleasures of the shore—bathing, fishing, or boating—here you have every facility for your diversion;
if rather you would explore the inland country, few
districts afford more glorious landscapes than the
delightful woodlands of Hackness and the neighbouring dales, or than the lofty hills and the far-spreading
heathery grouse - moors; should your mood be for
society and its fashionable diversions, Scarborough, in
its high season, has surely enough to gratify you; if,
on the contrary, historical memories should lure you,
here there unfolds a long and a stirring history indeed;
if you are a brother of the angle, there are within
reach trout and grayling streams enough; if geology
and botany are your pursuit, nowhere can you find
grander sections of the secondary strata than in the
seaward scarps and inland cliffs that lie within easy
reach of Scarborough—in few places will you discover
more varied examples of plant life than adorn the
lovely neighbouring glens or cling to the hoary scarps
and broken cliffs by the sea. In short, the resources
and interests of Scarborough are great and varied in
a singular degree.

The castle hill, its most remarkable feature, rising with precipitous acclivities between the boulder cliffs of the north and south bays, is thrust out far from the shore-line as a peninsula, and presents a magnificent section of the Middle Oolitic rocks. On the northern face the cornbrash and upper estuarine series of the Lower Oolite are exposed ; but these sink on the harbour side, where the Kelloways rock is at the base of the cliff. The stratification is so curved that this forma-tion sinks below high-water mark on the seaward front, rising again to the north, and in this way the thick formation of the so-called Oxford clay (here a gray argillaceous earth), which lies upon the Kelloways rock, is depressed to the foot of the cliff. The Oxford clay is surmounted by the lower calcareous grit and the Coralline Oolite; and in one place a singular dis-location occurs, by which a narrow vertical section has been thrust up, bringing the Kelloways rock into juxtaposition with the lower part of the calcareous grit. Naturally, by wind and water, the huge cliff is being gradually eaten away; since the castle was built the upper area has, indeed, been materially reduced, and so recently as the autumn of 1890 there was a con-siderable fall on the northern side.

The position is one of such exceeding strength—of far greater importance, indeed, than any other on the Yorkshire coast—that we cannot doubt that even the Celtic inhabitants had a camp upon its crest, and certainly—though visible traces have been destroyed by the later works—we may feel sure that the Romans, who seized upon Eston Nab, Dunsley, and the Peak as points of vantage, had a stronghold also here. Scarborough was, in fact, a 'scar,' with a 'burgh' upon it long before history has record thereof. Harald Hardrada, as we have seen, having made the coast of 'Kliflond,' fared southward to 'Skardaborgar,' and there he lay to, and, fighting with the burghermen, captured the height, whereon he caused a great pyre to be set aflame, from which, with forks, blazing brands were cast upon the wooden houses below, and these were thus destroyed, and many men were slain. The existing castle—as we learn from William of Newburgh, the Yorkshire Augustinian, whose chronicle covers the period from 1154 to 1198, in which he lived—was built, in Stephen's days, by William le Gros, Earl of Albemarle and Lord of Holderness, a grand-nephew of the Conqueror, and a comrade of Walter l'Espec at the Battle of the Standard. 'Seeing this to be a fit place to build a castle upon,' says the chronicler, 'helping nature forward with a very costly work, he closed the whole plane of the rock with a wall, and built a tower within the very strait of the passage.' This powerful noble and abbey - builder, however, was constrained, after a siege, upon the accession of Henry II., *diu hæsitans, multumque æstuans*, to give up his castle into the king's hands, who thereafter fortified it anew, and built 'a great and splendid keep.'

In the reigns of the early Plantagenets Scarborough was already a place of considerable importance, and its fairs began to be thronged by Osterling and Fleming traders from Ghent, Ypres, and the Baltic. Two representatives of the borough sat in the Acton Burnell Parliament of Edward I. (1283). The merchants were wealthy, and we find that they founded the hospital of St. Nicholas on the cliff of that name, to which was attached a Benedictine church, the sole remain whereof is the colossal effigy of a cross-legged knight in chain mail, with surcoat and basinet—believed to be that of Sir John de Mowbray, castellan of Scarborough *temp.* Edward II.—which is now preserved at the neighbouring museum. There was also in the town the hospital of St. Thomas, founded by Hugh de Bulmer in the reign of Henry II. The coming of the friars to England early in the thirteenth century brought to the town the Grey Friars (Franciscans), or Friars Minors, and the Black Friars (Dominicans), or Friars Preachers, who, at Scarborough itself, and at Pickering, Bridlington, and Whitby, were preaching for the Crusade in 1291. It throws light upon the relations of the religious orders at this time that, in 1284, it had required the express injunction of Archbishop Wickwaine to procure for the Friars Minors of Scarborough the right to preach in the parish church, which was in the hands of the Cistercians, who had an alien cell here as early as the reign of John. A house of the White Friars or Carmelites is said to have been founded at Scarborough by Edward II.

It was at Scarborough Castle in 1312 that Piers Gaveston, the gay, scoffing Gascon, was taken by the

furious baronage. He fled thither with the king from
Teignmouth by sea, but Lancaster 'the Actor,' Pembroke 'the Jew,' and Warwick 'the Black Dog,' at
whom he had jeered, were resolved he should sway
the royal counsels no more. Pembroke therefore
besieged the castle, and, failing to capture it by assault,
reduced it by famine, and Gaveston came forth, despite
the terms of his capitulation, to his beheading at
Blacklow Hill. In the terrible incursion of the Scots
in 1318, the Black Douglas came wasting and slaying
through Yorkshire, and, having given Northallerton
and Boroughbridge to the flames, he reduced Scarborough also, and Skipton, to ashes; but the town
seems to have soon regained much of its importance,
and the castle probably did not suffer.

A piratical incident of considerable significance
occurred at Scarborough in 1377, when one Andrew
Mercer, a Scottish freebooter, had been captured by
certain northern ships, and lay in durance in the
castle. It was a period when England had lost her
command of the seas, chiefly by the defeat of Rochelle;
her waters were infested with Frenchmen, Spaniards,
and Flemings; and in that very year the Isle of Wight
was ravaged, and Hastings was burned by the French.
Mercer's son entered the confederacy against England,
and, with several Scottish, Spanish, and French vessels,
boldly entered the harbour at Scarborough, cut out
certain ships, and carried them to sea. A patriotic
citizen of London, however, one Alderman Philpot,
having taken upon himself the duty which the Govern-

ment neglected, had furnished a fleet of his own, and now put to sea, overhauled the enemy, gave him battle, and recaptured the Scarborough craft, as well as fifteen richly freighted vessels of the Spaniards. The gallant alderman was afterwards impeached for 'raising a navy without consent of king or council,' but was acquitted, and received some of the honour he deserved.

Our historical sketch may now be interrupted by a description of the castle itself, for none of the main features are of later than Edwardian times, the keep itself being of the reign of Henry II. The height upon which it stands is roughly lozenge-shaped, and the descents are very precipitous—in many places absolutely sheer—on three sides, the fourth or landward side, on the south-west, having a steep grassy slope. It is upon this face of the hill that the keep, the curtain wall, the fosse, and the dike are found. The fosse, which cuts off the height from the mainland, is exceedingly deep, and has beyond it the castle dike as a further protection. The sole approach to the castle is by a narrow, ridge-like causeway across the fosse, a steep ascent, with a barbican, repaired in the seventeenth century, at its foot, and shut in between massive zigzag walls, with the bases of flanking Edwardian towers, which, as Leland puts it, must be passed 'or ever a man can enter *aream castelli.*' A writer, whose technical description of the castle works is the most thorough that has appeared, and is based upon a close study of mediæval military architecture, describes this narrow causeway as cut through at its deepest part; 'and in the cut is built a lofty pier, which appears to have carried a tower and a gate, from which probably bridges dropped either way to guard the causeway. These seem to have worked, as at Dover, between parapets spanning the bridge-pits, so as to steady the pier, and to protect laterally those using the bridges.'*

As we ascend the causeway, the shattered shell of William le Gros' keep frowns above, presenting its broken side toward the steep. It stood, as was often the case with early castles, upon the curtain wall, overlooking the point of danger, and in a very commanding situation. It is square, and the seaward side is perfect, while parts only of the north and south walls still stand, and the western side has disappeared altogether, the destruction having mainly been wrought by gunpowder after the siege of 1645. The extreme height is about 80 feet, and the width some 50 feet, the keep thus being smaller than that at Rochester, to which it bears a resemblance. Externally there is, except on the south side, a deep plinth, and the angles had shafts, as at the Peak Castle in Derbyshire. The keep was divided into three stories. The entrance was on the west side, and there are evidences that it was protected by a square barbican with a machicoulis. The inner doorway was 7 feet wide, and had a segmental arch, and, in the thickness of the wall, there 9 feet 6 inches, is a staircase leading to the next floor. Early castles were often divided transversely by a wall rising to the floor of the uppermost story; but at Scar-

* 'Scarborough Castle,' by 'C.,' *The Builder*, Dec. 16, 1866.

borough its place seems to have been taken at the base by a round arch rising from corbels in the wall. There was a chamber in the south wall, and, on the east side, a fireplace with a round head. The chief apartments were above, and the next floor had two mural chambers and a fireplace, while the uppermost story seems to have formed one large room. The windows have two lights, divided by a shaft, beneath a semicircular arch, inclosing a plain tympanum, and there are evidences of doorways and machicoulis in the walls. The rugged curtain wall, which probably belongs to various periods, extends from the keep on the south - western face, and has drum turrets at intervals, and the hill has been escarped below it. There are traces of other works adjacent to the keep. The castle yard, or garth, has now an area of about seventeen acres, but much of it has crumbled away. There is from it a magnificent view northward along the coast, and as far southward as Flamborough Head, as well as of the inland country. From the seaward edge we look down to the chaos of rugged, weed-grown rocks that lie at the foot of the precipice, the evidences of its progressive downfall.*

During the Pilgrimage of Grace, in 1536, Aske besieged the castle, then held, with a garrison hastily got together, by Sir Ralph Evers (or Eure); but it

* At low water it is possible to scramble round the foot of the cliff from one bay to the other, but the way is exceedingly rough, and the rocks slippery and dangerous. It is unwise for a single pedestrian to attempt it, for, in case of a fall, help may be needed to get away.

stood out, notwithstanding a determined attack, great hardships being suffered by its defenders from want of supplies, and the Pilgrims fell back; but the king's fair promises found little trust among a large section of the Yorkshiremen. Sir Francis Bigod of Mulgrave (who, as we have seen, lost his life in the end for the cause), standing upon a hillock at Setterington, with the skill of a dialectician—for in subtlety of intellect he stood head and shoulders above his fellows, and was a friend of Latimer, Barnes, Crome, and other lights of the new learning, too—proved to the assembled commons that the pardon was a deception. It was upon this memorable occasion that one of them, convinced by the argument, cried out: 'The king hath sent us the faucet, and keepeth the spiggot himself.' Even as Aske returned from his southern journey disquieting rumours were spread that the king intended to throw garrisons into Hull and Scarborough; and Hallam, on the celebrated Plough Monday, at Watton, standing before the Lady altar there, declared to his friends: 'I think best to take Hull and Scarborough ourselves betimes.' Bigod had been determined to find out the truth of the matter, and so, during the Doncaster truce, he had seized a ship at Scarborough, with £100 of the king's money, and pulling the master, Edward Waters, by the beard, had threatened to cut off his head if he would not disclose the truth, and so had made him confess that the king did in fact intend to fortify both Scarborough and Hull, and thus to bring the country into complete subjection.

Of the attempt of Hallam to secure Hull we shall speak later in this book. The utter failure at that place drew off Bigod from Scarborough, and the attempt there was entrusted to George Lumley, son of Lord Lumley, who had attended Bigod's muster, but who had but half a heart in the matter. Lumley's hand had clearly been forced. 'I think,' Bigod had said to the commons, 'you should command Mr. Lumley here to go with you to take Scarborough Castle and town, and to keep the port there.' Lumley entered Scarborough with six or seven score men, but was careful to adjure them to be peaceable, and by no means to make an attempt upon the castle, for that it was the king's house. However, he set a watch about the castle, but . sent a messenger to old Sir Ralph Evers at midnight to warn him that young Sir Ralph, the keeper of the castle, should not for his safety seek to enter just then. The next day, with his own company, he incontinently went home, and John Wyvell and Ralph Fenton became captains in his stead; but these, upon the approach of Sir Ralph Evers, abandoned the siege. However, they were taken and put in ward, and on February 12, 1537, within a month of their attempt, they were indicted at gaol delivery, and received with others the sentence of death; and, from a memorandum of Norfolk to Cromwell, dated on the next day, we learn that Wyvell was hanged in chains at Scarborough, and Fenton at York. Bigod himself, with Lumley, Sir Thomas Percy, the abbots of Fountains and Jervaulx, Hamerton, Sir John Bulmer, and Nicholas

Tempest, did not suffer at Tyburn until the following June.

Scarborough furnishes an example also of the searching inquisition which was made at this time into the most trivial, foolish, or gossiping utterances of private individuals that might be construed to imply sedition. John Borrowbie, the prior of the White Friars there, invited the warden of the Grey Friars in the town, and the Vicar of Muston, to his chamber, and there showed them a certain prophecy, which the vicar seems to have ascribed to Merlin and to Thomas of Erceldoune, the 'Rhymer,' as well as a prophetic 'jargon,' which William Langdale of Scarborough had given him. Nothing might have happened, perhaps, if the vicar had not scandalized his parishioners by alluding to the prophecies in his church porch, but then a diligent inquiry was ordered. The references in the Record Office papers seem, at this late date, very obscure. There is mention of an eagle, understood to imply the emperor, who should 'spread his wings over all this realm'; and of a 'dun cow,' believed to be the pope, who should 'set the church again in the right faith'; and there is a rhyme, forecasting the downfall of Cromwell, beginning :

'When the crumme is brought low,
Then shall we begin the Christis Cross row.'

Another 'jargon,' supposed to refer to Lord Lumley, began : 'When the cock of the north hath builded his nest.' Point was given to the matter by the fact that, according to the vicar, Merlin and Bede, being inter-rogated as to the time of the fulfilment of the prophecies, had answered: 'About the year of our Lord God a thousand v. hundred and xxxvij.' It may be that certain of them buoyed up the hopes of the Pilgrims who followed the younger Lumley to Scar-borough, for, when Langdale fled into the castle, he left them on the window-sill of his house in the town, and, with certain books, the commons carried them away.

And now, while the bones of Wyvell were whitening on the scaffold as a ghastly warning to the Scarborough men, the angry jealousy of Henry was stirred afresh by strange news concerning the neighbourhood of their port. The strained relations of Henry and his nephew, the King of Scots, are sufficiently well known. On January 1 in this year 1537, with supreme indifference to the susceptibilities and wishes of Englishmen, James made Magdalen de Valois his bride; and an applica-tion that he might pass with her through England having received no prompt reply, he resentfully set sail, with four Scottish and ten French ships, ac-companied by the French vice-admiral and the Bishop of Limoges, for Leith. On the night of May 13 he lay at anchor half a mile from Scarborough harbour, and divers fishermen saw him aboard his ship, and one man gained speech with him. Norfolk, the king's lieutenant in the North, who had all along urged that the spectacle of English wealth might have a beneficial influence upon James, in communicating the intelligence to Cromwell, remarked that he had been in hopes the king and queen would land and taste his wine at Sheriff Hutton. Less satisfactory intelligence, however, reached the court from Sir Thomas Clifford. It was stated on the word of a certain James Crane, who had come from France with James, that he (Crane) had gone ashore at a village near Scarborough in order to buy provisions there ; and that twelve Englishmen from the village and surrounding country had come aboard the Scotch king's ship, and, kneeling before him, had thanked God for his safety, and had implored him to come in to them, 'as they were oppressed and slain.' Similar occurrences were reported to have taken place further north along the coast, and James himself was heard to say, when opposite Berwick, that ' if he lived one year he would himself break a spear on one Englishman's breast.' Norfolk was instructed to search out this matter to the bottom, which he did with no very satisfactory result ; but, inasmuch as Crane mentioned places as near Scarborough that did not exist, he did not give credence to his story. However, it contributed to fan the smouldering embers to a blaze in the subsequent war that ended disastrously for the Scots at Solway Moss.

We pass on from these curious illustrations of local feeling in the time of the Northern risings to a not less curious event that happened at Scarborough during Wyatt's rebellion (1553), when the castle was secured by stratagem. One market-day there strolled into the town a number of countrymen, as countrymen do, apparently to buy such things as they needed. As evening fell, these men wended their way up the castle hill, and suddenly, for every man was a soldier disguised, they fell upon the guards at the barbican gate, and, rushing in with their leader, Thomas Stafford, second son of Lord Stafford, overpowered all resistance, and captured the castle. The stratagem was effective, but the triumph short-lived, for three days later the Earl of Westmoreland appeared, and retook the castle without loss. Stafford's ruse is said to have given rise to a proverb, 'A word and a blow, like a Scarborough warning,' but the hero himself lost hishead for it at the Tower.

From this time until the Civil Wars, in which it played a prominent part, the history of Scarborough was uneventful. At the outbreak of the war the castle was held for the Parliament by Sir Hugh Cholmley, but he declared for the king, and was besieged there by Sir John Meldrum, with a body of Scottish and English soldiery, in February, 1644. The town was stormed on the 18th by four distinct columns, with a loss of only eleven men ; and the ships in the harbour were made prize of war, being released to their owners upon payment of a fourth of the value, but many of them were dismantled and made unseaworthy. Batteries were also placed to play upon the castle, and a lodgment was effected in St. Mary's Church, where eighty prisoners were taken. The Parliamentary commander then brought guns up the hill, with which

14

he placed a battery in the church choir, and on the next morning opened fire from the east window upon the main works of the castle. The defenders were not slow to reply, and in the end the choir of the church was destroyed, and has never since been rebuilt. Several determined attempts to carry the castle by storm failed, owing to the long and strenuous defence of the Royalists, among whom Lady Cholmley remained until the last, nursing the sick and wounded. On June 22 Sir John Meldrum died from wounds received during the siege, and was succeeded in his command by Colonel Sir Matthew Boynton. The garrison was at last reduced to great extremities, and it surrendered honourably on July 22, 1645, the men issuing in a most pitiable condition. The Commons thereupon ordered a 'day of thanksgiving.' During the siege rectangular silver coins, of the value of five shillings and half a crown, were issued, being inscribed with the castle and the words 'Obsidium Scarborough.'

A second siege of Scarborough took place in 1648, when Colonel Matthew Boynton (the successor of the officer of the same name who reduced it in 1645) declared for the king. On December 23 it surrendered to Colonel Bethel under most honourable conditions, it being provided that the governor, officers, gentlemen, and soldiers should march out wearing their uniforms, colours flying, drums beating, and 'bullet in mouth,' to Scarborough Common, and should there lay down their arms. Colonel Boynton, who was afterwards slain in the fight at Wigan, spent his estate in defence

of the castle, and Charles II. granted life pensions of
£200 a year to his widow, and £100 a year to each of
his two daughters.*

With that consistent belief in the utility of maritime
power which was the wisdom of the Stuarts, though
here their strength was insufficient for their purpose,
they commissioned privateers, by letters of marque
from Prince Charles, during the Civil War in aid of
their operations upon land (a side of the struggle to
which very little attention has been given), and so
effective was their action, that, in 1646, the people of
Scarborough complained that, within eight days, they
had lost as many as nine vessels. Seven ships of war
were thenceforward stationed upon the Yorkshire coast,
but seem often to have been outmatched by astute
privateers, manned largely by Yorkshire seamen, who
knew their own coast exceedingly well. One of the
most notable of these was one John Denton, master
of a ketch carrying one gun and a company of about
thirty men. With this craft he committed great
depredations about the year 1650, boarding and
capturing the *Amity* of Scarborough in the neighbourhood of Filey, and carrying it near Flamborough,
where he released it on payment of a fine ; looting a
vessel aground in Tees mouth, laden with alum and
butter ; and being captured himself in action when he
was attacking a ship of Whitby. Some coblemen of
Bridlington were instrumental in his defeat on this
occasion, for, lying in York Castle, he declared that,

* State Papers, (Domestic Series), Charles II., 1660.

if it had not been for the company he was with, he
would have landed in revenge and burned Bridlington
Quay. The political character of Denton's piracy is
proved by the warrant of Bradshaw, as President of
the Council, authorizing his detention in York Castle
on a charge of piracy and bearing arms against the
Parliament, as also by the fact that he was one of four
who proclaimed Prince Charles as King of England,
at Malton, in 1651; but his careless, or it may have
been his sympathizing, custodians allowed him to go
abroad, though with a keeper, to dine with a certain
Captain William Thornton, and, horses being in
waiting at Walmgate Bar, he made his escape.

Another very remarkable episode took place at
Scarborough on April 1, 1650. A privateer, named
the *St. Peter of Jersey*, Captain Joseph Constant, which
had been commissioned by Prince Charles, set sail
from Dunkirk with a crew of about thirty, mostly
Dutchmen, and hovered about the Yorkshire coast.
The strange craft being observed, and her character
being detected—either by her build, for she is styled
a 'vessell of warre,' or her suspicious movements—
one Robert Colman, master of a North Sea fishing-
smack, volunteered to Colonel Bethel, then Governor
of Scarborough, to effect a capture. Accordingly he
was provided with a proper vessel, well armed, and
manned by twenty-five seamen, as well as by as many
soldiers under the command of Captain Thomas
Lassells. The Scarborough craft put out from the
harbour towards dusk, so that her character could not

be distinguished, and approached the privateer, the commander of which, thinking he had an easy prey, fired upon her, hove alongside, and hailed them, 'Strike, ye dogs, for King Charles!' Colman thereupon gave the order to board, which was done; a hot skirmish took place, himself and three seamen being wounded, but the strangers were outmatched, five of them slain or drowned, and the rest brought with their vessel as prisoners into Scarborough harbour.

A few years later, in 1655, George Fox, the founder of the Society of Friends, was imprisoned in Scarborough Castle, and has left a record of his painful experiences. The first cell in which he was confined he described as a purgatory, because it was filled with smoke; in the second his body was benumbed, and his fingers became swollen owing to cold, for he had no fire wherewith to dry his clothes; while the third was so open to the weather that 'the water came over his bed, and he was fain to skim it up with a platter.' Moreover, he tells us, his gaolers provided him so scantily that a threepenny loaf had to last him three weeks, and, out of pure malice, they mixed wormwood with his water. Three years later, however, he was free, and was invited to preach in the very castle where he had been confined. The castle was somewhat repaired in the time of the Jacobite rising of 1745, but its later history has been uneventful, and the elements have carried on the destructive work begun in the Civil Wars. Unsightly barracks were built there during the last century, and now, upon the castle hill, volunteers are from time to time encamped in the summer-time.

With the Civil Wars, the older history of Scarborough, which was intimately bound up with its castle and harbour, may be said to have ended. A new history opened with the discovery of the spa-water about the year 1620, which has led to the building of the new town, and ultimately to the attractions of modern Scarborough; but there is a radical distinction of character between the old town and the new, and so let us now describe the former before we enter upon the circumstances that relate to the latter. The old town of Scarborough will remind you a good deal of Whitby, its quaint red-tiled houses closely packed upon the steep between the hoary castle and the sea. You may be assured that, though there is much that is new here, and contrasts abound, yet, in general character, the place has changed little even since John, or Edward I., or Richard III. was here. In that quaint way known as Sand Side, that lies on the flank of the old harbour, just below the castle hill, and leads out to the piers, where you may see coasting-craft, and Norwegian barques discharging ice or timber, and on one of which the ducking-stool was placed that still remains in the museum, there yet stands a house in which very credible tradition alleges that Richard III. and his queen were lodged in 1484. It presents merely an ordinary appearance from the roadway, but an inscription upon it records the tradition, and the window openings on every side show that it once was

isolated. Forty years ago it had older evidences
within, and an ancient oak bedstead, cupboard, and
table.* Hereabout there are the characteristic features
of a fishing port—a forest of the masts and cordage
of smacks in the harbour, the briny scent, the fishermen,
in blue jerseys and oilskins, standing by, or hauling at
ropes by the pier, men and women laden with baskets
of fish, the eager chaffering in the early morning of
those who buy and sell. A network of steep and
narrow roads, with stairways in places, leads up the
hill between the fishermen's houses — old - world
dwellings of brick, with red roofs and with Dutch
tiles, many of them, within, lying between the green
dikes of the castle and the harbour.

Such a narrow way, and a flight of steps, will bring
you from hence to the old church of St. Mary, which
still bears considerable evidences of its battering in
the Civil War. Anciently it was a possession, with
the chapel within the castle, of the abbey of Citeaux,
granted thereto by Richard I., and Cistercian monks
were resident here; but these were dispossessed as
aliens by Henry IV., and the church was granted to
the priory of Bridlington. Leland thus speaks of it:
'There is but one Paroche Churche in the town, of
our Ladye, joyninge almost to ye Castle. It ys verye
fayre, isled on the sides, and cross-isled, and hath
wythout towers for belles, with pyramids on them,
whereof two towers be at the west ende of the Churche,
and one in ye middle of the cross-isle.' The choir, as

* Illustrations of these may be seen at the museum.

we have said, was destroyed during the siege. The central tower also was so damaged that it fell four years later—as it now stands it was rebuilt in 1669, when the north aisle was added—and the western towers have also disappeared. The existing church is therefore the nave of the old one, and a restoration was creditably effected in 1850. The west end, with its three lancets and a wheel window, is mostly modern, and a modern Decorated window has been inserted in the east end of the shallow chancel, which is formed at the base of the old central tower. The original features of the church are Transition Norman and Early English. The piers on the north side, except the two westernmost ones, and the two eastern piers on the south side, are of the Transition, but the others are pure Early English. One pillar is characteristic in having six detached shafts round a central pier, banded in the middle. Vaulting shafts rise between the single-light Early English clerestory windows, and there are clustered vaulting shafts at the west end between the bases of the old towers, which open to the nave with clustered pillars and arches. The south aisle is noteworthy, having a chantry chapel opening out of it in each bay, the several chapels being separated from one another by solid walls. These chapels, though additions to the original structure, are still Early English. Each has an altar-recess, and a piscina in the south wall, and an aumbry in the east wall. The modern windows are Curvilinear Decorated. On the south side of the chancel is a Decorated chapel. The north aisle, added, as we have said, in the seventeenth century, has late Decorated pillars with grotesque capitals, which are said to have been brought from one of the monastic churches, now destroyed, in the town. The church, as will be seen, is a very interesting one, and before the Civil War must have been a fine structure.

We may now turn to the history of modern Scarborough, which begins with the discovery, about the year 1620, of the beneficent qualities of the 'Scarborough Spaw' water by that 'sensible, intelligent lady' Mistress Farrow. From Dr. Witty's curious book on the subject, we learn that the water erelong became 'the usual physic of the inhabitants.' Its fame soon spread through the country, and visitors began to resort to Scarborough to 'take the waters,' as they did to Harrogate, Buxton, and Tunbridge Wells. Dr. Witty, whose 'Scarborough Spaw' was published in 1667, attributed the virtues of the water to its containing vitriol, iron, alum, nitre, and salt. He was not, however, left in undisturbed possession of his beliefs, for Dr. Simpson, in his 'Hydrologia Chymica,' attacked his theory, as did Dr. George Tunstall of Newcastle, in his 'Scarborough Spaw Spagyrically Anatomized,' published in 1670. An amusing controversy followed, for Witty replied, calling his last-named assailant a mountebank, in his 'Scarborough's Spagyrical Anatomizer Dissected,' and this again provoked a bitterly worded 'New Year's Gift for Dr. Witty; or, The Dissector Anatomized,' from Tunstall, published in 1672. At this time the corporation of

Scarborough was in possession of the waters, and was wont to appoint governors. As we write, we have before us an engraving, made by one F. Hornsey in 1806, presumably from an old painting, of 'Dicky Dickinson, the first Governor of Scarborough Spaw.' He is represented wearing a long-bodied coat, with a hat of extraordinary character; his face hideous, with very small frontal development, and overspread by a foolish smile, and his legs curiously deformed. Doubtless he was a 'character,' if not a 'natural,' and we imagine that it was in satire of his 'pretty wit' that it was said of him :

> ' Samos unenvied boasts her Æsop gone.
> And France may glory in her late Scarron,
> While England has a living Dickinson.'

A cistern for the waters was made about 1698, but, owing to an earthquake or landslip, they were lost for a time in 1735, after which a spa - house was built. During the century the number of visitors grew, and, at the close of it, the Scarborough season was established, and had a reputation for 'all the refined amusements of polished life.' Sheridan's 'Trip to Scarborough,' produced at Drury Lane in 1777, is evidence of the success of the place. It is in the second scene that Lord Foppington exclaims : 'Well, 'tis an unspeakable pleasure to be a man of quality— strike me dumb! Even the boors of this northern spa have learned the respect due to a title.' Before this, however, we hear of sea-bathing at Scarborough in ' Humphrey Clinker,' in which the energetic Clinker, thinking his master is drowning, drags him ashore from a machine in the midst of the people. The spahouse was wrecked by a gale in 1836, and in the following year the Cliff Bridge Company, which had already connected the spa with St. Nicholas Cliff, across the opening of the Ramsdale Valley, began reconstructive work. By the year 1858 the Spa and promenade were completed, with their delightful grounds; but, in 1876, a disastrous fire laid the buildings waste. Reconstruction and rebuilding followed at a cost of £77,552, and the very successful Palladian building that now graces the foot of the South Cliff, including a grand hall, theatre, picture-gallery, refreshment rooms, and other features, with its splendid sea-terrace, its tower, and the delightful walks that wind up the hillside, overshadowed by beautiful trees, and amid a profusion of flowers, as well as the existing Cliff Bridge, result from the energy, skill, and taste that have been bestowed upon the work.

The Spa is the centre of the life and gaiety of Scarborough; and in the season—which begins, one would think, too late, and ends too early—when its terraces are thronged with a fashionable crowd, especially at night, beneath the flashing lights, when the sea rolls against the terrace-wall, and the strains of music— here always of the best—float upon the air, and you look out to the dim form of the castle hill, and the line of lights sweeping round the bay, it presents a scene unique of its kind in England. And what can be more delightful than, from the Spa grounds or the cliff-top, to look out over the sunny bay, dotted with varied craft, shut in by the bold form of the castle hill on one hand, and a fine headland on the other, and to watch the busy scene upon the sands, or the children playing upon the dark talus of the Black rocks that skirt the southern hill ?*

Let us now mount the hill to the crest of the South

* A full and particular account of the Scarborough Spa, and of the fortunes of the Cliff Bridge Company, will be found in 'Scarborough and Scarborough Spa,' by Mr. Francis Goodricke, the company's manager. The pump-room for the spa-water is at the north end of the terrace, and is very commodiously arranged. The following is Dr. Sheridan Muspratt's analysis of the two wells :

	North Well. Cubic inches.	South Well. Cubic inches.
Nitrogen gas	7·4864	7·9792
Carbonic acid gas	43·3112	38·0400
	Grains.	Grains.
Carbonate of lime	42·354	34·841
Carbonate of magnesia	2·844	4·051
Carbonate of iron	1·465	1·996
Carbonate of manganese	Trace.	Trace.
Sulphate of magnesia	98·952	90·092
Sulphate of lime	69·120	69·537
Sulphate of soda	7·060	2·015
Chloride of sodium	19·287	19·540
Chloride of potassium	3·002	2·416
Chloride of magnesium	1·941	·920
Iodide of sodium	Trace.	Trace.
Bromide of sodium	Trace.	Trace.
Organic matter	Trace.	Trace.
Silicic acid	·859	1·063
Total solid matter	246·884	226·471

Specific gravity of waters 1·0033069   1·0028378
Mean temperature, 48 degrees.

Cliff. (There is an ingenious tramway, with balanced cars, the motive force being gravity, obtained by pumping sufficient water into the car required to descend, which thus draws up the other.) Here is the fashionable part of Scarborough, where terraces of fine houses continue to spring up, and where—as well as on St. Nicholas Cliff — the best hotels are found. It is delightfully breezy at the top, and there is a magnificent sea-view. Moreover, southward of the Spa, the cliff and undercliff have been laid out in skilfully contrived paths and beautiful gardens, about a delightful cove which is there, and, between the hills and the sea, you will find a quiet and retirement acceptable sometimes in the bustle of the season. The grassy steep of Oliver's Mount, otherwise known as Weaponness (500 feet), dominates the South Cliff, and has the appearance of a blunt truncated cone, but is in fact the 'nab' of a long narrow ridge that shuts in the Ramsdale Valley on the east. From the crest there is a magnificent marine view, extending from the cliffs in the neighbourhood of Cloughton to far-off Flamborough Head.

Ramsdale is that valley which separates the South Cliff from the rest of the town, and opens to the sea between the Spa and St. Nicholas Cliff. The bottom and the slopes of it are well planted, and have been laid out as a park, with pleasant winding paths amid the trees, and a sheet of ornamental water below. Near the seaward end of the valley stands the Museum —a prominent object, in the form of a well-designed

round temple of the Roman Doric order. It is
singularly rich in illustrations of local history, especially
of the primeval life of the neighbouring moors, as well
as of the geology and botany of the district. To a
large oaken coffin exhumed at Gristhorpe, one of its
chief possessions, we shall refer in a subsequent
chapter. Close by the Museum the Cliff Bridge spans
the valley, and it is crossed higher up by the Valley
Toll-Bridge, which leads from the South Cliff to the
business part of the town. Beyond the valley lies the
railway station, and, near by, the principal theatre, the
Londesborough, and the road to Falsgrave (the
Walsgrave of Domesday), which, from a rural village,
has become an integral part of the town.

The beautiful North Bay, lying between the arms of
the castle hill and Scalby Ness, has also now gained
a large measure of popularity among visitors. You
may live here more cheaply than on the South Cliff,
and there is very good accommodation, and the broad
sands are specially delightful. The cliff here, too, has
been laid out in gardens, with winding paths, flower-
beds, and pleasant seats, with great success. There
is a pier also in the bay; and a new and splendid drive
from Peasholm round its bold curve to the foot of the
castle hill, takes its name from the late Duke of
Clarence, who opened it not long ago.

And now as we abandon Scarborough, with its
unrivalled situation, its long history, its modern attractions, and its many sharp contrasts of the old and the
new, the conventional and the picturesque, we may be

inclined to exclaim with Dr. Witty, the erewhile advocate of the spa, *Felix qui potuit boni fontem visere lucidum!* We may find pleasure, too—as we look upon the harbour of Scarborough, crowded with varied smacks, and the quays busy with men, while the gray cliff rises behind, crowned with its crumbling walls and · shattered tower—to remember a verse from a Robin Hood ballad which, exaggerating as it does no little the prosperity of the Yorkshire fisher-folk, sends even the brave outlaw himself from beneath the greenwood tree to join the Scarborough fishing-fleet.

> ' The fishermen brave more money have
> Than any merchants two or three ;
> Therefore I will to Scarborough go,
> That I a fisherman brave may be.'

NOTE.—The following table of *return* driving distances to favourite resorts near Scarborough may be useful : Ayton, Forge Valley and Hackness, 15 m. ; Lady Edith's Drive and Forge Valley, returning by either Ayton or Hackness, 13 m. ; Seamer and Ayton, 11 m. ; Seamer and Cayton, 9 m. ; Seamer, 8 m. ; Scalby, 5 m. ; Scalby Mills, 3 m. ; Scalby and Burniston, 8½ m. ; Scalby and North Cliff, 7 m. ; Hayburn Wyke, 13 m. ; Robin Hood's Bay by Burniston and Cloughton, 26 m. ; Filey, 15 m. ; Hunmanby, 20 m. ; Flamborough, 38 m.; Cornelian Bay, 5 m. ; Yedmandale, 12 m.; Wykeham, 14 m. ; Beedale, 16 m.; Harwood Dale (Mill Inn), 18 m. ; Thornton-le-Dale, 34 m.

CHAPTER XII.

THE REGION OF THE UPPER DERWENT.

Seamer—Sir Thomas Percy and the Pilgrimage of Grace—The
Rising of 1549—The Aytons—Forge Valley—Raincliff Wood
—Everley—Hackness—The Monastic Cell—The Passing of
Hilda—Hackness Church—Lowdales and Highdales—Silpho
and Broxa — Troutsdale — The Black Beck—Deepdale—
Langdale—Harwood Dale—Yedmandale — Hutton Buscel—
Beedale—Wykeham and its Priory—Brompton—Snainton—
Ebberston—The Scamridge and other Dikes—Allerston.

In our descriptive journeying we shall now wend westward from Scarborough, in order that we may explore
the glorious region of the Upper Derwent, and say
something of certain interesting places that lie beyond
that river. No dale completely intersects the calcareous
hills, that lie along the northern side of the Vale of
Pickering, between Thornton Dale and Forge Valley,
which is the way of the Derwent. The gathering
ground of that river is remarkable, and merits a little
description. As will be seen by a glance at the map,
the elevated land that bounds Stainton Dale on the
west turns inland certain streams that rise within a
couple of miles of the shore, and these, meeting other

brooks which flow down from Fylingdales Moor, from
Wykeham High and Low Moors, and from the High
and Low Moors of Allerston, constitute the vigorous
flood of the youthful Der.vent. This network of
streams, in short, converges to Forge Valley from
many quarters, even as the ramifications of an ivy-
leaf converge to the stem. Issuing from this narrow
cleft, where it is within four miles of the coast, the
Derwent is turned inland by the gentle heights that
flank the shore between Scarborough and Filey, and
winds a sluggish course across the almost level Vale
of Pickering, where cornfield succeeds cornfield, and
meadow, meadow, in monotonous succession, to its
confluence with the Rye; and to that other narrow
cleft through the southern range of the calcareous hills
in the neighbourhood of Castle Howard, without which,
as we have already said, the Vale of Pickering would
be a vast lake.

The railway from Scarborough to Helmsley has now
made accessible not only Forge Valley, but the whole
of the tributary dales of the Derwent and the Rye,
and we may therefore reach the foot of the valley by
the station named after it at West Ayton; but during
the season at Scarborough very many drive thither.*
For ourselves, in this wayfaring we may take either of
two courses: we may leave Scarborough by the Fals-

* In the season three and four horse char-à-bancs regularly
traverse the valley, driving by Seamer and Ayton to Everley and
Hackness, and returning to Scarborough by Suffield and Scalby,
though some return by a shorter route through Raincliff Wood.

grave road, and, passing through that erewhile rural village, climb the steep hill beyond to Stepney (whence there is a splendid retrospective view of the town and of the twin bays, giving a better conception of the position than can be gained elsewhere), and cross Irton Moor, by the road, to Ayton; or from Scarborough we may traverse the Ramsdale Valley (with the railway), and proceed by Seamer and Irton. In either case the Aytons, East and West, lying at the foot of Forge Valley, are the 'objective.' Leaving Scarborough by the Ramsdale Valley, the Oliver's Mount range is on the left, with the Mere (a boating lake) at its foot, representing an older marshy mere now drained, and an equal range rises on the right; and, as we issue from the valley, there is a wide prospect of the flat country to the south, and of the level edges of the Wolds beyond, with dark plantations upon their crests here and there.

Seamer, which lies out in the open, takes its name from the Mere, and is a place of historical memories and present interests. It was a location of importance in Saxon times, and ornaments of the precious metals belonging to that period have been found there. There was a church, with a priest, at the Conquest, and the existing edifice has some very characteristic Norman features. The chancel arch is fine, and there is Norman work in the nave. The place was a lordship of the Percys, who gave importance to it, procuring for it a fair in the 5th Richard II. It was a 'great uplandische toune' in Leland's time, and its markets aroused the envy of the burgesses of Scarborough, who ultimately secured their suppression; but Seamer has now become a rural village. The castle, or house, of the Percys, at present a mere heap of ruins near the church, was probably being built or enlarged in 1424, when license was issued to the Bishop of Dromore to dedicate the Earl of Northumberland's chapel and altars there. Sir Thomas Percy, who died at Tyburn for his share in the Pilgrimage of Grace, was at Seamer with his mother when he heard that the commons were up in Lincolnshire, and that Aske had cried out, 'Thousands for a Percy!' at the gate of Wressel. Thereupon, disguised as a servant, he prepared to steal homeward, but, on the way, he met a certain Percey, who asked him if he knew where Sir Thomas Percy was (to whom, wishing to get away, he answered that he heard he was with his mother at Seamer), and who further told him that the commons were up at Malton, and were watching for Sir Thomas, and would have him among them, or would 'never leave his mother a penny.' With this sorrowful news he returned to Seamer, and told his mother, who thereupon 'wept and sore lamented'; and presently there came a party, who swore him to the cause, and he departed with them. It was the constable of Seamer, too, whom George Lumley warned to raise the commons of Pickering Lythe for the intended attack upon Scarborough Castle. The strong feeling of the district at this time is also shown by the fact that in 1549—when the Devonshire and Cornish men were

' up ' for the restoration of the old Liturgy, and when the unpopularity of the Protector Somerset led to risings in various places—there was an obscure revolt also at Seamer, inflamed chiefly by the parish clerk, who, with two more, lighted Staxton Beacon, three miles away on the Wolds, and thus brought together a band of some 3,000 men, who attacked the house of a certain Mr. White, dragged him, with others whom they took, including the Sheriff of York, from their beds, to the Wolds, and there slew them. The rabble, however, was dispersed by troops sent from York, and the leaders were captured and hanged.

Passing the neighbouring hamlet of Irton upon the left, a journey of two miles more along a country road, between flowering hedges and cornfields, with woods in front, brings us to the Aytons, East and West, which lie upon either side of the Derwent at the foot of Forge Valley. The double village is picturesque, rural and ancient, and a church is named in Domesday as existing there. The interesting little edifice at East Ayton, indeed, still preserves a Norman chancel with an enriched doorway, and a massive and beautiful font. The shattered and picturesque late Edwardian square tower, which still stands upon the slope in a very important position commanding the Derwent, is the sole remain of a castle of the Evers (or Eures), a Yorkshire family of great power in the time of Henry VIII., of whom was the Sir Ralph who was Governor of Scarborough Castle when the Pilgrims made their attempt upon that stronghold.

Forge Valley gains very much from the sharp contrast suddenly presented by its umbrageous woods to the open pastoral country we have been journeying through. It is in the nature of a cleft, and the hills on either side rise to a height of about 300 feet above the bed of the stream, clothed from base to summit with a rich woodland ; but, owing to the narrowness of the dale, they impress one as being much more lofty. At the bottom, the youthful Derwent—a famous trout and grayling stream — rolls over its rocky bed, and, even when it is hidden by the overhanging foliage, you will hear its voice in the woodland. The leafage of the ash predominates, but there are many oaks and a great variety of firs, and all the glades are carpeted with ferns, and bright or sweet-scented with primroses, bluebells, and lilies of the valley in the springtime ; but perhaps more glorious still are the woods when autumn has changed them like a wizard, and they are vested in every hue of brown, russet, and gold. A wayfaring of two miles through this delightful valley, a huge scarp of the calcareous rock being exposed at one point on the right, brings us to the place of the forge that gave to it its name, where of old time the monks of Hackness were wont to fashion their iron. And now, beyond, the country opens, the hill on the right trends away north-eastward, and who would can return that way to Scarborough by Lady Edith's Drive through Raincliff Wood, or can climb the hill by Lady Grace's Ride and explore Seamer Moor, where ancient earth-works may be observed. The moor has been extraordinarily rich in tumuli, many urns and other primeval remains from which are in the Scarborough Museum, and in the collection of the Earl of Londesborough. The woods of Raincliff are as rich and beautiful as those of Forge Valley, and there are many delightful paths through them, which, through the kindness of Lord Londesborough, the public are free to use.*

Issuing from the northern end of Forge Valley, the wayfarer will perceive that its richly-wooded steeps were, after all, but a fair preparative for the more varied loveliness of the Vale of Hackness, which lies beyond. Here the dale is wider ; there are spreading cornfields in the hollow ; the heights are everywhere crested with woodlands ; and the hills, as we go forward, assume a wondrous variety of noble contours. In the midst of the vale is the hamlet of Everley, consisting merely of a house or two, with a wayside hostel, the only one, we are informed, within several miles ; and here, in the bright afternoons of the late summer, it is a most picturesque sight to see the many vehicles from Scarborough drawn up beneath the trees, while the ostlers are watering the horses—excellent horseflesh, too—and the bright costumes of the ladies add points of new colour to the greenness of the dale. It was a different concourse of people, we may be sure, that was assembled here in 1652, when, as a York Castle record

* Lady Edith's Drive is so called from Lady Edith Somerset, daughter of the seventh Duke of Beaufort, and now Countess of Londesborough, and Lady Grace's Ride is thus named in honour of Lady Grace Augusta Fane, daughter of the twelfth Earl of Westmoreland, and now wife of Lord Raincliff.

hath it, a certain John Peacock, a gentleman of East Ayton, did kneel down in the presence of many and drink a health to the beheaded king, and exclaim : ' I hope the sun will once again shine on me ; there are 40,000 cavaliers coming into England, and upon their coming I will make some persons rue it.'

A mile beyond Everley we reach Hackness, which is a picturesque hamlet most sweetly placed by the river, and at the very heart of the 'sister vales,' nestled amid the hills, and surely one of the most beautiful villages in Yorkshire. It is, besides, a place of high antiquity, filled with memories of the earliest times of Deiran Christianity. It was here that Hild founded a monastic cell—' quod ipsa eodem anno construxerat, et appellatur Hacanos,' as Bede tells us—and hither sent certain of the sisterhood of Streoneshealh about the year 680. Here Bede records that, when Hild, after her long sickness, died, the nun Begu, afterwards known as St. Bees, witnessed her passing in vision. Thus he speaks of it :

'That same night it pleased Almighty God, by a manifest vision, to make known her death in another monastery at a distance from hers, which she had built that same year, and called Hackness. There was in that monastery a certain nun called Begu, who had served God upwards of thirty years in monastic conversation. This nun, being then in the dormitory of the sisters, on a sudden heard the well-known sound of a bell in the air, which used to awake and call them to prayers when any one of them was taken out of this world, and, opening her eyes, as she thought, she saw the top of the house open and a strong light pour in from above. Looking earnestly upon that light, she saw the soul of the aforesaid servant of God in that same light, attended and conducted to heaven by angels. Then awaking, and seeing the other sisters lying round about her, she perceived that what she had seen was either in a dream or a vision, and, rising immediately in a great fright she ran to the virgin who then presided in the monastery in place of the abbess, and whose name was Frigyth, and with many tears and sighs told her that the Abbess Hilda, mother of them all, had departed this life, and had, in her sight, ascended to eternal bliss, and to the company of the inhabitants of heaven, with a great light, and with angels conducting her.   Frigyth, having heard it. awoke all the sisters, and, calling them to the church, admonished them to pray and sing psalms for her soul, which they did during the remainder of the night ; and, at break of day, the brothers came with news of her death from the place where she had died.   The sisters answered that they knew it before, and then related how and when they had heard it, by which it appeared that her death had been revealed to them in a vision at the self-same hour in which the others said she had died.   Thus it was by Heaven happily ordained that, when some saw her departure out of this world, the others should be acquainted with her admittance into the spiritual life which is eternal.'*

Of the monastic cell of Hackness, as the Angles knew it, we know little more, but it seems to have been destroyed by the Norsemen at the time when Streoneshealh itself was laid waste. Its history was associated with that of Whitby after the Conquest, for William de Percy, who refounded the abbey, possessed also, as the successor of Earl Gospatric, the manor of Hackness; and his brother Serlo, the abbot, obtained from him the right to build a Benedictine cell here, to which, when Whitby was plundered and injured by pirates in 1088, Serlo retired with his brethren for a time. But, at the date of Serlo's succession to the abbacy, there was already a church at Hackness, for

* Bæda, 'Historia Ecclesiastica,' iv. 23.

his predecessor, Regenfrith, having been killed by
accident at Ormsbridge on the Derwent, the body was
brought to the church of St. Peter at ' Hacanos,' and
there buried in the chancel. This church is mentioned
in Domesday, and was perhaps rebuilt by William de
Percy, who had a house at Hackness.

At the village, the Derwent turns westward, and the
church of St. Peter stands about a quarter of a mile
north of it, near the gateway of Hackness Park.
Leaving the river for the nonce, let us make our way,
by the tributary Lowdales Beck, to where its spire
rises in the beautiful dale. The well-proportioned
tower is Early English, but the most ancient portion
of the structure is the plain chancel arch, with square
abaci, which is very early Norman, and to the same
period, but somewhat later, belongs the south side of
the nave. Three Early English pillars and arches are
on the north side, and the chancel has belonged to that
period, but has now a Perpendicular east window. A
splendid Early English arch also opens from the nave
to the tower. Earlier than any part of the structure
are the broken memorial crosses from St. Hilda's cell,
which have been found from time to time in the
churchyard, and are now preserved, with their Latin
inscriptions, in the church. They appear to be
memorials of the sisters Æthelburga and Hwætburga,
abbesses of Hackness, daughters of Aldwulf, King of
the East Angles, a nephew of St. Hilda, as well as of
Cynegyth, Bugge, and Trecea, who were correspondents
of St. Boniface. Other supposed inscriptions are upon

the fragments, assumed to be in the ancient Ogham character of Ireland.

Hackness Hall, the seat of Lord Derwent, is a fine structure of modern character, built towards the close of the last century, and has a central pediment and balustraded top. It lies in a most beautiful park, in which the Lowdales Beck expands into a glassy sheet. Those who continue their journey hence to Scarborough, ascend through the park—a most delightful way— where, above the grassy slopes, trees of huge growth clothe the heights, and beautiful woodland dells, opening on the left, give varied contours to the hills. The upward wayfaring is most pleasant amid such surroundings; and, when Suffield is reached at the top, there opens an enchanting prospect that crowns the whole journey, where suddenly, below, the cornfields burst upon the sight, with the village of Scalby in the midst, and the blue sea beyond, the bold headland of Scarborough uplifting the hoary keep far out on the right.

We, however, in our present wayfaring, instead of thus returning to Scarborough, shall make a brief descriptive journey from Hackness Church north-westward, up the Lowdales Beck, which brings us through country of like beauty—the broken wooded steep of Silpho Brow on the right, with the village of Silpho on the top, and a similar hill on the left, up which a pathway climbs to the beautifully situated hamlet of Broxa—to where a wooded nab facing us separates Highdales, down which a number of streamlets descend from Hackness and Silpho Moors, from the dell of the Whisperdale Beck, and its tributary the Breaday Gill. The beauty of this little nest of dales, with the finely-contoured hills, the rich woodlands, and running waters brawling over their rocky beds, is most enchanting.

But now we must return to the village of Hackness, and trace the Derwent upward, speaking, albeit briefly, of the series of upper dales, as each opens out in turn on the right and left. For a mile westward of the village the way of the river is beneath the very steep northern escarpment of the 'tabular' calcareous hills, which rise some 500 feet above its bed; and the tributary Trout Beck sweeps round the flank of these hills from High Scamridge through Troutsdale, a long, deep, and impressive cleft, diversified with wood and meadow, and, receiving a little tributary, the Freeze Gill, falls into the Derwent on its right bank. If we trace the river north-westward, something more than half a mile further, still in like beautiful scenery, we reach the foot of another nest of dales, where, upon our left, the Black Beck falls into the stream. The bold and massive forms of the hills, the deeply-cleft dales, and the rich woods make this country most delightful; but it is needless to expend superlatives upon that whereof the character has already been sufficiently indicated. Yet it must be noted that ever as we ascend the foliage becomes scantier, and that the purple of the moors grows nearer above the cultivated banks. Deepdale, well named, sends down its streamlet, the White Beck, rising in Ebberston

Low Moor, with a little tributary that joins it, sweeping round the base of the lofty nab of Bickley Moor, to the Black Beck.   Above this confluence the Black Beck has a course generally from west to east, and its way is known as North Side.   Here, from Wykeham High Moor, it receives the Hipper and Stockland Becks; further on it is itself known as the Cross Cliff Beck, and has its source, with its tributary, the Grain Beck, in the heather of Allerston High Moor, where chasm and moorland bank are overlooked by Blakey Topping.

From hence, to complete our survey of the Derwent, we must return to the confluence of the Black Beck with its stream, just beyond which, ascending the river, we reach Low Langdale End, lying below the sweet hamlet of Broxa upon the brow of the eastern hill.   From this point to High Langdale End, going almost due north, the distance is two and a half miles, during which we meet the youthful river, again amid dense woodlands, clothing the very steep banks, through which paths lead northward.   At High Langdale End the Derwent receives, on its left bank, its earliest nest of tributaries: the Lownorth Beck, known in its upper course as the Jugger Howe Beck, and still further up, at its source in Fylingdales Moor, as the Brown Rigg Beck, with its confluent streams, the Hollin Gill, the Helwath Beck (which rises in Stony Marl Moor, within a mile of Stoupe Brow, overlooking Robin Hood's Bay), the Castle Beck, the Keasbeck, and several more.   To trace these becks through Harwood Dale to the moors will well repay the hardy wayfarer, for the scenery is wild, impressive, and very beautiful, both of sea and land.   As to the youthful Derwent itself, we may trace it, through the heather, north-westward to its source, some three miles away, at Derwent Head, 800 feet above the sea, in a wild country, not far from the tumulus of High Woof Howe.

From this brief account of the dales of the Upper Derwent, it will be seen that the country is indeed rich in waters, and that, in reaching the sources, one meets with a rare and characteristic diversity of scenery, from fruitful cornfields, umbrageous wood-lands, and deep valleys, to the wilder and sterner beauties of the great rolling moorlands.   These heathery heights are covered with the evidences of primeval life, in tumuli, camps, and entrenchments, and many relics from them will be found in the Scar-borough and Whitby museums.   Upon Cloughton Moor, north-west of Scarborough, for example, is a so-called 'Druidical circle,' measuring 36 feet in extreme diameter, with the appearances of a small circle within, the whole occupying an elevated area some 60 feet in diameter.   Want of space, however, will not permit us here to dwell at length upon these curious and interesting evidences of a long-past age.

Having completed our survey of the many dales of the Upper Derwent, it remains in this chapter to deal only with certain places that have not so far fallen within our wayfaring, and that lie between Forge

Valley and Thornton Dale, at the foot of the southern slope of the calcareous hills.   We return, therefore, to Ayton, at the foot of the valley, and proceed south-westward to Hutton Buscel (or Bushel); but, before we reach that village, note must be made of a cleft in the 'tabular' hills, parallel with Forge Valley, some two miles in length, known as Yedmandale, which has some very pretty woodland scenery.   Hutton Buscel, a pleasant village stretching along the country road, takes its distinctive appellation from the great family of Buscel, or Busli, of whom Alan Buscel granted its church to the abbey of Whitby.   The existing church is of no great interest, though it has some good glass, and a monument of Richard Osbaldestone, Bishop of Carlisle 1747, and of London 1762.   It is interesting to remember, too, that at Hutton Buscel lived early in the century a typical Yorkshire squire, George Osbaldestone, always known hereabout as 'the old squire,' who was an ardent foxhunter and breeder of foxhounds, ever at home in the saddle, and fond of riding his own horses at steeplechases, and not less at home with his gun, in the cricket-field, or even on the river.

Half a mile farther along the road we reach Wyke-ham, a rural village on the Beedale Beck, which, in Beedale (its upper course), has some exquisite woodland scenery flanking its stream.   Wykeham is interesting from having once possessed a priory of Cistercian nuns, founded, about the year 1153, by Pain Fitz-Osbert of Wykeham.   This priory was entirely destroyed by fire in the reign of Edward III., and of the subsequent buildings scarcely a vestige now remains. The modern Wykeham Abbey is the seat of Mary, Vicountess Downe, and is situated in a fine and well-wooded park, wherein stands a modern church of good proportions by Butterfield; but the Early English tower of the ancient church still rises near by, with a cross to mark the site of the old high altar. As we leave the village of Wykeham, we pass the course of the Sawdon Beck, which descends from a shallow depression in the hills known as Sawdon Dale, near the hamlet of Sawdon, and have still as we go forward the same gentle wooded and pastoral hills on the right, and the same unpicturesque flat of the Vale of Pickering on the left.

Ere long our wayfaring brings us to the next village— that of Brompton—which is an exceedingly pretty one, well placed on the slope, with red-tiled and thatched houses, bright patches of garden, and an air of prosperity. The place is ancient, and Hinderwell says that it 'was a residence of the kings of Northumbria.' Certainly it had a church at the time of the Domesday survey, and the existing interesting edifice, in which Wordsworth was married in 1802, standing at the west end of the village, with a good tower and lofty spire, has a few Norman features and fragments. John de Brompton, the Benedictine chronicler, was possibly born here, taking his name from the place.

Something more than a mile further westward we reach the straggling village of Snainton, where, in the seventeenth century, was a clerk who sought to

set up a Gretna Green; but Robert Hendley of
Snainton had no 'peculiar,' and so was charged in
1649-50 with marrying couples without the consent of
their parents, 'nor doth he in any publique manner
make known the intencion of theire marriadge according to the lawes of the land, but in private places
and at unlawfull houres doeth make itt his practise to
joyne any men and women together in wedlocke not
of his parrish.'

The next village to which our hasty descriptive
wayfaring brings us is Ebberston, which lies, not along
the road we traverse, but at right angles to it along a
bridle-way that comes down from the hills by that dry
hollow known as Netherby Dale. The little church,
which has Norman features, like most of the churches
hereabout, lies apart from the village to the westward,
in a secluded woodland dell, to which the name of
Kirkdale is given. It was a chapel belonging to the
church of Pickering until 1252. On the slopes of the
'tabular' hills north of Ebberston is a series of
ancient earthworks of remarkable character. A long
entrenchment running north and south continues the
line of Netherby Dale; westward of this, and diagonal
to it, are the formidable Scamridge Dikes (concerning
which we gave General Pitt Rivers' opinion in the
introductory chapter); again, three-quarters of a mile
in the rear of these are the Givendale and Oxmoor
Dikes, and still another entrenchment is traceable in
the rear. The history of the many earthworks of the
Cleveland and 'tabular' hills, and of the Wolds, will,

it is to be hoped, one day be written more fully, for assuredly by them much light may be thrown upon the early conditions of the country, and presumably upon the warfare between the Celt and the Gael. In the hill above Ebberston is a small cave known as Alfred's Hole, wherein tradition—and an inscription once recorded it—avers that Ælfred of Northumbria, wounded in a great battle at the Scamridge Dikes, took shelter, only to be carried on the next day to Driffield, where he died.

More than a mile beyond Ebberston we reach Allerston, a pleasant village lying at the foot of Givendale, a hollow by no means rich in waters. A very interesting circumstance—if, indeed, it be an actual circumstance, for it depends upon the evidence of a single man — concerning the Civil Wars is associated with Allerston and its district. It appears from depositions at York Castle that, about a fortnight before Christmas, 1656, one Robert Awderson was riding a gray gelding when he met a certain Matthew Vasey of the Marrishes (which is a place about two miles south of Allerston, in the Vale of Pickering), who said to him that the gelding was a handsome animal, and that, if he would give it to King Charles, it would be £500 in his way some time. He further said that the other day three men from Bridlington-ward, one of whom was believed to be King Charles himself, had passed that way, and had gone to a house at Allerston, where 'the said men did lye downe on a bedd there, and gett some potchett eggs, and went

16

before day northward upon horses, each of about ten pounds price.' It would indeed be deeply interesting if it could be proved that Prince Charles was in Yorkshire in disguise at this time.

With a mere allusion to the retired hamlet of Wilton, upon the road between Allerston and Thornton-le-Dale, our descriptive westward wayfaring concludes, for the region beyond Wilton was dealt with in a previous chapter. The many historical, picturesque, and pleasant villages that lie at the foot of the 'tabular' hills are, as will be seen, evidence enough both of the importance of this district in early times, and of its prosperity at the present day.

CHAPTER XIII.

THE COAST FROM SCARBOROUGH TO BRIDLINGTON.

The Bays South of Scarborough—Geology—Filey—The Brig—
The Fishing Village—Filey Church—The Modern Watering
place — Neighbouring Villages — Flamborough Head — Its
Physical Characteristics — History — The Danes' Dike —
Capture of the Earl of Carrick off the Head, 1405—Paul
Jones—The Great Sea-fight of 1779—Flamborough Village—
The Constables—Caves and Rock Features—Bridlington Bay
—Landing of Queen Henrietta Maria and Bombardment of
Bridlington Quay—The Quay Town as a Modern Watering-
place—Bridlington Priory—Its History and Architecture.

To the south-east of Scarborough are three bays, to
be explored with care and discretion by the sands, or
with safety by the cliffs—Cornelian Bay, Cayton Bay,
and the bay at Gristhorpe. In all these the rocks are
boldly featured and, in their geological characters, full
of interest. The rough scars of the Black Rocks which
lie along the shore south of the Spa at Scarborough
are of the calcareous and ironstone beds of the estuarine
series of the Lower Oolite, and the cliffs are of the
carbonaceous sandstones and shales. The wayfaring
at low water is rough but exhilarating, and it is
interesting to notice the curious appearances of the

sandstones, which, with sharp flexures and inter-
mixtures of the shale, show that they have been
deposited by disturbed waters. Beyond the White
Nab, which is about a mile and a quarter from the
Spa, we enter Cornelian Bay, with its broken cliffs of
the same series, and the rugged scar may be sought
for its treasures of cornelian, jasper and moss-agate,
though these are not now so easily found among the
pebbles. The bold projection of Osgodly Nab stands
out at the other end of the bay, and separates it from
the greater sweep of Cayton Bay, where the Middle
Oolites, which have formed the grand northern escarpment of the 'tabular' hills, strike the coast. The
wayfarer will be well advised not to venture the
treacherous coast south-east of Cayton Bay, but there
to ascend the cliff to the highroad from Scarborough
to Filey. The Red Cliff (285 feet), at the northern end
of Gristhorpe Bay, consists of the Kelloways rock,
surmounted by the so-called Oxford clay, which is
capped by the lower calcareous grit. On the southern
side of this cliff is a dislocation, beyond which the
upper estuarine rocks rise to the high-water level, and
the tide sweeps round a lofty detached mass. Gristhorpe Cliff itself, which is separated from the Red
Cliff by a hollow partly filled with drift, has an elevation
of 280 feet at its northern end, sinking gradually along
the shore by Club Point to the long spur of Filey Brig,
and being gradually more and more thickly overlaid
with glacial deposits.

The sea views along this coast are wide and im-

pressive, and the cliffs, especially in the neighbourhood
of Gristhorpe, with the broad reefs below, and their
detached masses, though lower than those north of
Scarborough, have a very striking character, especially
when the north-easter blows hard, and the sea is white
with the serried ranks of the incoming waves, which
break upon the rocky scars, and throw up columns of
spray that are blown inland by the whistling wind.
The fringing country, which is well known to those
who take the pleasant drive from Scarborough to Filey,
falls gently from the cliffs to the foot of the Wolds,
the level edges and plantations of which, advancing
towards the shore from the southern flank of the Vale
of Pickering, are the most remarkable feature in the
inland prospect. The country is agricultural and
fruitful; and adjacent to the sea lie the tiny hamlet
of Osgodby, opposite Cayton Bay, and, upon the road
from Seamer to Filey, the rural villages of Cayton,
Lebberston, and Gristhorpe. It was upon the height
of Gristhorpe Cliff, about a mile from the village, that
the ancient oaken coffin, with its skeleton, which is
now in the Scarborough Museum, was discovered in
the year 1834, in a large tumulus. The skull, which has
been described by Retzius in the 'Crania Britannica'
(1849), was brachycephalic, and with a greater frontal
development than is common in skulls of like date.
With it were associated weapons, and objects of
bronze, bone, flint, and wood.

The coast has so far faced the north-east, but at
Filey, whither our wayfaring now brings us, it turns

at a right angle, and Filey itself faces the south-east, the long promontory of oolitic rock, and the natural breakwater of the Brig, protecting it on the north. The beautiful sweep of the great bay is over-looked by broken cliffs of boulder clay, and margined by the broad firm sands of Filey, Muston, and Hunmanby, and far out to the south runs the great chalk headland of Flamborough. Between the sea-ward termination of the oolitic rocks in the great reef of the Brig, and the chalk cliffs to the south, the sea has eaten out the bay, and it is worth while to mention that a lacustrine deposit is exposed upon the cliff. The Brig, which has made a natural harbour at the north end of Filey Bay, is a long spur of the sand-stone, dry at low water, its rocks deeply channelled, shattered, and worn. As Phillips says, it delights the naturalist with its many fucoids, corallines, radiata, and mollusca. 'After storms the shore is frequently one vast collection of the beautiful productions of the sea.' Nothing can be more exhilarating than to stand at low-water on a breezy day at the end of Filey Brig, with the waves dashing in silvery spray over the rocks, and eddying in the hollows, and a splendid prospect extending from Scarborough to Flamborough Head. The Romans recognised the importance of the place, and roads appear to have been directed upon it, and here was perhaps the 'well-havened bay' that Ptolemy speaks of. Indeed, jutting out at right angles from the Brig, some traces of an artificial pier have been found, assumed to be Roman, with certain shaped stones

THE COAST AT FILEY.   DRAWN BY ALFRED DAWSON.

above, whereof one was carved with figures of animals, these probably having served to support a beacon. . So obviously fitted is the bay for a harbour of refuge, sorely needed on this stormy coast, that many proposals, with the purpose of forming one, have been made, and the House of Commons even has adopted a resolution in favour of the project, but still no step is taken.

The cliffs of the bay are cleft by a number of small ravines, one of which, nearly a mile south of the Brig, now very picturesquely wooded, and laid out in pleasant grounds, separates the old fishing village of Filey from its church, and is spanned by a bridge. The village, inhabited by a race of hardy fishermen, who have manned their lifeboat in many a gale, is rather curious than picturesque, with its trim whitewashed cottages flanking the narrow streets and courts, and has something of a Flemish aspect. Crossing the bridge, we reach the church—a notable structure, with fine trees in its neighbourhood. There are evidences, in carved stones built up in it, that Filey was a religious centre in Saxon times, when it was a possession of Earl Tostig, and probably had an early church; but the origin of the existing structure may be ascribed to the care of the early canons of Bridlington, who served at Filey, and, indeed, had a small establishment there. The edifice consists of chancel, nave, aisles, transepts, and a low, broad central tower, and is mostly Transition Norman, and Early English. It was mutilated in 1839, but a restoration was effected with care and discretion a few years ago. The broad tower, with its corbel-table of grotesque heads, and its coupled lancets under round arches, has upon it weatherings which show that the roofs of the church were once very lofty, when the tower rose little above them, and the edifice must then have presented an appearance uncommon in Yorkshire. The Early English chancel, too, is remarkable, with its lancets and angle buttresses stepped from top to bottom. The church has no western door, there being a lancet and buttresses at that end; but, within the north porch, is a fine semicircular arch, of four orders of mouldings and shafts. The nave pillars are alternately round and octagonal, and support pointed arches, above each of which is a narrow, deeply-splayed, round-headed clerestory window. The tower is supported by fine ribbed columns. The transepts, like the chancel, are Early English, with rich arcading in the one on the south, but much of the aisle walls is modern.

The modern town of Filey lies upon the cliff to the south of the old fishing village, and is an excellent resort for those who love quiet, and the charms of a beautiful bay, margined by firm sands, along which one may gallop for miles. In front of the terraces are well-kept gardens and tennis-courts, from which paths lead down to the shore, and, as one stands at the top, columns of spray are seen rising from the Brig even in calm weather, as the waves break upon it, while their thunders are plainly audible in the storms. And yet, though at Filey there is rest and retirement, there lie within reach, as the readers of this book know, and will further see, not only a number of interesting and beautiful places, but all the attractions of modern Scarborough, too.

And now, in our descriptive wayfaring towards Flamborough Head, certain villages in the neighbourhood of the coast call for a few words from us. The rural hamlet of Muston, at the foot of the Wolds, a mile and a half from Filey, needs no special note. It was here that the vicar, in the days of the 'Pilgrims,' made common talk of those prophecies of 'Merlin and Thomas of Erceldoune' to which we referred in the chapter on Scarborough. Hunmanby, with an unmistakable Danish name, a mile and a half beyond Muston, most beautifully placed beneath the woods, looks across the cornfields to the white cliffs of Flamborough far out at sea. It has a church with a Norman tower and chancel arch, Early English pillars, and windows of both the Geometrical and flowing Decorated. The farmsteads hereabout are embowered amid trees, and in the summer evenings you will often see 'the many-wintered crow, that leads the clanging rookery home,' with his far-stretched followers, winging his way thitherward across the cornfields. Two miles south-eastward along the road is Reighton, finely placed upon the height that the Wolds here throw out towards Flamborough, and looking far out across Filey Bay. There is a small church, with Norman features in its massive nave arcades and its doorway. Other rural hamlets on the landward side of Flamborough Head, pleasantly situated upon the chalk hills, are Speeton, with geological characters presently to be alluded to, Buckton, Bempton, through which the road from Scarborough leads out to the headland, and Marton. The railway line between Scarborough and Hull makes the whole of this country accessible.

Flamborough Head is the last splendid feature of the Yorkshire coast that it falls to us to describe. Here, in one of the boldest promontories of the British coasts, the chalk, which constitutes the rounded hills of the Wolds, reaches the sea, and presents to it those sheer, white, water-worn cliffs which, though they lack the animation of the Lias and Oolite scarps to the north, have yet a massive and solemn grandeur peculiarly their own. As we proceed south-eastward along the sands of Filey Bay, the first new formation reached is the everted end of the Speeton (Neocomian) clay, which, with a southern dip, presents a cliff 200 feet high, and has given up the teeth and vertebræ of saurians, and many beautiful ammonites, hamites, and nuculæ, as well as other fossils. It passes beneath the red chalk, and this again beneath the white chalk, that gives all its character to Flamborough. The chalk cliffs attain their greatest altitude, with sheer scarps (436 feet), near Speeton, owing partly to the accretion of drift upon the top. A mile further on there is a curious flexure of the stratification; then we reach the northern end of the Danes' Dyke, and shortly the cliffs sink to a height of some 150 feet. It is here, on the northern side of the headland, that they are so curiously water-worn. On the southern side the cliffs are still lower, and the chalk sinks below high-water level half a mile beyond Sewerby Hall.

A position so remarkable as this, as a stronghold and vantage-point, would not escape the attention of the earliest inhabitants. We may believe, with General Pitt Rivers, as we have already said, that the so-called Danes' Dike is a defensive work, thrown up by some invader who had gained a footing in the promontory— perhaps of the Celtic incomer who displaced the still more ancient Gael.* On the southern side, the double earthen ramparts follow the eastern flank of a deep and precipitous valley, which opens to the sea between cliffs 109 feet in height, and which answered as a fosse in front of them; and a formidable defence is continued across to the edge of the cliff on the north, the work being in all two and three-quarter miles long. It seems not improbable that the Romans had a camp here, but it is certain that the Angles occupied the promontory, for it was they who gave it its name, from the beacon-light they maintained upon it. The Northmen, too, to whom the Dike has been ascribed, doubtless established themselves upon it, and the part between the earthwork and the head has sometimes been called 'Little Denmark.' Before the Conquest it was a possession of Harold, and afterwards came to William le Gros; but throughout the Middle Ages it was a lord-ship of one branch of the great house of Constable, of certain of whose members we shall presently speak.

* Pages 7 and 8 *ante.*

By its very position upon the coast, Flamborough has witnessed many seafaring incidents, whereof two only need be alluded to here. It was off the Head in 1405 that, in disregard of the truce, the young Earl of Carrick, afterwards James I. of Scotland, was captured by an armed merchantman of Wye as he was being conveyed, for his education, to the court of France.

Coming to more modern times, one of the most important naval actions that ever took place near the Yorkshire coast was that off Flamborough Head on September 23, 1779, which was witnessed by crowds from the headland. The celebrated pirate Paul Jones had spread terror along the coast, and it is still related that whenever he sailed by Mappleton, in Holderness, he was wont to salute Mr. William Brough—a former marshal of the Admiralty, who had superintended the execution of Byng — for whom he had a particular enmity, with a well-shotted gun fairly aimed at that gentleman's house, which was a conspicuous object upon the coast. The action of 1779 has been graphically described by Cooper in the ' Pilot.' It was a period of decline in the English naval power, and Jones, with a squadron sailing under the stars and stripes, had swept along the Yorkshire coast and driven the trading craft to port. He was in command of a French East Indiaman, which had been renamed the *Bonhomme Richard* out of compliment to Franklin, whose ' Poor Richard's Almanack' had just been translated into French, under the title of ' La Science du Bonhomme Richard.' She was frigate-built, with this peculiarity, that she had a lower battery, and she carried a scratch armament of forty guns in all. In her company were the *Alliance*, an American bomb-frigate of thirty-six guns; and the French vessels *Pallas*, thirty-two guns, and *Vengeance*, twelve guns. A convoy of merchant-men, escorted by the *Serapis*, forty-four guns, Captain Pearson, and by the *Countess of Scarborough*, a hired vessel mounting six-pounders on a flush deck, Captain Percy, coming over from the Baltic, was sighted, and Jones with his force gave chase, for as soon as the English naval officers saw the American, they stretched to the southward with the wind at south-west, sending the convoy inshore. The battle was fought with great valour by the two Englishmen, and, in her engagement with the *Serapis*, the *Bonhomme Richard* lost three hundred killed and wounded, and sank after the battle, carrying many wounded with her. Pearson, however, though a brave man, was no match for Jones, but would probably not have hauled down his colours, which he did in the end, but for the presence of the *Alliance*, which had taken small part in the battle. The *Countess of Scarborough*, after a gallant struggle, struck her flag to the *Pallas*. As, however, the convoy had escaped, the material advantage was held to have been on the side of the English. The London merchants, therefore, gave Pearson a sword, and the king knighted him, whereupon Jones made the characteristic remark : ' Should I have the good fortune to fall in with him again I'll make a lord of him.'

So much of the general features and maritime history

of Flamborough Head being before us, it will be well to take a descriptive journey to some of its more interesting scenes. The approach is usually made by vehicle from the station at Marton or from Bridlington Quay, and a very pleasant drive it is, between green fields and tangled hedgerows, passing the Danes' Dike, to the fishing village of Flamborough.* There is a Decorated church, restored, dedicated to the patron of Northumbrian fisher - folk, St. Oswald, with a splendid Perpendicular screen and rood-loft of carved oak, once richly painted and gilt. You will see near the village, too, the square and ruinous keep of a former castle, now known as the Danish Tower, but probably the last relic of the house of the Constables of Flamborough. In the year 1320, Sir Robert Constable of this place went with the Earl of Richmond on state business into France, and Archbishop Melton commanded the prior and convent of Bridlington to hold over a lawsuit they had against him until his return. There remains, too, in Flamborough Church, the epitaph of Sir Marmaduke Constable, who fought

---

* It is possible, under exceptionally favourable circumstances of tide and season, to walk from Bridlington Quay, along the narrow strip of beach, past the South Landing, to Selwicks (or Selex) Bay below the lighthouse ; but the author very strongly advises no one to make the venture, for there are many places hereabout from which there is no escape from the incoming sea. In fact, the exploration of the Flamborough caves should never be made except with the advice of the fishermen. Moreover, a tide-table should always be carried, and it should be remembered that the tide flows nine minutes earlier at the Head than it does at Bridlington Quay.

in France under Edward IV. and Henry VII., and who, being then of the age of seventy years, was present at Flodden Field, named in the inscription ' Brankiston Feld,' with ' his sonnes, brothers, servants, and kynsmenne.' There lingers also at Flamborough the memory of that Sir Robert Constable who was concerned with Aske and Darcy in the Pilgrimage of Grace. After the ' pardon,' Norfolk was in fear lest he should escape from Flamborough by sea, but the knight fell into the toils. Aske wrote, indeed, to Henry VIII. that Constable had ' stayed the people ' subsequent to the ' pardon,' and he, before he was hanged in chains at Hull, asseverated the same thing; but the charge against him was that he had been guilty of treason, with Bigod, Bulmer, and the others, at Flamborough and elsewhere, on January 17, 1537.

The sheer cliffs of Flamborough, gleaming dazzling white in the sunlight, with their faces scarred, seamed, and rifted, and the sea breaking in glittering spray at their feet, or thundering in some huge cave, whereof you see from your boat the dark opening below, while above, on the ledges, sit myriads of gulls, cormorants, auks, grebes, guillemots, puffins, razor-bills, gannets, petrels, and other seabirds, is a sight never to be forgotten. The caves are most usually approached, and the spectacle is most readily gained, from the North Landing, where boats are easily procurable, and whither the conveyances drive from the village. It is not difficult from this point to reach the largest of the caverns—Robin Lyth's Hole, said to derive its name from a terrible freebooter—which is nearly fifty feet high, and is approached by a steep, narrow path from the landward. The pathway is easily practicable as you descend at low water, but there are hidden pools within, avoiding which you go down to where the seaward opening frames a glorious prospect of the waters, and, looking back, see the walls of the cave above glistening with weird effect. Not far away, on the other side of the landing-place, is the rocky arch known as Bacon Flitch Hole, and Thornwick Bay may be reached by the cliff-tops, crossing the Ghaut Ravine. The headland is very curiously waterworn at Thornwick into little inlets and coves, and the huge cliff lies upon the water like the heavy paw of some colossal beast, while the great cliffs of Speeton lie beyond, where the sea-fowl mostly have their haunts. On the other hand, between the north landing-place and the point of the headland, the cliffs are curiously indented, and in one cove stand the two remarkable detached pinnacles known as the King and Queen. Further on is Selwicks (or Selex) Bay, with a curious pillar at either end of it, and hereabout the chalk is water-worn in a very curious and fantastic manner. The beauties and marvels of Flamborough will be best discovered by exploration under the guidance of some fisherman of the headland. There are, indeed, a multitude of other caves, arches, and projecting masses, many of which can best be seen from a boat. The lighthouse, too, above Selwicks Bay, at the eastern point, may be visited. It exhibits a revolving

THE KING AND QUEEN ROCKS, FLAMBOROUGH HEAD.   DRAWN BY ALFRED DAWSON.

white and red light, visible at a distance of nineteen miles, while from the rocket station at the cliff edge a dynamite rocket is discharged every five minutes during foggy weather.

Flamborough Head protects Bridlington Bay, which lies to the south of it, from all the north-eastern storms, and creates what was known of old time, perhaps—though whether Filey has the better right to it, who shall say?—as the *Portus Felix;* and, of Ptolemy, the ' well-havened bay ' or ' bay of the Gabran-tovici,' perhaps a misreading for ' Brigantovici '— Γαβραντουικων ὁ και λεγομενος Ευλιμενος κολπος. The bay, however, is not so well-havened as to secure absolute immunity from danger, as is witnessed by a memorial in the Bridlington churchyard, a mile inland, which records the burial of forty-three sailors and three ship-masters who perished, with many companions, in the terrible storm of February 10, 1871, when twenty-three vessels foundered in the bay. But it was a harbour of the priors of Bridlington, and has long been a favourite landing-place.

The Stuarts, as we have seen, having strong support in the North, had naturally recourse to the Yorkshire coast, and in 1643 Queen Henrietta Maria, returning from Helvoetsluys under convoy of Van Tromp and seven Dutch men-of-war, bringing with her the arms and supplies which she had purchased in Holland by her disposal of the crown jewels, landed at Bridlington Quay. Batten, the Parliamentary admiral, who had been on the look-out to intercept her, had been out-

17

witted, but he put into Bridlington Bay two days later with four ships, and cannonaded the town—the queen, still lodged in a house in Queen Square, being compelled to seek shelter, half naked, in a ditch. Van Tromp, however, whose vigilance had been strangely relaxed, then hove in sight, and drove off the outnumbered Englishmen. A rumour was spread abroad in 1666 that the Dutch had landed at Bridlington Quay, in relation to which a certain William Hunsloe of Walkington remarked in public that 'the Dutch had got the better, and were landed upon the coast at Bridlington, and that hee would lead them on.' 'What was the king?' he asked. 'Hee was but a chimney-sweeper, and hee would justifie it,' for which traitorous expression the said pot-valiant hero was pilloried at Bridlington, as well as at York and Beverley.

In these days Bridlington Quay is a popular watering-place, which, with its firm level sands and generally calm waters, affords every facility for boating, fishing, and bathing ; and it has the attractions of its two piers, inclosing the harbour, a sea parade, and many entertainments in the summer, as well as in its nearness to Flamborough Head, Bridlington Priory, and a number of interesting villages. Itself an ancient fishing village, it still has the quaint red-tiled cottages of the fisher-folk, and the modern hotels and terraces of houses are an engraftment upon its original character, not quite so happy in their effect as like engraftments at Whitby and Scarborough, where the old and the new stand side by side. Hilderthorpe, on the south sands, though an ancient place, has the aspect of a modern suburb.

Bridlington, sometimes called Burlington, about a mile from the Quay town, glories in a splendid ecclesiastical remain, save Whitby and Rievaulx the most remarkable to which our wayfaring has brought us, and worthy in many ways to be compared with Beverley, which we have yet to describe. The Augustinian canons were established at Bridlington by Walter de Gant, grandson of Baldwin, Count of Flanders, in the reign of Henry I. The Yorkshire baronage showered possessions upon them; they were greatly favoured by many kings; and they reared and perfected a splendid house, bringing the stone from Filey, by favour of Ralph de Neville. The prior was summoned to Parliament by Henry II. When the Archdeacon of Richmond, it is interesting to learn, chose to make his visitation of their house, bringing with him a cavalcade of ninety-seven horses, as well as twenty-one dogs and three hawks, whereby, in a single hour, provisions were consumed that would have long sufficed for the whole house, Innocent III. forbade him thenceforth to journey with greater attendance than was permitted by the Council of Lateran. William of Langtoft, the mediæval chronicler, was a canon of Bridlington, as William of Newburgh, a native of the place, had at one time been before him, and it is singular that the sole historical mention of him that seems to remain, apart from his literary work, shows him in not a very favourable light, for in 1293 Archbishop Romanus bade the prior call him back from the south, whither he had gone, pretending, contrary to the fact, that he had an archiepiscopal license so to do.* The priory probably suffered from the attacks of pirates, for, in 1388, Richard II. gave license to inclose and fortify it. Prior John de Thweng, who died in 1379, had a great reputation for sanctity, and miracles were said to have been wrought at his tomb; and it would appear that the proceedings for his canonization were completed, for the prior was venerated as St. John of Bridlington, and the Archbishop of York and other prelates translated his relics to a shrine behind the high altar. Sir George Ripley, the alchemist, who died a Carmelite at Boston in 1492, had been a canon of Bridlington. The last prior, William Wood, died at Tyburn for his share in the Pilgrimage of Grace, and also Dr. John Pickering, a preaching friar of Bridlington, who had composed verses held to be treasonable, beginning, 'O Faithful people of the Boreal region,' making reference to the 'naughty Cromwell,' and comparing him to Haman for persecuting the commons as Haman persecuted the Jews.

> 'If this Aman were hanged then der I well say
>   This realm then redresséd full soon should be,
> And the bishops reformed in a new array.'

These verses were said to be in everyone's mouth at Bridlington and Pontefract. We have some precise

* 'Reg. Archiep. Romani,' apud Ebor., 44 b.

information as to the destruction that went on at Bridlington shortly afterwards. Cromwell instructed Norfolk that the shrine was to be taken down, the plate and jewels sent up to London, and the corn and cattle sold. On June 5, 1537, Norfolk sent to Henry all the adornments of gold from the shrine, and other objects—'and if I durst be a thief, I would have stolen them to have sent them to the queen's grace; but now your highness having them may give them unto her without offence.' On the same date Norfolk sends a letter to Cromwell, touching this spoliation, with certain personal touches which we will refrain from reproducing, but which are enough to damn the characters of both.* Richard Pollard was the minion sent down to carry on the work of destruction. He described the house as out of repair, and said he never saw people so needy as in those parts. He had 500 marks offered for the lead from a single barn, and thought the lead from the whole priory would be worth little less than £1,000. So was the priory stripped, the lead cast into sows, and the whole made money of. Richard Bellasis carried on the sordid work. In November, 1537, he described how much he had accomplished at Jervaulx, and was minded to let that house stand until the spring. 'As for Byrdlington, I spare it till next March, as the days are now so short.'

The church at Bridlington, as we now see it, is

* 'Letters and Papers, Foreign and Domestic, of the Reign of Henry VIII.,' vol. xii., part ii., Nos. 34, 35.

therefore but the wreck of the splendid fabric that the Augustinians reared — the sole fragment that was spared, not from the fury of iconoclastic zeal, but from the shocking, sordid, calculating destruction that was wrought at the bidding of Henry by Bellasis and his fellows. It is to be observed that the relationship between the houses of the Canons Regular of St. Augustine and parish churches was regular and normal, and, in fact, the canons of Bridlington adopted and re-edified the church which had existed at the time of the Domesday survey. It was upon the choir, as more especially reserved to the monks, that the hand of the destroyer fell. This, in fact, was taken down at the Dissolution, and the great central tower, being thus deprived of proper support, fell, and destroyed the transepts also, so that, of a great cruciform structure once 360 feet in length, there remains little more than the nave, the existing east end being patched up from the fragments. The Decorated window inserted therein was designed by Sir Gilbert Scott at the restoration, when the present roof was put up. The north flanking tower is very early Decorated, with earlier work at the base, where is a walled-up round arch. The rest of the west front is of very fine Perpendicular character, strongly resembling that at Beverley. The deep panelled buttresses of this front, the many canopied niches, now tenantless, together with the richly-carved and moulded doorway, and its ogee canopy, and the lofty west window, filled with good modern glass, which has a transom projecting

in an unusual manner, give exceeding richness to
the whole work. The south - western tower is of
like character, the details of its buttresses and windows being exceedingly rich; but its upper works
and crocketed pinnacles are recent—a hideous brick
octagon, which once crowned it, having been removed.
The wall of the north aisle is Early English, with
lancet windows; but the clustered piers, triforium, and
clerestory on that side are early Decorated. This triforium has, in the eastern bays, two two-light arched
windows within a circular arch, enriched with trefoils
and quatrefoils in the tympana, the main triforium
arches westward being pointed, while there are single
geometrical windows of fine character in the clerestory.
On the south side the easternmost piers are early
Decorated, the others having been cased in the Perpendicular period. Above is a triforium passage
behind a range of tracery, and the triforium itself is
united with the clerestory. The windows are of the
geometrical Decorated, somewhat later than that of
the north side, and the eastern aisle windows are of
the same character; but the aisle wall to the west,
against which the prior's lodge was built, is blank.
The cloister was on this side. On the other side, the
north porch will be noticed as a splendid work, exceedingly rich and elaborate, with its dog-tooth and nail-
head mouldings, and with carvings of a king, queen,
and bishop in the shafts of the portal. The wayfarer
whose journey brings him to Bridlington may spend a
long time in the examination of the splendid detail and

interesting features, which here want of space will not permit us to describe. The shattered Bayle Gate, with a chamber over it, is the last relic of the fortifications erected for the defence of the priory in the reign of Richard II. It passed, after the Dissolution, by purchase to the Bridlington men, and its chamber was used as a town-hall, and its cellars, known by the name of Kidcote, as a gaol. The fair which the canons of Bridlington were authorized to hold by King John is still held between the Bayle Gate and the church. Enough, then, has been said to show that, though Bridlington is sadly shorn of its magnificence, and all its domestic offices have disappeared, it yet possesses more than enough of architectural beauty to attract the wayfarer thither.

CHAPTER XIV.

THE COAST OF HOLDERNESS.

In faring southward from Bridlington, in this descriptive
journey, we leave behind us all that is impressively
picturesque on the Yorkshire coast to traverse the
monotonous seaward fringe of Holderness, and this
we must speak of somewhat briefly. Holderness is,
indeed, full of attraction for the geologist; it possesses
also in many parts a certain picturesqueness of its
own, and it has many interesting places. Beverley,
more interesting than any of them, will occupy us in
the next chapter, and we shall here deal chiefly with
places that neighbour the shore.

The geological history of Holderness speaks plainly
of a time when the sea beat against the chalk hills of
the Wolds just as now it does against the white cliffs

of Flamborough ; for Holderness itself, resting upon the cretaceous formation, here sunk far below the sea-level, is a vast deposit of the great glacial drift, consisting of boulder clay and gravel, which has filled what must once have been a great bay lying between Flamborough Head and some promontory answering to the Spurn, and which has brought with it worn and shattered fragments of rocks from Scandinavia, Scotland, Cumberland, Durham, and many parts of Yorkshire, sweeping down also with these the characteristic corals of the mountain limestone, the fossil plants of the coal series, ammonites and other shells from the lias, and many fossils from the chalk, as well as the bones of the mammoth and other antediluvian animals, which, from their being little worn, appear not to have been transported far.   There supervened upon this age a period in which, under favourable climatic conditions, the many meres left by the retiring waters of the glacial deluge—of which Hornsea Mere is now the sole considerable representative—were embosomed in dense forests, in which the great Irish elk, and boars, wolves, red and fallow deer, wild oxen, and other animals, had their haunts.   Again the conditions changed, and the dense forests and marshes were overlaid, in some places very thickly, with silt, sand, and clay, which is now found resting upon a bed of peat, wherein lie the trunks of great trees of the ancient forest.   Exposed to the action of the sea, the boulder cliffs have been progressively eaten away, and whole villages have been engulfed.   The sedimentary deposits of the ancient lakes are now exposed upon the beach, and every cliff is hastening to its fall; while the rolling fragments washed from the further north are swept along the shore to build up the pebbly isthmus of the Spurn.

Before, however, we go southward along the coast, certain places near Bridlington, and upon the borders of the Wolds, demand our attention. Some two miles west of the town, in a pleasant wooded country watered by the Gipsy Beck, lies Boynton, where the church has a good Perpendicular tower and modern nave and chancel. The Hall is the seat of Sir Charles W. Strickland, baronet. The family was established here by William Strickland, whose portrait is at the Hall, a comrade in American discovery of Sebastian Cabot. Further on is Rudstone-on-the-Wolds (the Rodestan of Domesday), named from a great 'standing stone' of fine oolitic grit, probably from the moors near Scarborough, which is 24 feet in height (it is proved to be as long below ground), nearly 6 feet broad, and 2 feet 3 inches thick—a strange weird object, as you see its dark form against the western sky at sunset. The restored church, too, is noteworthy, with its Norman tower and tower arch, and characteristic font of the same period, and its early Decorated chancel, with fine geometrical 'roll tracery' in its east window, and three two-light windows on each side. On the road from Bridlington to Driffield, at the foot of the Wolds, and with a wide prospect of the flat country of Holderness to the south, lie Bessingby, a pleasant, but not otherwise notable, village; Carnaby, with a

church of some interest; and Burton Agnes. It is well
worth while to pursue the wayfaring to the last-named
place, where there is a noteworthy church, 'restored'
by Archdeacon Wilberforce, who set the fashion of
'restoration' hereabout. The late Norman and Early
English arcades, and the Perpendicular work in the
tower, are good, and the Elizabethan monuments remarkable. Burton Agnes Hall, the Jacobean seat of
Sir Henry S. Boynton, baronet, built of brick, with stone
coigns, and with a very picturesque gateway, standing
amid its woods, is a fine object in the landscape. Inigo
Jones added to it in 1628. In the middle compartment
of the façade the bays are square, while in the wings
they are octagonal. Within, the hall is rich with carvings of Scriptural subjects in wood and alabaster; the
dining-room has a curious carved 'Empire of Death'
over the mantel; and the 'long gallery,' approached by
a picturesque staircase, has a ceiling elaborately carved
with climbing roses and other flowers upon a trellis-
work.

It is a distance of nearly three miles along the sands
from Bridlington Quay to Auburn, by the little hamlet
of Wilsthorpe; and the yellow sands and blue sea,
and the fresh sweet air, must suffice for the pedestrian,
for the cliff, which is of clay and gravel, rises at most
about 30 feet, and at Auburn, and for some distance
further still, sinks to a height of 7 feet only. Auburn
yet holds a feeble remnant of its former self against
the incroaching sea, which for centuries has been
sucking its seaward houses down, in the ruins of one

of which, as William Strickland of Boynton wrote to
Cecil as long ago as 1571, coins of Vespasian and
other Roman emperors were found.   Hartburn, a mile
further on, has altogether disappeared, like Elestolf
and Widlafeston, which, though named in Domesday,
are believed now to lie somewhere in the sands of
Bridlington Bay.   At the site of Hartburn, the water
of the Earl's Dike reaches the sea, and a mile and a
half further on, past the small elevation of Hamilton
Hill, we reach Barmston, set back a little from the
shore, in a richly cultivated country, for nearly the
whole of Holderness is very fruitful.   Barmston has
an interesting church, with a hagioscope between the
south aisle and the chancel; and the recumbent effigy
of a knight, said to be of Sir Martin de la See, who
died in 1497 (but apparently earlier), clad in plate
armour, with a jewelled baldric, and the words ' Jesu
Nazare ' upon his basinet.   In like armour, and with
like inscription, is the half-length effigy of Sir Thomas
de Wendesley, 1403, in Bakewell Church, Derbyshire.

About half a mile south of Barmston the Barmston
water opens to the sea, bringing with it, by means of
an artificial drain, the water of the Stream Dike, which
rises further south near Hornsea Mere, and, flowing
north, would otherwise, after joining the Old Howe
water, turn southward to the Hull.   Ulrome Grange,
standing upon an elevation of the boulder clay near
the shore, is separated by the Stream Dike from
another small elevation (25 feet), known as Goose

Island, and there seems to be no doubt that, in a long-
past age, the Dike was a waterway between two of the
Holderness meres. The deeply interesting discovery
was investigated a few years ago by Mr. Boynton, of
Ulrome Grange, while the artificial drainage was being
deepened, of a lake-dwelling, upon the course of this
water. At a depth of 3 feet below the ground level,
and some 10 feet above the bottom of the old lake,
the surface of a platform, in size about 75 feet by
50 feet, was found. This platform consisted of felled
trunks, not squared, some of them 15 or 18 inches
in diameter, of oak, birch, two varieties of willow, alder,
ash, and hazel, with brushwood, placed in alternate
layers at right angles to one another, and stayed by
stakes and buttress - like piles. The platform was
assumed to be of two periods, for the lower construction gave rude and unusual implements of flint, bone,
and stone, with fragments of dark pottery, while a
bronze spearhead was found in the upper portions,
which also showed traces of the use of metal tools.
Bones of the ox, horse, deer, wolf or dog, sheep, boar,
and presumably of the otter and goose, were associated
with the platform. Traces of other lake-dwellings
have been discovered in the same waterway, and may
be compared with that of the pile-dwelling at Barton
Mere, Bury St. Edmunds.* The hamlet of Ulrome,
which preserves for us the name of some Danish Ulf,

* At Driffield is a museum very rich in the prehistoric evidences
of this region, built by Mr. Mortimer, who has given up many
years to patient exploration of them.

perhaps of the great Ulf to be referred to presently in relation to Aldborough, has a small church with some very ancient portions, including a round - headed doorway. In relation to Ulrome, it is melancholy to note, as at a great many other places in Holderness and elsewhere in the neighbouring country, that Dr. Heneage Dering, Archdeacon of the East Riding, though a scholar, inaugurated in 1720, and carried out, a barbarous destruction of chancel-screens, which stripped many churches of much of their interest.

More than a mile south of Ulrome, the coast continuing of the same character, marked here and there by fresh-water deposits exposed upon the low boulder cliffs, we reach Skipsea, standing a little back from the shore. Here is a restored church, with Early English arches resting upon octagonal piers, and Perpendicular walls and tower. The place is separated from the hamlet of Skipsea Brough by a drained marsh, through which the Stream Dike flows; and here rises a mound, with an encircling rampart, known as Albemarle Hill, which was almost certainly the site of the castle - keep of Drogo de Beurere, the Conqueror's Flemish companion, to whom he gave most of the possessions, in Holderness, of Morkere, Tostig, and Ulf, and who here had his *caput baroniæ*. A witchcraft story, it may be mentioned, lingers at Skipsea. It is on record that, in 1650, one Ann Hudson of that place was charged as a witch, and it was said that a sick person, having 'scratched her and drawn blood,' had recovered.

In a fresh-water deposit exposed at Skipsea, bones of the great Irish elk have been discovered. Further south the boulder clay rises to the comparatively considerable height of nearly sixty feet at Skirlington Hill, but falls again to Atwick, where the tusk of an elephant has been found, and the cliffs thence to the great depression of Hornsea Gap are of the height of some forty feet. Hornsea aspires to be a watering-place, and is chiefly resorted to by the inhabitants of Hull, with which it is in railway communication. For those who love quiet, with the pleasures of a level shore, though one in no way picturesque, and of an agricultural country, it is not without attractions in the summer-time, and it affords excellent opportunities of studying the evidences of the boulder clay. The Mere, too, is interesting, as the last considerable lake of Holderness, and, dotted with wooded islets, is not unpicturesque. It is slowly tending to the same end as its fellows—filling gradually with earthy deposits and vegetable accretions, and being approached almost perceptibly by the all-devouring sea. It is now scarcely two miles long, some five miles in circumference, and, at its broadest, three-quarters of a mile in width, and it is well stocked with coarse fish. A curious legendary story concerning it has been circulated, but is of very doubtful authority, though it has recently been repeated.* It is to the effect that, in the time of Henry III., upon a dispute between the abbots of

* 'Yorkshire Legends and Traditions.' Second Series. By the Rev. Thomas Parkinson. 1891.

St. Mary's at York, and of Meaux, touching the right of fishing in a portion of the Mere, trial by battle having been adopted for decision as to the rival claims, the champions of Meaux, after fighting a whole day, were utterly defeated, and that the Mere remained thenceforth, as it certainly did, a possession of St. Mary's Abbey. The church at Hornsea was restored by Sir Gilbert Scott. It has many Decorated features, and its Perpendicular clerestory and chancel are excellent. Places of some interest in the inland country are Sigglesthorne, where there is a restored church with an Early English tower, and Brandsburton, where the church has fine brasses of Sir John St. Quintin and his lady, and of William Darell, all of the second half of the fourteenth century.

Two miles south of Hornsea stands Rowlston Hall, whereat Paul Jones was wont to discharge well-shotted guns whenever he sailed thereby, as was mentioned in the last chapter in relation to the great sea-fight off Flamborough Head; and beyond it Mappleton, where is a restored church, with Early English and Decorated features. Here the boulder cliffs, which are being eaten with exceeding rapidity, maintain exactly the same character, and are some sixty feet in height, as they continue to be for some miles more. The pleasant, rural village of Aldborough is set a little back from the shore, more than three miles south of Mappleton, and appears to have retreated inland, as its seaward portions were washed away. Here probably dwelt that Ulf, son of Thorold, lord of much of

18

Holderness before the Conquest, who so richly endowed with lands the cathedral church of St. Peter at York, including in his grant Godmundham, where Coifi brake the idols of Thor and Woden, and placing his horn upon the altar in token thereof.* There is a stone built up in the existing church at Aldborough—an inscribed dial, divided like that at Kirkdale, which we have already described, into eight hour-spaces — which shows us that a church stood here before the Conquest, built by this same Ulf. It bears the following inscription :

VLF HET ARÆRAN CYRICE FOR HANVM AND FOR GVNTHARD
SAVLA.

(Ulf had this church built for the souls of Hanum and Gunthard.)

The church of Ulf, however, was probably washed away, for a new structure was erected in the middle of the fourteenth century, and this, again, has been mostly rebuilt, though apparently in imitation of its predecessor. There remain a fine and colossal effigy of Sir John de Meaux (ob. 1377), the last of his race, with a helmet hanging above it (which, as they say, in the evil time, was used as a coal-scuttle !), and another of a lady, probably the wife of Sir John, both of them somewhat defaced.

* This celebrated 'horn,' which is in reality formed from an elephant's tusk, and is enriched about the mouth with carvings of griffins and other animals, is still preserved at York. It was lost during the Civil Wars, but was restored by one of the Fairfaxes, who obtained possession of it, not, however, before its ornaments of gold had been stolen. In 1675 it was banded, and provided with a chain of silver-gilt.

We might pursue our wayfaring inland a few miles
from Aldborough to the great and stately wooded park
of Burton Constable (Sir F. A. Talbot Clifford-Constable,
baronet), with its red and fallow deer, and its great
house, the historic seat of the Constables, dating from
the time of Henry VIII., with Jacobean fronts, and
many splendid apartments within, including a great
and notable library, concerning all which very much
might be said. As for the coast southward of Aldborough, it preserves exactly the same unpicturesque
character by East Newton, Ringborough, and Grimston Garth, where are traces of the ancient home of
the Grimstons, now replaced by a modern house not
far away. At Hilston Mount the cliffs rise to a height
of some eighty feet; and upon them an octagonal tower
of brick, built, about 1750, by Admiral Storr, whose
family mansion here has disappeared, forms a prominent mark upon the long low coast-line. At Hilston
is an exquisite modern church, of small dimensions,
erected in memory of Lady Sykes of Sledmere, which
retains the south door of a Norman structure. The
cliffs now begin to fall, by Tunstall, where is an un-
important church of Early English and Perpendicular
features, to Sandley Mere, over part of whose ancient
bed the sea deposits its sands. The sea is here kept
back only by a reedy flat, and by a broad tract of sand
and pebbles washed up the beach, and sometimes a
high tide will rush over the barrier, and, but for an
artificial bank, would flow down the country beyond
to the Humber. In this lacustrine formation bones

of oxen and deer, with stag-horns, have been found, while, from time to time, the teeth of elephants, worn by attrition, are washed out of the boulder clay.

Still further south is Owthorne, crumbling rapidly away beneath the ceaseless wearing of the sea, and just beyond it a curious lacustrine deposit. Phillips's remarks concerning this are worth quoting: ' This deposit ends towards the north, near the little project-ing cliff which is all that remains of the churchyard of Owthorne, the church having been sometime washed away, and the churchyard so rapidly wasted that all the gravestones have been removed. The buried bones of former generations, which are seen projecting from the crumbling cliff, have a singular appearance, and, combined with the falling of the cliff and the roar of the destroying waves, fill the con-templative mind with solemn and awful reflections.'* This lacustrine deposit lies between Owthorne and Withernsea, and greatly resembles that already described at Sandley Mere. It consists of blue clay, with a bed superimposed of peat, full of hazel-nuts and branches, with some animal remains. A tragic and singular incident is associated with Owthorne. ' In the vicarage of Owthorne,' says ' Murray's Guide,' ' the Rev. Enoch Sinclair was murdered in 1788 by his two nieces and a servant named Alvin. Alvin afterwards married the elder niece. Her sister, four years after-wards, confessed the crime on her death-bed. Alvin was taken and condemned; but during the preaching

* ' Illustrations of the Geology of Yorkshire,' 1829, p. 63.

of the "condemned" sermon at York he protested his
innocence aloud. The shock proved fatal to the
preacher, a Mr. Mace, who fell dead in the pulpit.
The murderer declared that the hand of God was
evident, and the "vox populi" supported him; but he
confessed his guilt the next day on the scaffold!'

Withernsea is a watering-place in direct railway
communication with Hull, and is a pleasant seashore
resort, where boating and bathing with pure and
healthful air can be enjoyed; but its utter want of
picturesqueness deprives it of other attractions. Here
again is the melancholy record of land washed away
by the sea, for the spot upon which stood the ancient
church of Withernsea lies under water, and the present
pleasing late Perpendicular edifice was consecrated in
1488.

There is a great deal of excellent church architecture
in Holderness, and we shall here step aside from our
wayfaring along the coast to describe the magnificent
edifice at Patrington, which lies between the coast
and the Humber. This splendid fane—due doubtless
to the Archbishops of York, who possessed the manor—
is known as the ' Queen ' of Holderness—of the ' King '
(Hedon) we shall speak in our last chapter—and is a
prominent landmark for all the country-side, as well
as far out at sea. It consists of nave and chancel,
with aisles, north and south transepts, also with
aisles, and a remarkable central tower and spire; and,
saving that the vast east window is a Perpendicular
insertion, the whole edifice belongs to the late Decorated

period. The singular and graceful features of the
tower and spire will at once attract attention. The
bell-chamber is lighted by two square-headed windows
on each side, pierced beneath two arches of an arcade
of four, which graces the tower on each face at this
stage. Supported by flying buttresses above the tower
rises an octagon, most gracefully finished with a
parapet and with sixteen crocketed finials, and from
within which the spire, also octagonal, rises to a
height of 180 feet. The west window, itself somewhat
later in style than the others, and the windows
throughout the church, excepting the fine Perpendicular
one at the east end, have all curvilinear Decorated
tracery, those in the chancel being very elaborate.
Externally, throughout the church, buttresses terminating in foliated pinnacles, and with grotesque
gargoyles, separate bay from bay. The doorways, too,
are much enriched, and both porches are noteworthy,
the southern one having a parvise over it. Within,
the aisles are separated from the body of the church
by clustered columns, with enriched capitals, carrying
graceful arches, and those supporting the tower are
exceedingly fine.

The roofs have their original pitch. From the south
transept the Lady Chapel projects in the form of a
three-sided apse, and is so vaulted that the central
boss forms a pendent, enriched with carvings of the
Annunciation, St. John, and St. Catherine; while
facing the altar it is open, so that it would hold a
light—an arrangement singular, if not unique. The

eastern aisle of this transept is also groined. There remain to be noticed the very fine polygonal font of granite, much carved, and the Easter sepulchre, which is one of the most remarkable in the county. It has four compartments arranged vertically. Two of these are blank, but, of the others, one represents the soldiers watching by the tomb, and the other the Resurrection, angels with censers being represented on each side of our Lord. Reference may here be made to the interesting church at Welwick, two miles south-east of Patrington; and to the little church of Skeffling, within the Spurn, which has Early English features.

From this excursus we return to Withernsea, and pursue the unpicturesque coast further, with its low boulder cliffs and occasional lacustrine deposits upon the shore, by Holympton and Out Newton, where everywhere is the melancholy evidence of land-decay. But now the country rises, and Dimlington Height, the greatest elevation in Holderness (146 feet), swelling with a long sweep, looks far out both to the sea and the Humber. 'Here,' says Phillips, 'the wasteful action of the sea is very conspicuous; the sand and pebbles being removed from the base of the cliffs by the southward set of the tide, vast masses are undermined, and fall in wild and ruinous heaps; these, as they gradually reach the base, are washed away, and the process of destruction is repeated.' Dimlington Height sinks gradually to Easington, where there remains a small church with good Early English and Perpendicular features. Beyond this point the coast grows weird and lonely—the long sea-bank stretching far before, covered with rough grasses and sea-holly, the narrow strip of sand, the vast stretch of brown mud, and the threatening sea, with a few sea-birds flapping their white wings heavily by the shore. Here, too, you may still see at times some solitary buzzard winging homeward his lonely way across the sands.

We are now approaching the Spurn, and Kilnsea is the last place that intervenes, where, the ancient church having been swept away within living memory, you may see a modern edifice of brick. In this lonely spur of Holderness the Quakers had a strong following in the seventeenth century. Thus we learn that on Sunday after Lammas Day, in 1663, as Henry Lalley (or Lathley), minister of Hollym (which is a little hamlet between Patrington and Withernsea), was setting out to preach at Kilnsea, a certain Johnson, who doubtless belonged to the sect, called out to him many times : ' Harry, art thou going to Kilnsea to tell lies as thou hast done at Hollym? Repent, repent ; thy calamities draw near!' This same Johnson, it seems, at Michaelmas in the same year, seized hold of one John Thompson at Hollym, 'gripte him and shakte him, and tould him tythes should quickly be put downe, and if the Lord would put the sword into their hand, wee should see they would fight the Lord's battle.'

And now, with this historical notice of a characteristic feature of seventeenth-century life, we fare forward along the low pebbly isthmus from Kilnsea toward the

Spurn. It has been surmised that this narrow causeway may some day be swept away, and leave the Spurn itself an island. It is, indeed, but a shifting bank; yet, as we have noticed so much of the destructive work of the sea, we are here able to adduce its constructive work also, so true is it that nothing is ever lost. For, if the whole coast of Holderness is in motion, it is hitherward that its elements are rolled, and these, besides, as we shall show in the last chapter of this book, being washed up in part upon the shores of the Humber, build up the narrow causeway that leads out to the Spurn, and to Smeaton's lighthouse thereon, and, as Phillips well says, 'it is out of the ruins of Holderness that the Spurn is constituted and maintained.'

CHAPTER XV.

BEVERLEY.

Early History—St. John of Beverley—King Æthelstan—Beverley Sanctuary—The Frithstol—Mediæval Life—Religious Institutions—The Banner of St. John—The Minster described—The Recently discovered Chapter-House—The Percy Shrine—St. Mary's Church—Beverley and the Pilgrimage of Grace—The Civil Wars—Seventeenth - Century Incidents—Witchcraft—The Surrounding Country—Meaux Abbey—Leconfield Castle.

WE may say of Beverley what has been said picturesquely of Pontefract, and even with greater truth, perhaps, that it is in all our histories. What a sufficient picture of English life have we here in this quiet, reposeful East Riding town! How many historical figures, shades of good men and great, move thereon! The very name of Beverley speaks, as we well may believe, of the far-off time when beavers built their dams in an expanse of the river Hull; and we think, too, of the Angles forcing their way up from the salt marshes and mud flats of the Humber estuary, to make their settlement where perhaps had been the Petuaria of the Romans, amid the rich woodlands that came afterwards to be known as the Sylva Deirorum

—the Deirwald, or Wood of the Deirans. Here, with full access to the sea, by a river then easily navigable to vessels of light draught, they had a rich soil for the tiller, an unfailing supply of wood and water, thickets in which their swine could crunch the mast, and everywhere an abundance of game. As seafarers, Beverley became their port, protected from every storm, and screened from every pirate; as husbandmen, here, on the almost imperceptible western slope of the central valley of Holderness, through which the Hull winds slowly between the distant edges of the Wolds and the low cliffs of the shore, the forest clearings gave up rich fruit to their tillage.

Upon this peaceful scene there comes the figure of Archbishop John, born at Cherry Burton, near by, and we see him found here the monastery for men and women, like that of Hilda at Streoneshealh, whereto, worn out by his pastoral cares, he betakes himself, that he may end his days in meditation and prayer. Much is told of his holy life, and men hear without questioning of his wondrous deeds, and soon the country is filled with the news of miracles wrought at his tomb, and crowds of pilgrims erelong resort to his shrine. What a picture of the ages of faith do we gain when we see Æthelstan, Ælfred's golden-haired grandson, turning hitherward as he marches North with his men, incited thereto by returning pilgrims, to kneel at the tomb of the blessed John of Beverley, and carrying with him the standard of the saint, under which he wins the victory of Brunanburh!

Small wonder, filled with such enthusiasm, that he returns to redeem the promise, made when he laid his knife upon the altar, by richly endowing the church (still languishing from the onslaught of the Danes), and founding therein a college of secular canons, and vesting it with the celebrated privilege of sanctuary.

The history of Beverley is an ecclesiastical history, for its archiepiscopal lords long continued to wield the great privilege, whereby, in a savage age, they were able to baulk revenge, and to temper justice with the sweets of mercy and discipline. Happily, there remain to us particulars of the confession the man seeking sanctuary was required to make, and of the oath he was compelled to take. The archbishop's bailiff, we are told, causing him to put his hand upon the book, called upon him to swear that he would be faithful to the spiritual authorities, as well as to the bailiff, governors, burgesses, and commoners of the town; that he would 'bere no poynted wepen, dagger or knyfe, ne none other wepen ayenst the Kyng's pece;' that he would assist in quelling strife and extinguishing fire, and would be 'redy at the obite of Kyng Adelstan at such tyme as it is done at the warnying of the belman of the towne,' and would do his 'dewte in syngyng, and for to offer at the messe on the morne. And then gar hym kysse the book.' The traditional words used by Æthelstan in making his grant are recorded on a quaint old picture, repainted in the time of James I., which hangs in the south transept of the minster:

' Als Fre make I The
As hert may thynke,
Or Egh may see.'

The privilege of sanctuary extended to within a radius of about a mile from the minster, but the church itself was the great refuge, more especially its choir, and the last resort of all was the ' frithstol '—the chair carven out of a solid block of stone, now broken and clamped with iron, which stands in the choir. The penalty for breaking sanctuary was heavy, and grew heavier according as the place in which the sanctuary-man was seized was more sacred, until, if hand was laid upon him as he sat upon the ' frithstol,' the offence became ' boteless,' no ' bote ' or penalty sufficing to redeem it, and the offender was visited with grave spiritual and civil punishments. It is on record, as an example of such an act, that, in the year 1331, certain persons, in violent contumely of St. John, incurring thereby the greater excommunication and other grievous pains, broke into his sanctuary by night, and carried thence by force a frithman, one John Acreman of Bruges, who, having slain a certain Sir John Nele at Courtray, and having done other ill deeds at Norwich, had been admitted to the sanctuary.

But it is not only by reason of its sanctuary of St. John that the history of Beverley is ecclesiastical, for the Archbishops of York were both the patrons of its minster and its civil lords; and to the wise and benevolent jurisdiction of the Northern primates, con-

trasting so markedly with the extortionate dominion
of the barons, is it due that a rich and prosperous
merchant community grew up at Beverley.   It was
the archbishops who obtained for the townsmen their
markets and fairs, their municipal privileges as free-
men, and the establishment of their merchant guild.
In 1269 Archbishop Giffard procured the removal, by
Dame Joan de Stuteville, of all her locks and dams
in the river Hull, whereby the navigation thereof was
impeded, to the intent that thenceforward, without
let or hindrance, ships and boats might ascend from
the Humber to Beverley; but it was provided—and
the circumstance throws light upon the insecurity of
the coast at the period—that Dame de Stuteville
might, in time of war or public disturbance, for the
security of the realm against pirates and marauders,
place a chain across the river at Stanford rake from
sunset to sunrise; while her men at Hull were to have
the right to take earth for the building and maintenance of their sea-dike.   It was Archbishop Neville
who, in 1380, granted to the men of Beverley that
pleasant resort known as the Westwood, which is still
their delight, and wherein, in these days, there is
perhaps the finest golf-link in Yorkshire.   But, inasmuch as the archbishops had rights and the burgesses privileges, it could not but happen that disputes
should arise between them at times, and so we find
that, in 1282, so incensed were the men of Beverley
against the austere Archbishop Wickwaine, although
he was a benefactor to the town, that, with unseemly

behaviour, they prevented him from preaching in their minster, whereupon he laid the town under an interdict, which Martin IV. confirmed.

Under the fostering care of the archbishops, who often resorted to Beverley, it became one of the great religious centres of the North. In addition to its collegiate society of St. John, with its splendid minster, it had the magnificent cruciform church of St. Mary, which still remains, and those of St. Martin and St. Nicholas, which have disappeared. The Grey Friars had their house without Keld Gate; the Preaching Friars, who were favoured by Archbishop Walter de Grey, who held their provincial synod at Beverley in 1286, and who were preaching for the Crusade in 1291, were located near the minster; the Commandry of the Hospitallers stood in the Trinities, where now the railway-station is; and there were in the town the hospitals of the Holy Trinity, St. Giles, and St. Nicholas, besides other religious institutions. Throughout the Middle Ages many were the strangers and pilgrims who resorted to the shrine of St. John, and not a few learned men issued from its schools or ministered in its churches—Alured of Beverley, sometime treasurer of the minster; John Alcock, bishop in succession of Rochester, Worcester, and Ely, who died in 1500; the saintly John Fisher, Bishop of Rochester, beheaded in 1535; and many more. Legend says that when the Conqueror harried Yorkshire with terrible vengeance, smitten with fear at the death of one of his servants, he shrank from despoiling the shrine, and Beverley remained untouched; but Professor Freeman has rejected the story. The banner of St. John, which Æthelstan had carried to victory at Brunanburh, was one of those which gave its name to the Battle of the Standard. The concourse of pilgrims continued to grow, and among them knelt King John; and Edward I. came there several times, and we learn that, after ' waking a night ' before the shrine, he took with him the sacred banner, and floated it in his war against the Scotch. Edward II. was more than once at Beverley, and he also, in his northern campaign, had with him St. John's banner, borne by John de Rolleston, the archbishop's vicar at the minster. Other royal visitors to Beverley were Henry IV., and, after Agincourt—on the day whereof the shrine is said to have distilled holy oil, 'like drops of sweat '—Henry V., as well as Henry VI., to whose interest the town was firmly wedded, and who came thither from the neighbouring castle of Leconfield, where he was visiting the Earl of Northumberland. In these centuries Beverley was a thriving town, supported in great part by the clothing industry, and it had wealthy merchants and considerable shipping. It appears to have been protected by a ditch—some say a wall—and, of its bars, the North Bar alone remains—a picturesque object neighbouring the market-place. It had returned two members to Parliament as early as the reign of Edward I.

The centre of ecclesiastical influence in Beverley was the great minster of St. John, which is still the chief attraction to the visitor. As we see it now, it belongs wholly to a period subsequent to the year 1188, in which, by a calamitous fire at night, the old church was wholly destroyed. The work of building the present minster seems to have been soon begun, but the canons suffered grievously from want of funds, and we find that, in 1311, persons were going about the country fraudulently representing themselves as authorized to solicit donations for the chest of blessed John of Beverley. Nothing, however, was spared in the beautification of the glorious fane; and, in the exquisite charm and delicacy of its details, it certainly ranks among the choicest examples of English mediæval art. Unfortunately, in the limited space of this chapter, but an imperfect account of it can be given. The plan of the structure is cruciform, there being, in addition to the great aisled transepts, a second and smaller intersection one bay removed from the east end—an analogous arrangement to that which is found at Canterbury, Rochester, Salisbury, Lincoln, and in other Early English examples. At the intersection of the great transepts are massive piers, evidently intended to support a central lantern, but, the foundations probably having been distrusted, this was never built. The chief internal measurements of the church are: total length, 332 feet 4 inches; extreme breadth at the main transepts, 167 feet 2 inches; width of the nave and aisles, 63 feet 1 inch; height of the vaulting, about 65 feet.

With the exception of the Percy Chapel at the

east end, the whole of the choir and transepts
are Early English, with notable insertions and later
enrichments; the nave generally Decorated, and the
west end, with the north porch and lofty towers,
Perpendicular; but the impression received upon
entering the structure is of its extreme uniformity, the
general arrangement of triforial space, clerestory, and
vaulting having been preserved throughout. This
impression, however, to some extent, passes away when
the rich and varied detail and characteristic features
of the construction are examined. The typical bay of
the chancel—and, as has already been said, the arrangement is throughout analogous—consists of an exquisitely - proportioned arch, deeply moulded, and
resting upon lofty clustered pillars; above it a triforial
space, enriched with an arcading of trefoil arches, cut
with the toothed ornament, resting upon slender
detached and clustered shafts, there being behind this
arcade another one, attached to the wall, the plain
arches whereof have their apices behind the caps of
the detached shafts, and a quatrefoil occupies the
interspace between the two sets of arches; and, again,
the clerestory above, with a passage, has a series of
pointed arches in front of its lancet window, enriched
like those of the triforium, and resting upon slender
marble shafts. The east window of the Lady Chapel
is a fine Perpendicular insertion, but the exquisite
character of the Early English detail is here very
noteworthy. There seems to be no doubt, from the
construction, that the last bay of the minster, though

Beverley Minster.

approximately of the same date as the rest of the choir, was not originally contemplated. Another extremely beautiful Early English feature is the double staircase (embodying most charmingly the dog-toothed, trefoil-arch arcading of the aisle wall), on the north side of the chancel, which has recently been shown to have been the entrance to the chapter-house, a building of which the foundations were discovered not long ago. Like the chapter-houses of Wells and Westminster, the one at Beverley was erected upon a vaulted crypt or undercroft, and was an octagonal building, some thirty-eight feet in diameter, vaulted, as in the instances named, from a central shaft.

It is very remarkable that, in the lofty nave of Beverley, which maintains the character of the Early English choir, we arrive without transition at the curvilinear Decorated. The adaptations, also, are singular, and something has been forfeited of the characteristic features of the Decorated style. The character of the clustered columns is the same, but foliage is introduced in the capitals ; the arcade before the clerestory windows has three arches instead of five, and the ball-flower replaces the dog-tooth ; the Early English arcading of the aisle wall is continued on the south side, but the windows have flowing tracery. Externally, the buttresses of the nave are connected with the clerestory by flying buttresses, and on the south side are ornamented with niches, while the parapet is enriched with Decorated panelling, which is carried right round the Early English transepts and choir. The Perpendicular west front of Beverley has been inspired by that of York, from which, nevertheless, it differs, compensating for what it lacks in magnificence by an air of slenderness and grace that gives a soaring character to its towers (160 feet 7 inches to the battlements), and the panelling and niche-work are very beautiful. To the Perpendicular period also belongs the splendid north porch, with its buttresses, pinnacles, and niches, and the parvise over, as well as the Percy Chapel at the east end. Of the monuments, the most celebrated is the glorious Percy shrine—supposed, though its recumbent figure has disappeared, to be that of Idonea, wife of Henry, second Lord Percy (died 1365)—which stands beneath the arch between the choir and the north-east transept. The lovely enrichments of the ogee arch and gabled canopy of this shrine—the boldly-carved crockets and finials, the grotesque heads and figures of men and angels, with fruit and foliage, magnificently designed—certainly entitle this to be considered the most splendid Decorated monument in England. Other beautiful carvings exist in the choir, and the *misereres* have much that is curious. If the minster lost something at its restoration, it unquestionably gained more at the hands of Sir Gilbert Scott, and many of its later defacements and obstructions were removed.

It is singular that Beverley, possessing a minster so splendid, should have also, in the parochial church of St. Mary, an edifice almost as remarkable and scarcely less interesting. The beautiful conception and splendid

detail of the west front, representing admirably the
transition from the Decorated to the Perpendicular,
with its lofty octagonal turrets, enriched with niches,
panelling, and battlements, its large window, and
charmingly-moulded doorway; the great clerestory,
with its long series of three-light traceried windows;
the elaborate beauty of the south porch, with its
lateral traceried windows and its pinnacles; the extent
and character of the transepts, the rare charm of the
choir, and the massive character of the central tower,
with its panelled battlements and many pinnacles, and
the unusual traceried circular windows in its lower
stage—all mark this as one of the most noteworthy
parish churches in England. Within, the Decorated
arches of the chancel have circles enclosing trefoils
in the spandrels, as well as the enrichment of niches:
and the ball-flower and nutmeg ornaments add much
to the beauty of the east end. The transepts are
Perpendicular, much earlier work, however, being used
up in them. A quaint inscription records the fall of
the original central tower: ' Pray God have marce of
al the sawllys of the men and wymen and cheldryn
whos bodys was slayn at the faulyng of thys ccherc
. . . . thys fawl was the 29 day of Aperel . . . . 1512.'
The six bays of the nave, which are chiefly Perpendicular, are somewhat heavier than those of the
chancel, but the enrichments are many, and the lofty
clerestory gives a fine character to this part of the
church. Angels at the terminations of the hood-
mouldings of the arches bear shields, quaintly recording

the donors of portions of the structure hereabout. 'Thes to pyllors made gud wyffs—God reward theym.' 'Thys pyllor' (one with a curious row of minstrel figures sculptured upon the capital) 'made the meynstryls' (members doubtless of a fraternity of gleemen known to have flourished at Beverley in the Middle Ages). 'Xlay and his wyffe made thes to pyllors and a halffe.' The ceilings throughout the church are panelled, there being some richly-carved bosses, and are nearly flat; and on the panels in the chancel are curious painted figures of English kings. Many hands have been engaged upon the restoration of St. Mary's Church, including those of Pugin and Sir Gilbert Scott. The chief benefit has been that it has been strengthened, and that many of its encumbrances have been removed.

The ecclesiastical history of Beverley may be said to have ended with the terrible events that attended the risings of Aske and Bigod, which caused great heart-stirring thereabout, and with the dissolution of the Collegiate Society of St. John in the first year of Edward VI.

The news of the Lincolnshire rising was brought to Beverley by one Woodmancye, who afterwards fled, and was excepted from the pardon. 'From that time forward,' as Hallam said at his examination, 'no man could keep his servant at plough, but every man that could bear a staff went forward towards Hunsley.' During the 'truce,' as we read in a letter of Dame Dorothy Darcy, certain ships came to Hull 'with wine,

Lenten store, and corn,' but it became noised abroad that they were laden with ordnance, with which the king intended to fortify Hull. At once Holderness was 'up,' and the commons hastened to Beverley, where Hallam was at their head; but Aske hastened to 'stay' them, and assured them in the common hall of the king's grace, and of how a Parliament was to be held at York, and the queen crowned there; but Hallam, less trustful, asked why, then, were the tenths to be collected. Soon Bigod's influence became manifest, and, while Lumley attempted Scarborough, Hallam marched upon Hull, and was taken there in the dramatic manner to be related in the next chapter. Thereupon, with a strong body, Bigod hastened to Beverley, and demanded that Hallam should be given up. But it was too late. The rising had failed. Sir Ralph Ellercar had entered Hull, and Bigod fled from Beverley—else, as Matthew Boynton wrote to his father-in-law, Sir John Bulmer, 'he had been ffotten wytt all'—towards Mulgrave on foot, for his horses were taken by Gregory Conyers, and soon thereafter he was captured. We have elsewhere alluded to his fate.

The seventeenth century saw many dramatic incidents in the history of Beverley. Charles I. held his court there, at the house of Lady Gee, during the siege of Hull; and after the failure to reduce that place he returned to Beverley. A body of the Parliamentary forces pursued, and, taking a circuitous route, entered the town by the North Bar Gate, whereupon a fight

took place in the streets, in which they were driven
back, Charles having meanwhile taken refuge in the
hall garth near the minster. Afterwards Beverley was
occupied by the Parliamentary party; but, when Newcastle advanced for the second siege of Hull, it was
abandoned, and plundered by the Royalists. The
Cavalier feeling seems to have run very high in
Beverley, for, in 1651, even a common sergeant-at-mace
of the town was indicted for adding to a proclamation
of Cromwell's, which he had cried, the words, 'God
save the King and Parliament!' while in the same
year another Beverley man was charged, before
Thomas Hudson, the mayor, with saying: 'I will drink
a health to Prince Charles, King of Scots, and to his
good success into England, and to the confusion of all his
enemies,' as he quaffed a silver beaker of ale, and with
pulling off the cap of one who refused to pledge him,
saying it was 'a health that deserved to be un-
covered.'

A curious illustration of religious feeling occurred
at Beverley in 1663, when two sectaries, probably
Quakers, were indicted for attempting to disseminate
their opinions by circulating printed matter, one of
whom—who said he dwelt with God, and was commanded by God to witness forth the truth—affixed a
paper to the Beverley market-cross, which seems to
have begun with the words: 'Oh, all you hireling
priests, cursed lawyers, and corrupt magistrates, take
notice!' A strange scene took place also in the
minster in 1662, when the burgesses, having elected

a minister said to have been a person of scandalous
life, and an enemy of the Government, refused to
admit another licensed by the official of York. They
assembled within the sacred edifice, and attempted
to break open the chancel doors, whereupon a proclamation was read to them to keep the peace, and
a troop was brought in. In the end their leader, an
alderman of the town, was arrested.

In addition to such typical instances as these of the
North Country occurrences of the seventeenth century,
Beverley affords us also an illustration of the strange
recrudescence of the belief in witchcraft that characterized it. In October, 1654, John Greencliffe of the
town deposed as follows—his deposition is at York
Castle—and we give his own words, merely modern-
izing the spelling: 'On Saturday last, about seven in
the evening, Elizabeth Roberts did appear to him in
her usual wearing-clothes, with a ruff about her neck,
and, presently vanishing, turned herself into the simili-
tude of a cat, which fixed close about his leg, and
after much struggling vanished, whereupon he was
much pained at his heart. Upon Wednesday there
seized a cat upon his body, which did strike him on
the head, upon which he fell into a swoon or trance.
After he received the blow, he saw the said Elizabeth
escape upon a wall in her usual wearing apparel.
Upon Thursday she appeared to him in the likeness
of a bee, which did very much afflict him, to wit, in
throwing of his body from place to place, notwithstanding there were five or six persons to hold him

down.' The woman charged denied all knowledge of
the offences alleged, and we are unable to say if the
affair ended as disastrously for her as such allegations
did for some other Yorkshire witches at this period.

Thus Beverley is a town about which many memories
of bygone times are clustered, and almost every stone
of the place has its history. A picturesque, quiet place,
you will think, too, as you traverse its old roadways,
or linger in its market-place, or see it from a distance
across the cornfields, with the noble towers of the
minster and St. Mary's Church soaring out of the plain.
De Wint has depicted it thus most delightfully in one
of the three of his works in the Dixon Bequest at
Bethnal Green, as it lies amid trees beyond the yellow
flat, and with a dim blue distance beyond. The
country all about it, though without any striking
features, is pleasant, rich, and fruitful. Away beyond
the Hull, amid beautiful woods, lies the site, and very
little more—for a few broken walls and a gateway,
with the evidences of moats, are all that remain—of
the Cistercian abbey of Meaux, which was founded,
in satisfaction for his not having joined the Crusade
as he had vowed to do, by the same William le Gros
who built Scarborough Castle. It is on record that
the Abbot of Meaux and twenty-two monks succumbed
in the Black Death of 1349. Their house is reported
to have been very fine, as in such a neighbourhood we
should have expected it to be, but the destruction
thereof has approached near to completeness. On the
other side of Beverley, two and a half miles away to

THE MARKET PLACE, BEVERLEY.   DRAWN BY ALFRED DAWSON.

the north-west, is the pretty village of Leconfield, with
the site, marked by its moat, and nothing more, of
Leconfield Castle, a great house of the Percys, to
whom the estate came by marriage with one of the
sisters and co-heiresses of the last Peter de Brus of
Skelton, upon the division of the Brus fee. Leland
saw the house, and describes it as built partly of
timber and partly of stone and brick. The neighbourhood of Beverley, besides these, has many other
places of interest, too, but to these it is beyond our
scope to refer.

CHAPTER XVI.

HULL AND THE HUMBER.

WHATEVER the Yorkshire coast has possessed of commercial activity, in its dealings with countries beyond the sea, has fallen, in these later times, to the busy port of Hull. The Flemings, Easterlings, and Danes, who were wont to resort to the ancient mart of Scarborough; the Netherland and Florentine merchants who came to buy the wool which the Yorkshire Cistercians and sheep-farmers produced; the argosies with their fine fabrics that, from Bruges, Ypres, Ghent, and Antwerp, resorted to the quays of Ravenser, Hedon, and Beverley; the active trafficking that the

men of Whitby carried on later with the ports of the
Baltic—all these are represented in these days by the
ships and men that have recourse to the great port in
the Humber. The reasons for this change of direction
in the commercial stream are manifold, but the chiefest
of them are natural. The sea, whose ravages upon
the coast of Holderness we have already to some
extent described, did its most impressive work of
material destruction within the point of the Spurn,
where the important port and town of Ravenser or
Ravenspur—the Ravenspurg of Shakespeare—has
altogether disappeared, with its island of Ravenserod.
Yet here was a place so considerable that it had many
merchants and considerable shipping, and returned
members to Parliament, in 1305. The ravages of the
sea continued, nevertheless, and, as the houses of the
burgesses were washed away one by one, the merchants
betook themselves to the rising port of Hull; and
when, in 1399, Bolingbroke landed there—when, as
Shakespeare has it,

> ' The banished Bolingbroke repeals himself,
> And with uplifted arms is safe arrived
> At Ravenspurg '

—Ravenser was already almost abandoned, and he found
a hermit building an oratory there. But the decayed
port continued to be a landing-place still, and it was
thither that Edward IV. came before the battle of
Barnet, in 1471. Not a vestige of it now remains.

But, if the sea has worked thus destructively within
the estuary of the Humber, it has operated otherwise,

with the river itself, in a very marked manner thereabout. The network of rivers that water Yorkshire
and a part of the Midlands discharged themselves, in
the early Middle Ages, through a vast morass of mud
and marsh, into the Humber. Of that fenny tract
a great part has now been reclaimed for agriculture
by the labour of Cornelius Vermuyden, the Dutchman,
and many others; and, by the ingenious process of
'warping,' the waters are now made to drop their
fertilizing ooze upon the soil. But a vast amount of
alluvial mud is carried out into the Humber estuary,
where, but for the steam dredges, the docks at Hull
would soon be filled; and it was here, out of this
'warp,' and the soil washed away from Ravenser, that,
by the action of the river and the tide, a vast deposit
was gradually formed, between Patrington and the
river, which rose gradually, until it was at length
reclaimed in the time of the Stuarts, was formed into
a parish in 1831, and is now the fruitful cultivated
tract known as Sunk Island. The process which thus
went on affected also the water-way of the Hull, which,
with the increased draught of vessels, at length became
impracticable for merchant craft, and thus Beverley
was cut off from direct communication with the sea.
The same thing happened also at Hedon—a thriving
borough chartered by Edward III., which returned
representatives to Parliament even until the time of
the Reform Bill—now, outrivalled by Hull, and with
its water silted up, remaining a quiet, decayed little
place, some two miles away from the Humber. You

may see the evidence of its former greatness in its splendid church, which is known as the 'King of Holderness,' just as the sister church of Patrington, already described, is spoken of as the 'Queen.'*

And we may trace the rise of Hull, too, to the unrivalled advantage of its situation in regard to the inland country, for while, in the Middle Ages, the marshy water-way of the Esk was scarcely available for the conveyance of moorland wool to Whitby, and long journeys by pack-horse or wain awaited those who would carry their produce to Scarborough, or other places on the coast, the rivers that converge to the Humber—the Ouse, the Aire, the Don, and the Trent — with their network of tributaries, made it possible to float down the produce of a vast and

* Of this splendid church, the chancel and transepts are Early English, the nave Geometrical Decorated, and the lofty central tower Perpendicular. In the north transept are three pairs of lancet triplets—its old eastern aisle, like that on the south, has disappeared —and a triforial clerestory, which ran also round the chancel (of the same character), but this has been broken by the insertion of the five-light Perpendicular east window, as well as originally round the south transept. The church has been restored, not happily, and the south transept retains less of its original character than the one on the north. The piers of the nave are clustered, and have plain capitals, supporting graceful arches, above which are two-light clerestory windows, and most of the aisle windows in the nave have exquisite geometrical tracery. A Perpendicular window has been inserted at the west end, and the western portal externally is very fine. The beautiful Perpendicular tower, resting upon pillars and arches of the same date, has admirable three-light windows, and rises to a height of 129 feet, with an elegant open-work parapet. There is much exquisite detail in the building.

fertile country to Hull. Be it remembered that, from
the twelfth century until the time of Edward III. or
later, our export trade was chiefly in wool, as a raw
material for manufacture, to the great Flemish port of
Bruges, and, when that had decayed through the
action of Maximilian, to Antwerp, and that it was not
until later that we began to export fine fabrics ourselves.

When Edward I. returned from the battle of
Dunbar, in 1298, and was staying, it is said, at the
castle of the Stutevilles, at Cottingham, he saw, as he
passed with a hunting-party, with a keen eye, the
splendid advantages of the situation of Hull. There
was, indeed, as we might have expected to find, a
harbour already at the mouth of the Hull, at Myton,
and the village of Wyke, where, by the grants of
Matilda Camin and Benedict de Sculcotes, the Abbot
of Meaux was established in possession in the twelfth
century. The place was sometimes called Hull, and
we saw in the last chapter that the men of Dame
Joan de Stuteville were working at their sea-dike there
in 1296. Edward I., moved by his scheme, bought
the little port from the Abbot of Meaux without hesita-
tion, conferred upon it the name of Kingston-upon-
Hull, and issued a proclamation offering favours to
those who should settle there. The town was created
a free borough in 1299, and the harbour was improved,
and an era of scarcely interrupted prosperity began. It
has been pointed out that the original plan of Kingston-upon-Hull resembles, as a long though irregular

parallelogram, that of other towns established by Edward I. in Guienne and Aquitaine, as well as of New Winchelsea, which he also founded. The town was walled and ditched for protection against the raids of pirates, who were often insufficiently provided against afloat.

Among the merchants who took up their residence at Hull in answer to the proclamation were the De la Poles, rich burgesses of Ravenser, of whom William de la Pole was the first mayor of the town, in 1332. The De la Poles became merchant princes, were high in the favour of successive sovereigns, and played no small part in the history of England. The family received many honours, including the dukedom and earldom of Suffolk, and John de la Pole married Elizabeth Plantagenet, eldest sister of Edward IV. They had a palace at Hull, and their connection with the town was a considerable factor in its development. By some authorities it is said that Richard de la Pole was associated with Edward I. and Sir Robert Oughtred in establishing the White Friars at Hull. What is certain is that Michael de la Pole, afterwards Earl of Suffolk and lord chancellor, founded a house of Carthusians in the town in the reign of Edward III., of which, however, not a vestige now remains, as well as a hospital. Hull had likewise houses of Black and Crutched Friars, and several other hospitals, including one known as the Maison Dieu, and the Trinity House, an establishment for the relief of distressed seamen, to which reference will presently be made.

20

So considerable was the importance of Hull by the reign of Edward III., who in an ordinance concerning mints named it as a place for a furnace, that, in 1359, it was able to furnish 16 ships and 466 men for the French expedition, the quota of London being but 25 ships and 662 seamen. A strong castle was erected on the east side of the Hull River, and the fortifications were repaired by Richard II. The town had by this time a very large trade with the Hanse towns and Flanders, which continued to grow, and Henry VI. constituted its government afresh, and styled it 'the Town and County of the Town of Kingston-upon-Hull,' and, in 1445, its mayor became 'Admiral of the Humber.' The place was very strongly attached to the Lancastrian party in the Wars of the Roses, and it is said that, when the common funds had been wholly expended in the cause, other money was raised even by the sale of the market-cross. Hull continued to prosper, though it suffered severely from plague and the inundations to which its position made it liable, and by the reign of Henry VIII. was one of the most thriving seaports in England.

To the Pilgrims of 1536 and 1537 it seemed of capital importance that Hull should not be made a stronghold against them. In the former year, however, Brandon, Duke of Suffolk, kept his forces against the place, as Aske said, 'contrary to the appointment,' and Sir Robert Constable (who subsequently was hanged in chains there) was sent thither as ruler by Aske. The country-- we are quoting Aske's deposition in the Record Office—

was also put to the charge, through the action of
Suffolk, of finding 200 soldiers ; and the siege of
Scarborough, and the taking of Waters and his ship
by Bigod at that place, to which we have alluded, were
the further result. Their seizure of Hull in 1536 ended
unfortunately for the commons, but they were never
content to be dispossessed of the place. The readers
of this book are informed (page 204) of the manner
of the new agitation which was felt when it was
rumoured that the king after the pardon intended to
throw forces and munitions of war into the town, and
of the matter of Hallam's speech on the celebrated
Plough Monday at Watton. It was Hallam himself
who, on January 16, 1537, made the new and futile
attempt upon Hull, in which he was taken by the
burgesses, with several of his companions. The mayor
and aldermen were on the alert. An armed body was
discerned approaching, and, before the gates of the
town could be closed, one Fobere, coming up to
Alderman John Eland, pointed out the leader to
him.

'An you look not shortly of yon man Halom,' he
said, ' he will subdue you all.'

To which Eland replied, ' I knaw him not.'

' Yon is he,' said the other, ' that is on horseback
in the yeatts, and ye may see people assemble hastily
till him.'

Recognising Hallam by this, Eland plucked Alderman
William Knolles by the arm, saying : ' Go way, for
we will have him.'

They thereupon went up to Hallam, and, seizing his bridle, demanded his name.

'My name is Halom,' he replied.

'Then thou art the false traitor that I look for!' exclaimed Knolles.

A struggle ensued. Eland on one side of the horse and Knolles on the other smote at Hallam with their daggers, but they could not penetrate his coat of fence. Then some of Hallam's companions came to his aid, and Knolles was struck to the ground, but quickly he 'gat up,' and, with other help, 'bykerd with them, and part of them took.' Meanwhile, Hallam on horseback and Eland afoot were waging battle together. The alderman, in smiting a heavy blow at the Pilgrim leader, severed his bridle-rein, whereupon it seemed that Hallam would have fled ; but, probably because of the pulling on one side only, the horse ran against a 'ditch bray' at the Busse ditch, and he was forced to alight. Then the struggle was renewed, and Eland and Hallam fought on and 'bykered together till he was taken and hurt'; but the alderman himself was 'hurt,' too, with several of his servants and others on both sides. Such is 'the very truth of the taking of that traitor Halom,' as Eland and his fellow-aldermen set it down in writings preserved now in the Public Record Office.

Two days afterwards, Sir Ralph Ellerkar, the younger, reached Hull, and in the afternoon there came three messengers from Sir Francis Bigod, who was at Beverley, as we said in dealing with that place, demanding the release of Hallam and his fellows. The request was refused ; two of the men were put in ward, and the third sent with an answer to Bigod, ' which, I think,' wrote Ellarkar to Henry VIII., ' made him and his company to flee out of Beverley.' So ended the rash and ineffectual attempt of Bigod and Hallam to wake anew the slumbering fires which Aske, Constable, and others of the leaders in the first rising were doing their utmost to quell. The consequences to these devoted men were terrible, and are like, in the light of recent investigations, to cast new obloquy upon the administration and methods of Henry VIII.

The king was at Hull in 1540, and, upon his instructions, a new water-supply was secured for the town, and Suffolk Palace, the house of the De la Poles, then in the royal hands, was put in repair. A citadel was also built, with additional fortifications. These defensive works, with those erected by Charles II., have now entirely disappeared, and certain of the Hull docks cover the site of them. The mediæval fortifications, probably of brick, seem to have been largely on the left bank of the Hull ; those of Henry VIII. were upon the right bank.

Our brief survey of the history of Hull brings us down now to the well-known events that took place there during the Civil War. In 1642 the town was one of the greatest arsenals in the kingdom, and the Commons resolved to secure it, with Portsmouth and the Tower, by vote. Sir John Hotham was the new governor, and, though he was expected by the Royalists

to side with the king, when Charles appeared before
Hull, on April 23, 1642, he closed the gates and raised
the drawbridges, at the same time, upon the Beverley
gate, protesting his loyalty upon his knees.   This act
was the first of overt hostility to the king, who thereupon, proclaiming Hotham a traitor, withdrew to
muster a host.   A plot was now formed for giving up
the town, which Hotham and his son were found to
have concealed, and for this doubtful dealing they were
branded as traitors to the Parliament also, and, being
removed to London, there lost their heads.   The host
which the king brought against Hull numbered 3,000,
but a determined defence was made, and, by cutting
the dikes, the town was laid under water for two
miles round it, and the attack failed.   In September, 1643, Hull was again besieged, this time by
Newcastle ; and Fairfax, the new governor, made a
strenuous defence.   Batteries were thrown up against
the town, and a heavy cannonade was kept up, red-
hot shot being thrown into it ; but the dikes were
again cut, and Fairfax made desperate and effective
sorties, so that, after a leaguer of six weeks, during
which much damage was inflicted upon the town,
Newcastle was compelled to raise the siege.   In the
very nature of things it was scarcely possible for him
to succeed, for the Parliament had secured open com-
munications upon the sea by seizing the very fleet that
Charles had created by means of the ship-money the
Parliament men had themselves so fiercely opposed.
    Hull was the scene of another act of treachery at

the time of the Revolution of 1688. James, knowing
well the importance of the place, and thinking that
William of Orange might even land there, had
garrisoned it with trusty troops. Viscount Montgomery's regiment (now the 11th Foot or Devonshire
Regiment) was quartered in the town, and a company
of grenadiers, commanded by Lord Langdale, the
governor, was attached to it. Lieutenant-Colonel
Hanmer and Colonel Copley, Lieutenant-Governor of
Hull, therefore concerted measures with the magistrates
of the town ; and, suddenly seizing Lords Montgomery
and Langdale in their beds, they 'put the Roman
Catholic officers and gentlemen of that persuasion in
the town into custody, and declared for the Prince of
Orange.' These were, however, released when the
town and citadel had been made secure.

The Civil War, with the troubles which it brought
upon Hull, inflicted, with pestilence and inundations,
considerable injury upon the commerce of the port ;
but prosperity was soon resumed, and Hull grew still
more flourishing through the eighteenth century ; and
the great development of our export trade at its close
caused an enormous increase of shipping in the
Humber. Hull, too, had, as it still has, a considerable
fishery. Vessels from the port were the very first to
engage in the Greenland whale fishery, as long ago
as 1598. The whalers of Hull discovered, and made
a whaling centre at, the island of Jan Mayen ; and
even well into the present century the whale fishery
continued of some importance. It was the master

of a Hull whaler, the *Isabella* (Captain Humphries), who, with his crew, was able, in 1833, to rescue Sir John Ross and his companions after their sojourn of four years in the Arctic regions.

The original harbour of the port of Hull was in the lower reach of the Hull River, and it was not until the year 1778 that the basin now known as the Queen's Dock, entered from that river, and covering an area of nearly ten acres, formed on the site of the old fortifications, was opened.* It is now used mostly for the timber and general trade. The Humber Dock (more than seven acres), resorted to chiefly by Dutch trading-craft, was opened in 1809, and these two docks were connected in 1829 by a third, now known as the Prince's Dock (something more than six acres); while the small Railway Dock, entered from the Humber Dock, was opened in 1846. All these basins are on the right bank of the Hull; but the great Victoria

* The increase of shipping in the Humber during the second half of the last century cannot be considered apart from the growth of the West Riding towns at the same time, nor from the immense development that was given by a large body of public-spirited gentlemen in that district—the pioneers of its present prosperity— to the inland waterways by which its productions were carried down to the port of Hull. This is a history that has yet to be written. No one interested in it can afford to overlook a series of articles by Mr. Francis A. Leyland (*Halifax Courier*, November, 1886, to March, 1887), in which he has traced minutely the remarkable history of the improved navigation of the Calder, with the associated canals. In this work a moving spirit was that open-minded statesman Sir George Savile, of Rufford (of whom a portrait is in the Trinity House at Hull), who was also greatly concerned in the erection of Smeaton's lighthouse at the Spurn.

Dock, devoted chiefly to the Baltic timber, grain, and guano trades, with its annexed basins and timber ponds, is upon the left bank. Other more recent basins, extending along the bank of the Humber, west of the landing quay, are the Albert, William Wright, and St. Andrew's Docks, while further east lies the great Alexandra Dock. Vessels from every country in Europe may be seen in these basins, and a babel of tongues may be heard upon the quays; but the chief concourse of ships is from the ports of Russia, Germany, Sweden, Norway, Denmark, and Holland, which bring all the produce of Northern Europe to our shores. From hence, too, are exported to Europe and the Eastern world vast quantities of manufactured goods from the great industrial communities of the North. Hull, in short, is in constant communication not only with the countries named, but also with all Western Europe, and the ports of the Mediterranean and the Black Sea, as well as with many of those in the Far East, and in America. A considerable ship-building industry, too, is carried on at the port, and many fine vessels of our merchant marine, and certain war vessels for our own and foreign navies, have taken the water at Earle's shipbuilding yard.

The old town of Hull lies inclosed between the Hull, the Humber, and the Queen's, Prince's, and Humber Docks—formed upon the line of the ancient fortifications—by which the two rivers are connected. The street-names hereabout bespeak the mediæval life of the place—Whitefriargate, Blackfriargate, Mytongate,

Posterngate, and Bowlalley lane. Here, in the midst
of the town, is the market-place, with the fine church
of the Holy Trinity; and, on market days, when the
space is filled with stalls, and an eager crowd are
chaffering over the produce of Holderness, looking up
at the brick walls of the church, you will be reminded
of some market scene in the Low Countries, and you
may often hear, too, the tongue of Dutchmen and of
Danes. It is the choir of the church that is chiefly
built of brick, the transepts, nave, and tower being of
stone. The work of building was begun in 1312, and
Edward II., who, like all our Plantagenet kings, had a
great interest in Hull, contributed largely to it. The
transepts, central tower, and choir are of the Decorated
period, the latter considerably later in style, while the
nave is of Perpendicular character, and, in general
features and spaciousness, is an imitation of the choir.
The great east window is fine in character, with three
tiers of lights below the tracery, and approaches much
more closely to the Perpendicular than the large east
windows of the church aisles. These three windows,
with four fine buttresses with niches, and terminating in
floriated pinnacles, and a rich parapet, give a splendid
aspect to the east end, which has a rectangular outline.
The lateral windows are also good. Within, the
characteristic feature of the choir is great spaciousness, the arches being lofty, and there is a high
clerestory; but a certain slightness about the piers
contrasts unfavourably with the massive character of
most church-building of the date. The transepts, as

we said, are somewhat earlier, and it has been pointed
out that the north and south windows are good
examples, representing the transition from the geometrical to the curvilinear Decorated. From the
south transept a chapel opens, which has a vaulted
tomb resembling somewhat the Percy shrine at
Beverley. The nave very greatly resembles in aspect
the choir. It has similar lofty arches, and a like
clerestory, the windows, which are of unusual size,
having tracery of an uncommon character. The west
end resembles the east end in general arrangement of
windows and pinnacled buttresses (and, indeed, the
lateral buttresses are of similar type), and has a
remarkable squareness of appearance. At the restoration, the great west window was filled with good
stained glass by Hardman, at a cost of £1,000. Below
it is a fine canopied portal, richly moulded, and flanked
by enriched niches. The central tower has large
windows like the church itself, and rises to a height
of 140 feet, with an ornamental battlement and
floriated pinnacles. The church has some interesting
monuments in addition to the one already mentioned.
Picturesque the fine structure certainly looks in the
market-place, and its lofty battlements and pinnacles,
rising above the houses as you look up Queen Street
from the quay side near the Victoria Pier, add quaintness to the busy scene thereby. The church was
restored at a cost of £30,000 under the care of Sir
Gilbert Scott, when much of the decayed brick and
stone work was recased, and when the traceries were

renovated, and new panelled roofs put up in the choir and transepts, and when much other needful work was also done.

Not far away, in Lowgate, stands St. Mary's Church, a Perpendicular edifice, which has been a great deal altered, and, in fact, was almost rebuilt at its restoration by Sir Gilbert Scott. It is but the choir of the original church, one ill-supported tradition asserting that Henry VIII. pulled down the nave and tower, having need of stone for one of his new defensive works. The church dates originally from the beginning of the fourteenth century, and the existing tower, spanning the causeway with its arched base, was built in 1696. The edifice is wide, for there is a double south aisle, and it is comparatively short. The east window, which is of very great size, is filled with excellent modern glass, and, indeed, the church is particularly rich in fine glass of recent date. Within, the church has a very striking and fine appearance.

The father of Andrew Marvell, who was born at Winestead, near Hull, was minister of this church, and the boy was educated at the grammar school on the south side of the church of the Holy Trinity, founded in 1486 by John Alcock, Bishop of Ely, and rebuilt in 1583. From this school also came Thomas Watson, Bishop of St. David's, and William Wilberforce. Wilberforce, the philanthropist, who brought about the abolition of slavery, represented his native town in Parliament, and is the greatest of its modern worthies. He was born at a quaint house of some-

what Dutch aspect in the High Street, in which, at
an earlier date, Sir John Lister had entertained
King Charles I. The Wilberforce monument, erected
in 1835, a Doric column upon a high square base,
surmounted by a statue of the statesman, stands at
the foot of Whitefriargate Bridge.

It is beyond our scope here to speak of all the great
institutions and public buildings of Hull, but certain
of them demand attention. The Trinity House, near
the Prince's Dock, originally and still an institution
for the relief of decayed seamen, had its beginning
with the guild of the Holy Trinity, founded in 1369,
and incorporated with the Shipman's Guild in 1457.
The brethren were charged with the care of the
'haven' of Hull, and, through the concession of
Charles II., became very wealthy. They have now
care of the beacons and buoys of the Yorkshire coast
and the Humber, with the appointment of pilots, and
are a corporation of great influence in the town. In
the hospital itself thirty younger brothers and master-
mariners' widows have accommodation, while more
than a thousand out-pensioners receive allowances. A
marine school was established in the House in 1785,
and there about 140 sons of sailors are trained, and
receive a nautical education free. In addition, the
brethren have hospitals and almshouses in other parts
of the town, where a great number of decayed master-
mariners, their wives and widows, have their homes.
The Trinity House, which extends from Trinity House
Lane to the Prince's Dock, was rebuilt in the Tuscan

style round two courts in 1753, and these are separated
by a Grecian chapel, rich in its marbles, opened in
1843.   There is a quaint, sequestered aspect about the
place, and it is kept bright and spotless as the deck
of a man-of-war, and the council chamber is still strewn
with rushes in the ancient manner.   The house has
many pictures, including portraits of Captain Cook
(by Webber), Alderman Ferris, a great benefactor—the
same to whom the Beggar's Bridge at Glaisdale End
is ascribed (page 94 *ante*)—Andrew Marvell, Sir George
Savile (by Hudson), Queen Victoria (by Sant),
George III. (by Sir G. Chalmers), and William, Prince
of Orange, as a young man (by C. Netscher), in a fine
carved oaken frame, besides representations of the
' Battle of the Nile' (by Smirke and Anderson), the
' Landing of William III. at Brixham,' as well as much
fine and some curious plate.   There are but two other
like Trinity Houses in England—namely, at London
and Newcastle.

Among the many other hospitals which Hull possesses
—the one founded by John Gregg, a wealthy merchant
in Posterngate, dates from the year 1416—is that of
the Charterhouse, which is a memorial of the munifi-
cence of Michael de la Pole, Earl of Suffolk, founded
in 1384, and so called from its relation to the Carthusian
monastery, which he also established.   It stands in
Charterhouse Lane, a little north of the old town, and
adjacent to the river Hull.   The foundation is for
twenty-eight poor men and women, and the present
brick building replaced the older one in 1780.   Of the

De la Poles, who were so thoroughly identified with the growth and prosperity of Hull, we have already spoken. Their mansion - house was in Lowgate, opposite St. Mary's Church, and here Henry VIII. lodged in 1540, after having beheaded many years before Edmund de la Pole, the last Earl of Suffolk of that family, who had been imprisoned for seven years in the Tower.

The aspect of the streets of Hull presents in these days little that is picturesque, yet here and there some old brick building or some quaint corner may be found that speaks of the former time. Of modern Hull it is not our purpose to write at length, though much might be said in description of the fine Italian town-hall, with its campanile and its statues, of the dock offices and the Royal Institution, of the recent churches, and of many other edifices in the town, and especially, perhaps, of the museum which is in the Royal Institution building. It contains many things that illustrate, not only history and geology generally, but specially the early conditions of Holderness which have been treated in this book, among the objects relating thereto being a curious carved representation of a serpent-boat, wherein were inserted originally the feet of eight human figures most primitively shapen, each carrying a club and two shields, and having, like the serpent-head, pieces of quartz inserted in the eyes. This relic, which has been damaged, was dug out of the blue clay at Roos, a few miles from Withernsea.*

---

* An account of it will be found in the *Reliquary*, xi. 205.

Beyond the limits of the old town Hull has spread in every direction, but mostly to the north and west, and here, in an endless succession of streets, are all the features of a large town—not much that is picturesque or beautiful, a good deal that is commonplace; but here and there some building of character, some example of architecture that is above the level, will attract the passing wayfarer. And beyond the great *plexus* there is the far-spread suburban fringe where the breathing space is freer, and the country about us greener ever as we go out from the throng. The modern merchants of Hull no longer, like their great predecessors, dwell in the High Street, or the ways that neighbour the ancient port, but have their pleasant villas away in the outskirts, or at Hessle, or Ferriby, or Anlaby, or Cottingham, or in the pleasant town of Beverley, or in some other of the agreeable places not too far away.

To realize that this is the third port in the kingdom, the wayfarer, having visited every dock, will return to the quay near the mouth of the Hull, and to the Victoria Pier, and will look out to the shipping in the river, 'where Humber pours her rich commercial stream.' Here the motley crowd that ever haunts a landing-stage makes a picturesque foreground to the great expanse of the river, thronged with varied craft, from the humble coasting-barge and river-boat to the man-of-war, which is there for the defence of the estuary; while far away beyond lies the low coast of Lincolnshire. It is difficult amid the shrill whistling of packet-boats, the rattling of cordage, and the babel of many tongues, to go back, as for a moment we would do for contrast, to the far-off time when the oozy flood had its course amid the dense forest that once lined the shore; or to think of the Hunnish king from whom, as legend hath it, the river takes its name :

'Or Humber loud that keeps the Scythian's name,'

as Milton speaks of it. The 'loud' Humber is so described from the 'bore' or 'eagre,' the tidal wave that at times disturbs its course. Thus does Drayton make the river itself proudly address us :

'What flood comes to the deep
Than Humber that is heard most horribly to roar?
For when my Higre comes, I make my either shore
Even tremble with the sound that I afar do send.'

And now, at the end of our pleasant descriptive journeying along the Yorkshire coast, and amid the interesting places that neighbour the shore, we may say that, if it cannot be said that the busy town of Hull presents much of interest to the lover of the beautiful, the picturesqueness that belongs to shipping it certainly has in a pre-eminent degree. The varied build and rig of the thronging craft, the tall forests of masts, and the quaint figures of the seamen, all contribute, indeed, under fine effects of light, to make of the Humber and the Hull docks a very striking and attractive picture. We may conclude by saying, too, that, wherever shipping is, there is scope for the artist's brush; and so whatever Beverley, with its ancient fellow-towns of the Yorkshire coast, has lost, has been the gain, in more senses than one, of the thriving port of Hull.

APPENDIX A.

The following is a table of the geological formations of the Yorkshire coast, and of the hills in the coast region. It will be remembered that the dip of the stratification is towards the south, and that therefore the formations are successively denuded in the order of this table as we go north.

	FORMATIONS.	LOCALITIES OF OCCURRENCE.
POST-TERTIARY.	*Recent and Post-Glacial—* Alluvium, Peat, Clay, etc.	River courses, moorlands. Holderness, with lacustrine deposits.
	Glacial— Boulder Clay, Sands, and Gravel	Holderness, Bridlington, Filey Bay, Scarborough (North and South Bays), Dunsley Bay, North Cleveland Coast.
SECONDARY. JURASSIC.	*Cretaceous—* White Chalk	Flamborough, The Wolds.
	Red Chalk	Speeton.
	Neocomian Beds	Speeton, Vale of Pickering.
	Upper Oolite— Portland Beds	Speeton.
	Kimmeridge (blue) Clay	Speeton, Kirby Moorside.
	Middle (Coralline) Oolite— Upper Calcareous Grit	Pickering and Helmsley, 'Tabular Hills,' (with the subjacent strata of the Middle Oolite).
	Do. Limestone and Coral Rag	Seamer, Ayton, Brompton, Kirkdale.
	Middle Calcareous Grit	Brompton, Pickering, Helmsley.
	Lower Limestone and Passage Beds	Forge Valley, Hackness, Troutsdale.
	Lower Calcareous Grit	Scarborough Castle, Oliver's Mount, Red Cliff, Gristhorpe Bay, Filey Brig, Hambleton End.
	Oxford Clay	Scarborough Castle, Red Cliff, Gristhorpe, Saltergate Brow, Rievaulx.
	Kelloways Rock	Scarborough Castle, North Cliff, Red Cliff, Hackness, Rievaulx.
	Lower Oolite— Cornbrash Limestone	North Cliff, Scarborough, Cayton Bay, Gristhorpe Bay.
	Upper Estuarine Series	Gristhorpe Bay, Scarborough, Cloughton, Staintondale Cliffs.
	Gray Limestone	Gristhorpe Bay, Scarborough, Cloughton, Peak Cliffs.
	Middle Estuarine Series	Gristhorpe Bay, Cloughton Wyke, Hawsker.
	Millepore Bed	Gristhorpe Bay, Osgodby Nab, Cloughton Wyke.
	Lower Estuarine Series	Peak Cliffs, Eskdale, Burton Head.
	Dogger (Ferruginous Sandstone)	Blea Wyke, Peak, Whitby, Boulby, Cleveland Hills.
	Lias— Upper Lias · { Alum Shale / Jet Shale / Gray Shale }	Robin Hood's Bay, Whitby, Runswick, Boulby, Cliffs near Guisborough, Roseberry Topping, Eskdale.
	Middle Lias { Ironstone Series / Sandy Series }	Hawsker, Kettleness, Staithes, Skinningrove, Head of Bilsdale, Eston Nab, Eskdale.
	Lower Lias	Robin Hood's Bay, Boulby, Redcar Scars.

APPENDIX B.

For information as to the sea-fishing of the Yorkshire coast, the very best course is to go to the fishermen themselves, who will be found uniformly courteous and obliging. Boats can be hired without difficulty. Excellent gurnards are taken late in the summer by means of the 'chopstick' and line, and there is capital whiting-fishing all along the coast. Mackerel, after the first week in August, but more freely in September, may be taken with the line. Billet are in abundance until the winter, and many codling are caught. Good winter codling grounds are in the neighbourhood of Whitby, the Peak, Cloughton, Cornelian Bay, and Cayton Bay. Par are about the coast through the year, and many flat fish may be landed at Whitby and further west, as well as in the neighbourhood of Scarborough Castle Hill. Those who would like a rough night's experience with the herring fleet will find no difficulty in gratifying their taste by applying to the fishermen. On the other hand, success will attend shallow water fishing from the piers at Whitby, Scarborough, and Bridlington, for those who like such sport.

In the rivers and streams the trout and grayling are very many, and nowhere can better sport be had, the trout rising from half a pound to three pounds or more,

and the grayling are also heavy.   The waters are clear,
and the fish 'educated,' so that the rodster may con-
gratulate himself warmly upon his success.   Still, very
good baskets are secured.   Pike and other coarse
fish may also be found in certain rivers, notably in
the Derwent, below Ayton, which has many of them.
As to the salmon, which enter all the streams that flow
down to the sea, these also may be caught, the angler
being properly licensed, and always having due observ-
ance of the season.   The Yorkshire Fishery District
includes all the rivers and streams running into the
sea between Trent Falls and the Thorney Beck,
Hayburn Wyke, *i.e.,* chiefly through the Humber
(clerk, Mr. J. H. Phillips, Scarborough); the Esk
Fishery District, those from the Thorney Beck to the
Skinningrove Beck (clerk, Mr. W. Brown, Whitby);
and the Tees District, those from the Skinningrove
Beck to Hardwick Hall (clerk, Mr. M. B. Dodds,
Stockton).   Information concerning the fisheries can
be gained from these gentlemen, as also from vendors
of tackle in all the towns.

North-east Yorkshire is threaded by such a number
of streams that only to the more important of them can
reference be made here.   Licenses for the salmon and
trout fishing of the Esk and its tributaries are issued
by the Esk Fishery District, and the Esk Angling
Association has done much for the quality and number
of the fish.   Tickets by the day, week, or month may
be obtained at the tackle-vendors' in Whitby.   There
is very good trout-fishing about Ruswarp and Egton
Bridge, as well as generally upon the tributaries of the
river.   Inquiry may be made at the village hostels.
The Rye is well stocked with trout and grayling, and
as a grayling stream there are few better.   The Rye-

dale Anglers' Club, which preserves the waters, has done splendid service to the brethren of the angle by improving the quality and increasing the number of the fish. It has an artificial breeding-ground for trout, and 30,000 or 40,000 fry are turned into the river every year. A considerable length of the river is rented from Lord Feversham and Sir George Wombwell. The Costa Beck, a tributary, is strictly preserved from Keld Head, near Pickering, to Kirby Misperton, and is a stream abounding in trout and grayling; but the waters are so pellucid and bright that fine tackle and a delicate hand are required, and there is often difficulty in landing the fish owing to the weed, which grows vigorously owing to a degree of natural warmth in the stream. Mr. J. H. Phillips, of Scarborough, can give information regarding the fishing hereabout, and particulars can also be gained at the inns at Pickering. In the Newton Beck, between Newbridge and Kingthorpe, where the stream is in the hands of the Duchy of Lancaster, no fishing is allowed.

The Derwent also is an excellent trout and grayling river, and one of the freest rising streams in Yorkshire. Its upper waters and those of its early tributaries swarm with small trout, but the fish are larger lower down at Hackness and in Forge Valley. Below Ayton the river has many pike, roach, dace, gudgeon, chubb, and some other coarse fish. The trout range from one to three pounds. The principal riparian owners in the upper waters are the Earl of Londesborough and Lord Derwent. The river is preserved from Hilla Green Bridge, where the Trout Beck falls into the stream, downward through Hackness and Forge Valley, to a point two miles below Ayton; and there is a breeding establishment in Forge Valley.

Above the club length Captain Johnstone has a private water, but beyond are several miles of free fishing, including the Helwath Beck, and other tributaries, with plenty of small trout. The season subscription to the club water is £4 4s., and Mr. Denison, of the Valley, Scarborough, is the honorary secretary; but day-tickets (fly-fishing only above Ayton Dam, 5s.; and below the dam, 2s. 6d.) may be obtained from Mr. Patrick, gunmaker, Scarborough. Good trout-fishing may also be had in the streams nearer Scar-borough—the Scalby and Burniston Becks, and in the beck at Hayburn Wyke, all preserved, in the last-named at a very moderate fee. Moreover, this water is free above the confluence of the Staintondale, and Thorney Becks, which discharge their waters into the Wyke. There are a few trout also in the Hertford River, which rises near Filey, and flows into the Derwent at Seamer Carr. The Hull River, also an excellent trout stream in its non-tidal length, is strictly preserved by a club.

INDEX

In cases where the pages are not given in numerical order, those placed first are the principal references.

Deira, 11, 283
Derwent River and its Tributaries, 224, 225, 229-237 ; Fishing, 325, 326
Devil's Bridge, Mulgrave, 56
Dimlington Height, 279
Doedalegrif, 179
Doubting Castle, 98
Dove River, 152 *et seq.*
Dowthwaite Dale, 153, 154
Duck Bridge, Eskdale, 107
Duncombe Park, 128-132
Dunsley, 60, 9, 89
Dunsley Bay, 60, 10

E

Eagle's Nest, Mulgrave, 56
Earl's Dyke, 269
Easby Moor, 42, 110
Easington, Cleveland, 52
Easington, Holderness, 279
Easington Beck, 51
East Newton, 275
East Row, 56, 13
East Row Beck, 57
East Scar, Robin Hood's Bay, 185
Easterside Moor, 112
Ebberston, 240
Ebberston Low Moor, 235
Edstone Church (allusion), 144
Egton, 92, 93
Egton Bridge, 91, 92
Egton High Moor, 89, 90, 101, 103
Egton Low Moor, 97, 84, 88
Eller Beck, Goathland, 90
Ellerburn, 179, 180
Ellerdale Beck, 65, 81
Elton Beck, 136
Eskdale and the Esk River, 79-112, 6 ; Fishing, 324
Eskdaleside, 87
Eston Moor, 36
Eston Nab, 35, 36, 22
Everley, 230

F

Fairy Cross Plain, 105
Falling Foss, 85
Falsgrave, 222, 226
Fangdale Beck, 119
Farndale, 152-159

Farndale Moor, 155
Filey, 247-249, 10
Filey Bay, 245-248
Filey Brig, 246, 247
Filing. *See* Fyling
Fillett Tail Scar, 55
Fishing, 323-326
Flamborough, 254, 17
Flamborough Head, 250-257, 10 ; Caves, 255-257
Flamborough Rigg, 9, 168
Flashes, East and West, Redcar, 23
Flat Scar, Huntcliff, 25
Flat Scar, Robin Hood's Bay, 185
Flax Dale, 179
Forge Valley, 229 ; Fishing, 325
Freeburgh Hill, 46, 12
Freeze Gill, 235
Fryup, Great, and its Beck, 104
Fryup, Little, 105
Fylingdales Moor, 82, 83, 188, 236
Fyling Thorpe, 188

G

Gandale Beck, 177
Geology, 3-7, 66 *n.*, 141, 147, 182, 185, 190, 197, 244, 265-267 ; the Basaltic Dyke, 7, 88 ; Table of the Stratification, 322
Ghaut Ravine, Flamborough, 256
Gillamoor, 154, 158, 153
Gilling (allusion), 117
Gipsy Beck, 267
Girrick Beck and Moor, 46
Givendale, 241
Givendale Dikes, 240
Glaisdale, 101-103
Glaisdale End, 93, 94
Glaisdale Moor, 90, 103, 112
Glaisdale Ridge, 101, 103
Goathland, 89-91, 178
Goat Hole, Redcar, 23
Goldsborough, 57
Goose Island, 269
Grain Beck, 236
Grimston Garth, 275
Gristhorpe, 245
Gristhorpe Bay, 244
Grendale, 47
Grosmont, 87-89, 9

THE END.

BILLING AND SONS, PRINTERS, GUILDFORD.